IF ONLY

IF ONLY

Judith
Arnold

This is a work of fiction. Names, characters, places, and incidents either are the product of the author's imagination or are used fictitiously. Any resemblance to actual events, locales, organizations, or persons living or dead, is entirely coincidental and beyond the intent of either the author or the publisher.

The Story Plant
Studio Digital CT, LLC
PO Box 4331
Stamford, CT 06907

Story Plant hardcover ISBN-13: 978-1-61188-315-2
Fiction Studio Books E-book ISBN-13: 978-1-945839-55-9

Visit our website at www.TheStoryPlant.com

First Story Plant printing: October 2021
Printed in the United States of America

If Only is dedicated to anyone who has ever passed a house and wondered: *What if...*

STORY PLANT BOOKS BY JUDITH ARNOLD

Love in Bloom's
Blooming All Over
Full Bloom

The Road Not Taken
By Robert Frost

Two roads diverged in a yellow wood,
And sorry I could not travel both
And be one traveler, long I stood
And looked down one as far as I could
To where it bent in the undergrowth;

Then took the other, as just as fair,
And having perhaps the better claim,
Because it was grassy and wanted wear;
Though as for that the passing there
Had worn them really about the same,

And both that morning equally lay
In leaves no step had trodden black.
Oh, I kept the first for another day!
Yet knowing how way leads on to way,
I doubted if I should ever come back.

I shall be telling this with a sigh
Somewhere ages and ages hence:
Two roads diverged in a wood, and I—
I took the one less traveled by,
And that has made all the difference.

Chapter One

If Only We'd Bought This House...

Ruth Singer knew chaos theory. Or, at the very least, she knew chaos. Chaos was her life. Chaos was her world. Chaos was her middle name.

As she understood it, what chaos theory boiled down to was: if a butterfly in Botswana flapped its wings, it could cause a tornado in Arkansas. Her father had educated her on this concept when she'd been a child. It had left her wondering what Botswana's butterflies had against trailer parks in rural America, since that seemed to be where tornadoes touched down with tragic frequency. But she hadn't questioned her father. For one thing, arguing with her parents, especially while they were enjoying their daily cocktail hour—which, in her mother's case, usually lasted about four hours—was futile. For another, her father had been a mechanical engineer, so she'd assumed he was an expert when it came to butterfly wings and funnel clouds.

She was a long way from her childhood. In fact, she was within shouting distance of her seventieth birthday, an age which had seemed positively ancient to her when she'd been young enough to believe that her father knew what he was talking about when he'd lectured her on butterflies and chaos.

These days, sixty-eight years old didn't seem old at all. Would an old person take regular five-mile walks for exercise? Ruth did; therefore, she couldn't possibly be old.

To keep chaos at bay, she took her walks in any weather that didn't require her to wear waders or mukluks. Now that she was retired, she could walk every day, and she walked a different route each morning so she wouldn't grow bored. Her Wednesday route led her past the Victorian she and Barry had almost purchased thirty-two years ago, when they'd moved to Brentwood. Every Wednesday when she passed the house, with its gray scalloped shingles, its wine-red gingerbread trim, its steeply sloping roof and its circular turret on the second floor, she contemplated how different her life would be if they'd bought this house instead of the neatly rectangular colonial on Jefferson Road.

One decision—that house, not this house—had changed everything, the way the quiver of a butterfly's wings could cause a tornado half a world away.

She'd loved the Victorian when they'd toured it. She'd loved the oddly shaped rooms, especially the round turret room, which she would have claimed as her own private retreat, a hideaway filled with overstuffed chairs and books and a "Do Not Enter" sign on the door so the kids wouldn't bother her when she was secluded inside. She'd loved the window seats in the living room and the wainscoting in the dining room and the brick fireplace in the den. The house radiated charm the way the July sun radiated heat. Which had been Barry's primary complaint.

"It doesn't have central air," he'd complained.

"You really don't need air conditioning in Massachusetts," Patti, their excessively chipper real estate agent had assured them.

"*I* need air conditioning," Barry had insisted. Years later, he would brag to Ruth about his wisdom and foresight in anticipating global warming. Thanks to climate change, everyone needed air conditioning in Massachusetts now.

"We can put in some window units," Ruth had said.

"Window units aren't the same as central air. And the garage isn't attached. You want an unattached garage? Every time it rains, you'll get soaked racing from the garage to the house. Every time it snows, you'll get buried. Or you'll slip on the ice and crack your head open."

"We could build a breezeway," Ruth had suggested. She'd had no idea just how difficult building a breezeway might be, but the door from the garage lined up pretty well with the door to the mudroom off the kitchen.

"You want to buy this house and then redo the whole thing? Doubling the cost? That's crazy."

Maybe it would have been crazy. But she would have had that round turret room. And she and Barry wouldn't have wound up buying their colonial—new construction, attached garage, central air—across the street from the Jarvises.

Everything would have been different if Maddie had never met Kyle Jarvis.

~

If only we'd bought this house instead...

A sweet little girl named Janet lives in the house across the street. No, not Janet. People don't name their daughters Janet anymore. But a simple, solid name, not a trendy name, not a cool name, because this little girl isn't trendy and cool.

This girl—Nancy? Mary? Anne—yes, Anne! Anne is Maddie's age, and they've been best friends from the day we moved in. Anne is smart and studious and just mischievous enough to hold Maddie's interest. I love watching them when they're together, completing each other's sentences, swapping T-shirts and friendship bracelets, competing to see whose life is more worthy of complaint—who has more chores, who receives smaller allowances, whose mothers are more oppressive. (Anne's mother—Marcia, yes, that's her name—Marcia and I compare notes on the conversations we overhear. We regularly get together for glasses of wine or iced tea and laugh at our fierce, histrionic, adorable daughters.)

Anne and Maddie sit together every day on the school bus. This is a known thing; other children sit near them and talk to them, but the only time the bus seat next to Maddie is available is when Anne has to miss school with strep throat or an ear infection. When the girls get home from school, they walk together from the bus stop on the corner, stand in the street talking for a few minutes, and then enter their respective houses to do their homework and practice their musical instruments. Maddie plays the piano, Anne the violin.

Over time, they start playing duets together, always at our house because it's a lot easier to carry a violin across the street than to push a piano across the street. I sit in the turret room above the living room, where the piano is located, and listen as they play together, earnestly, intensely, beautifully.

When they're done playing, I emerge from my cozy round hideaway, descend the stairs, and prepare a plate of sliced apples, or crackers with peanut butter, and the girls carry their snack out to the porch, where they nibble and talk, solving the problems of the world or, at least, the problems of Brentwood Middle School.

They discuss the books they've read. They complain about their teachers. They polish each other's nails and debate which boys in their classes are the cutest.

Years pass, but their friendship only grows stronger and sturdier. In high school, they double-date. They retreat to one or the other's bedroom so Marcia and I can no longer eavesdrop on their conversations—but that's all right. They're entitled to their privacy, and Marcia and I are entitled to our glasses of wine.

When they're eighteen, Maddie and Anne double-date to the senior prom, posing with their courteous, clean-cut prom dates, first on Anne's smaller porch and then on our larger one, while Chuck and Marcia and Barry and I snap photos of them. Several other prom couples join them, but Maddie and Anne are clearly the queens of the group, the prettiest, the savviest, the most confident and least giggly. They have a lot to celebrate on prom night. They've both gotten into their first-choice colleges—Oberlin for Maddie, Middlebury for Anne. Next year will be the first time since we bought this house that they'll be apart, but—lucky for them—they've got email and phones and they'll stay in constant touch, even as they expand their horizons and welcome more friends into their lives.

They do well in college. They graduate. They land challenging, well-paying jobs in Boston and share an apartment like the one Barry and I had in Brighton, only without the cockroaches. They date wonderful men, and when it's time to settle down, they're bridesmaids in each other's weddings. Chuck and Marcia attend

Maddie's wedding, of course, and Barry and I attend Anne's. We talk about how each young woman is like an extra daughter to us, the twins we share.

They settle in the Boston suburbs, not in Brentwood but just a couple of towns away, and give birth to magnificent children. Anne's children call Maddie "Auntie Maddie," and Maddie's children call Anne "Auntie Annie."

Barry and I contemplate downsizing, selling the Victorian and moving into a condo community for active seniors. Except that we don't feel like seniors, and I don't feel like giving up the turret room. And we spent all that money to build the breezeway between the garage and the mudroom, and the daffodils we planted have multiplied through the years so they create a solid row of yellow, like a stripe of bright sunshine underlining the porch.

All our children loved this house. Barry started loving it once we retrofitted it with central air conditioning, and he's loved it ever since. Buying it was the right thing to do. It was the perfect launching pad for all three of our children. Especially Maddie.

So we stay. Marcia and I sit on the porch the way Maddie and Anne used to, nibbling on cheese and fresh strawberries and sipping our wine, swapping memories instead of bracelets. Our friendship is as solid as that of our daughters. I will not leave this lovely house. It suits me too well. And it never really feels empty, with our children and their children visiting all the time. The grandchildren love the turret room, but they're only allowed to visit. It's my *room. I can close the door whenever I like.*

And I do.

~

But Ruth and Barry had bought the colonial on Jefferson Road.

It was a nice enough house, she supposed. Comfortable. Thoughtfully laid out, with no surprises, no unexpected alcoves, no quirky little nooks. No window seats or round rooms. Well insulated. Well applianced. Well air-conditioned. All in all, a very practical, sensible house, its design the antithesis of chaos.

She couldn't complain. Barry had insisted that they move to Brentwood because she was running the music education program in Brentwood's three primary schools. She had been so touched that he wanted her to have an easy commute. Only later did she realize that her easy commute benefitted him as much as her. "You'll be there to greet the kids when they get home from school," he'd pointed out. "You'll be close by if they have an emergency."

They had emergencies. Children always did. A gym-class injury, a stomach bug, a wardrobe crisis. Ruth could handle whatever catastrophe befell her children, because her job kept her in town, only minutes from the emergency's ground zero, able to find someone to cover for her so she could race to the rescue with a forgotten homework assignment or a misplaced lunch bag. She recalled the time Noah, then in second grade, had fallen into a mud puddle at recess—by accident, he'd sworn, though she didn't believe him—and his teacher had contacted Ruth and asked her to bring Noah a clean shirt, because he couldn't spend the next two hours in a wet, stained garment. Apparently, second graders could not absorb their arithmetic and penmanship lessons if they were dressed in something wet and stained.

At least she'd never had to run any of her children to the emergency room during school hours. She'd taken Noah to the ER when he'd broken his ring finger playing basketball in the Saturday morning league, and Jill one evening when she'd developed a suspicious cough that had turned out to be a mild case of pneumonia. And Maddie the summer she'd gotten bitten by a brown recluse spider which had, in fact, not been a brown recluse spider, or for that matter, any kind of spider. Ruth had researched brown recluse spiders after she and Maddie had gotten home from the ER, and she'd learned that they didn't live in Massachusetts. But Maddie had insisted her bite was from a brown recluse spider because Kyle Jarvis had told her it was. He'd scared the hell out of her, and she'd relished having the hell scared out of her by him. Kyle's melodramatic flare had found the perfect audience in Maddie, especially when she was not just the audience but the star.

As it turned out, Maddie's affliction had been a black-fly bite, itchy but requiring little more than calamine lotion and a dose of Benadryl. And for that, Ruth had had to rush Maddie to the ER.

If she and Barry had bought that Victorian house, Anne, the sweet little girl in the Cape across the street, would never have alarmed Maddie by claiming that her bite had come from a venomous spider. Anne would have supplied the calamine lotion herself, and then suggested that they distract themselves by biking down to the playground near the Community Center and seeing who could kick the highest on the swings.

~

Sometimes when Ruth walked, she listened to an audiobook or a podcast. Sometimes she stewed about an article from the morning newspaper and wrote a letter to the editor in her mind. Today she spent at least forty-five minutes of her hour-long walk ruminating on how her life would have been different if she and Barry had bought the Victorian. Less chaotic? No. There were enough butterflies in the world to create chaos regardless of where she chose to live. But she might have been more patient, more tolerant of the chaos. She might have been a better mother.

In the fifteen minutes of her walk thinking about something other than the house, she contemplated how to spend the rest of her day. This was the first autumn of her retirement, and she still hadn't found her groove. She was beginning to suspect that retirement didn't have a groove. It did give her the time to take her five-mile walks every day, instead of just on weekends and holidays or in the evenings during Daylight Savings Time, when the sky remained light after dinnertime. This, in turn, meant she could walk past the Victorian every Wednesday, and think about how much better a mother she would have been if she'd raised her children there.

Entering her own house, she was briefly startled to find Rainie in the den, watching a streaming episode of a TV series about a prison in which approximately fifty percent of the dialogue consisted of the word *fuck*. Ruth wasn't a prude. She knew the word. She herself used it on occasion. But she believed dialogue in movies and television shows ought to be more inventive. Figuring out ways to use *fuck* as a noun, a verb, an adjective, and an interjection was inventive to a point, but really, the show's writers could have done better. Rainie was only fourteen. She didn't need to hear all that swearing.

"I forgot you were home," Ruth said, peering through the doorway between the kitchen and the den.

"Teachers' enrichment day," Rainie said. Even though the early November morning was not particularly hot, she wore a short-sleeved cotton T-shirt and athletic shorts, her long, thin legs protruding from the hems of the shorts. Her toenails were painted black and her hair featured several pink streaks.

"Teachers' enrichment day." Ruth sighed. "That's as close as teachers ever get to being rich." She was thirsty from her walk, but she'd be damned if she drank any water before she stood on the scale. She always weighed herself when she arrived home from her walk—naked, after peeing and before stepping into the shower. If she drank water before she climbed onto the scale, she might weigh an ounce or two more. Her scale registered only pounds, not ounces, but if by going thirsty for an extra few minutes she could coax the needle a fraction of an inch further to the left, she would happily forgo hydration. Ruth's mother had often told her that getting fat was the worst tragedy that could befall a woman. Ruth knew that wasn't true, but it was hard to tune out a mother's nagging, even if that nagging reached Ruth from beyond the grave. Years after her mother's death, Ruth still monitored every fluctuation on the bathroom scale.

Before she could head for the stairs, Rainie sprang off the sofa in the den and entered the kitchen. "Grammy? Can we talk?"

"Of course. But first, I want to say that show you were watching relied way too much on curse words. I hope you noticed the weakness of the writing."

Rainie laughed. "Oh, I'm so shocked! All those dirty words! I'm gonna have a heart attack!" She clapped her hands over her ears.

Ruth rolled her eyes. "I'm just saying, there are better written shows on TV. Even better written shows set in prisons. And anyway, it's a nice day. You shouldn't spend it inside, watching bad TV."

"I'm getting together with Kelsey and Nina later today. We're doing something. We haven't decided what." Rainie swung open the refrigerator door, pulled out a bag of green grapes, and popped one into her mouth.

Ruth was really thirsty. She wanted to drink some water, and she wouldn't do that before stripping and standing on the scale, which wouldn't happen until Rainie had gotten whatever was on her chest off it. "You said you wanted to talk," Ruth prompted her, hoping she didn't sound as impatient as she felt.

"Oh, right." Rainie took a moment to refresh her memory. She chewed a grape, swallowed it, and plucked another grape from its stem. "After Mom marries Warren, I want to stay here."

Ruth opened her mouth and then shut it. Then opened it again. "Why?"

"I like it here. Warren is boring. He's, like, ugh. Besides, you're my grandma. You've got better food in your refrigerator." She popped the grape she'd been holding into her mouth.

Chaos, Ruth thought, taking a deep breath before she said the wrong thing—not that she had any idea what the wrong thing was. Or, for that matter, the right thing. Rainie was old enough to know what she wanted, old enough to have an opinion about her mother's upcoming marriage to Warren Schneier. Rainie and Maddie had lived with Ruth and Barry since Rainie was just a few months old, and Ruth had been more of a mother to Rainie than Maddie had been.

Ruth didn't spoil her grandchildren. She didn't wear a frilly blue apron and bake chocolate chip cookies for them. She had never let Rainie leave her toys all over the floor, or throw tantrums, or get everything she asked for the instant she asked for it. Ruth was a stricter mother to Rainie than Maddie was.

But then, Maddie was Maddie. She careened through life, swinging from impulse to impulse. Maddie was brilliant and talented and...chaotic.

Maddie had decided that her teenage daughter ought to be her maid of honor at her wedding to Warren. That alone indicated the quality of Maddie's parenting. A woman should not ask her fourteen-year-old daughter to be the maid of honor in a wedding about which the daughter's attitude was at best tepid and at worst hostile. Rainie could have been a bridesmaid, perhaps, but not the maid of honor. Not when Maddie was insisting on a full-blown, full-bore formal wedding with all the trappings, the maid of honor responsible for hosting a shower, a spa day, and a girls' night out at a male strip club, none of which Ruth would permit Rainie to do. It had become a contentious issue between Ruth and Maddie.

Why Maddie hadn't asked Jill to be her matron of honor, Ruth couldn't guess. Jill was Maddie's older sister, the perfect person to lead the squadron of bridesmaids Maddie had chosen. Maddie's only explanation was, "I don't want a *matron* of honor. I want a *maid* of honor." And of course, the person of honor had to be a blood relative. Asking one of her unmarried bridesmaids to step into the leadership role would have insulted Jill beyond measure.

Thank God for Noah. Compared to daughters, sons were easy. Chaotic, true, but chaotic more in a tornado way than in a permanent-emotional-scars way. Sons could demolish a toy or a car or a house without too much effort, but they could not demolish a family, not the way daughters could. Noah could be an usher, don a tuxedo, stand with the groom, and offer a humorous yet touching toast at the reception. He wouldn't throw a hissy fit over the design of the bridesmaid's dresses—really, Rainie was much too young for the strapless gowns Maddie had selected for her bridesmaids, and her bosom was much too small. Noah would look dashing as he escorted his wife Laura (who had more than enough bosom to hold up her strapless bridesmaid gown) down the aisle. He would not need a special session with a hairdresser and a cosmetologist before the wedding. He would do what he had to do, and be what he had to be.

There was chaos, and there was chaos. Sons were chaotic.

Daughters were...*chaotic*.

Chapter Two

Seated at her piano hours later, Ruth savored her solitude. Rainie had departed to do something with her friends, Barry and Maddie were at work, and so far, at least, Ruth had resisted all attempts to introduce a dog into the household. She loved dogs. The family had had a dog when her children were growing up. But dogs invariably added a layer of chaos to their surroundings. And Ruth was so tired of taking care of other creatures, so utterly tired of being a mommy. The very thought of having to clean up someone else's poop made her want to smash the piano keys with her fists. True, dogs could be trained to use the back yard more easily than children could be trained to use the potty—Ruth should know; she'd trained her own three babies and Rainie, too, because Maddie had been too busy to take responsibility for that—but even after dogs were trained, you still had to deal with their shit. You couldn't just leave it lying on the ground. Brentwood was an enlightened town. People cleaned up after their pets.

All the other humans were out of the house right now, and no dogs—or cats, or gerbils, or goldfish—were underfoot, not that a goldfish would ever be underfoot. At this precious moment, Ruth was responsible for no one but herself.

She really hoped Rainie would move in with Maddie and Warren when they got married. Ruth loved her granddaughter, but she was done raising children. Done, done, done. She'd been done the day Maddie had stormed down the front walk with a stuffed duffel slung over her shoulder, and climbed into Kyle Jarvis's Jeep. To this day, Ruth wasn't exactly sure whether Maddie had flipped her the bird before settling into the passenger seat and letting Kyle drive her away. Not that it mattered what Maddie had expressed with her hands. Her attitude had flipped Ruth the bird. Her facial expression had launched a nuclear f-bomb Ruth's way.

And Ruth had said to herself, *That's it. I'm done.*

She'd been done until Maddie reappeared at the front door a little more than a year later, her duffel a lot dirtier and a squalling infant in her arms. "This is Rainbow," Maddie had said.

Rainbow. Who named a baby Rainbow? Who, with the last name Singer, would do such a thing to a child? Rainbow Singer sounded like a cloying anime cartoon character, one of those wide-eyed creatures that spun off an expensive line of toys, dolls, and games which preschoolers pleaded for in shrill, whiny voices.

Whatever, as Rainie would say. Maddie had come home and brought a baby with her, and Ruth had discovered that she was not done raising children, after all.

She wanted to be done now. She wanted Rainie to live with Maddie and Warren, to form a family with them. Rainie could visit her grandparents whenever she wanted, but after she visited, she could leave, and Ruth could regain the solitude she craved, the peace. The tranquility. The order.

She stared at the piano keys, recalling how, as a child, she'd thought of them as teeth. They weren't real ivory, of course—she'd hate to have a dead elephant under her fingers even more than a live dog under her feet—but their faded cream color reminded her of her own teeth, and even more of her parents' teeth, which decades of coffee, tea, and wine had dimmed. She had been six years old when she'd begun piano lessons, and she had tearily insisted that the keyboard was a row of teeth, poised to bite.

"The pedals keep it from biting," her father had assured her.

That claim had made no sense, but he was an engineer, so she'd believed him. She had been greatly relieved when she'd finally grown tall enough to reach the pedals. She'd developed a bad habit of pumping the sustain pedal constantly throughout each piece she played, until her teacher, a prune-faced widow named Mrs. Demming, had placed a brick-sized block of wood beneath the pedals so they couldn't be depressed. Mrs. Demming had employed a full array of tricks to train Ruth. She would hold a square of cardboard above Ruth's hands to force her to keep her eyes on the sheet music and not on the keys. She would balance a pencil across Ruth's knuckles to force her to keep the backs of her hands level as she played. She would throw a fit whenever Ruth's fingernails extended a millimeter beyond the tips of her fingers. "Tap, tap, tap," she'd caw. "This is a piano, not a bongo drum. Why do I hear tapping?"

Mrs. Demming had been a bitch, but Ruth had learned how to play the piano.

She was an adequate pianist. She could sight-read. She could play sweeping arpeggios in any key without hitting any clunkers. She could maintain a steady tempo. She could play while standing, and strike the right notes while making eye contact with her students above the top of the console piano with which each primary school music room in Brentwood was furnished. She could simultaneously play the piano and conduct the singers lined up on the risers in a rousing chorus of "We Are the World" or "Hakuna Matata," directing the singers with one hand while the other pounded out the accompaniment.

She wasn't a virtuoso like Maddie—or like Maddie could have been, if she'd stuck with it—but she didn't have to be a virtuoso. She played the piano well enough to teach primary school students how to make music. At one time, she'd played well enough to be the keyboardist in a band. That was how she'd mastered the skill of playing while standing. True rock stars never sat when they performed.

If Rainie convinced her mother to let her remain with Ruth and Barry, how could Ruth preserve the solitude she needed to play like a rock star? She still remembered that awful year during the pandemic, when they'd all been trapped in the house together, twenty-four-seven. Barry had turned the den into a home office, Rainie had attended classes through her computer, Maddie had been temporarily furloughed—you couldn't scrape tartar off teeth remotely—and Ruth had been reassigned to supplement the classroom teachers, using face-to-face software to instruct young scholars on basic math and reading because, after all, there were no concerts to rehearse for, no school plays to direct, no instruments to distribute and demonstrate when her students attended school remotely. But now everyone was back where they were supposed to be, except for Ruth herself, since she was retired.

Retirement was wonderful. She loved having the house to herself. Loved being able to set aside her Bach and Chopin and Debussy sheet music and bang out rock music instead. Carole King. Billy Joel. Elton John. Alicia Keys. And Ruth Singer originals, songs she'd written fifty years ago for the band.

They'd met in high school. She had been one of the rehearsal pianists for the school's glee club when Jimmy Grogan had approached her at her locker one afternoon and said, "So, me and some friends have this band and we need a keyboard player. You interested?"

Jimmy Grogan had never spoken to her before. If pressed, she would have sworn he didn't know who she was. He'd been one of those hybrid kids—freaky yet cool, with hair past his shoulders, an incipient mustache that didn't quite gel, and a wardrobe featuring jeans with fraying hems and ridiculous embroidered vests that somehow looked good on him. Her high school had had tracked classes—A-track for the elite scholars, B-track for the majority of students, C-track for kids who had no chance in hell of attending college and were okay with that. Ruth had been A-track, Jimmy—she assumed—B-track. They might have been in the same driver education class, and glee club. That was about it.

"I play piano," she'd said. "Do you want a piano player?"

"An organ."

"I don't have an organ."

"We do."

"So you want me to play your organ?" That had sounded kind of obscene to her, but she'd managed to keep a straight face.

"And maybe sing back-up. Danny Fortuna is our lead singer. We're thinking, like, the Doors. That kind of thing."

Ruth could play Doors music. It wasn't that challenging. "Do I have to get stoned like the Doors?" she'd asked.

Jimmy had laughed. She'd never heard him laugh before—then again, she'd never really heard him talk before either—but his laughter was effervescent. She pictured it bubbling up into the air like flavored seltzer. "That's up to you," he'd answered her question. "As long as you can play."

"What about a drummer?" She'd known other kids in her high school who had tried to form bands. Drummers were always hard to come by. For some reason, every aspiring rock star opted for a guitar, not a drum kit, probably because guitars were easier to transport, or else because their parents had said no to drums.

"Nick Montoya is our drummer. We got Mike Radowski on bass, and me and Danny play guitar and sing. We need a keyboard player, though. Mike's older brother was our keyboard player, but he graduated last spring and got his draft notice, so he enlisted. He gave Mike the keyboard when he left for basic."

And they were asking her to be their keyboardist. Ruth Pinchas, a nice Jewish girl, an A-track student who had never talked to any of these boys before. A girl surrounded by four slightly dangerous boys in a rock band.

"Sure," she'd said.

Jimmy had torn a page out of his loose-leaf notebook, scribbled an address on it, and handed it to her. "We practice at Nick's house, because he's got the drums," he'd said. "Mike stores his brother's organ there. We practice Saturday mornings, ten o'clock."

"Okay." Ruth would have to come up with a story to tell her parents. Ever since her bat mitzvah, they hadn't fussed about her disinterest in Saturday morning services at the synagogue. To be sure, they'd been pretty lackadaisical about *shabbat* services themselves. Ruth and her older brother had attended Hebrew school at the temple regularly until they'd each turned thirteen, done their bit before the congregation, had their fancy receptions, and reaped their rewards—mostly savings bonds from aunts and uncles, and assorted birthday presents from their friends. Once those rituals had been accomplished, the Pinchas family's participation at Temple Beth Elohim had amounted to paying membership dues and showing up for the High Holy Days.

But would Ruth's parents be upset if she said she was going to a band practice on Saturday morning with a bunch of boys they didn't know? They'd probably be more upset about band practice than about her skipping services. In their minds, band practice equated to getting stoned.

Like the Doors.

Ruth would come up with an excuse. She'd bike to Nick's house, wherever it was. Her parents wouldn't have to know.

~

Nick's house was on the other end of town, five miles away. Back then, bicycles weren't equipped with twenty-one gears. Ruth's bike had fat tires and a wire mesh basket bolted to the handlebar. She'd never gotten around to removing the pink streamers from the rubber handlebar grips.

Fortunately, that autumn Saturday morning was sunny, and a light jacket kept her warm. No helmet, of course—cyclists didn't wear helmets in those days—and she didn't bring any sheet music because she had no idea what the guys would want her to play, other than maybe "Light My Fire," which, to Mrs. Demming's dismay, Ruth could play by ear.

After telling her parents she was biking to the library to do some research for a US history term paper, she tossed a spiral-bound notebook into the handlebar basket to make her story seem credible and coasted down the driveway of their split-level tract house. In case her parents were spying on her through a window, she waited until she'd steered around the corner before pulling the wrinkled loose-leaf paper Jimmy had given her out of her pocket and studying the directions she'd scribbled onto it. She had to bike through the center of town and into alien territory, a neighborhood of small houses, some in need of paint and repairs, some surrounded by weedy lawns and chain-link fences. Nick literally lived on the other side of the tracks—the commuter line ran through her town—and her bike bumped and jerked as she pedaled over the railroad crossing.

She hadn't discussed this outing with anyone, not even her best friend. Debbie would have squealed in delight and shock at the thought of Ruth hanging out on a Saturday morning with the likes of Nick Montoya, Mike Radowski, Jimmy Grogan, and especially Danny Fortuna, who actually looked a little like Jim Morrison. But Debbie, much as Ruth loved her, wasn't the most discreet person in the world. She might let something slip in front of someone else, who'd mention it to someone else, and eventually it would get back to Ruth's parents. Depending on where she was in her multi-hour cocktail hour, Ruth's mother would either ground her for lying to her and spending a Saturday morning with four boys she didn't know and thus didn't approve of, or she'd erupt in a scream-fest with Ruth's father, accusing him of being negligent and letting his daughter become a juvenile delinquent.

Neither was true. Both her parents were adequate (her father more adequate than her mother) and Ruth was well behaved. If she felt it necessary to lie every now and then, she would lie.

Eventually she found Nick's house, a squat, shingled bungalow at the end of a short driveway. She bumped her bike over cracks in the driveway cement and parked it next to another bike that leaned against the side of the house. Even though it was private property, she locked her bike with a chain, just in case. This wasn't her neighborhood; she had no idea how safe it was.

Tucking her notebook under her arm, she strolled up the front walk, sidestepping the grass that sprouted through the cracks in the pavement, and rang the doorbell. And waited. The street was too quiet. She wondered if people were peeking through their windows at her, thinking she looked out of place. She wondered if she'd gotten the date wrong, or the time, or the address. She wondered if this was some sort of elaborate practical joke, and there was no band, and Jimmy Grogan had lured her here to rape her.

Then the door swung open and Nick Montoya, big and beefy, his black hair flopping into his face and his T-shirt emblazoned with the lips-and-tongue logo of the Rolling Stones, said, "Hey. Our keyboard player is here."

She followed him down a narrow flight of stairs to a basement that was half-finished. The floor was covered in indoor-outdoor carpeting, the walls painted a pallid green, the ceiling a maze of exposed pipes and ducts, with two rectangular fluorescent fixtures spreading a glaring light through the small room. Nick's drum kit took up much of the floor space, the rest of which was cluttered with amps, cables, and a compact electric keyboard resting on hinged metal legs.

The other boys were already present, clad in scruffy jeans and baggy shirts. In her beige cotton-knit sweater and neatly ironed bellbottoms, Ruth was clearly overdressed. But then, they were *boys*. She'd spent a lot of time fretting over her outfit that morning. Ever since she had hit puberty, her mother had impressed upon her the importance of dressing nicely for boys.

A faint blue haze hovered in the air, smoke from cigarettes, not marijuana. Ruth recognized the smell, and more significantly, she saw an ashtray heaped with cigarette butts balanced on top of an amp next to Nick's drum kit. The sight stunned her. She had classmates who smoked, but they sneaked their cigarettes. They would never smoke at home, under the same roof as their parents.

Maybe Nick's parents smoked, too, and didn't care that he did. Or maybe his parents weren't home.

If her parents knew she was in a house with four boys and no adult chaperones, they would freak out. She'd have to make sure they never knew.

Jimmy stepped forward. "You all know Ruth Pinchas, right?" he asked. "She plays piano for the glee club at school."

"Do you sing?" Danny Fortuna asked.

Her gaze lingered for an embarrassing moment on Danny's dark eyes, his hollow cheeks, his kiss-shaped lips. "I can sing," she said, turning away so she wouldn't have to think about how good-looking he was.

"So, here's the organ," Mike said, ushering her to the keyboard.

Hugging her notebook to her chest, she stared at the instrument. It spanned only five octaves. Colorful buttons ran in a row above the keys. The keys didn't look like teeth to her. Some were white, some gray, some black.

A wave of anxiety washed over her. "I've never played one of these things before," she admitted.

"It's just like a piano, only electric," Mike told her. He clicked a button, then pressed a key. A bright, buzzy middle-C emerged from one of the amps, and he shrugged as if to say, *See? Just like a piano.*

"Is there a stool I could sit on?" She scanned the room, noting the milk crates stacked sideways along one wall to create shelves, which were filled with ragged folders of paper and LPs in tattered sleeves. A few posters featuring psychedelic designs were taped to the walls. An adjustable round stool stood amid the array of drums, but there was nothing to sit on near the keyboard.

"You have to play standing up," Mike said. "Can you do that?"

"It's not cool to play sitting down," Jimmy elaborated. "You wanna look like Neil Sedaka or something?"

"Or Liberace," Nick added.

"Jerry Lee Lewis had a piano bench," Danny said.

"Which was because he was at a piano," Jimmy pointed out. "Plus, he was, like, acrobatic, bouncing around. I think he was standing when he played, most of the time."

"That guy in the Dave Clark Five," Nick said. "He played standing up."

"Ooh, the Dave Clark Five!" Danny twisted his voice to sound like a swooning prepubescent girl.

"I can play standing up," Ruth said, hoping she would be able to. She could hear Mrs. Demming nattering inside her skull: "Proper posture! Head up. Eyes forward. Feet on the floor, not on the pedals." *Well, I'll have my feet on the floor*, she silently assured her piano teacher.

"So," Mike said, pointing to various buttons. "This is the on-off switch. These other buttons are for different effects. I'm not sure which is which. You can figure that out."

Great. How was she supposed to figure the buttons out? Was everyone going to stand around doing nothing while she tried this button and that button?

"Okay," she said, sounding braver than she felt. She would have to play standing up, on an instrument that looked more like an airplane cockpit than a piano—but at least it didn't look like teeth. And damn it, she was *not* going to make a fool of herself in front of these boys, who hardly knew her. She was *not* going to be a wimpy, delicate A-track girl. She was *not* going to be Liberace. They wanted her to rock? Fine. She'd rock.

"Play something," Danny said.

She hesitated. It dawned on her that she hadn't actually been invited to join the band. This was an audition. She would have to earn her place here.

Her nerves kicked into overdrive, tensing the muscles in her throat. She swallowed a couple of times, then lowered her eyes to the keyboard—Mrs. Demming and her damned cardboard weren't around, and anyway, Ruth didn't want to look at the boys as she performed for them. She launched into "Light My Fire," duplicating the keyboard solo that opened the song. She'd never seen sheet music for it, but she had a good ear, and the solo wasn't complicated.

When she played "Light My Fire" at home, she always sang along. It helped her to keep the rhythm, to hear the counterpoint between the melody and the accompaniment. There was no microphone near the keyboard—thank God—but she sang anyway, softly, more to herself than to the boys, just to keep the melody rooted in her head. When she got to the long keyboard solo in the middle, she riffed a little, throwing in a few grace notes, a few trills. Nothing fancy, just her own touches. If the guys didn't like it, they could kick her out of the band. She wasn't really in the band, anyway. She was just in a basement, playing an electric organ, being evaluated.

Playing while standing up was weird. The keyboard seemed too far away, her elbows too straight. Mrs. Demming wouldn't be able to balance a pencil across her knuckles. The keys felt too responsive against her fingertips, bouncing back up after she depressed them, as if they had springs underneath them. Playing this instrument was like typing on an electric typewriter when you were used to typing on a manual.

The notes didn't resonate the way a piano's notes did. They didn't echo. No felt-covered hammer was striking a string. The black keys played an octave lower than she expected, so she avoided them. The white keys produced toy-like sounds, tinkly and twinkly. She supposed she could change the tonal quality if she knew which of the buttons to push. But she didn't, so she just kept going, plowing her way through the song on the gray keys.

When she reached the end, mimicking the organ's final solo with a flourish, she lifted her hands and glanced up. Singing had distracted her; staring at the keys had distracted her even more. She hadn't quite forgotten that she was in an unfamiliar basement in an unfamiliar house, performing on an unfamiliar instrument for a group of unfamiliar boys, but she'd somehow closed off her mind enough to ignore her surroundings and her audience for a few minutes.

Now she was keenly aware of them again—in part because they were all staring at her. No one said a word.

Their silence unnerved her. She must have flunked the test—something that, as an A-track student, she was not used to doing. They were going to tell her to take her notebook and ride her bike back home, and stick to the Bach three-part invention she was supposed to be mastering for her next lesson with Mrs. Demming.

Nick pulled a Marlboro from a pack in the back pocket of his jeans and lit it. The smoke curling into the air irritated her nostrils. But drummers were hard to come by, so if he wanted a cigarette, she assumed the band had to let him have a cigarette. And it was his house, after all.

Jimmy was the first to turn from her. He grinned at the other guys and said, "So? Do we have a keyboardist?"

"She sings," Danny said.

"She's good," Nick said, "even if she's a girl."

Ruth hadn't realized her gender might be part of the equation. Being the only girl in an all-boy band—what did that signify? Would she have to wear sexy outfits when they performed? Would she *want* to wear sexy outfits?

Hell, yeah. Unfortunately, she wasn't the least bit sexy. She was of average height, kind of flat-chested and thick around the waist. Her hair was brown, her eyes were brown, her nose had a slight bump at the bridge, and she didn't know a damned thing about how to use make-up effectively. Her Aunt Edith once told her that her mouth was her best feature, but Ruth didn't think her mouth was anything special. Nothing about her was special.

Not even her voice. She sang alto in the high school glee club when she wasn't playing the piano. Her voice lacked the sweetness of a Joni Mitchell and the gutsiness of a Grace Slick. She could hold a pitch, but other than that... Nothing special.

However, if the guys in the band wanted her to sing, she would sing. If they wanted her to stand when she played, she would stand. If they wanted her to look sexy, she would figure out how to do that, too. She was in a band. An actual rock band. With a drummer.

"So," Jimmy said, "let's play 'Light My Fire.'"

~

The band's name, she learned, was Trouble Ahead. They had tried out three other keyboard players before her—all boys—and none of them had passed muster. They'd tried playing without a keyboardist, but they didn't like the sound. They had never played in public. They'd been planning to, but then Mike's brother had gotten his draft notice and headed off to basic training, and they'd had to rethink things.

Jimmy and Danny had written a few songs for the band. Musically, their songs were basic—three- or four-chord verses and a chorus. Their lyrics were all about getting laid, getting wasted, and getting in trouble. Danny had a terrific voice—a rock voice, unlike hers or even Jimmy's—and he could deliver even a trite song well. She could bang out the chords on the keyboard, and add a few flourishes, and the songs didn't sound too bad.

"Original songs are better," Jimmy insisted. "No one can compare you to how the song sounds on a record."

The first two Saturdays, Ruth focused on learning the songs Jimmy and Danny had composed (her spiral-bound notebook came in handy) and jamming with them on various rock classics and top-twenty songs. The second Saturday, she actually sang harmony with Danny on the chorus of a song he and Jimmy had written about getting wasted—she didn't feel comfortable singing about getting laid; the lyrics about looking for a fast chick who wanted nothing more than fun just didn't feel right rolling off her tongue—but she, Danny, and Jimmy managed to do three-part harmony in the chorus of a song about waking up hung over after a night of carousing.

The third Saturday, rain gushed out of the sky as if the clouds were doing an impersonation of Niagara Falls. No way could she bike to Nick's house. If her brother were home, she could have persuaded him to drive her to Nick's, but he'd left for his first year at Tufts on Labor Day weekend and was undoubtedly busy looking for fast chicks and waking up hung over on campus right now.

She would have to ask one of her parents to drive her. Over breakfast, she explained to them that she had to go to Nick's house because they were working on a project together.

"What sort of project?" her mother demanded to know. "Who is this boy? Nick Montoya? He's in your classes? I've never heard his name before."

"It's a music project," Ruth said. "We're in glee club together."

"What kind of project does glee club have? I never heard of such a thing."

"Glee club is a real class, Mom. We get grades and everything."

Ruth's mother scowled. "I never heard of this boy, Nick Montoya. Where does he live?"

Jesus. The third degree. Her mother should have been a police officer, grilling suspects in an ugly little room with a two-way mirror on one wall. Instead, she was a stay-at-home housewife with too much time on her hands, time she spent trying to design her children's lives, as if she were an interior decorator and they were empty rooms.

"The southern end of town," Ruth said. That sounded less ominous than the other side of the tracks.

Her mother scowled again, her eyes narrowing, her brow pleating with creases. "A glee club project? You can do that here. We have a piano."

"He's got other instruments at his house. A drum set. We need drums for this."

"You're in a band?" her father guessed. He actually looked intrigued. "What kind of band?"

"A rock band," Ruth mumbled.

"A rock band!" Her mother shook her head and heaved a sigh, as if Ruth had admitted to shooting her chemistry teacher. "Oh, my God. A rock band. What's gotten into you?"

"Hey, at least it isn't a marching band," her father joked. "Then she'd have to wear a bright green uniform and troop across the football field in a silly formation." He downed the last of his coffee. "I'll drive you, Ruthie. I need to get a fill-up, anyway. The gas stations are cheaper on that end of town."

During the drive, he decided to explain Zeno's Paradox to her. "You understand we're never going to get there," he said cheerfully. "According to Zeno's Paradox, you can never get where you're going."

"Why?"

"Before you can reach your destination, you have to travel half the distance to your destination. From there, you have to travel half the distance again. And half again. So you can *approach* your destination, but there's always a half-distance you have to travel first."

Ruth thought about that for a minute. "What if our destination is twice as far as Nick's house? Then traveling half the distance to our destination gets us to Nick's house."

Her father glanced at her, beaming. "My brilliant daughter. You solved the paradox. You should be an engineer."

Fat chance. She was going to be a rock star.

~

She wrote her first song for the band over the school's Christmas break. It wasn't very good, but the guys treated it the way they treated her—with respect and vague detachment. "I don't get what it's about," Jimmy had said hesitantly.

"It's about not letting people push you around," she said. "Or take advantage of you."

"I mean, like, what? Guys putting the moves on you? Because if it's a girl thing—"

"Not just girls. I didn't mean it that way," Ruth said, although she actually had. As the only girl in the band, and a back-up singer, she had to be subtle, indirect, obscure. She couldn't come right out and write a song about guys forcing themselves on girls, even though that was what guys did. Her band mates, like every other boy she knew, undoubtedly forced themselves on girls, although none of them forced themselves on her. Probably because they didn't see her as a girl. They saw her as their keyboard player.

"It's like—" she peered at the lyrics she'd written out, along with chords for the guitarists "—*You push me, I'll push back. I'm strong, I'm tough, I'm not just a hack.*" She wasn't crazy about that line, but it rhymed and it summed up the song, which she'd titled "Hack." "That could be about anyone."

"The wimp talking back to the bully," Danny said helpfully.

"Who cares what it's about?" Nick's words emerged on a stream of blue smoke as he puffed on a Marlboro. "Let's just play it, see how it sounds. You take the lead for now, Ruth, so we know how the melody goes."

She sang it. They all decided it was okay. They'd play with it, add some guitar solos, and see what they could do to make it really rock.

They set a date for their first performance: April twentieth. A neighboring high school was sponsoring a Battle of the Bands, and they'd registered to participate. Now they were committed.

Ruth would have to wear something...well, not quite *sexy*, but flashier than a cotton sweater and denim bellbottoms. She imagined

Jimmy would wear one of his embroidered vests, and Nick would wear one of his Rolling Stones T-shirts. Mike would wear an army-khaki shirt—his brother had sent him one for Christmas. Danny... Who cared what he wore? His face was so beautiful, his clothing almost didn't matter. If Ruth wasn't in his band—and if he wasn't way out of her league—she'd have a serious crush on him. Actually, she *did* have a serious crush on him, but it didn't matter, because they were bandmates and she wasn't going to mess up Trouble Ahead the way Yoko Ono had messed up the Beatles.

Ruth doubted they would play her song during the Battle of the Bands. They would play "Light My Fire," because they did it so well, and then two of the songs Jimmy and Danny had written. That would fill their allotted slot. Entering the competition cost fifteen dollars, but there was a one hundred fifty dollar prize. Ruth contributed some of her baby-sitting money to the entry fee, and the boys covered the rest. Guys always seemed to have more money than girls did.

Ruth's mother was appalled. "You're supposed to be saving that money for college," she'd scolded.

"Like three dollars and twenty-five cents makes much difference," Ruth said.

"The boys want you in this stupid competition, let them pay." Her mother was on her second martini when she said this.

Ruth didn't think it was worth arguing. "Fine. I'll let them pay," she said, knowing full well she was going to kick in the three dollars and twenty-five cents she'd earned babysitting for the Kleins over the past two months. Her mother didn't want her in Trouble Ahead. She didn't want her playing in the Battle of the Bands. She didn't want her borrowing a scarf from Debbie that had an Indian-print pattern and tying it into a headband to make her look a little more rock-and-roll-ish. Her mother didn't want Ruth to do any of these things, but the quantity of vodka she consumed in her martinis gave Ruth an excuse to ignore her. All those pimento-stuffed green olives, too. She put two in each drink. They looked like sickly eyeballs that had fallen out of the face of a corpse and into her glass.

Three weeks before the Battle of the Bands, things fell apart.

Mike showed up late to Nick's basement. He was never late—but he was late that Saturday, and when he arrived, he was pale, his eyes bloodshot, as if he'd spent the previous night living one of the band's getting-wasted songs. "My brother's dead," he announced.

The boy who'd played the keyboard Ruth now played. The boy who'd left the band because he'd gotten drafted. The boy who'd given Mike the army-fatigue shirt he loved to wear.

For the first time since she'd joined the band, she hugged the boys. All of them. They gathered together in front of the drum kit, arms around one another, hugging tight while Mike cried softly. The hug lasted a good five minutes, and then Mike said, "Okay. Let's play."

He couldn't play, really. The bass lines all sounded off, out of sync with the drums, half a measure behind Ruth and the guitars. She tried to cover for him, having mastered the black bass keys on Mike's brother's keyboard, but the song sounded terrible. "We can skip the Battle of the Bands," Jimmy said while Danny pulled a joint out of his shirt's chest pocket, licked it, and lit it.

They passed the joint around. Trying not to think about Danny's saliva all over the joint—and then deciding she actually liked the fact that Danny's saliva was all over it—Ruth took one hit, coughed mightily, and waved it off the next time it circled around to her. "I'm going to write a song for your brother," she promised Mike. "What's his name?"

Chapter Three

If Only the Band Hadn't Broken Up...

With no one home, Ruth could sing as loud as she wanted. She remained seated on the piano bench—no longer was she obligated to play standing up—and let the song she'd written so many years ago flow out of her. "*Come on, Joe; where'd you go? Good-bye, John; you're really gone. So long, Jack; you won't be back. All of them, all of them, over in 'Nam, never coming home, just like Tom.*"

The song was named "Tom." Mike's brother was named Tom. He'd died in a place called Quăng Ngãi. Tom Radowski, it turned out, had been a classmate of Ruth's brother. When Ruth had telephoned David at Tufts to tell him about Tom's death, David said he remembered Tom—mostly because Tom had talked a lot about whether he'd get drafted after they graduated from high school. Most of David's classmates had clung to their student deferments by enrolling in college, or else by seeking out doctors who would swear they had flat feet or a heart murmur and couldn't serve. Tom Radowski hadn't been like that. "I've got nothing better to do," he'd said, according to David. "I'm not going to college and I'm healthy. They're gonna get me."

They'd gotten him. And all these years later, the song Ruth wrote for him and for Mike, filled with anger and anguish, made her vision blur with tears.

She remembered how Danny had looked, crooning the song on the stage in that high school auditorium at the Battle of the Bands. He sang it solo, his voice rising from somewhere deep in his soul, husky and bitter as Jimmy's guitar riffs twisted around it, and then Ruth's keyboard riffs. Mike played a simple bass line—it was all he could handle, but he handled it well. Afterward, the guys would swear that was the song that had won the competition for them.

Getting the prize money had been exciting. But what Ruth remembered, all these decades later, was how Danny had looked when he'd sung her song, how he'd sounded. So much better than she did, playing the song today.

She sang to an empty living room. It was nothing like Nick Montoya's smoky basement, where they'd spent so many hours practicing and bickering and praising one another. No fluorescent ceiling fixtures. No indoor-outdoor carpet. The floor of Ruth's living room was hardwood, polished to a high gleam and partly covered with an intricately patterned area rug imported from some Middle Eastern country. The sofa and love seat were upholstered in a forest green brocade with dark red highlights; the tall six-over-six windows were framed by lush burgundy curtains tied back with matching swags. The mantel above the fireplace held framed high-school graduation photos of Noah, Jill, and Maddie.

It was the sort of room that reeked of privilege, of affluence. The piano was a baby grand.

But if she closed her eyes, she could pretend she was on a stage bathed in moody light, surrounded by acoustic panels, watching her footing around coiled nests of cables and stacks of cheap amps, surrounded by Nick and Mike and Jimmy and Danny. She could pretend Danny was singing, and she was layering a line of harmony beneath his voice, and Jimmy's guitar solo was sweet and melancholy, and in front of them an audience of two thousand teenagers sat rapt, listening to the song she wrote and thinking about an unlucky soldier who died in Quăng Ngãi so many years ago.

If only the band hadn't broken up...

Sometimes I think I'm too old for this, but when you're a rocker, you're never too old. Trouble Ahead still performs the occasional concert for fans who simply weren't willing to release their hold on us. Not regular touring—that's awfully tiring, and we're all in a different place—but every now and then, we emerge from retirement, set up on a stage somewhere, and play for our loyal followers. After our induction into the Rock and Roll Hall of Fame—oh, God, that was so cool, being introduced by Chrissie Hynde, and getting up on the stage together while the audience cheered and a few solitary voices shouted, "Play 'Tom'! Play 'Tom'!"

Which, of course, we did, the final song of our three-song set. Not a dry eye in the house, as the cliché would have it—although who knows? There might have been plenty of dry eyes in the house. On the stage, though, where I stood behind the keyboard, surrounded by my boys, no eyes were dry.

Being a semi-retired rock star is...surprisingly quiet. When I was younger and hungrier, I thrived on the screaming crowds, the bedlam, the sea of glowstick-holding fans spread beyond the edge of the stage, the boom and swirl and din of the music we created. But now I prefer peace, the sweet emptiness of the air, the sound of my own voice and my piano, unamplified.

I'm rich—not a billionaire, but wealthy enough that I don't have to think about money, about budgeting, about clipping supermarket coupons. I spend most of my retirement in a spacious house surrounded by trees in Colorado...no, Montana. The winters are rugged here, but that's okay, because I pay someone to clear the snow from my driveway and chauffeur me around if the roads are too treacherous for my comfort level. My daughter lives nearby and has a thriving organic skin-care business. My son is a record and film producer in Hollywood but spends much of his time in Montana, as well, escaping the fires and floods and the film-industry head-cases. My son looks uncannily like Danny Fortuna.

I have a dog, a rescue mutt named Trouble—although he's no trouble at all—and I have a housekeeper who takes Trouble for walks when I don't want to, and who cleans up the poop so I don't have to. I enjoy puttering around the kitchen but don't make a fetish out of it. I don't have much of a yard, because the house is surrounded by dense evergreen woods, which give me the privacy I crave. But there's a small, open patch beyond the front door, and the daffodils return every spring, bright and yellow and happy.

Every now and then, superstars of the music world phone me and ask if I'll do them the enormous honor of singing back-up on a song on their album. Of course I say yes. I love singing, and if James Taylor or Bruce Springsteen or Adele or Beyonce wants to do a duet with me, how can I say no?

Except, of course, that if I'm a rock star, maybe they aren't *rock stars. Maybe the entire universe of rock stardom is reconfigured, the balance shifted, the hierarchy collapsed and reconstructed in an entirely different shape, because some butterfly in—why not?—Quăng Ngãi fluttered its wings. Maybe Trouble Ahead occupies the stardom slot that Bruce Springsteen might have occupied. Maybe Springsteen runs a car-detailing garage in central New Jersey. Maybe Beyonce is a real estate broker, and James Taylor is a counselor at a residential rehab center, and Adele is a preschool teacher. And I am a retired rock star whose fans still appreciate me.*

I've endowed a community center in my town. I have the money to do that—money I invest locally in addition to the money I donate to various political and environmental organizations. The community center is named the Tom Radowski Memorial Center. In the entry, a photo of Mike's brother hangs next to a small showcase with artifacts from Tom's life: his uniform, some of the letters he sent Mike from Vietnam, some photos, and the dog tags Mike wore once Tom's body and his effects were sent home. I know Mike would have liked to keep them himself, but when I told him I was going to name the community center in memory of his brother, he insisted on donating them. People often ask me how I was connected to Tom. "He was a classmate of my brother's," I say. "I didn't really know him myself, but his brother Mike was like a brother to me. I wrote the song 'Tom' for him. A song isn't enough, though. We need to remember these men who went off to war and never grew old."

So I'm rich, but I use my money carefully and effectively. I'm not pretentious. I'm not promiscuous. I live a quiet life because I can. No scandals. No fleet of expensive imported cars. My hair is long and silver, and most days I just pull it back with an elastic and forget about it. I live in well-worn jeans and comfortable shoes—no, elaborately tooled cowboy boots. They're my one wardrobe indulgence.

I took the leap into chaos, and this is my reward. This sweet, quiet life.

I'm content. I love my children and grandchildren, and I love my solitude. I can sing as loudly as I wish, in any room in the house I wish, and no one judges me. I host dinner parties for dear friends, and after we've polished off the wine and the port, they go home.

All those years on the road tired me out. Those years when I'd occupy the little room at the back of the bus, so I could do my remote studies—music career or not, I was determined to earn a college degree—while the guys filled the rest of the bus with their arguments, their laughter, their poker and video games and marijuana fumes. I performed while pregnant. I performed after the babies were born, although I had to hire a full-time nanny to travel with us when we toured. Not a hardship. My children grew up fearless and confident and surrounded by music. Everyone in our entourage became honorary aunts and uncles to them. It worked out.

I thrived on the concerts and the noise and the miles of asphalt. I adored my Trouble Ahead family—my boys, the roadies, our manager (who was sane and honest and made us a lot of money without exploiting us). I still remember the tour, thirty years ago, during which we convinced Nick Montoya to quit smoking. I remember talking Mike out of getting that ugly tattoo when we were playing in Phoenix. I remember Jimmy hugging me tight when I got the news that my father had died. I remember Danny.

Of course I remember Danny. Of course. He lives in L.A. but comes up to Montana to visit several times a year, and his visits are always joyful. And then he leaves, and that's joyful too.

Because when you're a retired rock star, you can have anything you want. Company. Solitude. Music. Silence. Peace.

She finished singing "Tom" and let out a deep sigh. Before the song's melancholy mood completely released its grip on her, she heard sounds coming from the kitchen—a door slamming, footsteps, the thump of a bag being dropped onto the table. "I'm home," Maddie shouted.

How much longer would Maddie consider this house her home? She was an adult. So was Warren. Maddie could move in with him any time she wanted, even if the wedding wouldn't take place until next April.

But no. She wanted to be a blushing bride. Not a virginal one—it was way too late for that—but at the ripe old age of thirty-three, she had decided to embrace tradition. "The bride shouldn't live with the groom before their wedding," she insisted.

Ruth had lived with Barry for a year before their wedding. Jill had lived with Ben. Noah had lived with Laura—and before Laura with Cynthia, and before Cynthia with Michelle. Ruth believed living with your partner prior to tying the knot was a wise step. If Maddie didn't live with Warren before they got married, how would she know what temperature he liked to set the thermostat at night, or whether he left the bathroom door open when he peed? Marriages had crashed and burned over lesser issues than those.

But Maddie wanted *tradition.* A big, expensive, traditional wedding, during which she would wear a big, expensive, traditional wedding gown, even though she was the mother of a fourteen-year-old girl—who would be wearing an utterly inappropriate—but big and expensive—strapless bridesmaid dress.

Ruth pushed back the piano bench and stood. Shaking off the last of the somber mood "Tom" had draped over her, she left the living room for the kitchen. Maddie hovered beside the table, rummaging through her...what was it? Too big to be a purse, but too elaborate, with its thick russet-hued leather and its zippered compartments, to be a tote bag. She was still dressed in the scrubs she wore at work, navy-blue trousers and a smock printed with garishly colored flowers—hot pink, neon green, pop-your-eyes-out blue. According to Maddie, the dentist who owned the practice where she worked thought these cheerful scrubs would relax patients so they wouldn't squirm or wince while their molars were getting drilled and their gums were getting poked. Whenever Ruth saw Maddie in her scrubs, though, the colors reminded her of Day-Glo posters from her youth. Pastels might be more tranquilizing, if the goal of Dr. Bromberg was to sedate his patients.

How Maddie had wound up becoming a dental hygienist was a mystery Ruth had yet to solve. Maddie had stumbled into it the way she stumbled into so much. After she'd returned home from her year-long rebellion with Kyle Jarvis, she'd wanted to fly off to Oberlin College, where she'd been accepted early-decision two years ago. "You already paid the deposit," she'd pointed out. "So I may as well go there."

"You have a baby," Ruth had argued.

"I figure you and Dad can take care of Rainbow while I'm in school. I need a college education."

Nice of her to have figured that out two years after the fact. "In case you haven't noticed, Dad and I work."

"You can put her in day care."

"*You* can put her in day care," Ruth had retorted, although she didn't like the thought of farming out to a day-care center the beautiful little girl currently in the port-a-crib Barry had found blanketed in dust in the basement, scrubbed clean, and brought upstairs. This was her granddaughter, her very first grandchild. She didn't want a stranger taking care of her.

She didn't want to take care of her either. She had raised her children. She'd been enjoying her empty nest. She loved having dinner with Barry in the dining room rather than the kitchen, and lingering over a second glass of wine while they discussed their days. No children arguing over whose turn it was to take out the trash. No spills or stains or complaints that someone got a bigger piece of cake than someone else. No frantic reminders of a play rehearsal, a soccer practice, a study date, a *date* date that would cut the meal short.

Raising her children had been a tough job, noble yet demanding. Ruth couldn't say she'd loved every minute of it, but she'd loved the vast majority of those minutes. And now she was done. She did *not* want to raise Rainbow.

"If you'd like to go to college," she said, "we'll work something out locally. If you'd like Rainbow to live here with us, you will live here with us, too. If you'd like us to pay your bills, you will contribute to the household budget. We will not pay hundreds of thousands of dollars for you to go to Oberlin while we take care of your baby."

After a long week of histrionics, sulking, and vicious rants, Maddie decided to enroll in a local community college. Why she decided to major in dental hygiene, Ruth couldn't say—but then, why did Maddie do anything? As far as Ruth knew, no child ever said, "When I grow up I want to be a dental hygienist." An astronaut, maybe. A ballerina. President of the United States. A rock star, naturally. But a dental hygienist?

Whether or not she had the career of her dreams, Maddie seemed in good spirits as she pulled a few containers of food from the depths of her bag. "We did this perfect implant today," she said. "I swear, Dr. Bromberg is an artist. DaVinci has nothing on him. He matched that tooth so perfectly—"

"I need to talk to you," Ruth interrupted her. "Actually, you need to talk to Rainie."

"About what?"

"You should probably ask her."

"Is she home?" Maddie set a plastic tub filled with a milky liquid on the table beside her bag. "What do I need to talk to her about? Is she in trouble?"

"She told me she wants to live here with Dad and me after you and Warren are married."

That stopped Maddie. She stared at Ruth, frowning, her impeccably tweezed eyebrows dipping delicately above the bridge of her nose. "Why would she want to do that?"

"You'll have to ask her."

"That's ridiculous." Maddie shook her head and carried the food containers to the refrigerator. "I stopped in at the Asian Mart on my way home and bought her favorite miso soup. How could she not want to live with us?"

Ruth supposed there was more to domestic arrangements than miso soup, no matter how tasty it was.

"I can't believe this," Maddie fumed. Evidently she took Rainie's decision as a personal insult—which it probably was. "Warren is so good to her. She's not even his daughter, but he always treats her with generosity and respect."

Also with a bit of condescension, if Rainie's reports of her visits with her soon-to-be stepfather were accurate. According to her, he'd called the pink highlights she'd added to her hair "adorable," which they really weren't. Besides, Rainie was at an age where being called "adorable" was horrifying. And, Rainie had complained, she'd had the pink highlights in her hair for two weeks before he'd even noticed.

Beyond that, Warren was a bit dull. The only reason Maddie could possibly want to marry him was that he was the antithesis of Kyle Jarvis. Maddie had always been one to embrace extremes.

"Rainie is my maid of honor," Maddie said indignantly. "Of course she'll live with us."

Miso soup and maid of honor. How could Rainie not want to live with her mother? "I'm on your side," Ruth said, filtering the sardonic undertone out of her voice. "But you need to talk to her."

"I'll get Jill to talk to her," Maddie said, removing a few more items from her tote and stashing them in the refrigerator. Ruth had no idea what they were, other than that they were sealed inside ziplock bags or plastic tubs. Was Maddie still on her vegetarian kick? Maybe they were soybean stews, or gluten-free crackers that tasted like sawdust. Of course, she'd wind up eating Ruth's food, anyway—even meat—because Ruth's food didn't taste like sawdust.

"Why do you want her to talk to Jill?"

Maddie gave Ruth a look. She had been giving Ruth the same look since she'd hit puberty. It was a look that said, *Mom, you are such an idiot.* "Jill," she said, "is a psychotherapist."

"Jill is your sister. She's Rainie's aunt. Therapists don't treat their own family. Not that Rainie needs treatment," Ruth added, opening the refrigerator door and inspecting one of the containers Maddie had placed there. The label was printed in Japanese, or maybe Korean. Shrugging, Ruth shut the door. "You don't need Jill to run interference between you and Rainie. Just sit down and talk to her. Find out why she doesn't want to move in with you and Warren. It could be something as simple as her wanting to stay in Brentwood High School. All her friends are here."

"I think there's some paperwork we can fill out so she can stay a student here, even if she moves one town away," Maddie said. "If that's the only problem, she can keep going to Brentwood High."

"She won't be able to take the bus to school," Ruth pointed out. "The school buses won't cross town lines."

"Then I guess we'll have to drive her. It'll screw up my work schedule, though. And Warren's. Once the tax season starts, he won't have any free time." Maddie ruminated for a moment, then beamed a suspiciously bright smile at Ruth. "You're retired, Mom. You can drive her to school."

No, I can't, Ruth almost retorted. She was done. Done chauffeuring children around. Done being at their beck and call. Done with Maddie, done with Rainie, done with all of them.

"I'm going to take a walk," she said, even though she'd already walked five miles that day. Another mile or two, or five, or twenty-five, wouldn't hurt. If anything, it would take her out of this house, away from the demands of her family, off into a world where she could imagine what her life might have been like if a butterfly had fluttered its wings differently.

Chapter Four

If Only I'd Gotten My Tubes Tied...

"So let her stay here," Barry said.

He'd gotten home ten minutes ago. The first ten minutes of Barry's arrival home from work, after pulling into the garage, shutting off the engine of his beloved Audi TTS, and entering the house, were nearly always spent in the master bedroom with Ruth, where she sat on the bed while he shed his tailored business suit like a moth emerging from a chrysalis, replacing his office attire with a pair of jeans and casual shirt—flannel in the winter, polo shirt in the summer. He loved his job as a partner at Strom Strategies, loved the status, loved the income that allowed him to buy sporty, overpriced cars—but he loved his worn-out jeans at least as much. He'd been a hippie when Ruth had met him. He was miles from hippiedom now—a senior partner in a highly reputed consulting firm, a brandy connoisseur, someone who avoided signing petitions on the chance that going public with his politics might offend a client. But he still loved his jeans.

They'd both favored jeans when they'd met. They had been broke at the time, and jeans were relatively cheap and easy to patch when they tore. They'd been in graduate school, she in a master's degree program in education, he in a doctoral program in economics. He'd been shaggy and goofy and cute in those days—he was still cute, though no longer goofy—but after two years, he realized he would rather be practicing business than theorizing about it, so he'd switched over to an MBA program while Ruth supported them with her first teaching job, in a small private school that paid abysmally. They'd been young. They'd been spirited. They'd eaten a lot of spaghetti. It had all seemed romantic.

His hair was much shorter now than it had been during their graduate-school days. It was much grayer. His belly was bigger, but like many men, he had the amazing ability to continue wearing the same size jeans despite his paunch, simply hitching the waistband lower so his gut could bulge comfortably above his belt. Ruth could not do this. If she gained just a few pounds—the greatest tragedy that could befall a woman—she had to move up a size. Thanks to strict self-discipline and the voice of her mother nagging inside her skull, a voice she had tried unsuccessfully for the past fifty-plus years to vanquish from her memory—she'd managed to maintain her weight, never straying more than a few pounds above what she'd weighed in high school. She had also discovered the utter joy of comfort-waist trousers.

Barry didn't need comfort-waist trousers. He simply rearranged his flesh around the trousers he already owned.

"You really want Rainie to continue living here after Maddie moves out?" Ruth pressed him.

He smoothed his polo shirt into his jeans, adjusted the waist, and buckled his belt. "If it makes her happy," he said. He was a doting grandpa. Whatever made his precious grandchildren happy was fine with him. The more, the merrier, as far as he was concerned. Let all five of the grandchildren live in his house, forever if they wished.

Of course, he'd never had to juggle child care and career. He'd contributed to the potty-training of all his and Ruth's children and Rainie when he could, but he rarely could, because...well, there were always reasons. He had an important phone call with a client. The Patriots were playing a televised game. He had to review his and Ruth's investment portfolio to make sure the transaction he'd phoned in had gone through. He'd had a long, difficult day and was wrung out. He needed a nap.

Having Rainie continue to live with him and Ruth after Maddie and Warren got married wouldn't affect his life that much. He wouldn't be in charge of rousing her when she overslept, and hustling her out the door to catch the bus—or driving her to school if she missed the bus. He wouldn't have to help her manage her after-school schedule—the clubs, the soccer team, the get-togethers with friends—and nag her to do her homework, and listen to her whine about said homework, and discover that she was still awake at midnight, screen-chatting with the friends she'd already spent hours with earlier that day. He wouldn't have to yell at her to go to bed so she wouldn't oversleep again the next morning.

Maddie ought to take care of Rainie, but she didn't. So Ruth did. Someone had to.

She loved Rainie. She didn't begrudge her granddaughter a moment of her time and attention. Pink hair and Goth pedicure notwithstanding, Rainie was maturing into a lovely human being, for which Ruth believed she herself deserved much of the credit.

But she wanted to be done. She wanted to experience retirement the way most people did—actually *retired*. Free of daily responsibilities. Free of needy people making demands on her, the way the superintendent of schools, and her principal, and her fellow teachers, and her students, and their parents—to say nothing of her own children—all had. She wanted to wake up each morning, draw in a deep breath, and think, *today I will take care of myself and no one else.*

That had always been her vision of retirement: a stage of her life when she could be gloriously selfish. When she could put her own needs and whims first. When she could enter a room without surveying it and its occupants and thinking about what and who had to be taken care of before she could sit down and prop her feet up and shut her eyes for one blessed moment. When she didn't feel beset by the chaos of daily life.

I am turning into an old grouch, she thought—and worse, a bad grandmother. Barry was right. If Rainie needed to stay here with her grandparents, why shouldn't she? Maddie was right, too—if Rainie felt compelled to reject her mother, maybe she ought to talk to a therapist like Jill. Maybe the whole family ought to.

Maybe they were all insane.

When Ruth was pregnant with Jill, she told Barry she believed two children were enough. "My friend Sarah has three kids, and she said it was a mistake," Ruth told Barry as she waddled around the kitchen, looking as if she'd swallowed a watermelon whole and feeling twinges of envy as he slurped beer from an icy brown bottle. She hadn't allowed alcohol to pass her lips for seven months. A glass of wine, or even a cold beer like the one Barry was chugging, would have been a joy.

They were still living in Brookline at the time, in a flat on the second floor of a three-decker near Coolidge Corner. The neighborhood wasn't quite as chic as it would later become, but it was a step up from their graduate-school apartment in Brighton, which they had shared with a vast army of cockroaches and silverfish. The Brookline apartment was varmint-free, if you didn't count the occasional mosquito or yellow-jacket that buzzed through an open window. They had to keep their windows open all summer, because the apartment had no central air conditioning. Just one window unit in the living room which rattled like a decrepit truck with suspension issues whenever they turned it on high.

"Sarah knows everything," Barry muttered. He'd recently begun working at Strom Strategies, and he was still trying to figure out how to be a grown-up financial consultant instead of a shaggy, goofy graduate student. The effort made him cynical.

"She said the number of children should never exceed the number of available adults."

"So we could have three children if we hired a nanny," Barry calculated.

"Or if we invited my mother to move in with us."

He laughed. They both knew that if Ruth's mother ever moved in with them, Ruth would be forced to move out—by the police, who would arrest her and lock her in prison for having murdered her mother.

"Okay. We'll have two children," he said. He was always agreeable when Ruth launched into a discussion about something he didn't care one way or another about.

"So, I was thinking you should get a vasectomy."

Barry stopped being agreeable. He choked on a mouthful of beer, set the bottle onto the kitchen table with a thump, and gaped at her. His sudden pallor implied that merely thinking about the procedure caused excruciating pain in his groin. "No way," he said. "I don't want anyone messing with *that*."

That would have survived a minor messing just fine. Sarah's husband had gotten a vasectomy after their third child. According to Sarah, their sex life had been better than ever since he'd undergone the surgery.

Ruth would like her sex life to be better than ever. More than that, she wanted to limit their family to two children.

At her last ob/gyn appointment, her doctor had raised the subject of having her tubes tied. "It's a simple matter," he'd assured her. "We can do it while we're in there."

"In where?"

"After you've delivered the baby. Everything's all opened up. We can just go in and make a few snips."

She did not want her gynecologist to "just go in." She'd given birth to Noah naturally, and planned to do the same for her second child. No one would have to "just go in." She'd push and the baby would come out.

Besides, tubal ligation, especially if it was performed within minutes of her baby's birth, seemed like an insult to her body. It would be like saying, "Hey, uterus, nice job. Now we're going to decommission you."

She leaned against the Formica counter, arms folded, maternity blouse limp and damp with sweat. Barry remained at the table, his left hand molded to his beer bottle and his right hand resting in his lap, not quite cupped around his scrotum but near enough to fight off anyone who approached with the intention of tampering surgically with his precious testicles. "Why don't you want to have a vasectomy?" she asked. "You agree with me that we're going to stop after two children."

"Sure, we can stop," he said. "But what if you die and I remarry, and I want to have a baby with my new wife?"

"*That's* your best argument?"

"I didn't say what if we got a divorce. The only way I'd leave you was if you died. So don't get all pissy."

"You'd really want to have a baby with another woman?"

"Only if you were dead." He sounded a bit too eager for that possibility to materialize. "You don't want any more children? You can do that thing. The tube tying."

"Why does birth control have to be my responsibility?"

"You're the one giving birth," he pointed out, his reasonability irritating her. "Women want to control their bodies. They want to be the ones who decide to get an abortion—or keep the child and demand child support from the dad. You want autonomy over your body? Get your tubes tied."

Sighing, she pushed away from the counter and turned to prepare the hamburgers they were going to have for supper. Her swollen abdomen bumped against the edge of the sink, and the fetus gave a sharp kick in response. It was hard to remember how far her body extended in front of her. "All right," she conceded. "I'll think about getting my tubes tied."

She did think about it. Unlike Barry, she didn't hesitate out of a fear—or hope—that he would keel over and she'd remarry and want more children. But having someone *just go in and make a few snips* seemed so invasive. According to her doctor, it might take several weeks to recover. She would have to remain in the hospital for a few days, whereas a vasectomy could be done as an outpatient procedure. A tubal ligation would cost several times more than a vasectomy, too. She might suffer from abdominal pain, and after the abdominal pain of giving birth to her baby, more abdominal pain seemed unfair. Equally unfair, the procedure wouldn't put an end to getting her period.

She hated her diaphragm—glopping all that spermicide jelly into its rubbery little bowl was messy and it smelled antiseptic. Also, she didn't like the idea of having spermicide—technically a kind of poison—inside her. And a diaphragm seemed so archaic. It was barely an improvement over the ancient practice of jamming dead leaves or wads of wool into the vagina to prevent pregnancy.

She considered getting an IUD, but one of her friends had had a terrible reaction to having one, and wound up needing a hysterectomy. And two of her friends in college took birth control pills and wound up with blood clots in their legs, which scared her enough to avoid the pill. Barry wouldn't use condoms because, he said, he was no longer a teenager. He was an adult—and married. Married men didn't need condoms unless they were cheating on their wives, according to him.

So. Her choices were the diaphragm or the surgery.

She didn't want the surgery.

She would be careful, she resolved. She'd use copious amounts of the damned spermicide. She'd monitor the calendar and veto sex on her most fertile days, even though her period was irregular enough that she couldn't be absolutely sure which days those were. She really didn't want a third child.

For years, her caution worked. She and Barry and Noah and Jill made a statistically perfect family: son and daughter, two years apart, and the children didn't outnumber the adults. Noah was adventurous, physical, noisy. Jill was organized, observant, intellectual. Noah occasionally pushed Jill. Jill occasionally tattled on Noah. They loved music, satisfying Ruth's soul, and rough-housing, satisfying Barry's.

When Jill turned three, Ruth enrolled her in preschool. Noah was in kindergarten by then, freeing Ruth to search for a better teaching position. She quickly landed one, running the primary-school music program in the tranquil Boston suburb of Brentwood. She and Barry abandoned their Coolidge Corner apartment for a tiny, overpriced house in Newton so the children could have their own bedrooms, a fenced-in backyard, and the dog they'd been begging for, a rescue mutt Ruth wound up taking care of. She and Barry risked turning into their parents. They were now a textbook nuclear family, living the middle-class suburban life they'd once viewed with contempt through a haze of young-adult arrogance and marijuana smoke. But it wasn't bad, really. Ruth was content.

Her sex life wasn't better than ever, but it was good enough. Good enough, and pregnancy-free enough that she started using a little less spermicide—the odor really did turn her off—and not paying quite as close attention to her calendar. She got complacent.

She got pregnant.

Sometimes she wondered whether Maddie was the way she was because she'd been conceived with a spermatozoa headstrong and stubborn enough to fight its way through that contraceptive jelly and the latex barrier of Ruth's diaphragm. This was no lazy spermatozoa. It had overcome all obstacles, determined to get what it was after.

Noah was almost ten years old when Ruth got pregnant, Jill almost eight. Ruth hadn't purchased a box of diapers in nearly six years. When she learned she was expecting, she actually thought, for a few days, about getting an abortion. But of course she wouldn't. She didn't even raise the idea with Barry, and she often wondered if he'd also entertained that possibility without mentioning it to her. And she wondered whether Maddie wound up being as challenging as she was not only because the spermatozoa had been so obstinate but because somewhere in her cellular memory she comprehended that she might have been aborted.

But she wasn't. Ruth and Barry were married. They could afford another child. They decided having a new baby would be an interesting adventure.

Maddie was definitely an interesting adventure.

"I want to name her Magda," Barry said in the delivery room just minutes after she was born. "After my grandmother."

"You didn't even like your grandmother," Ruth reminded him. She'd met Barry's paternal grandmother a few times. The woman had been dour and wizened, with a faint, silvery mustache and a Bulgarian accent thicker than concrete. Her funeral a year ago had been a perfunctory affair, with less discussion about the deceased than about the quality of the lox served at the *shiva* reception (too salty) and the rabbi's speech impediment (a tendency to spray saliva when he chanted).

"I like my grandmother more, now that she's dead," Barry said. "I think we should honor her."

"Madelyn," Ruth suggested. "Not Magda. I can live with Madelyn." She was a fan of short names like her own, and Noah and Jill. But Madelyn had a nice flow to it. It was musical.

At first, Ruth figured her physical and emotional fatigue dealing with Maddie was her own fault. She was out of practice; she was too old to feel sentimental about nursing her baby at two a.m. and again at five a.m. The onesies she'd thought were so adorable when Noah and Jill were babies now seemed ridiculously complicated, and Maddie squirmed too much after her bath, constantly trying to jam her pudgy feet into a onesie's sleeves rather than its legs. Ruth had had to buy all new baby clothing. She'd donated the baby clothes Noah and Jill had worn years ago to a battered women's shelter, assuming she would never have any more use for them.

After a while, though, she began to realize that her fatigue wasn't simply the result of too much to do and too little sleep. Maddie was *different.* She was smart and aggressive and demanding. Noah and Jill had both seemed quite intelligent to Ruth when they were babies, but they'd been mellow. Noah could amuse himself for hours trying to fit his fisted hand into his mouth. Jill was content simply staring at the Winnie-the-Pooh characters in the mobile hanging above her crib.

Not Maddie. She wanted to move, to master, to conquer. If Noah was throwing a baseball, she wanted to throw a baseball, too, even though she still hadn't quite gotten the hang of sitting up unassisted. If Jill was braiding her hair, Maddie wanted braids, too, even though she didn't have enough hair to braid. She scampered after Noah and Jill, first on all fours, scooting around in a speed-crawl that would have taken first place in those baby races Ruth saw on TV, and then on her feet once she'd learned how to walk—a skill she'd mastered at nine months, just so she could keep up with her siblings. She was always hungry, and always picky. Pureed plums were fine. Pureed yams wound up on the floor, on the wall, and in her ears, but never in her mouth. By the time she was a year old, she'd figured out how to unbuckle the strap of her high chair and climb out of it. The first time she did this, Ruth barely caught her in time before she jumped off the chair's plastic tray. That was, in fact, the last time she did it, too, since Ruth decided the high chair was no longer safe and moved Maddie to a booster seat for her meals.

She loved banging on the piano so much, Ruth decided to start teaching her basic piano technique when she was three. Her fingers were too small, but she discovered that pressing one key at a time sounded better than slapping multiple keys with her palms.

She was wild, but she was beautiful. Ruth wasn't sure why. She considered herself passably attractive, and Barry was good-looking in a guy sort of way. Noah and Jill were healthy, energetic, normal kids. Cleaned and scrubbed, they photographed well in family portraits. Most of the time, they weren't clean and scrubbed, but to their mother, they were gorgeous.

Maddie's beauty, however, was of a higher order. Other children's mothers would come up to Ruth in the supermarket or at school events to comment on the length of Maddie's eyelashes or the delicacy of her dimples. Strangers on the street would ask if she was a model, and one mildly creepy man in downtown Newton Centre once told Ruth he ran a modeling agency and pressed a business card into her hand. When Maddie's hair finally came in, it grew black and thick. Her eyes filled half her face, and her mouth shaped the dictionary definition of rosebud lips. Sometimes, Ruth wanted to put a bag over Maddie's head, just to protect her from whatever danger her stunning appearance might bring.

Amazingly, blessedly, Maddie seemed totally unaware of her uncommon beauty. She was too busy tearing through life to pay attention to anything as trivial as her appearance.

Ruth had thought that enrolling Maddie in day care and resuming her teaching job would leave her doubly exhausted, but the hours she spent teaching music to the primary school students in Brentwood were actually restful compared to the hours she spent with Maddie. She would pick Maddie up from day care at three-thirty, and Maddie would babble the entire drive home, at first in gibberish and then in English, posing questions that taxed

Ruth's weary brain. "Does the universe have a bottom?" she'd ask. "Why do we have toes?" "If I put my head upside down, can I talk backwards?" Once they arrived home, she would demand a snack. She would want to ride on the dog's back. She would pull apart one of Noah's Lego constructions. She would beg Ruth to read her favorite book, Ludwig Bemelmans's *Madeline*. She would charge around the back yard until she fell and scraped her knees, and while Ruth bandaged her scrapes, she would ask, "Why do we have blood?"

She dominated dinnertime, yammering and playing with her food, one day refusing to eat broccoli and the next day refusing to eat anything *but* broccoli. She amused herself by racing around the kitchen after dinner, barreling into Ruth's shins and knocking her off balance while she cleared the table. Bedtime was hectic and draining; she wanted to stay up as late as Jill did, since they shared a bedroom, a fact Jill resented with good reason. Maddie loved to go through Jill's things—her barrettes, her books, her diary, which Maddie couldn't read but could scribble in with a red Sharpie. "I want my own bedroom," Jill whined. "It's not fair that Noah has his own room and I don't."

True enough. It wasn't fair. "We'll get a bigger house," Barry decided.

They could have bought that Victorian with the turret, but no. They'd wound up buying the colonial on Jefferson Road, because it had central air and an attached garage.

The day after the moving van had deposited their belongings and departed, Barry had waltzed off to his office in the city, leaving Ruth to oversee the unpacking. The schools were closed for summer vacation, and she'd told Jill and Noah to arrange their own rooms. For Noah, this meant dumping onto the floor of his closet whatever clothing hadn't remained inside his dresser drawers during the move, arranging his soccer and Little League trophies atop his bureau, and then pedaling away on his bicycle to check out the neighborhood. Jill spent the day meticulously organizing her every possession, arranging her shoes on a chrome rack inside her closet, shelving her books in alphabetical order by author, and emerging from her room only to forage for food, thank Ruth for finally giving her her own bedroom, and glower at Maddie and warn her not to enter Jill's bedroom without permission. "*Ever*," she emphasized. "Don't you ever, *ever* come in unless I say you can."

Three-year-old Maddie was too young to organize her room, so Ruth did it for her. She had a dresser. She had a small rocking chair for her stuffed animals to sit in. She had a comforter for her bed that featured a loud pattern of stars, comets, and planets—mostly Saturns, since the majority of the planets had rings around them—which Maddie had picked out herself during an outing to the mall a year ago. She had a tot-sized table and chair that would be replaced by a regular desk once she started attending school, although Ruth could not imagine Maddie sitting still at a desk. She would be much more likely to do her homework on the floor, with worksheets and colored pencils scattered all around her, or else on her bed, where she would undoubtedly get ink stains on her outer-space blanket.

Ruth was busy trying to put the kitchen together—a difficult task in the best of circumstances, and much more difficult with a three-year-old pulling open drawers, sloshing water out of the dog's bowl by the mud room door, and insisting the pots and pans Ruth stashed inside one cabinet really belonged in another cabinet—when the front doorbell rang. Neither Ruth nor Maddie looked presentable. Ruth wore an old striped shirt and denim cut-offs, and her hair was held in a ponytail by a scrunchy. Maddie had dressed herself that day, and everything clashed with everything else—and much of the fabric was wet, given her engagement with the dog's water bowl. Mother and daughter were not prepared to entertain visitors.

The visitors were a smiling woman a few years younger than Ruth, carrying a paper plate covered in silver foil, and a boy Maddie's size, with pale blue eyes and long, floppy hair the color of a deer's pelt. He lurked behind the woman's legs, peeking out from behind them when he spotted Maddie.

"Hi!" The woman beamed a two-hundred-watt smile. "I'm Darlene Jarvis. I live right across the street. Welcome to Jefferson Road!"

"Thank you," Ruth said, wishing she had enough energy to sound enthusiastic. She was pleased, really. Being welcomed to the neighborhood was a lovely thing. But she'd been unpacking boxes all morning, rearranging furniture, deciding which paintings would hang on which walls, and dealing with three children, one of whom was gonzo. "I'm Ruth Singer. This is my younger daughter, Madelyn."

"I'm Maddie," Maddie corrected her mother. The boy might have seemed shy. Not Maddie. "Who are you?" she asked him.

He peered up at his mother. "This is Kyle," Darlene said. "Looks like you two are about the same age."

"What's in the plate?" Maddie asked, deciding that looked more interesting than Kyle. *If only her focus had remained on home-baked goodies instead of that boy across the street...*

"Do you like snickerdoodles?" Darlene asked, handing the plate to Maddie.

Ruth whipped the plate out of Maddie's grip before Maddie could race off and devour the entire plate of cookies herself—or worse, feed them to the dog, who would undoubtedly devour them and then vomit all over the pristine hardwood floor in the living room. "I have two older children," she explained to Darlene before sending Maddie a pointed look. "These are for sharing." She raised her eyes to Darlene again. "Thank you so much. That's very kind of you."

"Well, we were hoping some new children Kyle's age might move into the neighborhood. Kyle, Maddie is your age," Darlene told her son.

He gazed at Maddie for a long moment, then said, "I have a swing set."

Maddie forgot about the cookies, grabbed Kyle's hand, and darted across the street with him to a shingled modern house with an oddly angled roof and a circular window above the front door. Ruth shouted after them to look both ways before they crossed, but they ignored her. Fortunately, Jefferson Road was not a heavily traveled boulevard. They made it safely to the opposite curb and then vanished around the side of the house, their hands still clasped.

And that was that.

~

If only I'd gotten my tubes tied...

No Maddie.

No years of exhaustion, frustration, exasperation. No teachers sending notes home that read, "She's quite smart but her behavior leaves something to be desired." No post-Ruth piano teacher, far more skilled than Mrs. Demming, saying, "She could be a virtuoso, if only she'd apply herself." No close-minded pediatrician declaring, "I really don't think she has ADD; that diagnosis generally pertains to boys, not girls." No early-decision acceptance to Oberlin College, where—maybe—she'd take piano lessons in the school's conservatory, or else commit herself to textile design or neurobiology or archery or whatever whim entered her brain the day she had to declare her major. No storming out of the house, just days after she'd graduated from high school, climbing into Kyle's Jeep, flipping Ruth the bird, and vanishing around a bend in the road... and returning a year later with Rainie.

Life is easier. Calmer. Simpler.

So much less chaos without Maddie. I live in a world where butterflies are butterflies, not tornadoes.

~

No. Ruth couldn't go there. What kind of mother would allow herself to dream such a thing? A life without one of her children... How could she even entertain a glimmer of the possibility? Even fantasizing about it for a fraction of a second made her feel like a murderer. Worse than a murderer.

Good mothers were supposed to love their children, love them equally, love them blindly, love them passionately.

Ruth was a good mother. She loved Maddie.

But God help her, sometimes she peered down that other path, that imaginary path, that path without Maddie. It looked so smooth, so easy, so relaxing, lined with daffodils, illuminated with sunlight, populated by graceful, gliding butterflies.

Yet she couldn't picture herself taking a step down that path. Even craning her neck to see what might be around the bend, when it vanished from view... She couldn't do it.

No, she could not have gotten her tubes tied. She could not have lived a life without Maddie. She could not have survived with that void in her existence—a void she wouldn't even have been aware of if Maddie hadn't been born.

Maddie had been born, and she occupied a significant chunk of Ruth's heart. She was a godawful tenant—always late with the rent, leaving dings on the walls and scuff marks on the floor, wasting heat and electricity and carousing day and night, disturbing the neighborhood. But she lived there, deep inside Ruth, and she always would. She and Ruth had signed a lifelong lease.

Chapter Five

Warren came over after dinner that evening. Ruth had told Maddie to invite him for dinner, but Maddie said no, he was very busy, this was a challenging season for him at work. Ruth wasn't clear on why that should be. He was an accountant, and the tax season generally started in January. But however busy he was, he was able to stop by after dinner for a confab with Maddie and Rainie.

Warren was pleasant, polite, and profoundly sincere. Tall and endearingly gawky, he always said, "Please" and "Thank you," and he held doors open for people and stood whenever a woman entered the room. None of that mattered as much to Ruth as the fact that he was smitten with Maddie and deeply devoted to her. If he could take good care of her daughter, Ruth would be satisfied.

Whether he could take good care of her daughter's daughter was a different matter. He had arrived carrying a large, bubblegum-pink teddy bear for Rainie. "I saw this and thought of you, Rainbow," he said sweetly, once Ruth led him into the den, where Maddie was watching a cable-news show and adding her own political commentary to that of the pundits, while Rainie sat curled up in one of the leather easy chairs, a tablet propped on her knees and her gaze riveted to the screen.

She looked up when Warren entered, and her eyes widened in horror at the sight of the stuffed bear. "Really?"

"The color," Warren explained with a tentative smile. "It reminded me of your hair."

He probably intended the remark as a compliment, a way to prove that he did pay attention to Rainie, or at least to her hair. Her grimace and exaggerated eye roll indicated that she did not take his words as a compliment. She curled deeper into the chair and wrapped her arms around her knees.

"Well," Ruth said, "I'll leave you to discuss things."

"No, stay, Grammy!" Rainie pleaded.

Ruth didn't want to insert herself into what was apt to be a difficult conversation about Rainie's future residence. Rainie probably wanted her there for support, to help her convince Maddie and Warren that she should remain with her grandparents in Brentwood after the wedding. She apparently didn't realize that Ruth was not wholeheartedly on her side in this debate.

She should have asked her grandpa to sit in on the discussion; he had no objections to Rainie's continuing to live with them. But he was off doing something important, as if he suspected that a diaper might have to be changed.

"Please, Mrs. Singer, stay," Warren said, courteous as ever. "You might be able to offer some insights."

Hardly, Ruth thought, but she reluctantly followed him into the room and settled into the other leather easy chair, leaving the couch free for Warren and Maddie. Maddie pressed the remote to shut off the TV. Her expression bore a brooding intensity, no doubt spawned by the pundits who'd been bloviating righteously about this or that political scandal. Even seething, Maddie looked beautiful, her hair falling in lush waves around her heart-shaped face, her eyes bright and her mouth, as always, a perfect rosy hue and naturally puckered into the shape of a kiss. She had exchanged her garish work scrubs for a dark sweater and darker jeans, and she looked like an artsy city dweller, not a suburban mother who worked as a dental hygienist.

Warren wore a cable-knit brown sweater vest. Other clothing, too, but the vest just seemed so *Warren*. Kyle Jarvis would never have been caught dead in a sweater vest.

Maybe that was why Maddie had chosen to marry Warren. She'd always been enamored of extremes. If Kyle was the epitome of wildness, Warren was the epitome of tameness. His vest was the human equivalent of a dog's harness leash.

Maddie was his human. She gave her head a slight nod, and Warren obediently said, "Rainbow, we'd very much like you to live with us after the wedding. You'd have your own bedroom and your own bathroom. Well, technically not your own—that bathroom would be the guest bathroom when we have guests. But we won't have guests that often, so it will be your bathroom most of the time. And we'll get all new towels for that room if you'd like. Would you like new towels?"

Rainie rolled her eyes again. At some point in their roll, she glimpsed the teddy bear, propped up next to Warren on the couch. She shuddered slightly. "I have nice towels here," she said. "This is my home. I've lived here my whole life. Right, Grammy?"

"Pretty much," Ruth said. Rainie had spent the first few months of her life in Maine, but luckily for her, she had no memory of that.

Rainie attempted a placating smile. "It's nothing personal, Warren—"

"Of *course* it's personal," Maddie snapped. "How can it not be personal? Warren is going to be your stepfather."

"I know that." Rainie sent Ruth a beseeching look.

"Perhaps you could explain why you want to stay here, beyond the fact that it's been your home for so many years," Ruth said. Rainie's answer might be tricky, it might be toxic, but sometimes, the only way to heal a sore was to lance it. Jill, who was a professional psychotherapist, had taught Ruth that lesson.

Rainie squirmed. She glanced at the teddy bear again and twisted her thin, long-limbed body even deeper into the chair. "Okay. So, this is my only home. Right," she said. "And I go to school here in Brentwood. And all my friends are here in Brentwood. And all my *stuff* is here in Brentwood. And forgive me, Warren, but you're going to be my stepfather, but you've never been a father. Grandpa has been a father. He knows how to do it."

Too bad Barry hadn't been in the room to hear that. It would have made his chest swell with pride. Of course, one of the things he knew about how to be a father was the trick of making himself scarce whenever a difficult situation involving children arose.

"I want to learn how to do it," Warren said earnestly, tilting his long, rectangular face in Rainie's direction. "You can teach me—but only if you come and live with us."

"And I already discussed the school situation with your grandmother," Maddie added. "We'll fill out some forms so you can continue to go to Brentwood High School. She'll drive you back and forth."

Ruth glared at Maddie. She had never agreed to chauffeur Rainie to and from school. She wondered if she would be willing to do that, though, if it meant Rainie moved into Warren's house after the wedding. Ruth did believe that a daughter belonged with her mother.

But Warren had brought that ghastly teddy bear. He might have an inkling about how to be a father to a toddler. Not a teenager. Especially not a pink-haired teenager. His learning curve was a miles-long, dizzying spiral.

"I'm your mother," Maddie reminded Rainie, muting her tone in an effort to sound gentle but mostly sounding slightly congested. "You're my daughter. We're a team, Rainbow. Daughters listen to their mothers. I always listened to my mother." She sent Ruth a smile.

It was Ruth's turn to roll her eyes. Yet Maddie actually seemed to believe what she'd said. Somewhere in her complicated brain, she had convinced herself that she and Ruth had a healthy, stable relationship, that she had never defied Ruth, never ignored her, never bolted out of the house stark naked when she was four years old and didn't want to wear the pajamas Ruth had set out for her after her bath. Never doused the dog with Ruth's hair mousse to see if she could make its fur stand on end. Never set her book of Hanon Piano Exercises on fire in the back yard so she wouldn't have to practice them anymore. Never broke curfew, never staggered across the street from Kyle's back yard at two in the morning, smelling of Cointreau, never told Ruth she hated her. Never flipped her the bird before running away with Kyle and vanishing for a good, long year and a half.

Ruth and Maddie shared a peaceful relationship now. Maddie wasn't the rebel she'd once been. She worked in a dentist's office, she was engaged to marry an accountant, she proudly sported a modest diamond solitaire on her left ring finger. Somewhere along the way, she'd embraced conventionality—more conventionality than even Ruth, who still liked to pound out rock tunes on the piano and howl when there was no one around to hear her.

Perhaps part of Maddie's transformation entailed deleting all those wretched childhood incidents from her memory bank.

"Mothers should listen to their daughters too," Rainie said, defiance burning in her eyes. "I'm a team with Grammy and Grandpa." Once again she turned to Ruth, searching for support.

"We're a family," Ruth said, sweeping the sofa with her gaze. "All of us. That's a little different from a team. With teams, you get to pick your teammates, or you can quit the team if you don't like how things are going. With family, you're stuck. But that's not always a bad thing."

Rainie shot Maddie a hostile look. "When is it not a bad thing?"

"When you have people who love you more than life itself," Ruth said. "That's what family is all about."

Rainie studied her bare toes, the vivid black polish she'd painted on the nails, the jutting, oddly beautiful bones of her ankles. After a long silence, she sighed, unfolded herself, and stood. "I'm not going," she announced. "I'm staying here." Then she strode out of the den. The teddy bear remained seated forlornly next to Warren.

Another heavy silence, and then Maddie smiled brightly. "She'll come around." Typical Maddie behavior: no matter how bleak things seemed, she always assumed that everything would turn out the way she wanted it to.

Far too often, it did.

Chapter Six

Ruth hosted Thanksgiving on the Saturday after the actual day. Every year, she volunteered to observe the holiday two days late so her children could spend Thanksgiving with their in-laws, Noah with Laura's family, Jill with Ben's, and this year Maddie with Warren's, even though they weren't yet married. Ruth figured someone had to be flexible, someone had to sacrifice, someone had to say, "Okay, they can have you for Thanksgiving." It might as well be her.

Her generosity about this won her points from her children and their in-laws, and of course she still got to have her entire family gathered around her dining room table for a huge turkey feast and a chance to give thanks a mere couple of days later. While frantic shoppers crowded the stores on the Friday after Thanksgiving, Ruth would busy herself in her kitchen, preparing her belated holiday meal. Then her family would gather on Saturday. The menfolk would do whatever it was menfolk did, the grandchildren would make noise and run around, indoors or outside depending on the weather, and occasionally storm the kitchen to ask when they could *finally* eat because they were *starving*, and Ruth and Jill and Laura would drink wine in the kitchen while they oversaw the final preparations, set the table, arranged the platters, and carved the bird.

Once Ruth instituted her Saturday Thanksgiving policy, she and Barry became regulars at a Thursday Thanksgiving hosted by her friend Coral and Coral's wife, Lee. Coral had been the art teacher at Longford, one of the three primary schools in the Brentwood district, and she and Ruth had formed an instant bond when Ruth was hired by the school district. Coral had retired a couple of years before Ruth, but their friendship transcended their jobs.

Now that Ruth was retired, too, she and Coral often met at a local restaurant for lunch, where they'd both lustfully eye the thick, fattening sandwiches being delivered to other tables, and then bemoan their weight and order salads.

Barry wasn't thrilled with Coral's Thanksgivings, in part because he was usually one of only two or three men present and in part because Lee was a vegetarian, so Coral's buffet included lots of dishes he didn't recognize and therefore didn't trust—oddly shaped breads, portobello mushrooms in dense, dark sauces, casseroles filled with beans and lentils and suspicious green things. Because Coral wasn't a vegetarian, the buffet always included a platter of sliced turkey breast, but none of the traditional fixings accompanied it. "Don't worry," Ruth would always reassure him. "We'll have stuffing and yams and butternut squash on Saturday." He would mutter, heap his plate high with sliced turkey, and sneak off with the few other men to catch snatches of Thanksgiving-day football games on their cell phones.

This year, Thanksgiving at Coral's was typical—Barry and his fellow male guests devouring turkey while avoiding the other dishes, and commenting in hushed voices about whatever football game they'd been watching before Coral announced that everyone should grab a plate and fill it while the food was still hot. During the drive home, Barry muttered about Coral's failure to serve pumpkin pie and about Lee's accessories: "Three piercings per ear is too many for a woman past the age of sixty," he declared, and Ruth could only smile in amazement that he'd even been aware of how many earrings Lee was wearing. True, she wore her hair in a near crew cut, exposing her earlobes, but Barry usually didn't notice details like that.

As soon as they arrived at their house, Barry raided the freezer for the tub of holiday-special pumpkin-spice ice cream Ruth had purchased earlier that week, and settled himself in the den to watch football on the huge flat-screen TV. Ruth remained in the kitchen, trying not to panic about how much work awaited her tomorrow and wishing she could flop down on a sofa and pig out on ice cream too.

But tomorrow would arrive, and with it a hell of a lot of work.

On Friday morning, Rainie announced that she would help Ruth with the preparations. "You ought to use an axe on that," she said, sweeping into the kitchen to find Ruth hacking at a solid butternut squash. She'd already peeled it, cut it in half, and scooped out the seeds. Chopping it into small cubes required strength, however. An axe might be overkill, but a buzz saw would have been welcome.

"You know, they sell those things already peeled and chopped up," Rainie said.

"It's not a *thing*. It's a butternut squash," Ruth lectured, ignoring the ache in her hands as she pressed down on the heavy blade of the knife she was using. "And buying it already peeled and chopped would be cheating."

"It would be easier."

"Easier isn't always better." It usually was, of course. But Ruth was determined to put as much effort as she could into cooking. It was Thanksgiving, after all, and she was the hostess. The matriarch. The grandma exerting herself so her family would give thanks for her efforts.

"I was hoping you were going to make the pies," Rainie said. "I want to help with the apple pie. Not with..." She gestured toward the partially dismembered squash on the cutting board and, in a teasing voice, said, "That *thing*."

"I figured I'd get this diced and then slice the apples. The crusts are already made." Preparing the crust dough had been Ruth's first project that morning, mostly because she hated making pie crusts and wanted to get that task out of the way so she could focus on the fun stuff—like chiseling the butternut squash into manageable chunks. Her pie crusts usually came out heavy and oily, nowhere near as light and flaky as store-bought crusts. But damn it, she was the Thanksgiving chef, and she insisted on making everything she could from scratch.

So yes, she'd made the crust for the apple and pumpkin pies. She hadn't rolled it out yet, though. It sat in two pale, dense spheres in a bowl on the counter, protected by a sheet of wax paper. Wedged side by side in the bowl, they resembled the plump, doughy cheeks of a naked tush, which struck Ruth as unappetizing but somehow appropriate.

Rainie noticed the angle of Ruth's gaze and crossed to the counter. She lifted the wax paper and peeked into the bowl. "You're such a good cook," she said. "You must really love cooking."

In truth, Ruth didn't love cooking all that much. But at least on occasions like Thanksgiving, she was determined to do the whole earth-mother thing and prepare everything—with love, she told herself. Her mother had rarely cooked, and Ruth had decided, once she'd created her own family with Barry, that she would do anything her mother rarely did. She would put in the labor. She wouldn't cut corners. She would be the exact antithesis of her mother.

Her grandmother had always hosted Thanksgiving when Ruth was growing up, which meant her mother didn't have to exert herself with prep work or cooking. The family would pile into her father's Buick and drive to her father's mother's apartment, which would be redolent with the aromas of roasting fowl and baking sweets. Ruth's grandmother had insisted it was no work at all, she loved cooking for her loved ones. "Eat, bubbela," she'd croon, spooning mashed potatoes and stuffing and green beans swimming in cream-of-mushroom sauce onto Ruth's plate alongside a couple of thick slabs of breast meat. "You're too thin."

Ruth had never in her life been too thin, but she'd loved that her grandmother *thought* she was too thin. And she'd loved that her grandmother put forth so much effort for her family.

Now Ruth put forth the effort, even if her pie crusts were mediocre. She wanted her family to feel her love in the food she served—and she didn't want to be like her mother.

"We are having apple pie, aren't we?" Rainie asked, placing the waxed paper back onto the bowl containing the crust dough. "Pumpkin pie, I know, because I know Grandpa loves pumpkin pie. But also apple pie, right? I want to try to make a lattice crust."

Ruth eyed her granddaughter with surprise. "You do?"

"Warren's mother had a pie with a lattice crust yesterday. It was a rhubarb pie so it tasted gross, but it looked great. If we're having apple pie, I think I can figure out how to weave the top."

Ruth considered. She never made a lattice top for her apple pie. Would it bake well? Would all the syrupy juice leak through the open spaces in the weave and dribble all over her oven?

Who cared? If Rainie wanted to attempt a lattice top crust, she should. Maybe it would make her feel closer to Warren's mother, and she'd agree to live with Warren and Maddie after they were married.

Rainie swung the refrigerator door open. She located the bag of apples and also the bag of cranberries. Ruth made her cranberry sauce from scratch, too. She didn't care for it herself, but Barry did, and it was easier to make than pie crusts. Easier, even, than chopping up the butternut squash.

"I can peel and slice the apples," Rainie offered.

"You can slice them in the food processer," Ruth told her.

"I know." Rainie shot her an impish look. "You think boys are the only ones who like to use sharp, noisy tools?"

Ruth laughed. "I like having you as my sous chef. Last year you went out shopping with Kelsey the day after Thanksgiving."

"Oh, God, yeah." Rainie grimaced at the memory. "What a zoo. We almost got trampled, all those crazy shoppers." She pulled a few apples from the bag. "How many should I peel and slice?"

"Four should be plenty. They're pretty big." Ruth decided she'd cut the squash into small enough pieces and dumped them into a bowl. She would microwave them and then mash them. No cream, no butter. Not everything she served on the holiday had to be fattening. "So tell me about your Thanksgiving at the Schneier house yesterday."

Rainie sighed deeply, as if the memory grieved her. "Other than the rhubarb pie? I mean, who makes a rhubarb pie? Who eats it? I don't think the indigenous people of Plymouth ate rhubarb pie. Pumpkins and apples, sure. But rhubarb?"

"Other than the pie, did you have fun?"

Another deep sigh. Rainie lined up four apples and returned the bag to the refrigerator. "Warren has this awful sister named Eleanor. I don't know if she's divorced or she never got married. I sure as hell wouldn't want to be married to her. She criticized my posture." As if that was the biggest insult Rainie could imagine. "I was the only kid there. And they wouldn't let me be excused from the table. I didn't want any dessert—I mean, *rhubarb pie.*" She grimaced. "But they made me sit there and watch everyone else eat it. Mom even said it was delicious. I asked her later, on the drive back here, whether she really thought it was delicious, and she said Mrs. Schneier was going to be her mother-in-law and she wanted to have a good relationship with her. So, she's starting off this marriage with dishonesty."

Of course, a certain amount of dishonesty was essential for keeping a marriage going—especially dishonesty about in-laws. But it struck Ruth as ironic that Maddie would exert herself to have a good relationship with Warren's mother when she had never gone out of her way to have a good relationship with her own mother. That Ruth and Maddie did have a passably decent relationship these days was a tribute to Maddie's having finally grown up and Ruth's having practiced tolerance with at least as much diligence as she'd once practiced her scales on the piano.

"You know, sweetie—everything is going to work out," she said.

Rainie eyed her curiously, then shrugged. "Yeah, I'll figure out how to weave the crust. It'll look great."

Had Rainie realized that Ruth wasn't referring to the apple pie? Of course she had. She wasn't stupid.

And she probably sensed that everything wasn't going to work out, at least not the way she'd like. Her mother would marry Warren and dishonestly flatter her mother-in-law, and Rainie would either be forced to move to Warren's house or she'd remain with Ruth and Barry and create an ugly schism with her mother.

Perhaps it was best just to focus on the pie for now.

Chapter Seven

Barry's attitude toward Warren could be defined as benign tolerance. He welcomed into his heart anyone who made his children happy, and if Warren made Maddie happy, Barry approved of the man. Ruth, like her granddaughter, found Warren a bit boring, but he was stable and sensible. After her rebellious youth, Maddie now seemed stable and sensible, too, but because her stability and sensibility had shown up rather late in her development, Ruth didn't quite trust how permanent these attributes were. If Warren reinforced them in her, Ruth approved of him too.

He was the first to arrive Saturday, not long after Ruth had hoisted the twenty-two-pound turkey, stuffed and dressed, into the oven. Rainie had vanished into her bedroom to chat online with her friends, and Maddie was running a load of laundry—her brightly colored scrubs had to be cleaned frequently—so after greeting Ruth shyly (he was always reticent around Ruth, which some women might find endearing but she found irritating), Warren settled in the den with Barry, on the hunt for a televised football game.

Jill and Ben arrived soon after Warren, their children shrieking as if they hadn't seen Ruth just a few weeks earlier. Emma and Nate were fraternal twins. They were adorable, Emma bearing an uncanny resemblance to Jill when she'd been six years old and Nate taking more after his father. They were also rambunctious. Although already in first grade, they still had not mastered the concept of "indoor voices." Jill considered it important that her children enjoy the freedom to express themselves, even if they felt compelled to do so at top volume. Since Jill was a psychotherapist, no one dared to question her judgment when it came to her children's behavior.

"Can we color?" Emma bellowed as Ruth bent over to give her a hug. The child's shrill voice, blasting so close to Ruth's ear, caused her head to buzz.

"Can we paint?" Nate bellowed even more loudly. Of course he would want to paint. Painting was messier than coloring with crayons or pencils.

"We're not doing arts and crafts today," Ruth said, resigned to losing grandma points because she didn't say yes to every demand her grandchildren made. She'd lost grandma points years ago, while raising Rainie. Having to be Rainie's mother as well as her grandmother had toughened Ruth up. On the doting-and-spoiling grandma ten-point scale, she probably rated no higher than a five.

"Can we do clay?" Nate yelled, as if Ruth hadn't just vetoed arts and crafts.

"How about a jigsaw puzzle?" she suggested. A nice, quiet activity that might be messy enough to satisfy them.

"Can Rainie babysit for us?" Emma asked.

Back when Rainie was twelve and thirteen, she'd loved babysitting for her younger cousins during their Thanksgiving celebration, keeping them entertained while the grown-ups did grown-up things. Babysitting had made her feel mature. Now that she was fourteen, she believed she *was* mature, and she no longer volunteered for jobs that would prove how mature she was.

"I think she's busy right now," Ruth covered for her. "She'll join you in a little while. Go ask Grandpa to help you pick out a puzzle."

The children scampered out of the kitchen. Ben remained in the room long enough to kiss Ruth's cheek and tell her everything smelled delicious, even though the turkey hadn't been in the oven long enough to start emitting aromas. After he left the kitchen—no doubt to join the manly quest for a televised football game—Jill hugged Ruth, shed her coat, and said, "What can I do to help?"

They got to work cutting vegetables for a salad.

Jill looked elegant, as always. She had the ability to look like a woman who was not the mother of rowdy six-year-old twins. Her hair was styled into a neat shoulder-length pageboy—dutifully pulled back with a clip before she scrubbed and peeled the carrots—and she accepted the apron Ruth offered her to protect the silky black jumpsuit she had on. Ruth was wearing a comfortable cotton sweater and wool slacks, and she didn't care if food spattered on the garments. She had never understood the appeal of jumpsuits, which required a person to get completely undressed just to go to the bathroom. She'd choose ease in peeing over high fashion, any day. Jill had somehow evolved into the sort of woman who would choose high fashion over peeing.

Tearing large leaves of romaine into the salad bowl, Ruth asked, "Are your kids going to eat salad this year?"

"Probably not." Jill shrugged. "I think they'll eat the squash, though. Who made that gorgeous apple pie I saw on the sideboard? You didn't do that, did you?"

"Rainie did," Ruth said. "I hope it tastes as good as it looks." She eyed Jill across the center island. "Has Maddie talked to you about Rainie?"

Jill met her gaze. "What about Rainie?"

Ruth figured it wouldn't hurt to prepare Jill, in case the subject arose later that afternoon. "Rainie doesn't want to move in with Maddie and Warren once they're married. She wants to stay here."

"Who can blame her?" Jill wrinkled her nose. "I mean...*Warren.* And *Maddie.*"

"Maddie is her mother."

"Maddie is *Maddie*. And Warren is an accountant."

"What's wrong with accountants?"

Jill wrinkled her nose again. "We need them. They serve an important function. But really, what kind of person would want to spend his working life adding up columns of numbers?"

"I think what he does is a little more complicated. He has to know all about tax laws. And if he's good, he saves his clients money. Nothing wrong with that."

"I suppose." Jill helped herself to a knife and the cutting board and began slicing a carrot into bright orange disks. "Why would Maddie want to talk to me about this?"

"Because you're a shrink. She thinks that if Rainie doesn't want to live with her mother, she must need therapy. It's not as if Rainie is acting out or anything. She just wants to keep living here. She's comfortable here. She wants to continue at Brentwood High School. She isn't crazy. I don't think Maddie thinks she's crazy, either. I *do* think Maddie thinks this is some kind of adolescent rebellion."

"What do *you* think?" Jill asked.

Typical psychotherapy talk—instead of sharing her professional wisdom, the therapist asked the client what *she* thought. It was a racket, shrinks charging their patients for the privilege of diagnosing themselves.

Ruth studied the salad bowl, trying to decide how much more romaine to add. "I can't say I blame Rainie," she said. "This is the only home she's ever known. But I think she should live with her mother. I'd like to be done raising her."

"So you and Maddie want me to convince Rainie that for her mental health and successful development, she should move in with Maddie and Warren?"

Ruth smiled. "If you wouldn't mind."

Jill smiled, too, but her smile was icy. "I would mind."

Fortunately, they wouldn't have to argue about this, because the bubbling voices Ruth heard floating into the kitchen from the front door indicated that Noah and his family had arrived. "Happy Thanksgiving!" Noah boomed.

His two sons, Aaron and Ezra, operated at a slightly lower decibel level than Jill's twins. Ten-year-old Aaron was almost old enough to take over babysitting duties, now that Rainie had abdicated that role. Ezra was seven, just a year older than the twins. At Thanksgiving last year, Emma had announced to the family that she and Ezra were going to get married when they grew up. Jill had whispered to Ruth, "Well, that's an improvement. For a while, she insisted she was going to marry Nate." Marrying her first cousin was nowhere near as incestuous as marrying her twin brother.

Ruth dried her hands on a dish towel and moved to the doorway to greet her son and his family. She saw only males—Noah in a neat ribbed sweater and khakis, his boys in more colorful sweaters and khakis, and Barry, who had let them in and was holding their jackets. "Where's Laura?" she asked.

"She couldn't make it," Noah said, his big, dimpled smile firmly in place.

"Is she okay?"

"Just a little under the weather," he said.

"What does that mean?" Ezra asked. "Is it like being under an umbrella? Because it isn't raining."

"It means she didn't feel up to coming," Noah said briskly, then sent Ruth an apologetic smile. "She was feeling poorly this morning, so we both thought it would be best if she stayed home."

Ruth smiled back, doing her best to hide her disappointment. Laura was a sweetheart, and better at overseeing festive meals than either Ruth or Jill. She always swooped into the kitchen on their delayed Thanksgiving day, robust and cheerful, and dove into whatever project needed tackling: folding the napkins into interesting shapes, stirring the lumps out of the gravy, cutting the radishes into flowers, and arranging the rolls in a napkin-lined wicker basket.

Laura was solid, unpretentious, and evidently content to be a full-time mother, running the PTA, managing her sons' schedules, sewing their Halloween costumes. She had herbs growing in pots on her kitchen window sills and cast-iron cookware hanging from the ceiling. She created elaborate meals, from appetizer to dessert, without resorting to printed recipes. She knew, without looking it up, how many tablespoons of sugar were in a cup, how many ounces of milk were in a gallon, how many grains of salt were in a pinch. Ruth was a little bit in awe of her.

"I'm so sorry," she said. "Maybe we can Skype with her later."

"We'll see. I don't want to disturb her if she's resting," Noah said, then nudged his sons. On the cusp of tween-hood, Aaron held back slightly, but Ezra hurled himself at Ruth, who gave him a crushing hug. She could feel the chill of the November air clinging to him, and rubbed her hands up and down his back as if that would warm him up.

Noah kissed Jill's cheek, then Ruth's. "Where are the twins?"

"In the den with Ben and Warren," Jill said.

"Doing a jigsaw puzzle," Barry added. "The one featuring a picture of the Cape Cod dunes. Five hundred pieces. It's gonna take a couple of geniuses to finish that puzzle."

Apparently, Aaron and Ezra were willing to be geniuses. They romped into the den, where the twins welcomed them with deafening screams.

Barry and Noah wandered off after the boys, the promise of a televised football game sucking them in like a black hole. Alone, Jill and Ruth surveyed the kitchen, assessing what preparations still needed to be done and whether they could manage without Laura's expertise. There would be no radish rosettes this year, no origami-elaborate napkins.

Ruth opened a bottle of Chardonnay and filled goblets for Jill and herself. Enough Chardonnay, and while they might miss Laura, they wouldn't miss the fancy radishes and napkins.

~

Rainie's housing situation didn't come up during dinner. Just as well; it wasn't the sort of subject anyone would want to discuss with four restless children seated around the table. Aaron entertained Ezra and his cousins by teaching them how to balance teaspoons on their noses. Nate and Emma didn't have noses pronounced enough to balance spoons on—their noses were cute little buttons that would undoubtedly morph into something more substantial once they hit puberty. Emma bleated that she might want to marry one of the boys in her first grade class, but maybe she could marry Ezra too. Ben courteously pumped Warren for information about recent changes in the federal tax code. Noah teased Rainie about her pink hair. Rainie looked aggrieved and long-suffering, and looked even more aggrieved and long-suffering when she asked if she could have a glass of wine and Ruth said no, cutting Barry off before he could pour one for her.

Ruth sat at one end of the long table, Barry at the other. She had a nice view of the table, set with a heavy linen cloth and her good china and laden with heaping platters of food. She also had a nice view of her husband. He had aged reasonably well, his paunch notwithstanding. He still had most of his hair. His jawline had grown rounder with the aid of gravity and the addition of a few pounds over time, but his eyes were still a glittering hazel, gentle with sentiment as he gazed at his family and eager with hunger as he gazed at all the food.

He was a pushover when it came to his children and grandchildren. He'd always been the good cop, Ruth the bad cop, when their children had found themselves in trouble. It amused her to think Barry was a hard-headed businessman from the moment he climbed into his sporty little Audi at seven a.m. until the moment he pulled into the garage in the evening. Once he shed his suit and tie and slid his legs into his comfortable jeans, his hard head gave way to his soft heart.

The adults at the table made an extravagant fuss over Rainie's apple pie. Warren snapped a photo of it with his phone, and when he said he would post the picture on Facebook, Rainie looked appalled. The children at the table said they'd rather have Oreos than Rainie's masterpiece for dessert. "That's okay," Barry said, bringing a package of chocolate sandwich cookies from the kitchen and distributing them to the children. "More pie for us."

A few cookies later, the children were excused from the table. They ran off to the den, Nate screeching about the puzzle while Ezra and Emma pleaded with Aaron to find a movie for them to watch. "Emma loves all those corny Christmas movies," Jill lamented. "I don't know why. She knows we're Jewish."

"There aren't many corny Hanukkah movies," Ben pointed out. "What else are they going to watch?"

"They could watch football," Barry said.

"Um..." Noah surveyed the table, his gaze pausing briefly at Rainie, who, deprived of wine, was drinking coffee heavily spiked with cream and sugar and trying not to wince after every sip. "I'm glad the kids are in the other room. I've got some news to share."

Ruth felt her heart lurch. Something to do with Laura, no doubt. Something awful. Laura wasn't "under the weather." She had something dire. Cancer, or multiple sclerosis, or kidney stones.

"Laura and I have separated," Noah announced. "We're getting a divorce."

Silence enveloped the table. The air molecules stopped shimmering. A *divorce*? Why on earth would they get a divorce? They were a wonderful couple, with two wonderful sons. Noah was a successful attorney. Laura kept everything running smoothly at home. Their fifteenth anniversary was coming up next year.

"Why?" Barry finally asked.

"We just..." Noah smiled faintly. His eyes were too bright, as if the bulk of the smile had risen through his sinuses to infect them. "We've had a good run, but we realized we were stagnating."

"Big deal. You're stagnating," Barry said. "Everyone stagnates. It's what marriage is all about."

If Ruth had been sitting closer to him, she would have kicked him under the table, hard enough to leave a bruise. Luckily for him, the table was about ten feet longer than her legs. "*We* haven't stagnated," she said.

"You know what I mean. I mean we're used to each other. We're comfortable," he clarified for Noah. "The excitement dies down, and it's replaced by comfort."

"I've had enough excitement in my life," Maddie declared. "There's a lot to be said for comfort. And stagnancy."

"Stagnation," Warren corrected her, beaming down at her as if she hadn't just implied that their relationship was unexciting. Was that why Maddie had decided to marry him? Because she was tired of excitement?

There were worse reasons to get married, Ruth supposed.

"Our excitement hasn't died down yet, has it?" Ben murmured to Jill.

Ignoring him, she stared across the table at her brother. "Let me guess," she said. "You had an affair."

Noah looked insulted. "I haven't had an affair!"

"Sure you have."

"It's not an affair," he defended himself. "I've met someone very special."

"Oh, my God." Ruth heard the words slip out of her mouth before she could stop them. "Someone special? Laura isn't special?"

"Of course she's special," Noah said, without much conviction. "She's the mother of my sons. I'll always appreciate her."

"You'll *appreciate* her?" Ruth felt a hysterical rage crowding her throat. "What kind of thing is that to say about your wife?"

"I appreciate you," Barry called down the table to Ruth.

Of course he did. He also thought they were stagnating. But she wasn't going to get angry with him, at least not right now. She could get angry with him later. At that moment, all her emotion was aimed at her son, her firstborn, that smugly handsome forty-three-year-old man sitting at her table, an empty pie plate and a half-full wine goblet in front of him, announcing he was getting a divorce as calmly as he might mention buying a new allen wrench.

"You're such a cliché," Jill said.

"Don't psychoanalyze me," he shot back.

"Let me guess," Jill goaded him. "Your new lady is fifteen years younger and fifteen pounds lighter than Laura."

Noah's smile faded slightly; he had the good grace to look abashed. "Well, come on. Laura has let herself go over the years."

Let herself go? Ruth gripped the arms of her chair to prevent herself from leaping to her feet, circling the table, and slapping Noah. She'd never spanked her children. Even though she was the bad cop, she believed spanking was wrong, both ineffective and abusive. But right now, insulting his wife that way just because she'd put on a little weight over the years...

Laura was *zaftig*. Ruth's mother might have considered this a great tragedy, but it wasn't. "Laura is beautiful," Ruth declared.

"Oh, she's an attractive woman," Noah swiftly agreed, adding modestly, "She'll probably find someone better than me, once this is all settled."

"You've set the bar pretty low," Jill muttered. "Someone better than you shouldn't be hard to find."

Ben tapped Jill's arm. "Jill, really—"

"What?" Jill spread her hands palm up, as if she were trying to lift the air around her. "He's a cliché."

"I'm sure it's a difficult situation for everyone," Ben said diplomatically.

"*He's* the one who created the difficult situation."

"It takes two people to make a marriage," Noah remarked, his voice gritty. Ruth wondered whether he sounded that way when defending a client in a legal negotiation. "It takes two people to make a marriage fail."

"You're a lawyer," Barry said. Ruth wasn't surprised that his thoughts had overlapped hers. After forty-five years of marriage—a marriage he thought was comfortable and stagnant—mind melds were not uncommon. "I'm sure you know something about the legalities here," Barry continued. "I'm a business consultant, and I know something about finances." He'd dropped his soft-hearted grandfather persona, replacing it with his hard-headed business persona. "Have you given any consideration at all to how this will work financially? You're a one-income household with two growing sons, and you're going to divide your single income between two households? You've got alimony, you've got child support—Warren, help me out here. You're an accountant."

"There are tax ramifications," Warren said. Not terribly enlightening.

"Laura gave up her career to raise your sons," Barry continued, his voice growing harder with each word. "You owe her financial support."

Noah snorted. "What career? She was a glorified secretary."

"She was a legal secretary," Ruth reminded him. "In your firm. Obviously competent enough to catch your eye."

"Right. Her 'career'—" Ruth could almost hear the air-quotes in Noah's tone "—was finding a lawyer to marry. She succeeded. She found me."

"I can't believe you're discussing finances," Jill broke in. "You have two children." She gestured in the direction of the den. "Have you given even a moment's thought to the psychological impact this will have on them? Their daddy rejecting their beloved mother, leaving her for some floozy—"

"Kim is *not* a floozy," Noah protested.

"Jesus Fucking Christ!" Maddie erupted, shutting everyone up.

"Don't use that word," Ruth said. "It's Thanksgiving."

"Thanksgiving was two days ago," Maddie roared.

"Shut up, Maddie," Barry snapped. "Stop being so damned dramatic. You're ruining our Thanksgiving."

"Didn't you just hear me? Thanksgiving was two days ago," she retorted. "And Noah's the one ruining Thanksgiving, not me."

"You're the one acting hysterical," Barry yelled.

"Me? *You're* hysterical!" Maddie's large, dark eyes blazed with indignation, and her delicate chin jutted forward, aimed like a lethal spear first at her father and then at Noah. "Why the hell did you choose now to do this? You couldn't have waited six months? You're going to ruin my wedding! Laura is one of my bridesmaids. She's already got her dress. And you're one of Warren's groomsmen, and the two of you are supposed to walk down the aisle together, you asshole! How's that going to work? Maybe you'll have Laura on one side of you and skinny Kim on the other? Jesus Fucking Christ!"

"It's a good word," Rainie whispered to Ruth.

"There are better words," Ruth whispered back.

"Not at the moment." Rainie flashed her a hint of a smile.

"So no, Noah, you can't get a divorce," Maddie announced. "You won't ruin my wedding. It's *my* wedding, and you'll just have to tell skinny Kim to wait a few months. If she's smart, she'll decide you aren't worth the wait." With that, she tossed her napkin onto the table, shoved back her chair, and stormed out of the room.

Chapter Eight

If Only I'd Learned How to Ski...

Ruth cut her walk short, thanks to the icy pellets the clouds were spitting out and spraying onto the earth. They clung to the parched, pale grass of neighborhood lawns, rattled and bounced against the pavement, and stung her cheeks and nose. The ground wasn't slippery, but the wintery weather made her feel old. Walking only two miles rather than her usual five made her feel older. A full five-mile walk might have helped to settle her nerves, but Mother Nature didn't give a damn about her mental state.

She had agreed to meet Laura at Hilda's, the café where she usually lunched with Coral. Laura had phoned her last night and asked if they could get together around noon. "Of course," Ruth had said, tamping down her trepidation. Why would her son's soon-to-be ex-wife want to get together with her?

Ruth hadn't spoken with Noah since their Thanksgiving dinner. She'd considered phoning him, but what would she say? "You're an idiot! Stop it! Grow up!" Sure, he'd really like to hear that from his mother.

He was her son. She loved him. Like Barry, she welcomed into her heart anyone who made her children happy. At one time Laura had made Noah happy, but not anymore. Did that mean Ruth would have to welcome this Kim person and no longer welcome Laura?

No. Her heart also welcomed anyone who made her grandchildren happy. That category included Laura, even if she no longer made Noah happy.

Laura was already seated at a table near the window when Ruth entered the café. Ruth waved away the hostess and crossed the small dining room to the table, anxiety jittering inside her skull as she neared her daughter-in-law.

She was relieved that Laura looked exactly like Laura—not tear-stained, not raging, not haggard and miserable, with shadows under her eyes from her sleepless nights. As relieved as Ruth was, though, she was also apprehensive. What was she supposed to say to the woman her son was replacing with a newer, more aerodynamic model?

Laura rose from her chair as Ruth approached, and gave Ruth a friendly hug. That eased Ruth's anxiety a little. "It's so good to see you," Ruth said, meaning it.

"You too." Laura sounded brisk, not overly emotional. Then again, she wasn't an overly emotional woman, at least not in Ruth's experience. She was always upbeat, always busy, laughing her booming laugh at the antics of her sons or the foolishness of her husband.

Ruth removed her jacket and draped it over the back of her chair before sitting. Laura sat as well, and lifted one of the two menus on their table. "I've never eaten here before," she said. "What do you recommend?"

Ruth perused the other menu. Everything looked delicious, but she generally avoided the heftier dishes. "I usually order one of the salads," she said.

Laura shot her an unreadable look. Did she think Ruth was commenting on her weight? Was Laura's weight really the issue that had driven Noah to end their marriage? Granted, she was pudgy, but there was a sweetness and warmth to her appearance. Her cheeks might be round, but they were nearly always lifted in a smile. Her arms and legs were plump, but they looked strong and pillow soft. And if men were attracted to big bosoms, Noah should be at the head of a mile-long line of lustily drooling men eager to admire the ample dimensions of her chest.

A slim young woman approached their table, pen poised above her pad. "Are you ladies ready to order?" she asked.

Ruth glanced once more at the menu, but she already knew what it said. "I'll have the mesclun salad with a grilled chicken breast," she requested. "Balsamic vinaigrette on the side. And decaf coffee."

Laura sent her another look, then lowered her gaze back to her menu. "I'll have the turkey-bacon-avocado wrap, and... God, it's so cold out. I think I'll have a cup of the French onion soup too. And... a glass of the merlot. And water."

"Yes, water for me too," Ruth said. She would never allow herself a lunch as hearty as the one Laura had just requested, but she experienced a twinge of envy hearing Laura recite her order. Everything Laura had asked for sounded delicious. Compared to Laura's lunch, Ruth's salad, with dressing on the side, was pathetically Spartan.

The server strode away. Ruth watched her from behind. Her tush was so small, Ruth wondered whether she could sit without toppling over, since she lacked much of a base. Evidently, she ate more dressing-free salads than turkey-bacon-avocado wraps.

Was Noah's new sweetheart that thin? That young?

Shoving the thought away, she gave Laura a sympathetic smile. "I'm so sorry you didn't join us for Thanksgiving last Saturday," she said.

"Yeah, well." Laura fidgeted with her fork until the server returned with the drinks they'd ordered. Laura ignored her water and took a sip of her wine.

Ruth forced herself to be patient. Laura had initiated this lunch. She would have to initiate the discussion, whatever it was bound to be.

Fueled by a few sips of wine, she finally did. "Madelyn is driving me crazy."

Ruth shrugged. "Maddie drives everyone crazy."

"She's phoned me twice and texted me God knows how many times. She says Noah and I can't get divorced until after her wedding, because she needs us to march down the aisle together. She's got it all planned out, the pairing of the bridesmaids and ushers, the order we're supposed to go in, where we're supposed to stand. I think she's got us arranged by height or something, I don't know. She says she wants no awkwardness or hostility at her wedding.

Well, big whoop. Tell her to give Noah a brain transplant if that's what she wants."

"She wants you in her wedding party," Ruth said, although whether Maddie wanted this because Laura was her beloved sister-in-law or because of her height-order choreography, Ruth couldn't say. The fact was, *Ruth* wanted Laura there. Laura had been a member of their family for fifteen years. She'd produced two precious grandsons. Just because Noah was going through some sort of mid-life crisis—a cliché, as Jill put it, but clichés became clichés only because they were true so often—didn't mean Laura ought to be exiled from the family.

"She's being a bridezilla," Laura declared. "I have enough on my plate right now without having to deal with her. Can you muzzle her?"

"I wish." Ruth laughed sadly at the futility of that demand. "I'm sorry she's adding to your stress. Laura, I'm just..." She reached across the table, hoping to take Laura's hand, but the server showed up at that moment with their food, and Ruth had to pull back before she could give Laura's hand a squeeze. Laura probably didn't want Ruth touching her, anyway. For all her characteristic geniality and cheer, there was an aloofness about her today, a chilliness Ruth knew the steaming onion soup would not thaw.

"This looks good," Laura said, using her spoon to break through the melted cheese blanketing her crock of soup.

Ruth sighed. She was aching. Upset. Once again wishing she could be done taking care of her children, but acknowledging that when you were a good mother—and she honestly hoped she was a good mother—you could never retire from that job. "Laura, I'm so sorry. I don't know why you and Noah have reached this point, and it's really none of my business—"

"True," Laura muttered, then lifted the spoon to her mouth, blew on the steaming broth, and slurped it.

"But it breaks my heart," Ruth persevered. "For better or worse, you're my daughter-in-law and you always will be. If there's anything I can do..."

"You can tell Madelyn to get off my back," Laura said.

"I'll try."

"Her wedding is in April. I've got more than enough to deal with before then." Even as she ate, Laura was able to vent. "I booked us a week in Aspen for the boys' winter break from school. I had to make the reservations last March. We've got the plane tickets, a condo rental, the package with the lift tickets and everything. Now what am I supposed to do? Go without Noah? Let him bring along his new girlfriend? Why couldn't he wait to spring this on me until after the vacation—or after Madelyn's goddamn wedding? And the house. He had this brainstorm that we should sell the house and each get our own place, so we could start fresh. I don't want to start fresh. I'm not giving up the house."

"Of course not."

"He wants to move out? Fine. Let him live in a trailer park somewhere. Or let him move in with his girlfriend. I don't care. He's going to get tired of her sooner or later—or she'll get tired of him. This is just craziness on his part."

"I agree." Ruth stabbed at her salad with her fork, but she lacked the appetite to eat it. Even if she doused it with the vinaigrette, she suspected it would taste like weeds.

"You want to come skiing with us? You can have his ticket," Laura said.

"I don't ski," Ruth said ruefully.

"How can that be? You're a New Englander. Everyone here skis."

"I'm afraid not. My parents weren't skiers, so my brother and I never skied." Ruth had come close to skiing once, back in high school. Her friend Debbie's parents had invited her to join their family for a long weekend at one of the mountains in Vermont. She had been tempted, but going away for the weekend would mean missing band practice. If Debbie's family was willing to leave for Vermont Saturday afternoon, Ruth could have spent a couple of hours at Nick's house, practicing, and then traveled to the mountains—and lost a full day of skiing. But of course they were leaving Friday, right after school let out, which meant Ruth would have to skip practicing with Trouble Ahead. She couldn't do that.

Debbie had never forgiven her for choosing the band over her. They remained friendly, but the best-friendship bond frayed and eventually tore apart. The guys in the band became Ruth's best friends, much to her mother's horror. "These boys—they aren't A-track," her mother would fume. "If they like you so much, why don't they ask you out on a date? Not that you should date boys who aren't A-track."

"I can't believe you've never skied," Laura said, shaking her head.

"I'm not much of an athlete."

"Noah says you walk ten miles a day."

"Five miles, and you don't have to be an athlete to walk."

"You should try skiing. You'd love it."

Ruth considered the suggestion, then shook her head. Skiing was dangerous. It was risky. If you were doing it right, you were going too fast. "I'm old, Laura. If I fell, I'd break something." She hesitated, then asked, "Are you serious about wanting me to go to Aspen if Noah doesn't go? I'd love to spend a week with Aaron and Ezra, but... I don't want to get in the middle of your marriage. Noah should go with you. Maybe the change of scenery would give you both a new perspective."

"I don't need a new perspective," Laura said, bitterness coloring her tone. "My old perspective is just fine."

"Well, maybe you should invite a friend to go with you and the boys."

Laura responded by biting off a hefty chunk of her wrap and chewing. Ruth observed her daughter-in-law's cheeks, lumpy with the quantity of food in her mouth, and thought she ought to take smaller bites. Yet she was jealous that Laura could eat with such gusto, without regard for calories and weight, not caring how she looked and what people thought of her. Ruth should have ordered a big, juicy wrap. She should have thought, the hell with whether she gained a pound, or five, or ten. It wouldn't be the worst tragedy that could befall her.

"I know this is a crazy idea," she ventured, "but have you and Noah considered seeing a marriage counselor?"

Laura managed to scowl while still chewing. "What would be the point? I'm committed to the marriage. Noah isn't. What could a counselor possibly tell us?"

"I don't know. I was just thinking...Jill doesn't do marriage counseling, although she does some family counseling. But she could recommend someone."

"Noah wouldn't go, anyway. He thinks his life is perfect."

"It isn't perfect. He's going to be living in a trailer park." And spending a fortune in alimony and child support. Ruth recalled Barry's warnings at their Thanksgiving dinner. Honestly, she wouldn't blame Laura for wringing Noah dry financially. He deserved as much.

"I'm not going to knock myself out trying to convince him to stay with me," Laura said, her voice bristling with pride. She took a hefty swig of her wine. "If he wants to leave—what's the expression? Don't let the door hit you on your way out."

"What about the boys? They need their father."

"They need a father who isn't making an ass of himself with some young chick that he met at the gym."

"He met her at the gym?"

"The health club. Her elliptical was next to his treadmill. They bonded over fruit smoothies in the lounge." Laura scowled.

Jill was right. Noah really was a cliché. At least he hadn't met this new woman through one of the online matchmaking services. If he had, that would have implied that he'd been actively searching for someone to have an affair with. A chance meeting, two sweaty people who just happened to connect...

It was still a cliché. Once again, Ruth was overwhelmed by the urge to smack her son. Luckily for him, he wasn't at Hilda's right now. Also luckily for him, she didn't believe in spanking.

"I think you should invite a friend to go skiing with you and the boys," Ruth said. She knew better than to suggest that Laura invite her own mother to join them. Laura insisted her mother was toxic. Ruth had met the woman a couple of times and had to agree. Laura's mother was a widow whose list of grievances ran into the thousands, many of which she'd recite at every opportunity. A significant portion of them revolved around her daughter, who, according to her, had failed in numerous ways. Laura didn't phone often enough. Her hair wasn't styled well. She didn't have a glamorous career. She'd replaced her wall-to-wall carpeting with hardwood floors just so she wouldn't have to vacuum frequently, and sweeping the floors seemed archaic, plus they were cold. You couldn't walk barefoot on Laura's floors without chilling your toes. Also, she spoiled her sons. And she ignored her sons. And she didn't smile often enough. (This last item Ruth found preposterous; she could hardly picture Laura's face without a smile radiating from it. But then, Laura probably didn't smile all that often when her mother was in the vicinity.)

At Laura and Noah's wedding, Laura had gathered Ruth into a hug and said, "Finally, I've got a mother I can love!" No matter how stupid Noah was, no matter what he thought of his wife, Ruth adored her and always would.

But she didn't ski.

"It could be a fun getaway if you took a friend," she suggested when Laura continued to consume her wrap in silence. "During the day you could all ski, and in the evening, maybe the resort has a babysitting service, and you and your friend could go out and have a peaceful dinner."

"Sure. Maybe we could pick up guys at the bar," Laura muttered. "Or hey, maybe I can meet a guy in the next couple of days and bring him with me. I guess I'd have to join a fitness center first, and drink fruit smoothies. Too bad I don't like them. They're so thick and sticky."

Ruth forgave Laura her sarcasm. "I'm really sorry. If you want me to come, I'll come. I'll stay in the condo and read during the day while you're out skiing with the boys. And I can babysit them in the evening so you can pick up guys in the bar." She hoped her humor would spark a smile from Laura. Right now, Laura was definitely not smiling enough.

"We paid for the lift ticket," Laura said. "I need to find a skier."

"Maddie skis," Ruth said.

That got a laugh out of Laura. "No, thank you."

"I'll see what I can do to calm her down," Ruth said.

"Please. I just can't deal with her right now."

"Of course." Ruth forced herself to eat a little more of her salad. "Call me crazy," she said, "but I'd like to think Noah will come to his senses and join you in Aspen. I'd like to think this is just some weird aberration, and he'll apologize and make it up to you and worship you the way you deserve to be worshipped."

"And I'll forgive him and take him back?" Laura snorted a laugh. "Dream on."

If only I'd learned how to ski...

Most kids learn to ski because their parents are skiers. But I stumbled into it thanks to my friend Debbie's family. They invited me to join them on a long ski weekend, and to everyone's amazement—especially mine—I took to it as if I'd been born with well-waxed slats where my feet were supposed to be. By the end of the weekend, I was zipping down the intermediate trail in perfect tuck position, my hair streaming behind me and my face pink and tingling from the wind.

I loved the exhilaration, the speed, the edge of panic. The ability to stay warm while surrounded by snow. The icy bite of the air and the blinding radiance of the sun. The vivid colors—the white ground, the dark green of the surrounding evergreens, the brilliant blue of the sky. The sense of triumph that swept over me when I reached the bottom of the mountain.

I had never thought of myself as fearless until that weekend. I'd never thought of myself as an adrenaline addict. But there it was. I was a skier—and fearless.

The more I skied, the more fearless I became in other areas of my life. Suddenly, I didn't care about dressing to appeal to boys. I spoke up in class, correcting my teachers when I thought they were wrong, and I faced off with the assistant principal in charge of discipline when one of my teachers sent me to detention for challenging him in class. When I performed with the band, I didn't sing sweetly. I growled and howled and went full Janis-Joplin. I attended college in Colorado so I could ski on weekends.

I burned calories like an olympian. I could devour salads with dressing on them. I could drink fruit smoothies—or chocolate milk shakes—and never gain a pound. Everything I ate, I burned off on the slopes.

Now, of course, I'm older. But the skiing made me hard and muscular. And fearless.

I still remember that glorious week when Barry and I took Aaron and Ezra to Aspen. Barry doesn't care for skiing; his parents introduced him to the sport, but he found it boring. "You stand in line for a half hour to ride to the top of the slope. Then you spend five minutes going down the slope. A lousy ROI, if you ask me." Leave it to him to reduce skiing to a return-on-investment calculation.

But he was happy to join the boys and me in Aspen, if only because it gave Laura and Noah a full week alone, without interruption or interference or any worries about anything other than each other and their marriage. It was clear, after Noah's foolish fling a few years ago, that his family, his lovely wife and beautiful sons, were all that mattered. He and Laura needed time alone, time to be romantic, to be devoted to each other, and Barry and I were happy to give them that time, whether by babysitting at Noah's house or bringing the boys to our house for a sleepover...or taking them skiing in Colorado.

During that week in Aspen, Barry spent his days at the townhouse condo we booked, his laptop in front of him and his cell phone pinned to his ear while he conducted business long distance. I spent my days riding up the slope and skiing down it with the boys. They were still pretty new at the sport, so we stuck to the blue-square trails. But I got in a couple of black-diamond runs while they sat in the lodge, sipping steaming cups of cocoa. Aaron loved being put in charge of his little brother while I took my solo runs. Ezra didn't love the arrangement as much, but the cocoa made Aaron's bossiness bearable.

I would fly down those black-diamond slopes as if my skis were wings, as if the snow were the sky. I would soar. The wind would slap my cheeks and hiss in my ears. I was free. Free of children, free of worry, free of thoughts about all the things I should *be doing. I was doing what I should be doing—hunching my shoulders, tucking my poles under my arms, focusing my vision through my goggles, leaning left and then right, using my edges. Being a daredevil, not a good mother. Not a good girl. Being fearless.*

In the evenings, we ordered take-out for dinner—pizza, fried chicken in a bucket, shrimp lo mein and mu-shu beef from a local Chinese place. Laura and Noah telephoned every night to chat with the boys, and then Barry would watch a video with them, usually some action film featuring car chases or spaceship acrobatics and lots of noisy weaponry. Then bedtime for them, and Barry and I would relax by the fireplace in the condo, sipping glasses of Port. It was romantic, for us as much as for Noah and Laura.

Skiing did that. It solidified a marriage—or several marriages. It gave Barry and me evenings in front of a fire, relaxing because there was nothing else to do, nothing else calling us away from each other. No chores to attend to. No football games to view. No business calls or demands from Maddie.

Just us. Just the peace of a cozy room and a crackling fire, and a world of snow outside.

~

"I'm a bad mother," Ruth said to Barry.

"No, you're not." Barry fussed with the trousers of his suit, draping them over a hanger so the pleats in the legs lined up. He seemed more focused on smoothing the pin-striped wool over the hanger's dowel than on Ruth, who sat on the edge of the queen-size bed in the master bedroom, watching his nightly transformation from a businessman to a rumpled, comfortable homebody.

Did he really think she wasn't a bad mother, or was he just saying that to make her feel better? "One of my children is getting a divorce," she said. "Another of my children became a single mother as a teenager."

"Jill turned out okay," Barry said.

If his intention had been to make her feel better, he'd failed miserably. "Look at us, Barry. Look at the example we set for our children. Shouldn't they emulate us? We've been married for forty-five years."

"Is that all? It feels longer." He shot her a smile so she'd know he was joking.

Except that he probably wasn't. He'd said at their Thanksgiving dinner that he thought they were stagnating.

Clad in just his dress shirt, his briefs, and a pair of argyle socks, he strode over to the bed and gave her a hug. "You're a good mother," he said.

Of course he had to say that. What else could he say? *You're a lousy mother. Your kids turned out like shit. Maybe Jill hasn't committed any humiliating lifestyle mistakes—no out-of-wedlock babies, no infidelities that you know of—but she's officious and judgmental, and her kids are demanding and they scream all the time.*

Maybe all three of Ruth's children were screwed up. Maybe *she'd* screwed them up.

Was it possible to be a mother without worrying? Ruth was so tired of the worry, so tired of the whole mother thing. She wanted to retire from that job, the way she'd retired from teaching. *Retired.* Perhaps it should be written "Re: Tired." This was about her being tired.

She wanted to be *done.*

Through the closed bedroom door, she heard a clattering noise, pots and pans colliding one floor below. "Maddie's cooking dinner," she told Barry when he glanced toward the door.

He tugged on his jeans and buttoned them beneath his belly. "I call the leftover turkey," he said. He wasn't a fan of Maddie's cooking, which often featured mysterious green things among the ingredients.

"There's no leftover turkey," she reminded him. "In case you didn't notice, your grandchildren hoovered everything up."

"Even the Oreos," Barry lamented. He gave Ruth a kiss on the cheek. "You're a good mother. The fact that you had a package of Oreos in the pantry proves it."

Ruth knew when she was being patronized. Glowering, she left the bedroom and descended the stairs, Barry trailing behind her.

Still in her garish floral scrubs, Maddie stood at the kitchen island, numerous pans arrayed on the stove burners. "Why don't you have a wok?" she demanded. "I'm making stir-fry."

"You can make it in a regular pan," Ruth told her. "Or you can buy a wok."

"There's a wok on my bridal registry," she said. "Why should I buy one when I'm going to get one as a wedding present? Or maybe at the shower." Arms folded across her chest, she scrutinized the assortment of cookware spread before her, clearly unsure of which pan most nearly resembled a wok.

Barry ignored the pots and pans and surveyed the spread of vegetables on the center island. Two bottles of soy sauce—two different brands, one marked low-sodium—stood like trees among the shrubbery of bell peppers, onions, mushrooms, broccoli, zucchini, and celery. He zeroed in on a plastic tub. "What's this?"

"Tofu," Ruth told him.

He glared at Maddie. "I hate tofu. Why are you making a meal with tofu?"

"It's healthy for you," Maddie said.

"Like you're a doctor? You know what I should eat?"

"I'm in the health care industry," Maddie told him. "Maybe you ought to take me seriously."

"I take you seriously. *Too* seriously," Barry muttered, then swung open the refrigerator, no doubt searching for a stray turkey drumstick that might have eluded the hungry horde last weekend.

"You also need a rice cooker," Maddie scolded Ruth. "And no, I'm not going to buy one. It's on my registry too."

"You may not get everything on your registry," Ruth pointed out. "And you can cook rice in a pot. I've done it many times." She moved across the kitchen and peeked through the doorway into the den. It was empty. "Where's Rainie?"

"How should I know?" Maddie shrugged. "She never tells me anything."

You're her mother, Ruth almost retorted, but she bit her lip. Maddie was clearly itching for a fight. Ruth didn't feel like giving her what she wanted.

A loud buzz from the laundry room off the kitchen prompted Maddie to put down the skillet she was evaluating. "I'm running a load," she said before vanishing into the laundry room.

"She's always running a load," Barry muttered.

There were worse things to obsess over than clean clothing. With a sigh, Ruth wandered into the living room and gazed through the window. The morning's sleet had evolved into a light snow, one of those snowfalls that miraculously stuck to unpaved surfaces while leaving the roads and sidewalks clear. Magic snow, she called it.

Headlights caught the swirling snowflakes in mid-descent as an SUV cruised to the curb. The back door swung open and the car's interior light illuminated Rainie as she climbed out. Her jacket hung open, her head was bare, and she lacked boots and gloves. At least she wasn't wearing shorts and flip-flops.

She leaned in through the open door to talk to someone in the back seat, then straightened, closed the door, and ambled up the front walk, her school backpack clutched in one hand rather than slung over her shoulders. Ruth moved to the entry and opened the front door for Rainie so she wouldn't have to stand on the porch, groping for her house key while her hair became crusted with snow.

"Thanks," she said, sweeping into the house on a gust of blustery air.

"Welcome home," Ruth said. "It's so late! Did you miss the bus?"

"No, I was at Nina's house. Doing *research*," she emphasized as she peeled off her coat and swiped a hand through her damp hair. "Her mother gave me a lift home."

"That was nice of her. But you should have let me know you weren't coming straight home. I didn't know where you were."

"I sent my mom a text," Rainie said.

Wonderful. Maddie ignored vital texts from her daughter. "Next time," Ruth said, planting a kiss on Rainie's icy cheek, "send *me* the text."

Rainie nodded. Her eyes were bright with excitement. "So, we got this assignment in English. We're supposed to write an essay comparing the way something was done fifty years ago with the way it's done today. We were looking up all this stuff about hairdos and shopping—did you know how hard it was for women to get credit cards back then?"

Ruth nodded. "I was alive then, Rainie. Not that I had a credit card when I was a teenager, but I remember."

"That's the thing," Rainie babbled, her enthusiasm geysering. "I suddenly thought, like, *duh*, Grammy was a teenager fifty years ago. *You're* my research! So, can I interview you?"

"About hairdos and shopping?" Ruth chuckled and shook her head. "My hair was a mess and I wasn't much of a shopper."

"I bet your hair was pretty." Rainie hung her jacket in the coat closet. Ruth pulled it out of the closet and hooked the hanger onto the closet's doorknob, where it would remain until the jacket dried off. "So, I was thinking, do you still have your high school yearbook? I could write about how different high school was fifty years ago."

"I think I have it somewhere." Ruth frowned, trying to remember where she'd stashed her and Barry's old school yearbooks.

Somewhere in the basement, she assumed. Somewhere stuffed inside a box, sitting on a dusty shelf, surrounded by the old, faded pup tent and sleeping bags, the wicker patio furniture, the beach umbrellas and the gardening tools they no longer used because they paid a lawn care service to mow and weed and fertilize the yard. During the pandemic, when the family had been confined to the house, Ruth had thought decluttering the basement would be a good group project. She'd suggested that some of the gardening gear—the power mower, the electric trimmer, duplicate rakes and spades—could be sold or donated or left at the put-and-take in the town dump, but Barry had insisted on keeping everything because, as he'd said, "You never know."

What it was she'd never know remained a mystery. Never evidently meant never. In the meantime, the basement remained a junk-yard scavenger's dream.

"We'll look for the yearbooks after dinner," she told Rainie. "Your mother is making tofu stir-fry."

Rainie made a face. "Is there any leftover turkey?"

Chapter Nine

Ruth's yearbook proved easy to find, stored inside a carton with the words "Ruth's high school memorabilia" printed neatly on one of the flaps. She couldn't remember when she'd labeled that box and lugged it to the basement, but it offered proof that, despite the frantic batting of butterfly wings somewhere on the planet, she'd managed to preserve at least a sliver of order in her world.

"Memorabilia. What a cool word," Rainie murmured, accepting the oversized hardcover book Ruth pulled from the carton, then peering into the box. "What else is in there?"

Ruth wasn't sure. Standing in the light of a naked bulb screwed into a ceiling socket near the wall of shelves, and ignoring the motes of dust that sliding the carton from the shelf had stirred into the air, she glanced inside. There was the tassel from the mortarboard hat she'd worn on graduation day (dangling your graduation tassel from your car's rearview mirror was a thing back then), and the twenty-two-page research paper she'd written for her senior English class on the plays of Arthur Miller, double-space-typed and held together with rusting metal clips (a large, red A+ was scrawled across the title page, along with the words, "Well done," which was probably why Ruth had saved the project), and her diploma, tucked inside a black leatherette folder with the her high school's name embossed in gold on the front. If she set the box down and investigated its contents more thoroughly, she would likely unearth plenty of other treasures—quite possibly her old report cards, her National Merit certificate, some sheet music from her stint accompanying the glee club, and her biology lab report on the pithing of a frog (on which, if she wasn't misremembering, she'd also received an A-plus). But she feared that if she started rummaging through the box, like an archeologist who'd discovered an interesting shard of pottery on a dig, she wouldn't stop until she'd exhumed an entire set of dishware for twelve, left behind by some ancient civilization that had loved to throw dinner parties. Hours would pass before Rainie had a chance to write her compare-and-contrast essay.

So Ruth slid the box back onto the shelf, pondered the word *memorabilia,* decided it was indeed cool, and headed up the stairs, Rainie trailing behind her with the yearbook hugged to her chest.

They settled at the kitchen table, where the light was good and they wouldn't be distracted by the televised football game Barry was watching in the den. Seated next to Rainie, Ruth opened the yearbook.

Row after row of faculty photographs filled the first few pages. Back when she'd been a student, her teachers had seemed so old. Staring at their crisp black-and-white portraits, she realized that they were much younger than she was now. Some of them looked barely past puberty.

Rainie stared at the photos along with her, searching each page for clues to what made Ruth's high-school era different from her own. Not that you could tell much about the teachers from their photos. Mr. Crockett had the most benign smile, yet he'd been a tyrant, telling his math students that they were morons and would never amount to anything. Miss Arpanian looked so delicately pretty in her picture but had a voice as abrasive as a wood chipper. Mr. Conklin—whose sideburns were so thick, they looked like dyed cotton balls glued to his cheeks—had a wild-eyed look about him, which was appropriate since he'd taught driver education and spent much of his time strapped into the death seat of the school's specially outfitted Ford while a novice teenager steered the car in crazy circles around the community center parking lot across the street from the high school. That Mr. Conklin hadn't suffered a stroke or a heart attack during the course of these practice drives had been a medical miracle. For all Ruth knew, he might have wound up in an insane asylum some time after she'd graduated, tugging at his sideburns and screaming, "Look out!

Slow down! Brake, brake, *brake!*" as he banged his head against the padded walls of his room.

"They're all *Miss* or *Mrs.*," Rainie observed. "No *Ms.*"

"The term was just creeping into usage around then," Ruth explained. "I guess back in the day, people felt it was essential to know a woman's marital status."

Rainie crinkled her nose and shook her head. "I'll have to include that in my paper."

After the faculty pages came photos of the office staff, the cafeteria ladies, and the custodians, none of whom looked remotely familiar to Ruth. She'd eaten lunch in the cafeteria; she'd ventured into the office on various errands. She had a vague memory of entering the girls' bathroom in the science hall with Debbie once and finding one of the male custodians inside, mopping the floor. With all the sophistication of fourteen-year-old girls, she and Debbie had bolted from the bathroom, shrieking as if they'd seen a zombie rather than a guy in coarse cotton work clothes, a plethora of keys jangling from his belt as he pushed his mop across the pink tile floor.

Interspersed with the staff photos were candid shots of students poring over books in the library, seated in desks arranged in precise rows, wearing protective goggles while pouring liquids from a test tube into a flask in the chemistry lab—photos designed to convey that Ruth's high school had been a citadel of great learning and serious purpose. Those photos didn't comport with Ruth's memories of high school at all. She recalled loitering in the halls, sneaking out of study halls to play poker with friends in the audio-visual room, arguing with her American history teacher, Mr. Gallagher, about the Vietnam War, racing through boring and apparently pointless homework assignments, and planning her life around Trouble Ahead practices and gigs. Sure, she'd enjoyed some classes—glee club, especially, but also Mrs. Klein's English class, in which she'd written her A-plus paper on Arthur Miller, and Señor Garcia's Spanish class, not because she was particularly skilled in Spanish but because Señor Garcia looked like George Harrison, appealingly gaunt and blessed with dark, brooding eyes and a brilliant smile that he flashed whenever Ruth made an effort to roll her r's. She'd liked driver ed, too, if only because she enjoyed watching Mr. Conklin fist his hands, turn pale, and stomp on the brake pedal on his side of the front seat as students swerved and skidded around the parking lot.

Several pages further, they reached the "Seniors" section, the photos of her classmates. Here were faces she remembered, names she knew. Precise, rectangular photos of the people she'd grown up with, all of them looking a bit neater, cleaner, and more put together in their photos than they ever looked in real life.

"Wow," Rainie murmured, studying each photo as if it held a secret, a code, the combination to a wall safe containing millions of dollars. "This is what eighteen-year-olds used to look like."

"Yes."

"All the girls have the same hair."

"Pretty much," Ruth acknowledged with a smile. All the white and Asian girls, at least: long straight hair, the majority parted in the middle but some parted on one side. The girls who didn't have naturally straight hair often straightened it artificially. She recalled girls in the locker room after gym class discussing various techniques: rolling your hair on empty orange juice cans after you shampooed it, or ironing it, or wrapping it around your skull and holding it in place with multiple bobby-pins so it would dry flat. Or brushing it and brushing it until all the moisture was gone, although that could take hours. No one owned hand-held blow-dryers in those days.

Some of the black girls had long, straight hair too. A couple of daring girls had Afros, as did some of the boys, both black and white. If the boys had curly hair and couldn't do anything else with it, they let it go wild.

Most of the boys wore blazers and dress shirts and ties. Many had floppy mustaches, bushy sideburns, Afros or Jew-fros or scraggly hippie hair. Others were clean cut. You could tell a boy's politics by his hair in those days. Not a girl's, though. The conservative girls had long, straight, parted-in-the-middle hair, just like the liberal girls.

The portraits were arranged in alphabetical order. A few pages into the "Seniors" section, Rainie reached the Fs. Ruth spotted Danny Fortuna as soon as Rainie turned to his page.

He'd been so good looking. Even now, from the perspective of her advanced age and her forty-five-year marriage, she still felt a twinge of arousal when she glimpsed his picture. The chiseled cheeks, the elegant mouth, the dark eyes fringed with thick lashes, the tousled, tawny hair rippling around his face... In their portraits, most of the students gazed past the photographer and into some nebulous future, their faces angled slightly to the left or the right. But Danny looked straight ahead, daring the viewer. Beckoning her. Seducing her with his smoldering eyes and his hint of a smile.

Rainie apparently responded to him the same way Ruth did. Not surprising, since every heterosexual female—and probably plenty of homosexual males—had responded to him that way when Ruth had been in the band with him. "Wow," Rainie said. "Who's *this*?"

"That's Danny Fortuna. A friend of mine," Ruth said with a totally undeserved surge of pride. Yes, she and Danny had been friends. More than friends. They'd sung together, played together, made sweet music together. That she could have been close to someone like him, someone so staggeringly handsome, someone who oozed talent and charisma, made her feel...well, maybe not as cool as the word *memorabilia*, but cooler than she had a right to feel.

Rainie moved on to the next page, and the next. Ruth recognized other faces—Linda Freedman had sat next to her in calculus, and, Ruth recalled, wound up attending MIT. Joe Gessler had been some kind of baseball whiz, and everyone had predicted he'd wind up in the pros, but he'd gotten drafted by the army and not by a baseball team, and Ruth had never heard anything about him after that. Debbie Glazer, her best friend until the band had devoured too much of Ruth's time and energy and Debbie had found other girls to be best friends with. Sometime between junior and senior year, Debbie had started lightening her hair, and by the day her yearbook photo was taken, it was bleached to the color of dry straw. Her complexion wasn't suited to blond hair—her eyes were brown, her eyebrows dark, her skin tone olive (although you couldn't see that in the black-and-white photo), but she'd felt so pretty as a blonde, Ruth had never told her the color didn't work for her. If Debbie were a student today, who knew? Maybe she'd be adding pink highlights to her hair.

Jimmy Grogan's photo appeared on the next page. In his photo, he looked pretty much the same as he'd looked the day he'd approached Ruth at her locker and invited her to join the band—tangled hair, freckled face, easy smile. He didn't capture Rainie's attention the way Danny had—of course, no one captured attention like Danny—and Ruth said nothing as Rainie flipped the page. She savored a private memory, but that was all it was. A memory. Private.

More photos. Girls she'd stood with in the alto section of the glee club. The orchestra kids she'd played poker with. Artie Marmelson, whose mother had played in a weekly mah-jongg game with Ruth's mother, and the two mothers had tried to match-make their children, but Artie had been a nerd, too conservative for Ruth's tastes, too straight. Nick Montoya, looking beefy and mildly threatening despite his dress shirt and necktie, which seemed to be choking him.

And then the P's. "There you are!" Rainie jabbed her index finger at Ruth's photo. Ruth Pinchas, with long, straight hair parted down the middle. She'd added a little mascara to her lashes for the photo, and they made her eyes appear intense and slightly smudgy. Her nose was still a bit too big for her face, her chin a bit too pointed. If her mouth was truly her best feature, it was no wonder the overall effect screamed *average*.

"You were so pretty," Rainie said.

"You're a bad liar," Ruth teased, "but a very sweet one. Thank you."

"No, really, Grammy. Look at you!" Rainie did just that, leaning in, squinting at the photo. "You were so young! I can see why Grandpa fell in love with you."

"I didn't meet him until years later," Ruth pointed out.

"You were the only Pinchas," Rainie observed.

"It's not a common name. I think my graduating class had three Cohens and four Smiths. Uncle David and I were the only Pinchases in the school."

"You should have kept the name when you married Grandpa. It's so...*pink*."

"Everyone mispronounced it," Ruth told her. "They used to pronounce it 'pinch-us.' They'd tease me—'*Hey, Ruth, pinch us!*' I couldn't wait to get married so I could change it."

"I don't think Mom should take Warren's last name," Rainie said. "Schneier. It's an ugly name."

"There's nothing wrong with it."

"Singer is much better," Rainie said.

Ruth grinned. "Especially if you're a music teacher."

Rainie shared her smile, then shifted her attention back to Ruth's senior photo. "What were you wearing in the picture? It looks like a sweater."

"It was."

"I mean, just a plain sweater. Girls wouldn't wear that sweater today."

Ruth recalled the point of this exercise: to contrast the way kids looked and acted during Ruth's high school days with the way kids looked and acted today. "We had to dress nicely for the photographer," she explained. "Most of the time, I wore bellbottom jeans and paisley shirts."

"What's paisley?" Rainie asked.

Laughing, Ruth flipped through the pages until she reached another section of candid shots and extra-curricular activities. The students weren't dressed for their portraits in these photos, and they would give Rainie a clearer idea of the apparel teenagers wore when it wasn't school-picture day. Tie-dyed T-shirts, patched jeans, blouses with oversized, pointy collars, mini-skirts hemmed to display acres of thigh, bulky leather sandals, bulkier leather boots.

Rainie studied each picture at length, her lips pressed together, her eyes glistening with what appeared to be rapture. Ruth suppressed a smile. She saw nothing the least bit rapturous in the photos. The kids looked like kids of that era—funky, silly, mostly comfortable, sometimes defiant.

Rainie devoured the pictures as if they were a gourmet feast and she hadn't eaten in days. Which wasn't a commentary on the tofu stir-fry her mother had made, although suffice it to say no one had gone back for seconds.

"Look, there's the glee club," Rainie said, studying a photo of the choral group arrayed on risers on the stage. So many students were in the glee club, it was hard to distinguish individual faces, but Ruth wasn't crowded on a riser with the rest of the vocalists. She stood beside the piano. She played only at rehearsals, but she supposed the photographer had asked her to stand by the piano, and she had. In the picture she was wearing denim bellbottoms, clunky shoes, and a paisley blouse.

"That's paisley," she said, pointing to her photo. "That pattern. It looks like paramecia."

"What's that? Para—what?"

"Paramecia. That shape. They're one-celled creatures, but they're shaped like that."

"Like a comma?"

"Right. It was a popular pattern."

Rainie shrugged, unimpressed. She turned the page and surveyed the photos there: the cheerleaders forming a human pyramid, the thinner, smaller girls perched on the shoulders of the bigger, sturdier girls. The auditorium stage, with the cast of that year's musical production, *Camelot*, posing in costumes that looked more like overpriced pajamas and bathrobes than royal gowns and armor. A school dance at the gym, with a few brave couples gyrating on the parquet floor and a rock band performing on a platform beneath one of the basketball hoops.

"Hey!" Rainie bowed over the page, her brow wrinkling as she squinted at the photo. "Is that you?"

The band playing at that dance was, indeed, Trouble Ahead. In the photo, Ruth wore a scarf head-band style around her head, an embroidered tunic she'd bought just for performing, and the same bellbottoms she had on in the picture of the glee club, although you couldn't really see them because she was standing behind the electric organ that had once belonged to Mike's brother.

Rainie turned to her, her eyes wide, her expression almost accusing. "You were in a *band*?"

"I was," Ruth admitted.

"Why didn't you ever tell me?"

Ruth shrugged. "It was a long time ago. And you never asked."

"How could I ask? I didn't *know*!" She sounded not accusing so much as awed. "Holy shit! You were in a band!" She looked back at the photo, studying it intently. "Wow! You were so cool!" She hesitated, then asked, "Isn't that that cute guy?"

"Danny Fortuna," Ruth confirmed. "He was our lead singer."

"Holy shit!"

"Language," Ruth chided gently.

"Oh, come on, Grammy! You were in a band. I bet you cursed all the time."

Well, of course. She'd cursed plenty back then. When she'd been Rainie's age, she'd talked like people Rainie's age did. She cursed now, too, when a curse was absolutely necessary. But the fact of her being in a band didn't seem like a cause for cursing—even celebratory cursing.

"So you played at your high school?" Rainie asked.

"We played at my high school and plenty of others. Junior high schools, too, if they were paying. We played at YMCA dances and community center dances, and county fairs...and some rock clubs."

"When you were in *high school*?" Rainie's voice rose to a near screech. "You played in *rock clubs*?"

"We were pretty good," Ruth said modestly. "Of course, we weren't served drinks at those rock clubs. Just soda." They'd sometimes smoke a couple of joints out in Danny's van before a performance, and they'd share a couple of beers afterward, but they never did that in a place where an authority figure might see them. They wanted those gigs. They earned what seemed to them like good money playing in clubs and at that outdoor clam bar—what was it called? Sam's, or Jack's, something like that.

"I was the band's bookkeeper," she told Rainie. "I divvied up our earnings and handled the band's budget, so we could buy equipment and gas. Jimmy Grogan got us the gigs." He booked them, anyway. Danny was probably responsible for many of the return engagements, just because he looked so good and delivered the songs so well.

"What kind of music did you play?"

"We did covers of a lot of the hits. 'Light My Fire.' 'Good Lovin'.' 'A Whiter Shade of Pale.'"

"Huh? I never heard of that one."

"We also wrote and sang our own songs. Frankly, I think we did them better than we did the covers."

"Holy—wow," Rainie caught herself before cursing again. "That is just so cool. Did you make any records?"

Ruth laughed. "No. Things were much less do-it-yourself in those days. To make a record, you'd need a contract and a studio." She reminisced for a moment. "We did make some tape recordings for practice purposes. Jimmy had a cassette recorder and we'd tape ourselves sometimes during rehearsals to see how we sounded."

"Do you have any cassettes? I'd love to hear them."

Ruth would love to hear them too—or maybe not. Maybe she'd be embarrassed by them. Maybe the band sounded amateurish and off-key, and she'd wonder why anyone had ever hired them to play.

They'd probably hired Trouble Ahead because people wanted to look at Danny Fortuna, she reasoned. "No idea where those cassettes are now. Probably in a landfill somewhere."

"That sucks." Rainie sulked for a minute. "So what happened to the band?"

"I went to college," Ruth said, aware of the wistfulness in her tone. "So did Jimmy. Mike went to Canada. We just moved in different directions after graduation."

Rainie shook her head. "You were good enough to play at rock clubs. You could've become famous."

Ruth had to laugh at that. "In our dreams. We were okay. We were—all right, we were good for a group of high school kids." Although the cassettes might disprove that claim. Thank goodness they were gone. "None of us were brilliant artists. There were a million bands like ours. We had other things we wanted to do with our lives."

"Like what?"

"Well, I became a teacher."

"How about the others?"

Ruth shrugged. "No idea."

"You don't keep in touch with them?"

Good God, why would she? That was all so long ago. "I have no idea where any of them are."

"You should look them up," Rainie said. "Just go on Facebook. Or Google them. Maybe some of them joined other bands and became famous."

Maybe they had. Nick Montoya had been a solid drummer, and bands always needed drummers. And Danny... Well, Danny.

Ruth had a Facebook account which she never did much with. She'd friended her children and checked every now and then to see if Noah or Jill had posted photos of Aaron and Ezra and the twins. But if she had a free half-hour, she'd rather spend it taking a walk or playing the piano or reading a book, not sitting in front of a computer scrolling through gossip about people she hardly knew, or else people she knew so well she could pick up the phone and call them if she wanted to hear how they were doing.

"Look your band up, Grammy. It's easy. You can find anyone online."

"There's no such thing as privacy anymore," Ruth muttered.

"Nope." Rainie folded the yearbook shut and pulled it into her arms. "Can I borrow this for a while? I have to write my paper."

"Of course. Let me know if you have any questions."

Ruth remained at the kitchen table after Rainie stood and waltzed out of the room, cradling the book as if it were a priceless artifact. It was, in its way. It was a trove of memories, a road map to Ruth's past. A collection of what-ifs, of maybes, of nevers, of if-onlys.

Of lies. Because all those orderly, rectangular photos, all those fresh-scrubbed students on page after page, all those candid shots of people smiling, people having fun, people apparently loving every second of their adolescence—none of that was true. The butterflies had been fluttering their wings then too. Things happened. Choices were made. You kept putting one foot in front of the other, never knowing whether you were headed in the right direction, but moving along, anyway. Hoping for the best, preparing for the worst, and generally learning that preparation was more useful than hope.

Chapter Ten

If Only I'd Slept with the Man from Santa Fe...

"Thanks for letting me walk with you," Coral said.

Ruth laughed. "I'm not *letting* you walk with me. You don't need my permission to take a walk. But I love having your company."

The morning was cold and tart, the air biting. A thin layer of snow covered the ground, but the roads and sidewalks were plowed. Ruth and Coral had already planned to meet at Hilda's for lunch later that day, but Coral phoned that morning and asked if she could accompany Ruth on her walk. "I need to lose some weight," Coral explained as they started down Jefferson Road.

Ruth glanced at Coral. No one looked slim wearing a puffy coat quilted with down, and even without her coat, Coral wasn't exactly skinny. But she wasn't obese either. Maybe just a little stocky. Not a tragedy, although Ruth's mother might have thought it was. "You look fine to me," she said.

"I need to lose my Thanksgiving weight before I start adding my Christmas weight," Coral explained. "Besides, Lee's been bitching at me that I'm getting fat. I think she's just pissed because I eat meat."

"How long have you two been together?" Ruth remarked. "She ought to be used to the fact that you're not a vegetarian."

"We had a stupid fight yesterday over mung beans. I told her I thought they were tasteless. She went on and on about how I need to eat less meat and more plants." Coral sighed, her breath creating a plume of white vapor in the chilly air.

"Well," Ruth said, "we had a good time at your Thanksgiving. All the food was delicious."

"Especially the meat," Coral muttered.

Ruth grinned. "Barry loved the turkey. So did I." In retrospect, Ruth considered the holiday feast at Coral's house more pleasant than the blowup at her own house two days later, even if the food she'd served had tasted better. "Barry was impressed by Lee's ear piercings," she went on, not bothering to mention that he was *negatively* impressed. "She's wearing her hair shorter these days. You can really see all those earrings. Were there mung beans in any of the vegetarian dishes in your Thanksgiving buffet?"

"Who knows? I was too busy eating turkey to bother with all that vegetarian stuff." They turned the corner and moved apart so a muscular young man in floppy shorts, long leggings, a fleece vest, and ear muffs could jog between them. "How was your Saturday celebration?" Coral asked once he had passed and they could move closer together again.

Ruth's smile faded. "Noah announced he and Laura are separated."

Coral halted and twisted to face her. "No!"

"He says their marriage is stagnant. He also admitted he's having an affair. I guess he got bored with Laura. Honestly, I want to slap him upside the head. So does Maddie. She says he's ruining her wedding. Be grateful you don't have kids."

It was Coral's turn to chuckle, although her expression quickly turned pensive. "Marriage spoils everything. Lee and I never argued about mung beans before we got married."

"I'm sure you argued about other things."

"No. We were together—you're right, a long, long time. Close to twenty years. Then same-sex marriage became legal in Massachusetts. We were so excited when we could finally get married. We tied the knot that first year it was legal, remember? We couldn't wait. But..." Another long sigh, sending a cloud of white breath into the air. "Before our wedding, there was something, I don't know, illicit about our relationship. We were living in sin, and it was fun! We were together not by law but by choice. You get married, and suddenly you're legally bound. It isn't a choice anymore."

"Of course it's a choice. You can always choose to get divorced."

"Which is an enormously complicated thing, and expensive. And exhausting. Not that I'd ever divorce Lee. We're fine, mung beans notwithstanding. But before we got married, she'd always get so excited about my paintings. She'd say they were gorgeous. She'd say she wanted to hang this one over the fireplace, or sell that one for thousands of dollars. Not that any of my paintings ever brought four figures, but... She was so enthusiastic. Now I'm retired, and I spend practically every day in my studio, and she doesn't even peek through the door. Over dinner, she asks if I had a good day painting, and I tell her yes or no, and she goes back to eating her mung beans."

Sometimes Ruth's dinners with Barry were like that, too. Not that they had many dinners alone. Before Maddie began dating Warren, she'd usually joined them for dinner, and even now that the wedding was just a few months away, she ate dinner with them more often than not. And of course, Rainie almost always ate with them.

That was one reason Ruth wanted Rainie to move to Warren's house with her mother after the wedding. She wanted to enjoy intimate dinners with Barry. During which—who knew?—maybe they would argue about mung beans.

Barry thought marriage was about stagnating. Also comfort. And it was true: the excitement was no longer there. But at their age, did they really want excitement anymore?

They'd made love last night. Sex was no longer a frequent feature in their relationship, but they got around to it every couple of weeks or so. Barry might wish to have sex more often, Ruth less often. But she was Barry's wife. She wanted him happy, and she didn't want him chasing after a thin young woman named Kim whom he'd noticed on the elliptical next to his treadmill—if he ever joined a fitness center.

Unfortunately, due to his aging, aching knees (which probably meant the treadmill was out), *happy* for Barry meant he got to lie on the bottom while Ruth humped and pumped on top of him. It didn't seem fair; she did most of the work and he received most of the pleasure. Lately, she'd had to start using creams and ointments on her aging body parts. She felt like an old automobile engine, constantly in need of lubrication just so she could chug across town to the supermarket. No joy rides anymore. No top-down cruising toward the horizon. Just add oil and run an errand.

She read books and articles that claimed maintaining an active sex life was essential even in one's later years, not just for the sake of marital satisfaction but for one's physical and mental health. If sex was, in fact, essential for her physical health, why did she have to grease up her dry vagina just to make it happen? Why did it take an eternity for her to come—if she was fortunate enough to come? Her orgasms were nothing to write home about, either. As if they'd ever been an appropriate topic to write home about.

Last night, as she'd huffed and puffed and Barry had lain beneath her, alternately smiling and grunting and clutching at her tush, she'd closed her eyes and pictured Danny Fortuna. She'd felt disloyal doing that, but after having paged through her high school yearbook earlier that evening with Rainie, she'd had Trouble Ahead on her mind. Trouble Ahead and Danny. Imagining herself on top of him instead of her portly, mildly arthritic but blissful husband had made the event moderately more enjoyable.

Of course, she'd imagined Danny as he'd been in high school—eighteen years old, lean and virile. Today, he was probably portly and mildly arthritic too. Maybe bald and double-chinned. Maybe flatulent. Maybe obnoxious.

But he hadn't been any of those things back in high school. And imagining him at age eighteen allowed her to imagine herself at age eighteen, when her flesh was taut and her skin was smooth and she didn't have to juice herself up artificially. When she'd taken a few risks, sacrificed her best friend for the sake of the band, defied her mother, biked over the railroad tracks.

She'd felt almost sexy, thinking about Danny while she made love with Barry. Or maybe what had made her feel sexy was remembering that brief time in her adolescence when she'd taken a few risks.

Never in her life had she cheated on her husband. The mere idea caused her spine to tense, her stomach to clench. It just wasn't done. What little wildness she had inside her was directed toward wishing her children would leave her alone—which seemed shamefully unmaternal. She'd married Barry. She'd made a promise. She'd taken a vow.

There were temptations, of course. Not that she was a temptress, but, well...Danny Fortuna.

~

She and Coral talked about school business—what they missed about their jobs, what they definitely didn't miss now that they were retired—for the rest of the walk. Ruth contemplated asking Coral whether she and Lee still had regular sex, now that they were seventy years old. Whether lesbian sex was as good for one's physical health as heterosexual sex supposedly was. Whether Coral had to buy lubricants to get the job done. Whether she considered it a job.

But as close as Ruth felt to Coral, she didn't feel comfortable broaching that particular subject. Sex simply wasn't something she talked about with her friends. She recalled how uncomfortable she used to feel when Darlene Jarvis would casually, crudely chat about her sex life with her husband Glenn, and later, after they got divorced, with various boyfriends. Ruth had always wanted to silence her by saying, "We're neighbors, not sisters," but Darlene hadn't really treated her like a sister, anyway. Ruth suspected that Darlene blabbed about intimate subjects to anyone who happened to be handy: her pedicurist, a fellow passenger on the commuter rail into Boston, or Ruth when she wandered across the street to collect her daughter from an afternoon-long play date with Kyle. At the time, Ruth had often wondered if Darlene's frankness equated to licentiousness—and, more importantly, if Darlene's son viewed sex as casually and crudely as his mother did, and if he imparted that attitude to Maddie. Were Kyle and Maddie experimenting? Exploring? Playing doctor?

To ask would have made Ruth seem prudish. So she'd resorted to giving Maddie as many sex-ed lectures as she could, droning on and on about responsibility and self-respect, integrity and autonomy. A hell of a lot of good that did. Maddie ran off with Kyle and came home with a baby.

Ruth had tolerated Darlene's bawdy monologues, because she'd wanted to check on the kids, to see if they were, in fact, playing doctor. Whenever she rang Darlene's doorbell, though, the woman had always steered her away from wherever their children were playing, pressed a glass of wine into her hands, and ushered her into the oddly shaped living room of her oddly shaped house, where she'd plop onto one of the sleek leather sofas and yammer about the *Kama Sutra* or bondage games. When Ruth would interrupt her to ask what Maddie and Kyle were doing, Darlene invariably said, "Homework." Ruth had doubted that, but she'd had no discreet way of confirming her suspicions. The children were not in the oddly shaped living room, hunched over their school books, discussing the Peloponnesian War or polynomial equations.

Darlene had sold her house barely a month after Kyle and Maddie had graduated from high school, and driven off into the sunset, or, more accurately, into a slightly overcast mid-morning. Maybe Darlene had gotten sick of Ruth's phoning her and demanding to know where their children had gone—"How should I know? You think Kyle tells me anything?"—and decided the best way to avoid Ruth's constant questions was to sell the house and drive off, just as Kyle and Maddie had. Jenny Trofucco, who lived next door to Darlene, had said she'd heard that the Jarvises' divorce settlement had freed Glenn from paying the mortgage on the house once Kyle had finished at Brentwood High School, and Darlene couldn't afford to keep the house on her own. That explanation made more sense than Ruth's paranoid worry that Darlene had packed up and departed from Jefferson Road simply to get away from Ruth.

Either way, with Darlene gone, Ruth had lost her best chance to track Maddie down. Maddie had refused to answer her cell phone when Ruth or Barry called her, nor would she respond to the emails they—and Jill and Noah—sent her. Barry had suggested hiring a private investigator to track Maddie down, but Ruth had feared that if a detective located Maddie, she'd be so resentful that she might sever ties with her family forever. Ruth had figured—she'd hoped—that when Maddie was ready, when she decided she'd had enough of Kyle, when she realized he could not support her in the manner she was used to, she'd come home.

Ruth had been right.

"We're still on for lunch at Hilda's?" Coral asked as they rounded the corner to Ruth's street. Coral's SUV was visible in Ruth's driveway.

"Of course."

"I feel so virtuous after all that exercise," Coral said, her cheeks pink and her eyes slightly teary from the cold. "Maybe I'll splurge and get ranch dressing with my salad."

Maybe Ruth would splurge and get a turkey-bacon-avocado wrap. Laura had eaten her wrap with so much enthusiasm, while Ruth had picked abstemiously at her undressed salad. Barry wouldn't leave her if she gained a few pounds—not only because he didn't go to a fitness center and wouldn't have an opportunity to meet a slim young elliptical-user, but because Ruth generously lubed herself and went on top when he requested it.

After bidding Coral goodbye, Ruth entered her house, peeled off the layers of clothing she'd donned to keep warm during her walk, and showered. She'd be meeting Coral at the restaurant in two hours, and no one besides her was home; Rainie was at school, Barry was charging clients a fortune to consult with him, and Maddie was chiseling tartar off teeth. The conditions were perfect for playing the piano.

Ruth settled on the bench and sighed. Banging out Trouble Ahead songs would only make her feel nostalgic—or guilty about picturing Danny while she'd made love with Barry last night. She really ought to tackle some of her old classical pieces. The sheet music for Debussy's "Clair de Lune" sat atop the pile of music books beside the keyboard.

She had learned "Clair de Lune" back in high school. She'd been able to play it adequately. Maybe if she'd been more committed to it, she would have elevated the quality from adequate to decent or even good, but by the time Mrs. Demming had assigned that piece to her, her heart had already shifted to rock and roll. As she played the opening notes now, she could hear Mrs. Demming's voice cawing in her ear: "Put some grace into it, Ruth. This is an ethereal tone poem, not a funeral dirge. And for God's sake, stop using the pedal. You're muddying all the notes."

Just to spite Mrs. Demming's long-ago critiques, Ruth defiantly pressed her right foot down on the pedal.

It didn't make the piece sound better. She managed to get through it, but if she were forced to evaluate her performance, she would have dropped her grade from a gentleman's C to D-minus.

Maddie used to play "Clair de Lune" beautifully.

It was one of the final pieces she'd learned before she'd quit playing piano in a huff, insisting that it bored her. Ruth remembered getting dinner prepared in the kitchen and eavesdropping on Maddie as she swept through her piano practice in the living room. She remembered, especially, this piece, the delicacy of Maddie's touch, the way the notes created a gossamer image of silver moonlight dancing across water in Ruth's mind.

She also remembered the final, faint notes and then the thump as Maddie slammed down the keyboard guard and muttered, "Fuck this," before shouting, "I'm going to Kyle's." Probably to play doctor. Or, as Darlene Jarvis insisted, to do homework. Right. Fat chance.

"Fuck it," Ruth grumbled, echoing Maddie as she set aside the Debussy sheet music. No one was home. She rose to her feet, banged out the moody opening chords of "Tom," and sang, "*Come on, Joe, where'd you go? Good-bye, John, you're really gone...*" And closed her eyes, and pictured Danny. And felt disloyal. Unfaithful. And just a little bit wicked.

The man from Santa Fe was named Cord. An unlikely name, but that was what was printed on the ID tag that hung from a lanyard around his neck. She'd met him at a conference sponsored by a national organization for music teachers. It was the only conference of its kind she'd ever gone to, although she'd submitted requests for funding to attend similar conferences numerous times. That one year, the school system had gotten some sort of grant to be used for faculty development, and she'd been one of the lucky recipients.

The conference, unfortunately, was in a hotel in Reno, Nevada. As she recalled, the hotel rooms and meals were ridiculously inexpensive—which might have been why the school board had decided to send her that year. The hotel was vast and glitzy, decorated with ostentatious crystal chandeliers, gold-veined mirrors, and velvet-flocked wallpaper, giving it the ambience of a high-class whore house. But the food and room charges were cheap, undoubtedly because the hotel profited so heavily from all the gambling taking place in its lobby.

Ruth had hated that lobby. The haze of cigarette smoke thickened the atmosphere with a blue-gray smog, and the air vibrated with the gongs and chimes and bells of numerous slot machines doing what slot machines did. To get from the elevator to the conference rooms, Ruth had to navigate an ocean-sized expanse of black-jack tables, roulette tables, and row upon row of slot machines. All day and all night, the lobby was jammed with people talking, shrieking, smoking, drinking, cheering, weeping...and gambling.

However, the music education organization's workshops had been interesting. Honoring the faith the Brentwood School Board had placed in her by sending her to this conference and footing the bill, Ruth had dutifully attended as many workshops as she could cram into a day.

The final day of the conference, she staggered out of the last workshop on the schedule at four in the afternoon, weary and bleary. Entering the hallway, she was greeted by the now-familiar cacophony of casino noise blasting from the lobby. Instinctively, she clapped her hands over her ears and grimaced.

The man who followed her out of the workshop room tapped her shoulder. Turning she saw him mouth something. Or maybe he actually spoke. It was so noisy in the hallway, she couldn't hear his voice, especially with her hands pressed against her ears.

She lowered her arms. "What?" she shouted.

"Let's get coffee. I want to talk to you."

He stood a good half foot taller than her, his blond hair threaded with silver, his face pleasantly craggy and his eyes an attractive mix of gray and green. His smile cut dimples into his cheeks. He looked friendly enough. He was wearing a lanyard that identified him as a fellow music teacher. Coffee with a colleague, out of the blasting noise of the casino, sounded like a lovely idea.

They wandered through the lobby in search of a café that might be closed off from the casino. At the far end, beyond the elevators, they found a small lounge with empty tables. The lobby's din seemed distant once they were seated in the dimly lit room. It lacked the chandeliers and bordello décor. Ruth wished she'd discovered this lounge earlier during the conference, a semi-quiet oasis from the gambling mania on the other side of the elevator bank.

She set down her official conference tote and squinted at his name tag. "Cord?"

"My parents were weird. Thank God they didn't name me Rope," he joked, peering at her tag. "And you're Ruth Singer? Now *that's* a good name for a music teacher."

Ruth noticed a few other people with conference IDs filtering into the room, taking other seats. A bar occupied one corner of the room, but thanks to her end-of-conference fatigue, coffee sounded more appealing than liquor. Cord ordered two cups, then leaned back in his chair. "I was intrigued by what you said in that last workshop," he told her.

She felt her cheeks warm—not from his compliment but from embarrassment. "I was rude," she confessed. "It's the end of the conference, and I'm all workshopped out. I shouldn't have argued with the speaker like that."

"No, I think you were right," he said. "Why would that guy think elementary school kids were too young to grasp the concept of harmonics? Especially if you teach them using a guitar. They can practically see the vibrations of the strings and understand that if a string is vibrating as a whole, it's also vibrating as two halves, and three thirds."

"It's not that they need to understand the physics of it," Ruth said, "but they can learn that overtones are what give music its richness, and they're the basis of the western scale."

"It would be harder to demonstrate on a wind instrument," he said. "But let's face it—music *is* physics. It's math. It's just physics and math made beautiful."

They sipped their coffee and talked. It turned out Cord was a clarinetist—hence his interest in wind instruments—and was the director of a high school band and orchestra in Santa Fe, New Mexico, which seemed quite exotic to her. His wife, he told her, was a potter, which also seemed exotic. Santa Fe was a beautiful city once you got used to its high elevation, he said. Lots of galleries, lots of culture, lots of Native American and Mexican influence.

Ruth didn't argue, although she felt obliged to boast a bit about the gorgeous ocean beaches of Massachusetts. Conversation flowed easily. A couple of conference attendees spotted them, pulled two chairs over to their table, and ate dinner with them—the café sold sandwiches and light meals. After dinner, Cord ordered a bottle of wine for the table. The other two attendees said they had early flights in the morning and departed.

Ruth and Cord talked. They schmoozed. She could no longer remember about what, but the conversation flowed as easily as the wine. She'd made a new friend.

When she looked at her watch, she was startled to see that it was past ten o'clock. "Wow," she murmured. "How did that happen?"

"It happened because we're in good company," he said, covering her hand with his and giving it a squeeze. "I've really enjoyed talking to you."

There was nothing pushy in his touch. Nothing offensive about it. Nothing even remotely sexual. Except...

Except that their eyes met above their hands, and his eyes were so pretty, framed in laugh lines. And those dimples, and his ruggedly carved chin, and his long, lean body...

"We leave tomorrow," he said. "We go back home to our families. No one would have to know."

True. No one would have to know.

Except her and Cord.

She was tempted. Not because she was angry with Barry, not because she wanted out of her marriage. At the moment, she was madly in love with Barry. He was home dealing with the kids and the dog, keeping everyone reasonably fed and bathed and on schedule, while she was two thousand miles away, doing something she never, ever did at home: focus completely on herself. Be a professional. Be an adult, not a mommy. Be herself, by herself, for herself. Not take care of anyone else.

And yet...

"I wish I could say yes," she managed, "but I can't."

If only I'd slept with the man from Santa Fe...

One night, that's all. One wild, giddy night.

I haven't had sex with anyone except Barry since he and I met, back in graduate school. I know everything about his body—his aches, his pains, his movements, his rhythm, his smell. I know the freckles and moles marking his skin the way an astronomer knows the night sky.

But tonight—just one night with someone entirely new... As Cord said, no one will have to know.

I wonder if he's done this before, if he's done it dozens of times before. I wonder if, while his wife is in her studio in Santa Fe, shaping mounds of clay on a pottery wheel, he's schtupping women in cheap motels, in the back seat of his car, in bedrooms filled with floral-patterned bed linens and chintz curtains. He doesn't seem like a floral-chintz kind of guy, but then, for the sake of a cheap roll in the hay, who knows what he'll put up with? He's putting up with me, right?

This doesn't feel cheap. It doesn't feel like a roll in the hay.

And anyway, when his wife is doing her pottery, he's at his high school, conducting the school band or giving clarinet lessons or battling the school board for a bigger budget so he can buy more music stands or rent better instruments. Do band students actually have to buy their own tubas? Tubas aren't an issue in elementary school; the children are way too small for instruments that huge. They can handle trumpets, flutes and clarinets, as well as half-size student violins. Not stand-up basses. Not harps. Certainly not tubas.

Of course, I have little to do with the instrumental stuff. I'm the choral teacher. Children carry their voices inside them. No need to haul a massive tuba onto the school bus, no need to ring a tuba around those petite nine-year-old bodies. Voices are the perfect instrument, because you're never without them. They travel everywhere with you, more efficient than a harmonica, more lyrical than castanets, sweeter than a kazoo.

And I shouldn't be thinking about work right now, even though I'm at a music educators' conference. I should be thinking about Cord.

Silly name, but he's not a silly man.

His mouth feels different on mine, tastes different. His kisses excite me. I refuse to worry, refuse to feel guilty. I'm daring. I hurtle down mountains on skis, right? I can hurtle into the glorious darkness of sex with a near stranger.

His unfamiliarity is more thrilling than the act itself. Just the newness of it. I wouldn't want to run away with him, leave Barry for him, tear him from the grip of his potter wife. That's not what this is.

It's an adventure. It's one night. It's a chance for me not to be who I always am: wife, mother, chauffeur, cook, scheduler, mediator, nurse, dog walker, inventory manager. It's a chance for me to be just a music teacher, a conference attendee, a woman whose only label is what fits on the laminated card attached to my lanyard. It's a chance for me to take a chance. To do something wild and chaotic and risky.

Afterward, we laugh a bit, and then we smile shyly. He says, "That was nice," and I agree. Then I say I should go back to my own room and he agrees.

The next morning, we see each other waiting to check out of the hotel. The lobby is a blur of clanging slot machines, flashing lights, and chattering people. He tips an imaginary hat at me, and I nod and smile in response. I think about that advertising slogan—"What happens in Vegas stays in Vegas"—except we're not in Vegas. I suppose Reno is close enough.

We each check out, turn in our room keys, and wheel our suitcases to the curb of the circular driveway outside the hotel. The air is hot and dry and the sun glares, a painful contrast to the windowless gloom of the casino on the other side of the automatic glass doors. Taxis queue up, waiting for fares, and a bellhop in a flashy scarlet uniform, complete with braided epaulets and a double row of gold buttons up the front, making him look like a member of Sgt. Pepper's Lonely Hearts Club Band, suggests that since there's a long line of people waiting for cabs and most of us are heading to the airport, we ought to share cabs. Sensible advice.

Somehow, Cord ends up with two other people in the cab behind the one I'm in. Just as well. Last night was last night. Today is today.

Barry is waiting for me at Logan Airport when I land in Boston seven hours later. During the flight, I experienced twinges of apprehension—no, bouts of apprehension. Would Barry sense that I'd been with another man last night? That for the first time in our marriage, I had cheated on him? Would seeing him make me wish I was back in Reno?

*No, I'd never want to be back in Reno, at that ghastly casino-hotel. But with Cord. That one night with him had been so...*different, *as if I'd somehow left my body and my identity and become someone else. Or, like those testimonials from people who'd briefly died on the operating table and claimed they'd floated up to the* *ceiling and looked down at themselves, at their bodies being sliced and shocked and prodded back to life by the surgeons and nurses.*

I'd been somewhere else last night, spiritually as well as literally. I'd been someone else. Would Barry still recognize me? Would I care if he didn't?

Much to my surprise, seeing him standing by his car at the curb outside the terminal, watching for me, fills me with joy. My Barry. My familiar half-hippie, half-fierce-businessman husband. I know who I am now—not a disembodied spirit floating through the air, watching my body do things below, but a person, unified, body and soul. Barry's partner. His wife.

He gathers me in a bear hug before he stows my suitcase in the trunk of his car. "Thank God you're home," he says as he eases into the flow of traffic outside the terminal. "I missed you."

"You missed having me prepare dinner and yell at the kids and walk the dog," I tease.

"No. I just missed you." He ruminates for a moment, then grins. "Yeah, all those other things too. How do you do it? How do you keep the house and the kids functioning so smoothly?"

"It's my secret power," I say, returning his smile and thinking, yes, I have power. And I have secrets. Having secrets makes me feel even more powerful.

Barry will never know about what I did in Reno. He'll never have to know, because what I did, ironically, made me realize just how much I love him.

Cord was my walk on the wild side. My bad-girl adventure. My moment of ecstatic disorder. But now I'm home. The disorder is past. I'm safe.

Chapter Eleven

"It's kind of like an intervention," Jill said as she backed her Volvo crossover SUV—her official Mommy car, as she called it—out of the driveway. Ruth sat beside her. Maddie and Rainie occupied the second row after moving the twins' child seats into the rear of the car.

Ruth didn't believe Rainie should have been included in this outing, but Rainie had argued that since she was Maddie's maid of honor, she deserved to be a part of it. "It's going to be boring," Ruth had warned.

"No, it's not," Maddie had said.

Ruth had to admit that Maddie in full battle mode was never boring. And when it came to Noah's marital mess, Maddie was a four-star general prosecuting a world war.

At least Maddie and Jill were in agreement for a change. They both felt compelled to confront their brother, even if their reasons differed. Jill wanted to save his marriage. Maddie wanted to save her precisely arranged bridal party.

Rainie wanted...Ruth wasn't sure what. Not to be bored, maybe. Her soccer season was done, none of her friends were available to hang out with her today, and if she'd stayed home she might have felt obligated to do homework, or else watch college football games on TV with her grandfather. Big Ten, Pac-Ten, ACC—this was how Barry spent his autumn Saturdays. Witnessing her mother and her aunt as they screamed at her uncle had to be less boring than that.

Ruth had obtained Noah's new address from Laura. They'd had a telephone chat yesterday afternoon before the sun set. Laura, apparently, was finding solace these days in embracing her faith and honoring the Sabbath. "I'm making a pot roast and drinking a lot of wine," she'd told Ruth. "But I can't talk long. Once the sun sets, I have to hang up."

And drink wine, Ruth had completed the thought. Not that she blamed Laura. When life disintegrated into chaos, wine could be therapeutic. It could also add to the chaos, but if things were already chaotic, who cared?

Jill had entered Noah's address into her GPS, and now a mellifluous female voice chirped directions out of the computer in her dashboard. "In half a mile, turn right. In a quarter of a mile, turn right. Turn right." The smooth voice reciting these directions repeatedly broke into the vigorous discussion between Jill and Maddie, who, despite their shared mission, had vastly different agendas. "If he ruins my wedding, I swear, I'll never speak to him again," Maddie muttered.

"This isn't about your wedding," Jill argued. "It's about emotional maturity."

"You think you're going to get him to grow up in the next fifteen minutes?" Maddie argued. "Give me a break. He's a guy, which means he's got the emotional maturity of a two-year-old. This is about him fucking up my wedding."

"In a quarter of a mile, turn left," the GPS voice purred before Ruth could chide Maddie about her language. Not that it mattered. Rainie was clearly familiar with the f-word.

"I'm thinking about salvaging his marriage," Jill said. "His family. Those two sweet boys."

"Who are going to grow up and start shaving and learn to drive and get married and wind up with the emotional maturity of two-year-olds," Maddie said. "Thank God I only have a daughter. If I had a son, I'd kill myself."

"Does Warren have the emotional maturity of a two-year-old?" Rainie asked. She'd added a few streaks of turquoise to her hair sometime between yesterday and today. To Ruth's surprise, she thought the additional color looked good. It looked kind of rainbow-y.

"Warren is different," Maddie said, her voice crisp and dry. "He's very mature."

"Grampa isn't mature at all," Rainie said. "That's why I love him. He's like a little kid."

True enough. At work, Ruth assumed, Barry was a hawk, an eagle, some razor-sharp raptor spotting a chipmunk on the ground from hundreds of yards away and swooping down to capture it. That was what his clients paid him vast sums of money to do—spot the problems in their companies, swoop down, and take care of them with bloodless efficiency. But when he came home, when he traded his business suit for faded blue jeans, when he flopped onto the leather sofa in the den with a tub of Ben & Jerry's resting atop his paunch, or a bag of potato chips, or a package of Oreo cookies, he regressed. He slurped the ice cream, dribbled potato chip crumbs over the upholstery, separated the sandwich cookies and sucked the cream filling.

Ruth exerted herself not to mind that he behaved like—well, not a two-year-old, but definitely a prepubescent boy. It was who he was. If Maddie was right, it was who all men were. Probably Warren, too, although Maddie was not prepared to admit that.

The GPS guided them to a bland apartment complex off Route 30, a few three-story brick buildings with rigid rows of tiny balconies protruding from their façades. The complex had no landscaping unless you considered black asphalt adorned with white parking-space stripes landscaping. "Which building is his?" Jill asked, now that the dulcet-voiced lady on the GPS had delivered them to their address and fallen silent.

Ruth pulled from her purse the square of paper on which she'd jotted the address. "Building C," she said. "Apartment 302C."

"Great," Maddie grumbled. "It's on the third floor. These buildings won't have elevators."

"I think you can manage two flights of stairs," Ruth said.

"You could use the exercise," Rainie teased her mother. "You want to fit into your wedding dress, don't you?"

"I haven't gained a pound since I bought the dress," Maddie said. "Well, I gained a pound after Thanksgiving, but I lost it. I'm on my feet all day in the dental office. On the weekends, I like to relax."

"You sit on a stool," Rainie reminded her.

"You're looking for trouble," Maddie shot back.

Ruth considered intervening but instead only smiled. If anyone deserved to get harassed by her teenage daughter, Maddie did. Right now, she was probably thinking a daughter was more likely than a son to drive her to suicide.

Jill parked in a space marked for visitors near Building C, and they all climbed out into the cold afternoon. Ruth hugged her jacket more tightly around herself. Jill adjusted the cashmere scarf circling her neck. Maddie pulled the hood of her parka over her head. Rainie didn't bother to zip the sweatshirt she'd thrown on over her T-shirt. At least in the Singer family, teenagers tended to burn hotter than normal people. When her own children were growing up, Ruth used to beg them not to wear shorts and flip-flops to school when the temperature dropped below freezing. Sometimes they'd listened to her. More often, they hadn't.

Inside the building's vestibule, they found a panel with apartment listings and buttons. Jill pressed the button next to 302. After a pause, a metallic buzz alerted them that the inner door had been released. Noah hadn't even asked them to identify themselves. Ruth would have to discuss apartment safety and security with him. He was a lawyer; he should know better.

Then again, according to Maddie, he was emotionally two years old.

They ascended the stairs, Maddie muttering about how tired her legs were, Jill spritzing her hands with sanitizer from a travel-size bottle she had in her bag—a carry-over from the pandemic, Ruth presumed. She doubted the stairway railing was coated in germs, but the building did look a little defeated. The floating stairs and airy stairwell must have seemed quite modern when the complex was built, a good fifty years ago. Ruth had felt modern fifty years ago too. A lot less so now.

Only four apartments opened onto the third-floor hallway, so finding Noah's unit wasn't a challenge. Maddie raised her fist to pound on the door, but Jill nudged her aside, locating and pressing the doorbell. Maddie could save her fist for pummeling her brother.

The door swung open. Noah, clad in wrinkled khakis and an untucked flannel shirt, gaped at the four women on the other side of the threshold. His dark hair was mussed, his chin shadowed with an overnight growth of beard, and his eyes widened. "Oh! Hi," he said.

"You were expecting someone else?" Maddie asked.

"I was expecting Laura. I thought maybe she'd come to pick up the boys. It's too early, though."

"The boys are here?" Ruth experienced an odd mix of emotions: reflexive joy at the chance to see her two grandsons but worry that those grandsons might be bonding with Kim. Ruth didn't want them developing a relationship with Noah's skinny new girlfriend. That would imply that his relationship with the woman was serious, which in turn would imply that it might last long enough to do irreparable damage to his marriage, if it hadn't already done that.

"Laura had a hair appointment," Noah explained. "She said she was going to get a facial too. I don't know how long those take. So she brought the boys over. I guess she gave you my address?"

"She did," Jill said briskly. "Can we come in?"

"You should have called first," Noah objected, but he stepped aside and waved them inside.

Ruth, her daughters, and Rainie entered the apartment. It looked exactly like what it was—a way station for a straying husband living in exile. An arched doorway in the entry hall opened into a kitchen not much larger than a casket. Peeking through the doorway, Ruth saw a diminutive refrigerator, a cramped four-burner range with an oven barely big enough to bake a potato, and a microwave consuming most of the Formica countertop beneath a couple of laminate cabinets. Past the kitchen, the hall led to a square living room with white walls and nubby gray wall-to-wall carpet. The window, which opened onto one of those tiny balconies, was draped with vertical blinds. The furniture consisted of a bridge table and four chairs. The walls were a faded white, devoid of any sort of artwork. To call the room barren would have been a compliment.

Aaron sat at the table, a laptop open in front of him. Ezra had been sprawled out on the floor, viewing something on a tablet, but as soon as he saw his father's visitors, he sprang to his feet and launched himself at Ruth, flinging his arms around her thighs and pressing his face into her belly as he bellowed, "Grammy!"

She returned his hug, then eased him away from her so she could remove her coat. "Hello, Ezra! How are you?"

"We had pancakes for breakfast! With lots of syrup."

"It wasn't real syrup," Aaron commented from the table, his gaze wandering from aunt to aunt to cousin to grandmother.

"Yes it was," Ezra insisted. "It came out of a bottle."

"It wasn't pure maple syrup," Noah clarified. "My mistake. Apparently Laura only buys pure maple syrup, fresh out of a tree in Vermont."

"They tap maple trees in Massachusetts too," Aaron said. "From all over New England."

"I stand corrected." Noah kissed Ruth's cheek, eyed his sisters warily, and collected their coats. "To what do I owe the honor?"

"We need to talk," Jill said, glancing at the boys and smiling. "Is there another room where the boys can play?"

"I'm not playing," Aaron said. "I'm doing homework."

"We can go into the bedroom," Jill suggested.

"I'm not going into the bedroom," Maddie said. "I don't want to see the bed where he—"

"Okay," Ruth cut her off, shooting a look at Ezra and Aaron. How much did they know? Had skinny Kim spent the night here, and joined them for breakfast? Had she complained about the syrup? If she was so skinny, maybe she hadn't eaten any of the pancakes. Maybe she'd sat at that flimsy bridge table, nibbling on a grapefruit half while Noah and his sons indulged in their fattening, artificially sweetened breakfast.

"I can take the boys into the bedroom," Rainie volunteered, wandering over to the table. "What's your homework?"

"I have to write about this poem we read in class yesterday," Aaron said, sounding as enthusiastic as a driver handing his license and registration to a state trooper with blue lights flashing atop his cruiser.

"I love analyzing poems," Rainie said, beckoning him and Ezra toward a door off the living room. "Come on, Ezra. Bring your tablet. Let's leave the grown-ups to talk boring talk."

"Your hair is blue," Ezra said. "I thought it was pink."

"It's pink *and* blue," Rainie said as she led the boys into the other room. Ruth decided Rainie was her favorite person in the apartment, although Ezra, with his enthusiastic hug, ran a close second.

As soon as Rainie shut the bedroom door, Maddie launched into a tirade. "This bullshit has to stop, Noah. You have to grow up. I know you can't, you're physically incapable of it because you've got balls, which means you're male. At least I think you have balls. He had balls when he was born, Mom, didn't he? Maybe he lost them."

"Maddie," Jill attempted to stifle her. "Let's be reasonable."

"I'm reasonably asking him to do something he's incapable of doing, which is to think of someone other than himself for once in his life."

"Like you've ever thought of anyone but yourself," Noah retorted. "*My* wedding. *My* bridal party." He mimicked her high-pitched voice. "*My* wonderful party. *My* gorgeous bridesmaids' dresses."

"Noah," Jill broke in. "Please. We need to be reasonable here."

"He doesn't know how to be reasonable," Maddie retorted. "And I don't have to be reasonable. I'm the bride."

Somewhere in the recesses of her mind, Ruth could almost hear the sound of butterfly wings flapping, stirring the air, igniting a tornado. "I think I'll join Rainie and the boys for a few minutes while you all scream at each other," she said, crossing to the bedroom door and letting herself inside.

The bedroom looked moderately more inhabited than the living room. A queen-size bed filled most of the room, the blanket and linens rumpled, two pillows propped against the wall where a headboard ought to be. Several cartons and a suitcase stood along another wall, and a cheap-looking three-drawer dresser stood against a third wall. Ezra sat atop the dresser, kicking the drawers with his swinging feet as he played a computer game on his tablet. Rainie and Aaron shared the bed, sitting cross-legged, Aaron's laptop open between them. "The problem is, it's a stupid poem," Rainie was saying, although she paused at Ruth's entrance. "Hey, Grammy. Want to talk about a stupid poem?"

"What poem?" Ruth asked, lowering herself carefully to sit at the foot of the bed, doing her best not to jostle the laptop.

"*The Road Not Taken,*" Aaron told her. "By Robert Frost."

"That's a lovely poem," Ruth said. "Why do you think it's stupid?"

"Because," Rainie explained, "it's all about this guy taking the road not taken, but once he takes it, it's *not* not taken anymore. It's a taken road." She turned back to Aaron. "We had to do *The Road Not Taken* in fifth grade. I thought it was stupid then, but I wasn't sure why at first. Then, the more I thought about it, the more I realized it didn't make sense. As soon as the guy takes the road not taken, it's taken."

"I don't think that's what the poem says," Ruth said. "He takes one road. He doesn't take the other road. He can't help wondering what his life would have been like if he'd taken the other road. But he can only take one road. That's what life is all about. You take one road, and that means you can't take all the other roads that extend in front of you."

"You still remember the poem?" Aaron asked, gazing past Rainie at Ruth, his eyes wide with respect. "Did you have to learn it in fifth grade too?"

"I don't remember what grade," Ruth said. "It's memorable, though. You'll probably remember it when you're my age."

"I can never remember poems," Aaron said. "You must be very smart."

"I'm very smart too," Rainie said, although she was grinning so Aaron wouldn't take her too seriously.

"Anyway, that's just my interpretation of the poem," Ruth added. "What do you think, Aaron? What's your interpretation?"

"I don't know. You're a teacher. Your interpretation must be right."

"There's no one right interpretation. Maybe Rainie is right. She's very smart." Ruth shot Rainie a grin, then turned back to Aaron, awaiting his response.

He stared at the laptop screen for a minute, then sighed. "Okay, so why is the wood yellow? I mean, obviously he's talking about *woods*, not wood, but he wants it to rhyme with *stood* and *could*, so he writes 'a yellow wood.' But even in the fall, woods aren't yellow. They're green and orange and brown."

"Then that's what you should write about," Ruth said. "That Robert Frost chose words based on his rhyme scheme rather than their logic."

"And then the way it ends," Aaron continued. "*That has made all the difference.* All the difference about what? About what road he walked down? Like, okay, I walked down *this* road and the difference is I didn't walk down *that* road."

"It's meta," Rainie said.

"What does that mean?" Aaron asked her.

"Self-referential."

"Self-referential. Wow, that's cool." Aaron began typing.

"Okay," Ruth said. "Rainie is obviously smarter than me. She understands meta." She pushed herself off the mattress—it was a bit too soft; she hoped Noah wouldn't wind up with back problems from sleeping on it—and crossed to the dresser. "How are you doing, Ezra?"

"I killed three zorks," he informed her.

"Good for you. We don't want zorks overrunning the place." She moved toward the door. No screaming voices from the living room penetrated its vinyl veneer, so she risked opening it and rejoining the adults, wondering if their discussion had become boring. She'd prefer boring to hostile.

Her two daughters sat at the bridge table, facing each other. Jill was whispering to Maddie, who glowered. Ever since she'd been a toddler, she'd been able to pout with exemplary style. Her current pout was a masterpiece of outrage and resentment.

Ruth glanced toward the balcony, wondering if Noah was hiding there—or if, perhaps, he'd thrown himself over the railing to escape his sisters. But the balcony was empty, and after a moment he emerged from the minuscule kitchen, carrying two mugs. "You want some coffee, Mom?" he asked. "All I've got is instant, but it tastes okay."

"No, thank you." She was impressed that he'd extended this minor hospitality toward his sisters after they'd given him a verbal thrashing.

As it turned out, only Jill was on the receiving end of his hospitality. The other mug was for himself. "Did you bring me a piece of paper?" Maddie asked him, none too graciously.

"No," Noah snapped, equally nasty.

"Here's some paper." Jill pulled a spiral-bound notepad from her purse. A pen was attached to it, wedged into an elastic loop on the binding. The pad's cover and the pen featured the same pattern: pink paisley. Ruth shouldn't have been surprised that Jill carried an elegant notepad and pen in her bag—along with hand sanitizer and who knew what else. Jill was always well prepared.

Ruth contemplated summoning Rainie to check out the paisley pattern, but decided not to interrupt the poetry scholarship taking place in the bedroom.

Maddie impatiently flipped to a blank page and started drawing something on it. "So, the wedding cake is going to be tiered—the usual, although more elliptical than round. White icing, chocolate cake with almond ganache between the layers. But here's what I'm doing..." She sketched as she spoke. "The little bride and groom figurines will stand on the top tier, and then on the second tier I'm going to have figurines for my maid of honor—Rainbow—and our best man—Warren's cousin Charles. And then, on the next tier, we're going to have figurines of the rest of the bridal party. Jill, you and Ben are going to be *here*—" she drew a couple, outlining the female's strapless gown and the male's tuxedo, slightly to the left of the cake's center "—and Noah and *Laura*—" she gave the name added emphasis "—are going to be *here*. You and Laura, Noah. Together. *Here*."

"The cake's going to be covered with action figures?" Noah asked, then guffawed.

"They aren't action figures. They're bridal-party figurines. You'll be amazed at how well they resemble the members of the bridal party. I'm having my friend Alicia make them. She makes all the crowns and implants at the office. She can match a tooth like nobody's business. She's an artist, really. Even Dr. Bromberg says so."

"You're having someone who makes false teeth make your figurines?" Jill looked nonplussed. "Figurines of me and Ben?"

"And Noah and *Laura*." Maddie stared hard at Noah. "Your *wife*. A lot of effort is going into this. I provided Alicia with photos so she could get the faces right. I'm not going to let you fuck it up."

"Your cake is not the issue," Jill broke in. "The issue is...Noah, you have a *family*. You have responsibilities. You have sons who look up to you. Are you behaving in a way that merits their respect?"

"Would they respect me if I stayed in a marriage that stagnated?"

"Why couldn't you just have your affair, end it, and work things out with Laura?" Ruth asked. If, as Jill had stated earlier, the aim of this gathering was to be reasonable, it was a reasonable question to ask. If Noah had felt compelled to have sex with his svelte young fitness center buddy, okay. He'd done that. He could cross it off his bucket list. Would continuing to have sex with her make his life so much better? Was he in love with her? If not, why continue down that road? Why not take the other road?

"What are you saying?" Jill asked. "He's had an affair. Injury has been inflicted. To heal the marriage, he needs to make reparations."

"Does Laura want reparations?" Ruth asked. "As far as I know, what she wants is a nice family ski vacation in Aspen during the boys' school break. You should go, Noah. You should ski. You should spend time with your family. A family that skis together doesn't stagnate."

"How would you know?" Maddie asked. "You don't ski."

"I can imagine," Ruth said. "I have a very good imagination." She turned to Noah, who seemed obsessed with something in his coffee mug, staring intensely into it. "Noah. Your marriage was stagnating. So you did something to add some spark to your life. Fine."

"Not fine," Jill muttered.

Ruth ignored her. "Now it's time to find other, healthier ways to add spark to your life. Not that your fitness center isn't a healthy pursuit, but you need to figure out something that won't tear your family apart. You want Laura to lose weight? Work with her on that. You want to see your sons more often than on a Saturday afternoon when Laura's getting a facial? Figure it out. Look at this place." Ruth gestured with her arms, a wide wave. "It's awful. It's an empty room with a bridge table. Is this the life you want for yourself?"

"What he wants for himself is a young, skinny girl in his bed," Maddie said.

"He wants *something*," Ruth countered. "He wants to know what's down the road not taken. So he walked a mile down that road. Here's what you saw." She waved her arms around again. "Blank walls. A bridge table that could collapse any minute. A kitchen barely big enough to heat a can of soup. It's not a good road, Noah. Go back to the other road."

Her three children gaped at her, apparently bewildered.

She ignored their stares. "Think about what you *really* want, Noah. A cute young lady in your bed? Or your family?"

"Because if you don't work this out," Maddie added, "you're going to lose your youngest sister."

"Don't tempt him," Jill muttered.

"People have affairs for a variety of reasons," Ruth said. "They're bored. They're angry. They're lonely. Someone attractive makes herself available. None of these are good reasons. And then everyone acts as if this affair, this extramarital sex, is the biggest sin in the world. If you ask me, there are far worse betrayals in a marriage. A husband who gambles away all the money behind his wife's back, and then she can't afford to retire, and she has to work two jobs to pay off his debts? Or he's an alcoholic and he drove drunk while the kids were in the car? Or he embezzled at work? There are far worse sins than that he *schtupped* some girl he met at the gym. Ask Laura to forgive you. Ask her to join you at the gym so she can work out and get in shape."

"And keep an eye on you," Maddie said.

"I mean it. If your dad ever had an affair, well, if I didn't know about it—if I *don't* know—who cares? If I found out about it, I'd ask him why he had the affair. He'd tell me his reason—we were stagnating, he was too comfortable, he thought I was fat, whatever—and we'd work it out." She surveyed the room and spotted her coat, piled on the floor in a corner with Jill's and Maddie's coats. "Come on," she said, crossing to the pile and gathering the coats. "We've said our piece. Noah, sweetheart, I love you, and I know you want to do what's right. And I also know you don't want to live in this ghastly apartment." She gave his shoulder a motherly pat, distributed the jackets, and shouted, "Rainie? We're leaving."

The bedroom door swung open. "Email me your essay when it's done," Rainie called over her shoulder.

The clomp of footsteps followed her out of the bedroom. "Are you leaving, Grammy?" Ezra said. He didn't look particularly sad, or for that matter joyful. He was probably just seeking information.

"Yes." Ruth hunkered down and gave him a hug. A part of her wished he'd never get older, never outgrow his unabashed affection for his grandmother. But if he never got older, he'd wind up being an emotional two-year-old as an adult. Not a good outcome.

"What about my cake?" Maddie demanded. "I need to know. Alicia's making the figurines."

"Tell her to make some teeth," Noah retorted.

"You know someone who makes teeth?" Ezra asked, his eyes round. Clearly this news interested him much more than the departure of his relatives.

"Maddie," Jill lectured, "your cake decorations are not the most important thing here."

"I'm paying Alicia good money."

"Tell the baker to blob on some frosting flowers," Jill said. "I'm not sure I want a figurine of *me* on your cake either."

Incensed, Maddie turned on her. "It's special! It's unique! This is my one wedding, and I want a cake that's not just like all the other cakes. Frosting flowers? You've got to be kidding!"

With Maddie's fury aimed at Jill instead of Noah, departing the crappy little apartment became easier. Ruth ushered her daughters and granddaughter into the entry hall, then paused and shouted over her shoulder, "'Bye, Aaron! I'd like to see your essay, too, if you don't mind emailing it to me."

His voice floated through the open bedroom door: "Bye, Grammy. Thanks for explaining the poem to me."

"I like my explanation better," Rainie muttered. Ruth only smiled.

Other than Maddie's complaints about having to march down two flights of stairs, none of them spoke until they were settled in Jill's SUV. Jill ignited the engine, then twisted in her seatbelt to face Ruth, who was once again seated shotgun. "Really? You wouldn't mind if Dad had an affair?"

"If I didn't know about it, how could I mind?"

"If you *did* know about it?"

"She'd go ballistic," Maddie shouted from the back seat. "You're so full of shit, Mom."

"I wouldn't go ballistic," Ruth insisted. "I'd deal with it sensibly."

"That's you," Maddie said sarcastically. "Always so sensible."

"It *is* her," Rainie argued. "That's why I love you, Grammy. I can always count on you to be sensible."

"You love her because she's a good cook."

"That too." Rainie sent Ruth a beseeching look. It didn't convey pleasure at Ruth's cooking, or even respect for her sensibility. Instead it seemed to implore her: *Let me live with you when my mother marries Warren.*

Ruth might have pointed out that Warren seemed eminently sensible too. In fact, she wondered how Maddie could possibly love someone as sensible as he was, given her general antipathy toward her sensible mother.

Maybe Maddie didn't love Warren. Maybe she was marrying him because he indulged her, because he didn't ridicule her when she decided to personalize their wedding cake with little dolls that resembled the members of their bridal party. Maybe she was marrying him because he brought in a steady paycheck and he had a comfortable, if not especially gorgeous, house, and a calming manner. Maybe it was about the food; Warren's mother made woven crusts for her fruit pies, after all.

Maddie wanted to marry him, and she would marry him. Her reasons were not Ruth's business, any more than Barry's extramarital affairs, if any such affairs existed, would be her business. She doubted that he screwed around—how many women would be willing to be on top all the time, and listen to him moaning about his arthritic knees? He was a good man, a good husband, and Ruth loved him. But Casanova he wasn't.

What she didn't know wouldn't hurt her, however—just as what he didn't know wouldn't hurt him.

For better or worse, there wasn't much for him to not know. She hadn't slept with Cord from Santa Fe when she'd had the chance. She hadn't slept with anyone other than Barry once they'd met.

And she never told him that his complaints about his aching knees turned her off. She never would. He didn't have to know.

Chapter Twelve

Once the velvet voice inside Jill's GPS guided them back to Route 30 and familiar territory, Jill launched into a lecture on her credentials as a psychotherapist. Reparations had to be made, she insisted. Forgiveness had to be earned. Noah needed to recognize not just the folly of his ways but the emotional violence he'd inflicted on his family. If anyone could parse his situation accurately, it was Jill. She, after all, had the training, the expertise, the framed diploma on her office wall.

On a few occasions when she paused for a breath, Maddie shouted from the back seat that Noah was a dick. "I'm getting married only once in my life. Is it too much to ask my brother to keep his fly zipped until the wedding?"

"The wedding is in April," Rainie reminded her. "That's a long time for a guy to keep his fly zipped."

"What do you know about guys and their flies?" Maddie asked her.

"Mom. I'm in high school."

And she's very smart, Ruth thought, hoping that Rainie's knowledge of men's flies was theoretical for the time being. She never mentioned any particular boys to Ruth, other than as classmates or pals or obnoxious creeps who considered the sound of their belches amusing and referred to people with ugly gay epithets when no teachers were within earshot. That said, Rainie hadn't been immune to Danny Fortuna's sexual magnetism when she'd seen his photo in Ruth's yearbook. She might not have a personal familiarity with any guy's fly, but she knew what lurked on the other side of the zipper.

"My point is," Jill continued, her pompous tone temporarily silencing her back-seat passengers, "I'm a professional. Mom,

I know you meant well, but saying all Laura wants is a ski vacation... I mean, really."

"It's what she wants," Ruth said calmly. "She told me so herself."

"She was manifesting displacement," Jill said. "She thinks she wants a ski trip because she can't allow herself to acknowledge the pain Noah has caused her."

"I met her for lunch a few days ago. She didn't seem to be in that much pain then," Ruth said, recalling Laura's lusty enjoyment of her onion soup and turkey-bacon-avocado wrap.

"We call that masking. Out of pride, out of denial, out of fear, she masked her true emotions."

"Stop with the shrink jargon," Maddie boomed from the back seat. "You think you know everything."

"I think I know more about psychology than you do," Jill shot back. "And you know more about gingivitis than I do."

Ruth sighed. Maybe Rainie was lucky to be an only child. She had no older sister to condescend to her, and no younger sister to condescend to.

Ruth didn't regret having a brother. She and David had never fought much, mostly because they'd forged a mutually protective alliance against their mother, especially when she was in her cups. "She's on a tear," David would whisper to Ruth after their mother had refilled her martini glass and started raging about the length of Ruth's skirt or the length of David's hair.

"Let's just ignore her," Ruth would whisper back.

Their lives had diverged in adulthood, mostly due to distance. David and his family lived near San Jose, where he was a reasonably paid cog in a high-tech firm, his wife Sandy managed a bank branch, their offspring were all graduates of California's excellent state university system, and the modest split-level David had bought twenty-five years ago was now worth more than the gross national product of several third-world nations. Ruth and David—or, more often, David's wife, Sandy, emailed one another at least once a month, sending JPEGs of grandchildren and other items of interest: Barry's Audi when it had been new, for instance, or the magnificent Bundt cake Sandy had baked for David's boss's retirement party, devil's-food chocolate with glossy white icing drizzled over the top.

Although Ruth thought she'd raised her own offspring well, they still bickered like brats. She wondered whether her nieces and nephews—David and Sandy had produced two of each—quarreled the way Noah, Jill, and Maddie did. Just as she imagined David's California community sometimes as temperate and forward-thinking and sometimes as under threat from earthquakes and wildfires, she imagined David's kids as sometimes mellow and empathetic and sometimes as combative as her own children.

"I didn't say what I said at Noah's because I meant well," she defended herself now. "I said it because it's the truth."

"The truth as you understand it."

"She was cutting to the chase," Maddie said, a rare instance of her actually taking Ruth's side. "Noah needs to get back together with Laura. Screw all the bullshit about reparations and healing. Let them get back together. If they want to get a divorce after my wedding, fine with me."

"Of course," Jill said, her voice brittle. "As long as your little figurines line up nicely on the cake—"

"Almond ganache sounds delicious," Ruth interjected. "I'm looking forward to a piece of that cake."

Her daughters' voices were still echoing inside her skull when Jill pulled into the driveway of Ruth's house and let out her passengers. "I'm having dinner with Warren and his parents tonight," Maddie announced once Jill had driven away. "Rainbow, Warren's parents invited you to join us."

"I'll pass, thanks."

"It wasn't a question," Maddie warned.

"His parents will freak out when they see my hair. They already freaked out when it was pink."

"Your hair looks ridiculous. They're entitled to freak out."

"Ezra liked it." Rainie stormed ahead of her mother to the front door and into the house, shouting, "Hey, Grampa, we're home. What's for dinner?"

"I'm trying to get her used to eating her meals with Warren and me," Maddie told Ruth.

"Then maybe you ought to keep his parents out of it."

"They invited us."

"People are allowed to turn down invitations," Ruth said. "As long as they turn them down politely. Rainie did say thanks."

"I want her to come. She needs to get used to her new family."

"That's between you and her," Ruth said, letting Maddie precede her into the house. She was being sensible again, she knew. Sensible was something she excelled at. Sensible was often the antithesis of chaos, the best defense against it.

She thought about the poem Aaron was studying, the two roads. Had she always taken the sensible road? Had she always *not* taken the crazy road, the reckless road, the road with all the potholes and dead branches and black ice? The risky, exciting road?

She'd joined a rock band in high school and played in it for several years, until she'd left for Wellesley. Playing in a high school rock band was risky, not sensible. However, she'd been the most sensible member of Trouble Ahead. At the time, she'd assumed that this was because she was the only girl, and girls tended to be more sensible than boys (although Maddie had defied that generalization on more than one occasion). But maybe it was just because she was inherently, congenitally sensible. Maybe it was because whenever she had to make a choice, whenever she reached a fork in the road, she instinctively opted for the sensible path.

Maybe it was because when her mother drank she became argumentative and irrational, criticizing, whining, making grand statements about the tragedies that befell women. Maybe it was because when Ruth was growing up, she had sometimes felt her mother had the emotional maturity of a two-year-old, even if she wasn't a guy, and someone had to be the adult. If her father and David weren't around—and David became highly skilled at not being around throughout most of their adolescence—Ruth had to be the adult. She had to hold the chaos at bay.

Or maybe she was sensible because she was...afraid. Afraid of that chaos lurking just beyond the edge of her existence. Afraid to take risks. Afraid to strap on a pair of skis and fly down a mountain.

Chapter Thirteen

"You can be in charge of the money, Ruthie," Mike had decreed as soon as they'd earned some, a suggestion quickly seconded by the other guys in the band. At the time, their earnings amounted to the one hundred and fifty dollars they'd won in the Battle of the Bands.

After leaving the auditorium with their check, they drove to a nearby pancake house for a celebratory snack. The boys all ordered heaping stacks of pancakes, which Ruth found weird, since it was eleven-thirty at night and pancakes were a breakfast food. But then, pancakes served at eleven-thirty at night weren't the same as pancakes served at breakfast time. These pancakes came adorned with chocolate chips, multi-colored sprinkles, slivered almonds, and mountains of whipped cream. Still, they were pancakes, and she couldn't imagine eating pancakes at that hour. It didn't seem reasonable. Instead, tuning out the voice of her mother nagging her not to gain weight, she'd ordered a slice of cheesecake.

"We should pay for this out of our earnings," Nick suggested. "It's the band's money, right?"

"Maybe we should save that money to cover expenses," Ruth said.

All the boys stared at her. They were crammed into a booth designed for four. Ruth sat wedged between Danny and Jimmy on one banquette. Seated beside Mike across the table, Nick took up more than half of the banquette; he wasn't fat, but he was big. No way could three people fit on the banquette if Nick was one of them.

She pretended sitting so close to Danny, her thigh pressed against his, had no effect on her. He smelled of boy deodorant and sweat, and his shoulder bumped hers every time he shifted in his seat. She leaned slightly into Jimmy. He was cute, he was garrulous, and he was definitely safer to bump shoulders with than Danny.

"We've talked about buying another microphone and stand," she said. "Danny has his mic, and I've got that little mic by the keyboard. But when you guys are singing backup and you're all crowded around Danny's mic, your guitars start bumping into each other. We need another mic."

"She's right," Jimmy said.

"And then, down the road, there will be other expenses. If we want to keep doing this," she added.

"Of course we want to keep doing this," Danny said, sending her a dazzling smile. "We're winners! We're famous!"

The food arrived, and as they ate, the guys discussed what they could spend their money on while Ruth discussed ways they could earn more money. "Now that we've won this Battle of the Bands, we need to find some more competitions with prize money."

"Or gigs," Jimmy said. A dollop of whipped cream frosted his brave little mustache.

"What gigs?" Nick asked.

"I don't know. High school dances. Church youth group dances. Stuff like that. *Paying* gigs."

"How do we get those gigs?" Nick asked.

Jimmy volunteered to ask around and see what jobs might be available.

"You'll figure it out," Mike said. "You can handle our bookings and Ruthie can handle our money." She loved that they called her "Ruthie." No one else did, but the band—her colleagues, her fellow musicians—had chosen to give her this nickname. It made her feel special.

"Sounds good to me," Danny said. That he would trust her with the band's finances pleased her far more than it ought to.

"Yeah," Jimmy agreed, jamming his knee into her thigh when he twisted to face her. "I'll be the booker, and you can be the bookkeeper."

"I'm okay with you handling the money," Nick told her, making the decision unanimous. "You're better than me at math."

"She's better than you at everything," Jimmy teased him.

"Everything in school," Nick agreed. "I'm better than her at some things."

"Playing the drums," Mike said. "You're better than her at that."

"But she's gotta take care of the money and make sure we don't go broke."

"All right," she said, accepting her new responsibility graciously. "If we have gigs, we'll definitely need a new mic," she said. "And maybe gas money. Maybe a van so Nick can bring his own drum kit, instead of borrowing whatever is on the stage at a Battle of the Bands."

"Yeah. That drum kit stank. The hi-hat was, like, dead. No resonance at all."

"We brought our own instruments. Nick should bring his own instrument, too," she continued. Jimmy's older brother and Mike's father had driven them to the high school, and even with two cars, their guitars and amps and the keyboard had to be maneuvered and rearranged and wedged together to fit into the trunks. If the band was going to get gigs, they were going to need transportation to get to and from the gigs. And gas money.

As the oldest, Nick would be the first to receive his driver's license, although by the end of the summer, Jimmy and Danny would also be legal to drive. "I know I'll pass my road test," Danny said. "I drive my dad's car all the time."

"Where do you drive it?" Ruth asked.

Danny smiled. "Hey, it's illegal. Don't ask questions."

Ruth was glad he hadn't driven it illegally to the Battle of the Bands that night. What if, instead of standing on that stage and singing "Tom" with all the soul a white boy could muster, he'd wound up running a red light, getting stopped, and spending the night in a holding cell?

"If we're doing gigs," Danny continued, "we need to write more original songs."

"We can do that," Jimmy said, then twisted toward Ruth again. Her thigh was going to have black-and-blue marks on it from his knee. "Write us another song like 'Tom,' and we'll be famous."

"I don't know..." She smiled demurely. For one thing, she didn't want to seem as if she were taking over the band. It was one thing to be Trouble Ahead's bookkeeper—a stereotypical girl's job—and another to be its songwriter. Obviously, Jimmy and Danny would continue writing their songs about getting wasted and getting laid. But if she contributed to their repertory—well, she just didn't want them to think she was the most important person in the band. Because she wasn't. Any one of them had a greater claim to that role, Jimmy because of his nerve, Nick because of his drums, Mike because of his vulnerability, Danny because of his voice. And his face. And his all-around charisma.

She was just the keyboard player.

And now the bookkeeper. The organized, logical, good-at-math one.

And the one who'd written 'Tom,' she reminded herself. She was more than just the girl who played the keyboard and sang occasional backup. She'd written some okay songs and one really good song.

She'd have to write another really good song. And she'd have to be modest about it, because boys could feel threatened by a girl who did too many things well.

~

Ruth set up a bank account for the band's earnings. She was surprised to learn that none of the guys had their own bank accounts, and she offered to help them open bank accounts, too, although no one accepted her invitation. She had only a few hundred dollars in her own personal savings account, which her father had started for her with the money he and her mother had received as gifts from relatives in honor of Ruth's birth. She'd augmented the account with birthday money from her grandparents, and some of her babysitting earnings. And soon she started adding her share of the paydays from Trouble Ahead's gigs.

Perhaps she shouldn't have been surprised that Jimmy could line up jobs for the band. He had chutzpah. He'd marched right up to her one day at school, while she'd been standing by her locker, and invited her to join the band, despite the fact that they'd never spoken before and she would have bet he didn't even know who she was. With the same bravado, he called all those places he'd mentioned at the pancake house the night they'd won the Battle of the Bands—schools, YMCA's, church and synagogue youth groups. To her amazement, some of those places said, "Sure, we could use a band at our next teen night. If you won a Battle of the Bands, you must be pretty good."

After every gig, Ruth would take the check they'd earned, deposit it in the band's bank account, and pay each of the band members ten dollars from the account. They were actual professionals now.

The first purchase the band made as a group was a new microphone and stand. The second was a cassette tape recorder so they could tape their practices, listen to them, and critique their performances. Their third purchase was a bottle of Mateus rosé, purchased for them by Jimmy's older brother, so they could drink a toast to themselves after the band had passed five hundred dollars in earnings.

When the school term ended and summer vacation began, Jimmy found more varied gigs for them. They played in dingy little clubs with stages so small Nick's drum kit barely fit on them, leaving no room for Ruth's keyboard, so she'd wind up off to the side, in the shadows. They played in municipal parks; one local town featured a band in its park every Monday evening if it wasn't raining, and Trouble Ahead played there several times, serenading families on blankets eating cold fried chicken or crackers and brie while their children jumped up and down and waved bubble wands around. They played at a restaurant in Worcester that decided, after their first gig there, to book them for every Wednesday from nine to eleven, where they sang their hearts out for people busy slurping clam chowder, clinking their silverware against their plates, and yammering throughout the band's sets. They played at county fairs that featured almost-famous bands in the evening but needed no-name bands during the day to entertain passersby as they ate corn dogs and fried dough on their way from the Ferris wheel to the building where blue-ribbon quilts and first-prize zucchinis were on display.

None of the gigs paid much, but the money added up. Some weeks, they couldn't squeeze a rehearsal in on a Saturday morning, so they'd rehearse Sunday afternoon, or Thursday night. They'd learn a new song, tape it on their cassette recorder, and argue about whether Jimmy should get a guitar solo or Ruth should get a keyboard solo, whether Danny should hit a note squarely with his voice or slide into it, whether Nick's hi-hat was resonating enough.

Jimmy and Danny continued to write songs for the group. Mike composed a song about getting stoned which was mediocre, but it had a terrific bass-guitar underpinning, so they added it to their repertoire. Ruth wrote a few songs about adolescent love—also mediocre, but the band needed material. "What we really need," Danny told her after she'd played them a song she'd written about a jilted lover staring at a telephone that never rang—something he apparently couldn't relate to—"is another song like 'Tom.'"

Fortunately, none of the band members had experienced the death of a loved one since Mike's brother was killed in Vietnam. After the rehearsal where Danny had made that suggestion, Jimmy drove her home in the car he now shared with his brother, and she managed to avoid her mother, tiptoeing up the stairs to her bedroom. Eluding her mother was a lot easier with David home from college for the summer and consuming some of her attention. That night, as Ruth sneaked past the living room, she glimpsed David and her mother sitting on the couch. David appeared stoical, his face expressionless as their mother lectured him about a girl he was seeing that summer. Their mother clutched a glass of something clear, with ice cubes and two green olives in it. While

Ruth felt bad for her brother, she was relieved that, for a change, he was the target of her vodka-fueled criticism.

Once inside her bedroom, Ruth shut the door, muffling her mother's and David's argument. Their mother needed her own life. She spent too much energy focusing on David's and Ruth's lives. Maybe if she had a job, like their father, that would preoccupy her. Her offspring would no longer be her sole purpose in life, her only agenda.

But she didn't work. If she wasn't playing mah-jongg with her friends, she lolled around the house, watching game shows on TV and nursing her martinis until David or Ruth entered her field of vision, at which point she'd entertain herself by harassing them.

Ruth did her best to tune out her mother's voice. She sat on the carpeted floor of her bedroom, her back resting against her bed and a notepad balanced on her knees. She needed to come through with a good song for the band. A song as good as "Tom." A song born in some deep, emotional place the way "Tom" had been.

LuAnne Bricotti. Ruth knew LuAnne from glee club; during the school year, she'd stood next to Ruth in the alto section and held Ruth's scores when Ruth had to go to the front of the room to play the piano. They weren't close friends, but they got along well, and LuAnne had a dark, sassy voice with a bit of an edge to it, a voice Ruth envied. Last March, LuAnne announced that she was going to be staying in California with her aunt for a while, and she vanished from the school. It didn't take long for word to get around that LuAnne's aunt in California was actually a home for unwed mothers, where LuAnne would ride out the last few months of a pregnancy. According to the gossip hovering like a dense fog in the air of the history hall girls' bathroom, LuAnne had been dating a senior, a football player who'd been recruited to play at Rutgers next year. Marriage was out of the question. Abortions were illegal, although according to Debbie, you could get an abortion in Aruba or Jamaica or some other Caribbean island nation. LuAnne was Catholic, though, so flying to a tropical resort for an abortion probably would not have occurred to her.

Danny wouldn't want to sing a song from the point of view of a girl in a home for unwed mothers. But what about the football player? How did he feel about all this?

He struts around like the king of the world, Ruth scribbled into her notebook. *She goes into hiding 'cause she's just a girl. While she goes through hell, he doesn't think twice. She's the one who has to pay the price.*

Danny definitely wouldn't want to sing this. For all Ruth knew, he might have knocked up a girl himself. They all might have—Nick, Jimmy, Mike, and Danny. They were guys. They wrote songs about getting laid. They never wrote songs about what happened the day after they'd gotten laid, the week after, nine months after.

Danny...especially Danny. He attracted so much attention from girls during their gigs. Goofy junior-high-aged groupies liked to hang around the band when they played, giggling and asking for their autographs as if Trouble Ahead was famous. The giggling girls generally ignored Ruth, which was fine with her. They flirted with all the guys, but mostly with Danny, who welcomed their fawning with his dimpled smile, an occasional hand on a girl's shoulder, an occasional kiss on a girl's cheek, a lingering gaze with those bedroom eyes of his.

He *should* sing this song, Ruth thought. All the guys should sing this song. Maybe they'd learn something. Maybe they'd stop obsessing about getting laid.

In the hallway of his school, the girls flirt and the boys rule. His smile is so sexy, his body's so nice, and she's the one who pays the price. If he's the king, that baby is his prince, but he hasn't talked to his girlfriend since. He's moved on, stepped into tomorrow, leaving her with nothing but sorrow. Now they call her a slut and a whore, while he's the one they all adore. Because he's the king of the world, and she's just a girl.

She played with the words a bit, crossed a few out, added a few others, crossed them out and added more. She had an idea for a melody in her head, but she would have to wait until David and her mother cleared out of the living room and she could access the piano.

According to the alarm clock on her nightstand, it was nearly five o'clock. Her father would be home soon, and her mother would go into the kitchen to throw something together for dinner—in the summer, supper was often cold-cut sandwiches or tuna salad, because it was too hot for a real meal. Ruth suspected her mother didn't give a damn about the heat but simply didn't want to cook. They ate a lot of hamburgers and spaghetti in the winter because those meals didn't take much effort to make either.

She heard the rattle of the garage door opening beneath her bedroom and knew her father had arrived. Grabbing her staff-paper pad along with her notebook, she cracked open her bedroom door and peeked into the hall. David was climbing the stairs, shaking his head. "She's in a mood," he warned Ruth.

"Tune her out," Ruth whispered back, almost adding, *Lucky you, you get to go back to college in another month. I'm still stuck here.* But she doubted David felt lucky right now.

She heard her parents in the kitchen, discussing the bills that had arrived in the mail. Her father earned a decent salary; money was never an issue, as far as Ruth knew. He liked to tease her mother about how many phone calls she made, though, all of them listed on the phone bill, and that evening she wasn't in the mood to be teased. "I think David is sleeping with that girl," she told Ruth's father, evidently unaware that Ruth had emerged from her bedroom and descended the stairs to the living room, within eavesdropping distance.

Why shouldn't David be sleeping with that girl? He was a guy, just like the guys in the band. Sleeping with girls was what guys did. Paying the price was what girls did.

Ruth pressed on the soft pedal to mute the piano's volume—she still depended on those pedals, although in ways that differed from her childhood, when she'd been afraid the keys might bite her—and noodled the melody that had gone through her head while she'd been penning the lyrics. "Is that the Bach invention you're supposed to be practicing?" her mother hollered from the kitchen.

"I'll practice that in a minute," Ruth hollered back.

"Mrs. Demming is going to be here tomorrow. We're paying her good money. You should practice what she's teaching you."

Ruth made a face, safe in the knowledge that her mother was unable to see her from the kitchen. She could play the first three-part invention well enough, and she'd be happy if her parents stopped paying Mrs. Demming good money and let Ruth quit her lessons. She liked Bach, she liked the inventions, but she was never going to play in Symphony Hall. Surely she'd learned enough classical music to last her a lifetime.

Afraid her mother might abandon her exertions opening cans of tuna in the kitchen to spy on Ruth's practice, she jotted notes hastily onto the staff paper, scribbled chords below them, mouthed the words to make sure she had the rhythms correct. This couldn't possibly be how Lennon and McCartney wrote their songs, or Bob Dylan, or Joni Mitchell.

"I'm not hearing you practice," her mother shouted through the kitchen door.

Sighing, Ruth lifted her foot from the soft pedal and plodded through the Bach invention Mrs. Demming had assigned to her. She played it adequately, with absolutely no inspiration, no dynamics, no emotion. A player piano could have put more feeling into it. But she had to satisfy her mother, and she expected this mechanical rendering of a Bach masterpiece would do that. As soon as she reached the final measure, she pressed the soft pedal again and resumed working on her song, trying different chords, different progressions. Jimmy and Danny would need to know the chords so they could work their guitar parts into it. Mike would need to know the progressions so he could add a bass line.

Nick could just bang his drums. He always seemed to know where the downbeats were, where syncopation was called for, when to add a little cymbal or cowbell.

Two days later, with the band gathered in Nick's basement, Ruth played the song for them. She sang it with as much emotion as she could muster, wishing her voice was a little grittier, like LuAnne's. As she sang, Nick sat on his stool, smoking a cigarette. Mike played his left hand over the strings of his bass without plucking the strings themselves, apparently hearing the notes in his head. Jimmy and Danny just stared at her while she played. Even after nearly a full year of playing with the band, she still felt uncomfortable being watched while she performed. When they were doing a gig, she sang backup and no one paid her much attention. When they were in one of those seedy dives with a stage the size of a spearmint Chiclet, she could hide off to one side, in the shadows. Besides, everyone in the audience was busy admiring Danny. They probably didn't even notice her.

But now she wasn't playing for an audience. She was playing for the band. *Her* band, even if she still felt a little like an outsider. They let her handle the money; they must believe she was one of them, even if she was a girl and she played Bach inventions for Mrs. Demming, and she was only a substitute for a keyboard player who was dead.

Reaching the end of the song, she was met by a long, awkward silence. Then Jimmy said, "What the fuck?"

"It's a song," Danny snapped.

"I can't sing that song. Can you sing that song?"

"What, she gets knocked up?" Nick asked, snubbing out his cigarette.

"Like LuAnne Bricotti," Mike guessed. Apparently, the gossip must have made its way from the history hall girls' bathroom to the history hall boys' bathroom.

"Actually, yes," Ruth said. "I was thinking of her when I wrote this."

"She's gonna be back in school in September," Jimmy predicted.

"And Steve McDonough is going to be at Rutgers, thinking he's the king of the world," Danny said. "I think that's the point."

"I'm not saying it's a bad song," Jimmy said. "I mean, yeah. Okay. So the girl got knocked up. I can't sing that. Danny, you can't sing that. A guy can't sing that. I mean, come on."

"Ruthie can sing it," Danny said.

"She's not our singer."

"She can sing. It's just one song. We need more original stuff." Danny turned his glowing hazel eyes to Ruth. "You can sing it, right?"

She just *had* sung it. They'd all heard her sing it. Did she really need to answer that question? "I can sing it," she said softly, already getting nervous about the possibility that at some gig in the near future, a spotlight might abandon the Chiclet-size stage and locate her off to one side while she belted out this song.

"It's girlie," Nick said.

"Yeah, well, she's a girl," Danny retorted.

"But *we're* not girls. That's a girlie song."

"I'm thinking someone like Dionne Warwick could sing it," Mike said. "Or Dusty Springfield. Or—who's that 'Downtown' lady? Petunia Clark?"

"Petula," Ruth quietly corrected him.

"Marianne Faithfull," Jimmy suggested.

"She sang 'Downtown'?"

"No, but she's really hot."

"Oh, come on." Danny shook his head. "Ruthie is a girl. She could sing this song. You want to sing this song?" he asked her.

She wasn't used to being defended by anyone other than, on occasion, her brother. Or her father, when her mother was freaking out. Certainly not Danny. She could, and did, defend herself when she had to—in class, when a teacher questioned something she said. Or when a bitchy girl criticized her hair or her outfit—not that that happened all that frequently, but Ruth was seriously fashion-challenged, and her wardrobe was always about a year out of date. And there wasn't much you could do with plain brown hair except let it grow long and part it in the middle.

But this was the band. She still felt like a guest. And, face it, she *was* a girl in a band full of boys. They'd invited her in; they could just as easily invite her out. "If you don't like the song," she said, "we won't do it."

Another long, awkward silence. "Okay," Jimmy said. "Why don't we work on 'Stoned and Zoned.'" Which was a song he'd written, about getting wasted.

An hour later, when they were done practicing, Danny caught up with Ruth outside Nick's house as she was climbing onto her bicycle. "I'll drive you home," he said.

She gestured toward her bicycle. "I've got this."

"I've got a van. We can throw that in the back."

She couldn't pass up the opportunity to cruise through town seated next to Danny Fortuna, especially because she was feeling kind of melancholy. She'd thought her song was good. The band had thought it was good, too—or at least they'd pretended to think it was good. But they'd rejected it, and their rejection had reminded her that she wasn't one of them. As long as she had to sit down to pee, she would never be one of them. She understood that. She was a girl. Her song was a girlie song. They'd embraced "Tom" because it was about soldiers, about men, about war and death. It wasn't girlie. But if she wrote something from her own heart, on a subject that mattered to girls... Too girlie.

She pulled her notebook from the handlebar basket and Danny wheeled her bike down the crumbling driveway to a battered VW van parked where the curb would be if the street had curbs. He opened the back of the van, hoisted her bike and his guitar inside, and slammed it shut. The roof of the van was classic VW beige, the bottom a muted turquoise dulled by road dirt and rust. "When did you get a van?" Ruth asked.

"This guy who lives down the street from me sold it to me for two hundred and fifty bucks. He needed cash fast. I didn't ask him why." Danny shrugged and banged his fist against the door handle on the passenger side. "This door sometimes sticks." He had mastered the technique; the door swung open, its hinge whining.

Ruth climbed into the passenger seat. The vinyl upholstery was patched with thick gray tape, and the cab held the lingering scent of smoke—cigarette or marijuana, probably both. She might as well be back in Nick's basement, except that at least here she could sit. At band practice, she was always standing so she wouldn't be mistaken for Neil Sedaka or Liberace.

Danny circled the van and got in behind the wheel, giving his keys an important-sounding jingle. "So, I guess you got your license," she said.

He shot her a wicked grin. "Don't ask a question if you aren't going to like the answer."

All right, then. He didn't have his license. She was going to ride in a vehicle driven by someone who didn't have a license. If she was as sensible as everyone in the band seemed to think she was, she would have shoved that squeaky door open and jumped out.

But this was Danny Fortuna. She was seated next to Danny Fortuna in his van, just the two of them. She could smell his now-familiar scent mixing with the residual fragrance of smoke. She could feel the air growing warmer—already warm from the van's having sat for a couple of hours in the summer heat but now even warmer because Danny's body exuded its own heat. She cranked down her window and he cranked down his. He inserted the ignition key but didn't turn on the car.

"What's wrong with you?" he asked.

He didn't sound angry or exasperated. More concerned, like he expected her to tell him she had her period. She did, but she didn't consider that *wrong*. "What do you mean?"

"You wrote that song. It's a good song. We all thought it was a good song. But you didn't fight for it."

She couldn't look at him when he was accusing her of exactly what she was, which was spineless and passive and, she'd admit it, afraid. Afraid to rock the boat. Afraid to antagonize the guys. Afraid to make them confront the fact that she was a girl and they didn't want anything about Trouble Ahead to be feminine.

Instead, she gazed at her hands, folded neatly on top of her notebook in her lap. Despite the steamy August air filling the van, her fingers were icy. If asked to play the keyboard now, she wouldn't be able to. Her fingertips would be too numb. "It's not that good a song," she mumbled.

"Are you kidding? It's as good as 'Tom.' Maybe better."

"No it's not." As cold as her hands were, she felt heat crawling up her back, causing her neck to sweat. The hair at her nape would be wet soon, and it would start to frizz. "It's just a song."

"It's a good song. You should sing it."

"Okay—but not with the band."

"Why not with the band?"

"They didn't like it. I don't want them to kick me out." She shouldn't have said that last part, letting Danny see how insecure she was.

"They won't kick you out. They can't. You control the money." He laughed, and she forced a choked laugh out as well. "You should fight for that song. It's good. They just rejected it because it made them uncomfortable. I mean, yeah. That's what happens. The girl is called a slut and a whore, and the guy gets to go to college and play football. That song told the truth. You should fight for it."

"I hate arguing with people," Ruth said, realizing for the first time how true that was. "I argue with my mother all the time. I don't want to argue with you guys."

"We're not your mother," he said, at last starting the engine. "What's wrong with her? Why do you argue with her?"

"Because she's my mother," Ruth said, and laughed again, a little less nervously. "You know how mothers are."

"Not really." He pulled away from the curb. "My mom died when I was nine. My dad's girlfriends—he's burned through a bunch of them—I don't bother to fight with them. They come and they go."

"I'm so sorry." She hadn't known this about Danny. Maybe she could write a song like "Tom" about a young man who didn't have a mother.

He shrugged as if losing his mother was no big deal. Maybe to him it wasn't. At the very least, he was spared the ordeal of having a mother to argue with. "I don't really remember my mom," he said, driving very carefully, Ruth noted. "She had a heart condition. She was sick for like five years and then she died. She was in the hospital a lot, and sleeping a lot. My aunt used to come and take care of me, but she wasn't my mother, so we didn't fight." He shot Ruth another quicksilver smile. "My dad and I get along okay. He goes his way, I go mine."

"My dad and I get along okay too," Ruth said, surprised that it was easy to talk to Danny, despite the fact that he was intimidatingly handsome. "But my mom..." She sighed. "She does nothing. She's bored, I think. She drinks martinis and watches TV and meddles in my life and my brother's life. She's always criticizing me. She thinks I shouldn't be in a band. She only wants me to play classical music and get good grades, and lose five pounds."

Danny glanced at Ruth. Maybe she was just imagining it, but he seemed to zero in on her thighs, which looked thicker than usual because they were pressed against the scorching vinyl of the seat. "You don't need to lose five pounds," he said. "You could probably use a few extra pounds on top."

Then he wasn't just looking at her thighs. Maybe she should have been embarrassed or outraged that he was commenting on her rather puny bosom, but she wasn't. She felt oddly comfortable sitting beside Danny, letting him drive her home. If her mother glimpsed the van through the window as he dropped Ruth off at her house, there would be another argument, but she didn't care.

"My mother's overweight, and she thinks it's the worst thing in the world," Ruth said. "Maybe she'd lose weight if she stopped drinking martinis. There's a lot of calories in liquor."

"So she's a drunk?" Danny asked.

"No. She just likes her cocktails." Ruth sighed. "It's messy when we fight. I like things peaceful and orderly. There's nothing wrong with that, is there?"

"I wouldn't know." He shrugged again. "My house isn't peaceful and orderly. When things get too messy, my dad or I will get a trash bag and throw stuff out, or grab a broom and sweep. Sometimes one of his girlfriends will do that. What's your address?"

Ruth recited it, thinking, *now he knows where I live. Now he's a part of my life.* Having Danny Fortuna as a friend seemed a greater gift than even having him as a boyfriend. Boyfriends came and went. They got to be kings of the world, and then they departed for Rutgers to play football. Friends lasted, at least sometimes.

"I tell you what," Danny said as he turned onto her street. "We're going to do that song. I'll sing it with you. Then it won't sound so girlie."

"Really? You'd do that?"

"It's a good song." He braked to a stop in front of her house. "Don't let the guys shut you up. They aren't going to kick you out of the band if you argue with them."

"You're sure?"

"I've got your back."

She pulled the lever on the passenger door and had to ram it a couple of times with her shoulder until it opened. Climbing down, she turned and smiled at Danny. "Thanks," she said. "You drive very well for someone who doesn't have a license."

"You haven't seen me on the turnpike," he joked.

She shoved the door shut and watched him drive away. Only after he'd turned the corner did she remember that her bicycle was still in the back of the van.

That wasn't such a bad thing. Now he'd have to come back to her house again, to drop the bike off, maybe to drive her to the band's next gig or practice. He'd come back.

He had her back.

Trying not to grin like a lovesick idiot, she waltzed up the front walk to the house and let herself inside. Her mother was standing by the living room window, a glass in one hand and a scowl on her face. "Who was that?" she asked.

A band mate. A B-track kid. Someone who has my back.

"A friend," she said, and headed up the stairs, her mother's questions trailing behind her. She wasn't going to fight with her mother. It was true—she hated fighting. But if she had to fight, she'd save her energy to fight for her song.

Chapter Fourteen

If Only I'd Become a Concert Pianist...

Ruth was exhausted. Maddie had worn her out last night, spreading a seating diagram across the dining room table and penciling, and then erasing, the names of her wedding guests. Not that she'd sent out invitations yet, let alone received RSVP's, but she seemed to assume that anyone she invited to what she viewed as the greatest social event of all time would gladly rearrange their lives so they could attend.

Ruth thought Maddie could organize the seating chart herself, but no. She wanted her mother's insights and input. "I hate round tables," she lamented, staring at the circles penciled onto the broad sheet of paper. "I wish we could have long, rectangular tables, like they have in castles and manor houses. Remember that show set in the Regency era? They always ate at long, rectangular tables."

"Round tables are easier for conversing," Ruth pointed out. "At the long tables, you can really only talk to the people sitting on either side of you or directly across from you."

Maddie considered this and frowned. "But the long tables are classier. And then you have servants serving from the left and clearing from the right, and walking around the table with a gravy boat."

"I thought you were going to have a buffet," Ruth said.

"Servers are classier."

"If you're going with servers, you'll have to ask everyone on their RSVP cards whether they want beef, fish, or vegan," Ruth pointed out. "With a buffet, everyone can help themselves to what they want."

Maddie frowned again. "I guess," she said doubtfully. "But then people will be standing in line, waiting to fill their plates, instead of sitting at the table. It'll be like a cafeteria. Like in a hospital or a high school."

True enough. "What does Warren think?" Ruth asked. "Buffet or sit-down dinner?"

"He says I should do whatever I want." Maddie seemed less than pleased with this.

The discussion of the seating for her wedding dinner lasted until eleven o'clock without reaching any conclusions, other than her insistence that Noah and Laura would sit together because the entire wedding party would be seated at one table, and if Noah didn't like it, he could fuck himself. By the time Maddie rolled her paper into a scroll and fastened it with a rubber band, Ruth was weary enough to sleep standing up.

She'd climbed the stairs to bed and slept horizontally, however—and then arose at six-fifteen the next morning. Barry, who'd been spared Maddie's angst about the demographics of who sat where and in what configuration, had gone to bed at ten and awakened appallingly chipper while Ruth staggered around the bedroom, stubbing her toe on her closet door while she flung her arms into the sleeves of her bathrobe and fastened the belt with an uneven knot. Maddie woke up soon afterward, neither as energized as Barry nor as bleary as Ruth. Her neon-bright scrubs seared Ruth's sleep-deprived eyes. "I've got to run," she announced, filling her travel mug with coffee and racing to the door. "Make sure Rainie doesn't miss the bus."

The air had barely settled back into stillness with Maddie's departure before Barry filled *his* travel mug, pecked Ruth's cheek with a dry kiss, and murmured, "Make sure Rainie doesn't miss the bus." He was obviously parodying Maddie, but Ruth didn't smile.

When Rainie hadn't emerged from her bedroom by a quarter to seven, Ruth marched in and gave the girl's slumbering form a firm shake. "The school bus leaves in twenty minutes," she said. "I'm under strict instructions to make sure you don't miss it."

"I'm tired," Rainie groaned, burrowing under her blanket.

"So am I. Get up. I'm not driving you to school. If you miss the bus, you're walking, and it's a raw, icy day."

Rainie cursed. Ruth gave her shoulder one final shake, then left the bedroom, hoping her stern attitude would convince Rainie that she'd prefer to live with her mother and Warren than with her cranky, curmudgeonly grandmother, who would cruelly force her to walk to school if she missed the bus.

Rainie didn't miss the bus. She barely made it, racing out the front door with her backpack slung over one shoulder and a cold, unsliced bagel clutched in her hand. When Ruth went back upstairs, she peeked into Rainie's bedroom. The bed was unmade, a swirling tangle of sheets and pillows and quilt. Ruth briefly recalled Maddie's planet-adorned comforter. Rainie's wasn't terribly different, although it featured rainbows along with some planetary objects. Her down pillows had been punched and fluffed and dented. She must have tossed and turned a lot last night. She might well be as weary as Ruth was.

The silence enveloping the house once everyone was gone settled around her like a warm wool blanket, tempting her to return to her own bed. The wintery morning wasn't conducive to a five-mile walk. The time she would ordinarily be power-walking through town she could spend getting some more sleep.

But she'd never been one for naps. Once she was up, she was up.

Shaking her head at the messiness of Rainie's bedroom, she continued down the hall to her own bedroom and threw on some comfortable sweats. Then, she returned to the kitchen, refilled her mug with coffee, and flipped listlessly through the pages of the *Boston Globe*. Rainie and Maddie teased her for subscribing to the print edition—"Everyone reads the paper online, Grammy," Rainie chided, to which Ruth responded, "I'm not everyone." As far as she was concerned, the news was depressing whether she read it in print or online. The articles were tragic or irritating or silly. Congress did nothing. The president issued a statement. The state assembly did nothing. The governor issued a statement.

She tossed the news section aside and reached for the arts section. When Rainie was younger, Ruth used to take her into the city to see "The Nutcracker" every year in December, just as she'd taken Jill and Maddie when they'd been children. Noah had always refused to go. He'd insisted that ballet was for girls, even after Ruth pointed out that the Nutcracker itself was danced by a man, and that man probably had more muscles than most of the players on the Patriots.

Rainie had lost interest in "The Nutcracker" a few years ago, claiming she'd rather go to the Garden and watch the Celtics play basketball. Ruth admitted that basketball players had muscles too. Maybe next year she would take Emma and Nate to the ballet. This year, she wasn't sure they could sit still long enough, or remain quiet enough, to get through "The Nutcracker."

After draining her mug of coffee, she wandered into the living room, resolved to practice "Clair de Lune" until she could play it halfway decently. An abundance of pedal might muddy the sound, but it would hide her mistakes. She was retired. She had nothing better to do. She might as well wrestle Debussy's masterpiece to the ground.

She made her way through the score, not at all pleased with her playing. "Clair de Lune" was too schmaltzy, anyway. Rainie's bedroom was too messy. The weather outside was too sloppy. She needed something organized, something sensible in her life.

Tucked inside the piano bench were some of her music books, relics from her long-ago lessons with Mrs. Demming. She pulled out the book of Bach's two- and three-part inventions, its yellow cover faded, the corners bent, the binding shedding flecks of dried glue like brown dandruff. But the music was still readable, and her fingers remembered what her mind didn't. One thing about Bach's music: it was never chaotic.

Mrs. Demming should hear me now, Ruth thought with a grin as she worked her way through the first two-part invention. If Mrs. Demming heard her, she would probably have a stroke from how laboriously Ruth was playing the piece. How much easier it had been, during all those years of Ruth's professional life, to bang out the accompaniment to the songs her primary school choruses sang, to play chords with her left hand while conducting with her right. "This means louder," she'd tell the children, turning her hand palm up and lifting it toward the ceiling. "This means softer," and she flip her hand over and lower it, as if she were pressing down the vibrations of their voices. "Who remembers the musical words for loud and soft?"

Someone—some lucky child who took piano lessons, or some benighted child who took piano lessons—would shout, "Forte and piano!"

"Right! But we can play a piano *forte*, can't we? Because the real name for a piano is a pianoforte!"

And her students would sing—usually forte, and usually with at least a third of them flat or sharp or stumbling over the words, but they'd be smiling as they sang, and having fun, even if the only reason they were smiling and having fun was that music class gave them a break from spelling drills and math problems and history tests.

She'd enjoyed teaching, and she'd been good at it. Her evaluations had always been superlative, and parents still stopped her at the supermarket or the drug store to tell her how much little Taylor or Mackenzie or Riley enjoyed singing in her chorus. But it wasn't as if she had decided at a very young age that she wanted to be a primary-school music teacher, any more than she'd decided at a very young age that she wanted to be a rock star—which she'd never actually been. When she was eight or twelve or eighteen, she could have been anything. Her only goal back then had been to get out of the house like David, to go to college and not have to listen to her mother scolding her about her bellbottoms being too wide or her hair being too long, or her tush being too big, or the fact that she was wasting her time with that stupid band, or the fact that she never went out on dates because she spent so damned much time with that stupid band.

"I love you," her mother always said. "I only want what's best for you. I want you to have a successful life. Now go and practice the Bach inventions. We pay Mrs. Demming good money."

~

If only I'd become a concert pianist...

Everything changed when Mrs. Demming died.

I wouldn't wish death on anyone, even her. True, I didn't like the woman. I can still sometimes imagine the sting on my knuckles when she rapped them with her pencil because my hands were too arched over the keys. But it wasn't that I wished she was dead. I just wanted her out of my life.

And one day, she was out of my life, after having choked to death on a piece of steak. When I heard that, I swore off steak forever.

After a month, my parents hired Rosette Milleneaux to teach me piano. A teacher can change a student's life. Mme. Rosette changed mine.

"You are playing from your head," she told me, her voice colored by a faint but lyrical French accent, after I'd performed one of the Bach inventions for her. "You must learn to play from your heart. You must not worry about wrong notes. You must not worry about dynamics. Listen to the music here." She tapped my breastbone gently. "Feel the music here."

No smacks on my knuckles. No blocking the keyboard from my eyes. No fussing over my use and abuse of the pedals. All Mme. Rosette ever wanted me to do was feel *the music. Not think it,* feel *it.*

One encounter. One teacher. One epiphany.

So now I'm here, in my grand apartment on Central Park West in Manhattan, the living room windows overlooking that miraculous green acreage in the heart of the nation's most densely built, densely populated city. My Steinway Grand stands beside those windows so I can gaze out at them as I practice. I don't have to look at the keyboard, or even at the score, when I play. The music is in my heart, in my soul—and in my fingers.

I would never have predicted that Barry and I would wind up living in New York City. We're diehard Red Sox fans, after all. But I needed to be near Lincoln Center and Carnegie Hall, and

Juilliard invited me to give master classes every year. Barry can work with clients in the New York area as easily as with clients in New England. And of course, Maddie lives in New York, which is a major plus.

I still believe she has much more talent than I do. But she has her own career and I have mine. We share the same manager, and he occasionally books us together. So much repertory exists for two pianos—Liszt, Dvorak, Barber, Beethoven, Ravel—and we've mastered a fair portion of it. Lord, how the audiences love when we play Ravel's Ma Mère L'Oye *together. Our recording of that suite still sells steadily.*

I don't tour as much as I used to. It's exhausting, and we don't need the money. But I can usually fill Carnegie Hall or Avery Fisher Hall, and I still have a closet full of my concert wardrobe. Who would have guessed that Laura, my amazing daughter-in-law, would have designed so many gorgeous gowns for Maddie and me? Sure, Laura had always loved sewing—she was so enthusiastically domestic—but the first time she offered to sew me a gown out of silk chiffon that draped so comfortably over me, and gave my arms such an easy range of motion—I didn't want to wear anything else when I performed. "You can't wear the same dress every time you go on stage," she said, and went on to sew another dozen dresses for me, and a few for Maddie too.

Noah is so proud of Laura. He keeps asking her to sew him a tuxedo, but she says first he has to learn how to play the Bach inventions as well as I do.

Plunging into a career as a concert pianist was scary, but I did it. Mme. Rosette—well, she's eight-five now, and I call her just plain Rosette—encouraged me. She pushed me. She twisted my arm to audition for the New England Conservatory—and then untwisted my arm so I could play my audition pieces (which I didn't play flawlessly, but I did play from my heart). When I was accepted, she said there was nothing more she could do for me. Which was a crock, of course. She's my mentor and my muse. She's the mother I never had. She's both diligent and sentimental, and always positive, always finding something good in what I'm playing, even if I botch a piece. She still lives in the Boston area, but I travel up there to see her a few times a year, and we laugh and drink cognac and play Mozart and Stravinsky together in her studio. Even at her age, she can play beautifully—from her heart, not from her head.

So here I am, in a city I never expected to live in, with a career I never expected to have. I wasn't a prodigy. I didn't spend my childhood dreaming of this life, planning for it. But a woman entered my world and said, "You can do this if you wish. It is not the easiest path to travel, but it is a glorious path if you are willing to risk it. Teaching music is safe. I know, I am a teacher. But making *music... You must trust your heart, think with your heart, follow your heart."*

And much to my surprise, my heart led me here.

~

By the time Ruth reached the final measure of that first Bach two-part invention, she could almost believe she had never played it before. True, it had been years since she'd last opened her Bach book with its faded pages and its spine in desperate need of surgery, but Mrs. Demming had often lectured her about finger memory—"Even if your brain forgets how to play something, your fingers will remember."

Ruth's fingers remembered the songs she'd played with Trouble Ahead, especially the songs she'd written for the band. Even the crappy songs. But the classical music Mrs. Demming had forced her to learn, the music her mother was always nagging her to practice? She remembered how the pieces sounded, or at least how they *should* have sounded, if she'd played them well. But her fingers remembered nothing. They'd clearly developed amnesia, or maybe dementia.

She closed the book and rose to her feet. Singing "Tom" and "King of the World" was easier if she played standing up. Assuming the position of a keyboardist in a rock band who didn't want to be mistaken for Liberace or Neil Sedaka seemed to jog her fingers' memory somehow.

As she reached the end of the first verse of "Tom," she heard the doorbell ring. She glanced at her watch: nine-fifteen. Had she arranged to go walking with Coral today? Given the weather, she would have cancelled—if she'd remembered there was a plan to cancel. Did she have a walking date, or simply amnesia? Or dementia?

If Coral was at her front door, Ruth would invite her in, apologize for forgetting their scheduled walk, prepare a fresh pot of coffee, and warm up some bagels. If Coral was worried about her weight, she could skip the cream cheese.

She left the living room for the entry hall, and opened the door.

A strange man stood on her front porch. Not *strange*—he appeared perfectly normal, with light brown hair that cried out for a trim, a narrow face, thin lips, and pale blue eyes. He wore faded, loose-fitting jeans and a bulky maroon parka. A knitted yellow muffler circled his neck. "Mrs. Singer?" he said.

What was it about him? Something familiar. Something... *what?*

"You probably don't remember me." He extended a gloved hand. "Kyle Jarvis."

Chapter Fifteen

Holy fucking shit.

Fortunately, Ruth only thought the words—and if she'd mistakenly uttered them, Rainie wouldn't have heard her because she was at school. But they clamored inside her head, all three of them, in that order. Emphasis on the final noun.

Kyle Jarvis. Kyle, the kid who had grown up in the modern house across the street. The classmate who had absorbed Ruth's youngest daughter as if she were an ice-pop melting on his tongue, something sweet and tangy and easy to swallow. The boy who had been Maddie's partner in crime (sometimes literally; Ruth still remembered those nights when her underage daughter staggered home from the Jarvis house like a dragon, except that instead of breathing fire, she breathed fumes of booze). The high school graduate who'd driven his Jeep down Jefferson Road with Maddie by his side, and when Maddie came home a year later, she had a baby with her.

Kyle Jarvis, the father of that baby, now stood on her front porch.

"Can I come in?" he asked, his voice gentle and polite. He'd always been soft-spoken, Ruth recalled—certainly more well-mannered than Maddie. "It's kind of cold out here."

More than cold. A mix of snow and sleet spilled out of the heavy gray clouds, glazing the porch's bricks and frosting Kyle's hair. He was the father of her grandchild. She supposed she ought to let him into her house.

He wiped his thick-soled work boots on the door mat before entering. Standing in the entry, he unwrapped the yellow scarf, then shook it out. She pulled an empty hanger from the coat closet and draped his scarf and jacket over it, then hung it on the doorknob because the garments were wet.

Had Kyle always been this tall, or had she shrunk in the years since he'd absconded with her daughter? She recalled Noah growing an inch taller in college; boys did that sometimes, experiencing growth spurts into their twenties, taking forever to get through puberty. Some boys never seemed to outgrow puberty completely.

Kyle appeared reasonably adult now. She noticed a tiny scab on the edge of his jaw, undoubtedly left by a razor. When he'd run off with Maddie all those years ago, he hadn't looked old enough to shave. He'd still been all boyishness and peach fuzz.

All those years ago. Fifteen and a half years ago, to be precise. A lot had happened since then. Maddie had come back to Brentwood a mother. She'd enrolled in community college, gotten training, and become a dental hygienist. She'd met Warren on a blind date arranged by one of her colleagues at the dental office, accepted his marriage proposal, and now spent her spare time obsessing over who was going to sit where at her wedding reception and who was going to be represented by a figurine on her wedding cake.

Kyle no longer held any power over Maddie. To be sure, he hadn't held any power over her when she'd abandoned him and returned home with Rainie. The least Ruth could do, given his powerlessness, was return his courtesy. "Would you like a cup of coffee?" she offered.

"That would be great. Thank you." He rubbed his hands together briskly, and she resisted the maternal urge to scold him for not wearing gloves in this weather.

He followed her into the kitchen. No surprise that he knew where it was; he'd been in the Singer house hundreds of times, and while Ruth and Barry had renovated the kitchen ten years ago, replacing all the appliances and installing engineered stone counters and pale oak cabinets, the house's floor plan hadn't changed. He wouldn't get lost searching for the bathroom if he needed to pee.

"I wasn't expecting company," she said, waving vaguely at her faded old sweats and then busying herself preparing a fresh pot of coffee. "I do have some bagels, if you're hungry."

"Coffee's fine," he said. "Thank you."

Sheesh. Had he taken a course in etiquette at some point during the past fifteen years? Or purchased a gross of thank-yous on sale at the local dollar store?

She could fuss with the coffee maker only so long. Once it was brewing, she turned to face Kyle. Shaving scab and extra height notwithstanding, he hadn't changed much. He still struck her as thin and wan. His eyes were striking, but not much else about him was. She'd always wondered what about him had drawn Maddie to him. His personality, maybe—although that had always struck her as thin and wan too.

"Have a seat," she said, gesturing to the table in the breakfast nook. "Do you take milk? Sugar?"

"Black is fine," he said. She braced herself for another "Thank you," but he surprised her by not saying it.

Neither of them spoke. The coffee maker gurgled and hissed. Ruth gazed out the kitchen window; the sky beyond the glass pane was leaden and dreary, spitting icy flecks of snow onto the layer of white already blanketing the backyard. When the coffee maker beeped at the end of the cycle, she pulled two mugs from a cabinet, filled them, and carried them to the table. Settling into a chair across from him, she forced a smile. "So. Here you are."

"Here I am," he said. His smile looked much more natural than hers felt.

"Obviously, you're not in town visiting your mother."

He smiled. The house across the street had changed ownership twice since Darlene had moved out.

"How is she?"

He shrugged. "She lives in Florida. She says the weather is better there. I guess it depends on your definition of 'better.'"

Silence again. So much for small talk. "Why are you here?" Ruth said. What difference would an awkward question make, given all the awkwardness vibrating in the air?

"Rainbow asked me to come."

Thank goodness Ruth hadn't lifted her mug. If she had, his answer would have startled her into spilling its steaming contents all over the table. "Rainie asked you to come? What are you talking about? Rainie contacted you?"

"She found me on Twitter. I don't use it much, but I saw her message, and we started emailing."

You can find anyone online. That was what Rainie had told Ruth when they'd been thumbing through Ruth's high school yearbook. Evidently, Rainie had been speaking from experience. "So she found you on Twitter?"

"About a year ago. We've been emailing back and forth ever since."

Another shock. Of course Rainie had her secrets. She was a teenager. She probably had lots of secrets, thousands of them. Millions.

But emailing back and forth with Kyle Jarvis?

"I'm her father," he reminded Ruth.

"Yes, you're her father—biologically, anyway," Ruth said, wondering if he heard the edge of bitterness in her voice. "You've never seen her, you've never done anything to support her—"

"Once I got on my feet, I tried to contribute child support. I couldn't afford much, but I sent Maddie a check. She sent it back and told me she didn't want my money." His gaze circled the room and he gave Ruth a crooked smile. "She said you and Mr. Singer were supporting her and Rainbow just fine."

Wonderful. Maddie undoubtedly relished the opportunity to shove Kyle's money—his belated attempt at responsibility—in his face while allowing Ruth and Barry to cover her expenses. Of course, once she'd landed her job with Dr. Bromberg, Ruth and Barry had made her contribute to the household finances, more for her sake than for theirs. She paid a portion of the utilities and a fraction of the property tax bill, and she brought home unidentifiable foods in plastic containers from the Asian market near where she worked. "She has a job, you know," Ruth said. "She's a dental hygienist. I guess she figures she doesn't need any extra support."

"She's doing great, isn't she." He sounded wistful.

"If you came to see Rainie," Ruth said, wondering if it was Rainie or Maddie he truly wanted to see, "she's at school now. You should have come later in the afternoon." Not that Ruth wanted to encourage him, not that she wanted him to return to the house when Rainie and Maddie might be here. And Barry, who would probably be moved to punch Kyle bloody. If Ruth had been upset about Kyle's spiriting their daughter away, impregnating her, and doing whatever he'd done that would make her return home with her baby and without him, Barry had been livid. He had raged for months after Maddie had left, and months more after she'd returned home, although most of that second round of raging had occurred in the master bedroom after he'd gotten home from work and was changing from his suit into his jeans. He'd never raged in front of Maddie. Scolded, yes. Badmouthed Kyle, frequently. But only Ruth had the privilege of listening to him rant and fume with volcanic force.

Kyle was a good thirty-five years younger than Barry, though, and he had longer arms. If Barry took him on, Kyle could easily flatten him with a few well-placed punches.

"I thought I should come when Rainbow wasn't around, to kind of clear things with you," Kyle said. "She told me you're more of a mother to her than Maddie is. So I thought, you know, I should connect with you first."

Ruth would hardly consider this uneasy conversation *connecting*. But once again, Kyle was demonstrating an understanding of propriety and manners. "You didn't connect with me when you ran off with my daughter," she said.

"Yeah, well." His smile was vague and not terribly cheerful. "We were stupid kids, right?"

Emphasis on *stupid*.

"I have a good job now," he said. "I manage a bar just over the border in New Hampshire. I'm gradually investing in it so when the owner decides to cash out, I'll own the place. I'd like to be a part of Rainbow's life. She's told me she'd like that too."

Of course Rainie would like that. At the moment, her mother was planning to marry a man Rainie found boring, a man who tried to earn her affection with a grotesquely pink teddy bear and was pressuring Rainie to move into his house once he and her mother were legally wed. Rainie had made it clear that she didn't want to do that. And really, Ruth couldn't blame her. If Ruth declared that she wanted to retire as Rainie's de facto mother, would Rainie opt to move in with her father rather than wind up in boring Warren's boring raised ranch, where he would present her with boring stuffed animals in colors that matched her hair? If she had to change school districts, why not move all the way to New Hampshire?

Ruth wanted to be done being a mommy. Done, done, done. But still...a *bar*. Were Rainie's only choices boring Warren or a *bar*? Were Ruth's only choices being a mommy or letting Rainie move to New Hampshire? Why couldn't Maddie have been a bit less didactic, and Warren a bit less bland?

"Does Maddie know you're here to see Rainie?" Ruth asked Kyle. She had no idea what Maddie might do if she saw Kyle, but she'd bet Maddie would fare far better against Kyle than Barry would if the fists started flying.

"I didn't tell her. I don't know if Rainbow—you call her Rainie? I don't know if she told Maddie that we've been communicating."

"Yes, I call her Rainie and no, she doesn't tell her mother anything," Ruth said. The smile she and Kyle exchanged seemed almost conspiratorial. Ruth hated the thought that she and Kyle shared anything, not least an understanding of mother-teenage daughter relationships in general, or of Maddie's mercurial behavior in particular. She hastily dropped her smile.

"So when do you think would be a good time for me to see Rainb—Rainie?" Kyle asked.

Never. "That's between you and her, I guess." Ruth's cup was nearly empty, and a glance his way informed her that his was too. She suddenly felt a surge of curiosity—not about his showing up so unexpectedly, not about the way his appearance on her doorstep had yanked her out of her pretty dream of being a famous, successful concert pianist, someone whose fingers could dance through Bach inventions and Debussy tone-poems and magnificent classical duets with fantasy-Maddie. He had forced her to confront reality-Maddie, what had happened so many years ago, where she and Kyle had gone, why Maddie had come back.

Maddie would never tell her anything about those eighteen months she'd been gone, and Ruth's relationship with her was delicate enough that she would never risk shattering it by asking. But Kyle was being polite. He was drinking her coffee. He'd come to her house to see Rainie, but also, as he'd said, to see Ruth.

"What happened?" she asked, rising and crossing to the coffee maker. She refilled his mug without inquiring whether he wanted any more coffee, then refilled her own. "Why did you two leave home the way you did? And why did Maddie come back without you?"

"My fault," Kyle said. "It was all my fault."

Ruth highly doubted that.

"Where did you even go?" Ruth asked. "When she came home, she said you and she had been somewhere in Maine. But when she was gone, we had no idea. We called Maddie again and again on her cell phone, and she wouldn't tell us anything. Finally Barry got so pissed off, he stopped paying for her phone."

"I remember that." Kyle nodded, his gaze drifting as he reminisced. "That was a bad day. She was pretty pissed off too."

"It wouldn't have happened if she'd told us where you were."

"She thought if she told you where she was, you would come and get her."

Barry might have been tempted. Ruth had been pissed off enough to prefer that Maddie stayed away. They had already lost the deposit holding Maddie's place in the freshman class at Oberlin. If Maddie had wanted to spend her life screwing around with Kyle instead of studying at a fine liberal arts college, let her.

"We were living in a mobile home in the middle of nowhere." Kyle issued a short, sour laugh. "We thought it was romantic."

"I'm sure."

"We were broke. We had our savings, but it wasn't much and we blew through it pretty fast. And then she got pregnant." Another laugh, this one more philosophical. "We thought we were so daring, and there we were, like some family from a hundred years ago, Maddie home with the baby and me earning the money. 'Ozzie and Harriet,' my mom used to call that. I don't know what it means, but that's what we were."

"It was a TV show from when your mother and I were children," Ruth told him. "The family on the show was very conventional. The dad worked. The mom stayed home and raised the kids, cooked the meals, and cleaned the house."

"Yeah, that was us. Except Maddie wasn't real good about cleaning the trailer, and I wasn't real good at earning any money. I tried, honestly. I took any odd job that came my way. But it was never enough." He sipped his coffee, his gaze once again losing focus as he searched his memory. "The midwife charged us as much as a doctor would have. The baby cried all the time. And all those diapers. Diapers are expensive. *Babies* are expensive."

"No kidding."

"I started selling weed. Not a lot. It wasn't like I was selling to school children at the playground or trying to get people addicted to hard drugs or anything. Just a little recreational pot. It paid for the diapers." He shrugged. "I got caught."

"Well." Ruth wasn't going to sit in judgment. Marijuana was legal in Massachusetts now, and probably most other states, although she didn't care enough to research whether Maine was among them. Not that it mattered. It wasn't legal then, and Kyle had gotten caught. "Did you wind up in prison?"

"No. First offense. I got probation and community service. But Maddie packed up and left."

For once, Maddie had actually done something sensible. Ruth sighed, imagining how crazed life must have been in that trailer in the middle of nowhere—a messy trailer, given Maddie's antipathy toward housekeeping—with a screaming baby and a boyfriend in legal trouble. Growing up, Maddie had often been the source of the chaos in Ruth's life. How ironic that Maddie had fled the chaos of her life with Kyle when she couldn't stand it anymore.

"Do you have a criminal record?" Ruth asked. If he did, she wasn't going to let Rainie near him—as if she could keep Rainie away from her father. Rainie had found him, after all. She'd invited him into her life. But still...a criminal? Rainie was legally a minor. Ruth could say no.

"No. I stayed out of trouble for three years, did my community service, and the whole thing went away."

"That was fortunate."

He nodded. "I reached out to Maddie after that, got a job, sent the child-support check that she sent back to me. So I figured, that's that. She went her way, I went mine. I felt bad about Rainbow, but Maddie told me to stay out of their lives, and I figured I ought to respect her wishes."

If he'd wanted to be a father to Rainie, he'd had legal recourse. He could have gone to court, demanded joint custody or at least visitation. Of course, he would have needed enough money to hire a lawyer. Either he couldn't afford one or the idea hadn't occurred to him. Or he'd decided to honor Maddie's wishes and stay out of her and Rainie's lives.

"Maddie is engaged," Ruth informed him. "She's getting married in April."

"Yeah, Rainbow—Rainie told me. She said Maddie's fiancé is about as exciting as moldy bread."

"After all the excitement Maddie experienced with you, she clearly wanted something different."

"I don't blame her." He shrugged.

"And you?" Ruth asked. "Are you married?"

"I've got friends. Nothing serious."

Wonderful. A bar manager who had "friends." What a wholesome environment for Rainie. Living with an accountant stepfather and a dental-hygienist mother in a suburban raised ranch sounded a lot better to Ruth, even if it didn't to Rainie.

Kyle drained his mug. "I've taken enough of your time," he said. "I mean, you haven't even had a chance to get dressed this morning, and I'm sitting here drinking your coffee and running at the mouth."

Ruth almost argued that she *had* gotten dressed, that she was retired and the weather was nasty and she could wear any damned thing she wanted, even a baggy pair of maroon drawstring sweatpants and a matching maroon sweatshirt. But Kyle seemed to be ready to leave, and she was more than ready to have him leave.

"When can I get together with Rainbow?" he asked. "I'm staying at a motel on Route 9."

"I'll talk to her when she gets home from school," Ruth said. "Then...we'll see." Ruth knew she couldn't stop Rainie from contacting Kyle, but as long as he believed Ruth had some control over the situation, she wouldn't disabuse him of that notion.

Once he was gone, she bolted the front door and leaned heavily against it, as if that could keep him out of her life, and Rainie's. That lock was worthless against him, though. It always had been. It had never kept him from Maddie, never kept Maddie from him. Now it couldn't keep Rainie from him.

"Fuck," she said, just because it felt good.

She returned to the kitchen, ignored the coffee mugs still sitting on the table, and reached for the phone. She punched in Barry's office number—his personal one, bypassing his secretary.

"Ruth? I'm with a client," he said curtly. This was Barry in business-shark mode, not Barry in affable Grampa mode.

"Kyle Jarvis just walked out our front door. He was here. He wants to see Rainie."

A moment of silence, and then Barry erupted. "That son of a bitch! What the hell is he doing in our house?"

"He's not in our house anymore. He drank two cups of coffee and told me his life story."

"I have to call you back," Barry said, then hung up the phone.

Ruth stared at the dead receiver in her hand for a moment before she disconnected it and set it back in its cradle. He was with a client. He couldn't talk. She understood that. But being cut off like that infuriated her.

She walked back into the living room. Through the window she saw swirls of icy precipitation descending from the sky. The grim, foreboding vista matched her grim, foreboding mood.

She dropped onto the piano bench, her hands pressed to her knees. She knew the piano keys wouldn't bite her, but she couldn't bring herself to play. All she wanted was to go back in her mind to that gorgeous apartment with its Central Park views, that imposing concert grand with its lid propped open, the magnificent world she would have lived in if she'd chosen that road to travel down. A world with a kindly, inspiring Mme. Rosette unlocking talents Ruth doubted she possessed. A world in which Ruth dressed in elegant gowns and performed on elegant stages, not in smoky dives with stages too small to fit both her and an electric keyboard.

A world where there weren't millions of butterflies flapping their wings all around her.

Chapter Sixteen

Rainie stayed late at school for a meeting of the ski club, or so she claimed when she phoned Ruth to let her know she wasn't going to be coming home on the bus but would get a ride from her friend Kelsey's mother. Ruth couldn't help wondering—fearing, really—that Rainie was actually at some motel on Route 9, and that she'd be getting a ride home from Kyle. Rainie didn't ski. Why would she go to a ski club meeting?

But Maddie and Barry arrived home from work within minutes of each other, and when they heard that Kyle Jarvis had spent an hour that morning drinking coffee with Ruth in the kitchen of that very house, they exploded in rage. Mostly, their shouting emphasized their agreement that Kyle was an asshole, that he had some nerve, that he should crawl back under the rock he'd emerged from.

Yet even though they concurred on all this, they spewed plenty of invective at each other. Barry blamed Maddie for having run off with Kyle all those years ago when she could instead have gone to Oberlin and made something of herself. Maddie blamed Barry for being such a terrible father she'd had no concept of what to look for in a man, in a husband, in the father of her child. Barry called her spoiled. Maddie told him he'd ruined her life.

Both of them targeted Ruth, as well, because she'd actually allowed Kyle into the house. "It was sleeting outside," she justified her invitation. "I couldn't just let him stand on the porch."

"You could have sent him on his way," Barry railed.

"You could have kicked his ass to the curb," Maddie roared.

"You could have let him freeze to death," Barry said.

"You could have told him to fuck himself," Maddie suggested.

Ruth raised her hands, shook her head, and abandoned the kitchen for the den, where she hoped to tune them out. She didn't go upstairs with Barry to keep him company while he changed into his jeans and adjusted his belt beneath his belly. Listening to the two of them shout accusations of ruining each other's lives enraged and saddened her, and, as Kyle might say, pissed her off. She didn't want to spend a minute longer than necessary with either of them.

The atmosphere didn't improve much when Rainie arrived home. Hearing a car splatter through the slush puddles in front of the house, Ruth glanced out the window and saw Rainie emerging from a silver Lexus. She doubted that Kyle would be driving a Lexus. Wasn't he saving all his money so he could buy the bar where he worked?

"The ski club?" she asked, speaking in a low voice as she ushered Rainie inside and closed the door. "Or were you lying about that?"

Rainie looked bewildered. She glanced toward the kitchen, where Maddie and Barry had returned after changing out of their work clothes and were continuing their own verbal version of full contact karate.

"Why would I lie about it?" Rainie asked, mimicking Ruth's hushed tone.

"You don't ski."

"Aunt Laura asked me to go skiing with her and Aaron and Ezra in Colorado over the winter break. I think it was Aaron's idea. He wants to discuss poetry with me when we aren't on the slopes. Aunt Laura said she'd rent equipment for me and I could go on the bunny slope."

Ruth sighed. She'd been hoping, after the intervention with Noah, that he and Laura might have attempted to reconcile, at least enough to take their ski vacation together. A fun, romantic week enjoying the pristine snow in Aspen, and they might discover they really did love each other, and then they could be figurines on Maddie's wedding cake.

"Okay. Come with me," Ruth whispered, hoping to steer Rainie away from the kitchen.

"Is Rainbow home?" Maddie shouted, foiling Ruth's plan. Maddie stormed out of the kitchen, her hair wild and her eyes wilder. Barry followed close behind, but he didn't have as much hair as Maddie. His cheeks were flushed, however. Ruth hoped he wasn't on the verge of a coronary.

She instinctively positioned herself between the two of them and Rainie.

"You invited Kyle here?" Maddie charged Rainie, her shrill voice resounding in the entry hall.

"What?" Rainbow shot a frantic glance at Ruth, then stepped out from behind her. She was a brave girl. "I didn't invite him here."

"But you've been in touch with him?"

"Do you know what that son of a bitch did?" Barry chimed in. "How could you reach out to him?"

"He's her father," Ruth defended Rainie—and, she supposed, Kyle.

Rainie sent her another quick look and shook her head, as if to say she didn't need Ruth speaking for her. Then she said to Barry, "He's my father, Grampa."

"How did you even find him?" Maddie asked.

"You can find anyone on the internet," Rainie said.

"I should never have told you his name."

"I would have found it out anyway." Rainie lifted her chin, defiant. The pink and blue streaks in her hair glistened in the light from the brass ceiling fixture. "Grammy would have told me."

Ruth shrugged, not bothering to attempt to look innocent. If Rainie had asked, yes, she would have told her.

"He was here!" Maddie roared. "He was here, inside this house!"

"He was?" Rainie turned to Ruth again, this time meeting her full-face. "My father was here?"

"He is *not* welcome here," Barry declared, as if he spoke for the entire family. "He will *not* enter my house again."

"It's my house, too," Ruth retorted. Not that she wanted to argue on Kyle's behalf, not that she particularly wanted him in her house either, but she would not have Barry unilaterally deciding who could and could not walk through the front door. Besides,

Kyle had been awfully polite. A lot more polite than Barry and Maddie were right now. "Rainie is nearly fifteen," Ruth reminded him. "If she wants to meet her father, she has the right to meet him."

"Not in my house," Barry insisted, although his voice had dropped a level in volume.

"Oh, stop it," Ruth snapped. "Where is she supposed to meet him, at Starbucks? In a dark alley somewhere? She lives here too."

"Not for much longer," Maddie warned. "Maybe we should move into Warren's house now."

"I'm not moving into Warren's house," Rainie spat out, then broke away from Ruth and stormed up the stairs. Thirty seconds later, she slammed her bedroom door so hard the living room windows rattled.

"You're being stupid," Ruth scolded both Barry and Maddie. "If you tell her she can't see him, she's going to want to see him even more. If you tell her she can't see him here, she'll find somewhere else to see him. Maddie, you grew up knowing your father. Rainie deserves to know her father."

"*My* father didn't do what Kyle did. *My* father didn't drag me off to some shithole trailer in the wilds of Maine and then abandon all responsibility for me and my baby. *My* father had a good job and he paid the bills and he took good care of us."

"You chose to run off with Kyle," Ruth reminded her. "He didn't drag you off. You made a choice. You and he were eighteen, with no skills or advanced degrees. What did you think would happen? Money would cascade down from the sky? Some company would offer you both executive positions with corner offices? Someone would hand you the keys to a mansion and say, 'Here, I don't want this house anymore, it's all yours'?"

"I couldn't think straight when Kyle was around," Maddie said. "That's why I don't want him around. I want to be able to think straight." She wagged a finger at Ruth. "And don't call me stupid."

"You *are* stupid," Barry said. "Running off with him was stupid."

The two of them plunged back into their verbal brawl. Ruth clapped her hands over her ears, climbed the stairs, and entered the master bedroom, closing the door behind her. She didn't slam it; that was adolescent behavior, and at the moment she was the only adult in the house.

She ought to be preparing dinner right now, but she didn't feel like it. She had no appetite, and she certainly didn't want to feed Barry and Maddie. Let Maddie throw together a meal out of some of her plastic tubs with the Asian labels on them. Let Barry fix himself a sandwich, or pig out on a bag of potato chips.

She reached for her cell phone and tapped Jill's name in her contact list. After two rings, Jill answered. "Mom?"

"We have a disaster," Ruth said. "Kyle Jarvis came to Brentwood to see Rainie. Everyone is screaming at everyone, or else sulking. Or both."

"Is Maddie acting out?" Jill said, adopting her imperious I-am-the-expert voice.

"Yes. So is Barry. Rainie is just slamming doors."

Through the phone, Ruth heard whining and wailing. "Oh, shit," Jill said. "The twins are acting out too." In an even more pious, controlled voice, she said, "Emma, what have we discussed about making fun of Nate's action figures? Remember? We said we were not going to call them dolls."

"They *are* dolls!" Emma's voice blasted through the phone, as piercing as a smoke alarm.

"Are *not!*" Nate shrieked back. "Dolls are for girls!"

"Nate—" Jill now "—we have discussed gender assignment and toys, haven't we? There are no girl toys and boy toys. A boy can play with dolls."

"*I* don't play with dolls! Tell her to stop calling my space commandos dolls!"

"They *are* dolls! Dolls, dolls, dolls!" Emma bellowed.

"I've got to go," Jill told Ruth. "We seem to be having a disagreement here."

It was a flat-out fight, not a disagreement, and there was no *seem to be* about it. "Go take care of the twins," Ruth said. "Good luck." She disconnected the call, sank onto the bed, and sighed.

If only she'd become a concert pianist, she could be in that magnificent Manhattan apartment right now. If only the band hadn't broken up, she could be in Montana, walking her dog—or skiing, if only she'd learned how. If only they'd bought that charming Victorian house with the turret, Maddie would never have fallen in with Kyle, because he wouldn't have lived across the street. If only Ruth had gotten her tubes tied, Maddie would never have existed.

If only she'd run off with Danny Fortuna, none of this would be happening.

Chapter Seventeen

If Only I'd Run Off with Danny Fortuna...

By the next morning, no one was talking to anyone, which made life in the Singer house much more tranquil. Barry and Maddie both left for work without eating breakfast—and without saying goodbye to Ruth or each other. Rainie remained in her bedroom until they were gone, then emerged, grabbed a granola bar from a box in the pantry, and raced outside to catch the bus, mumbling a quick "'Bye, Grammy" on her way out the door.

Barry had spent the previous evening seething and stewing while a football game blared across the TV screen in the den. (How he managed to find a football game on TV nearly every night baffled Ruth, but he did.) Maddie had spent the previous evening in her bedroom, yammering to Warren on her phone; her voice could be heard through the door, muffled but brimming with indignation and outrage. Whether Rainie had spent the evening texting back and forth with Kyle, Ruth didn't know. After Rainie had stormed to her bedroom and slammed the door, she'd surfaced only once, sneaking downstairs to the kitchen in an apparent search for food.

Ruth had been in the kitchen, eating a bowl of soup, when Rainie found her. She'd filled a second bowl for Rainie, and they'd sat at the kitchen table, hunched over their respective steaming bowls, spooning salty chicken broth and overcooked noodles into their mouths. The only thing Rainie had said was, "I hate them all. I hate everyone, except you."

"I love you too," Ruth had assured her.

And then Rainie had risen, rinsed her bowl, placed it in the dishwasher, and vanished back into her bedroom.

Ruth had spent the evening...not hating them all, but not loving them either. She'd spent the evening on the comfortable couch in the living room, pretending to read a book while her mind simmered and bubbled, pondering what her life would have been like if she'd chosen the road not taken. That road would not have taken her here, in any event. Not this house, on this couch, with this book. With this family.

Now they were all gone for the day. Yesterday's storm had drifted out to sea and the roads were relatively clear, Brentwood's public works department having salted and plowed them overnight. Ruth dressed in layers, laced on her boots, and headed outside to take a walk.

She needed the cold, fresh air. She needed the silvery winter sunlight. She needed to put some distance between herself and her house—the house for which Barry had appointed himself the sole sentry. How dare he tell her whom she could and could not invite inside?

It was Wednesday, which meant her route took her past the Victorian. The house looked more fairy-tale magical than usual, its sloping roof frosted with white, its ornate eaves dripping with spiky icicles. If only she and Barry had bought this house when they moved to Brentwood, everything would have been different.

She was tempted to ring the bell, to ask whoever answered whether life was peaceful within its walls. Whether the matriarch of the household had claimed the turret room for herself and could shut everyone else out of that room whenever she needed solitude and serenity. Whether a little girl named Anne lived across the street.

Ruth wanted to be done with the residents of Jefferson Road—and Noah and Jill too. She wanted to be able to shut herself up inside a room—it didn't even have to be a round room—and not have to talk to any of them, listen to any of them, interact with any of them. She wanted not to be angry with any of them. She wanted not to be pissed off. She just wanted to be done.

She wanted to be sixteen again. When she was sixteen, Barry was a teenager in Rhode Island, unknown to her, and her children and grandchildren didn't exist. She wanted to live in a world where she could write songs about anything she wanted, even pregnant teenage girls hidden away in homes for unwed mothers while the boys who impregnated them got to live their lives unscathed, and she wanted to sing those songs in a band, with Danny Fortuna singing backup and telling the other members of the band her songs were good.

Her songs *were* good—at least, good by sixteen-year-old standards. The band agreed; they praised her songs even as they expressed concern about the appropriateness of the subject matter. What had Jill said last night? Something about not assigning gender to toys. Toys *did* have genders, though, and so did kids. And so did songs.

But because Danny championed Ruth's songs, the band let her sing them.

~

"Okay," Jimmy said. "With Danny singing backup, yeah, it'll work."

"It's still girlie," Nick grumbled.

"Well, guess what?" Ruth decided to assert herself. "I'm a girl."

"Uh-oh," Mike said, and grinned.

"You on the rag?" Jimmy asked her.

Danny elbowed him so hard, he nearly fell over. "It's a good song," he said. "Shut up."

"Next thing, she's gonna write a song about being on the rag," Nick muttered to Jimmy. "You shouldn't give her ideas."

"I don't need you to give me ideas," Ruth retorted, annoyed with Nick, with all of them except Danny. "I have plenty of ideas of my own."

"Uh-oh," Mike said again.

Ruth didn't have her period. She was just angry. Danny was right; she needed to stop thinking of herself as an invitee, an outsider the band had generously granted permission to hang out with them. She was a full-fledged member of Trouble Ahead. Her keyboard work contributed something essential to their sound. Besides, she'd written "Tom," the song that had won them the Battle of the Bands and turned them from a hobby into a group that earned a few dollars here and there when they played. More than a few dollars. She did the bookkeeping, and she knew they'd made over thirteen hundred dollars this summer, enough for each of them to pocket a generous amount of spending money (although most of hers went into her personal savings account for college) and to reimburse a portion of the cost of Danny's van and the shell Mike had bought to cover the bed of the old pick-up truck his father had passed along to him.

She hardly ever rode her bike to rehearsals anymore. Danny drove her back and forth. She appreciated having that driving time alone with him, not only because he was Danny Fortuna and what girl *wouldn't* want time alone with him, but because he would give her little pep talks that gave her the courage to stand up to the others in the band. She wasn't sure why he was so nice to her, but she didn't question her luck in having Danny on her side.

Would he acknowledge her in school once the fall term began? Would he wave at her when they passed each other in the hall? Would he seek her out in the cafeteria and sit next to her to eat his lunch? Would people stare at her and wonder how Ruth Pinchas, of all people, managed to become friends with the cutest boy in school? She was by no means the cutest girl. Not even close.

But school was still a couple of weeks away, and it had been a glorious summer. David distracted their mother enough that Ruth was no longer the woman's sole focus. David, his girlfriend, and Ruth's father even attended one of the band's gigs, one of those evening things in a neighboring town's park, where people picnicked on the lawn and children ran around chasing balloons and no one really paid much attention to the music. "Cool," had been David's assessment. His girlfriend, a round-faced doe-eyed girl named Heidi, had echoed him: "Cool." Ruth's father had pronounced the outing a lot of fun and reminded Ruth that even if she became a rock star, a college education was essential for success in life, and he expected her to continue her education.

She wondered what her father would think of "King of the World" if he heard Trouble Ahead perform it. So far, the band hadn't played it publicly yet, but Danny was pushing for them to add it to their repertory. She could guess what her mother would think if she ever heard the song: she'd assume Ruth had written it from experience, that Ruth had gotten pregnant and—who knew? Miscarried, or flown down to the Caribbean for an abortion when her mother wasn't looking.

Fortunately, her mother had no interest in hearing the band. "All these years we've paid good money to Mrs. Demming," her mother muttered whenever the subject of the band arose. "And this is how you're wasting your talent."

"I don't have that much talent," Ruth argued, which seemed kind of counterintuitive, but it usually shut her mother up.

The day Jimmy had accused Ruth of having her period, she left Nick's basement with Danny at the end of practice. "I'm going to write lots of girlie songs," she told him as they climbed into his van.

"You wouldn't know how," he disputed her. "You're not girlie enough."

She wasn't sure if that was a compliment or an insult. Unlike the girls who swarmed around Danny at their gigs, she wasn't flirty or overly feminine. She didn't know how to bat her eyes, and even if she did, her eyelashes were skimpy. She didn't dare to wear mascara at concerts, because it always smudged and smeared and she wound up looking as if she'd been crying. She didn't have a girlie body; she was average height and stubby, with small breasts and hips and a thick waist.

At least she had long hair, not only because most girls had long hair but because of something Meryl Dennison had said to her in the science-hall bathroom one day freshman year, well before Jimmy Grogan had approached her at her locker and asked her to play in his band: "Girls who aren't pretty should grow their hair in long, so they'll have at least one good feature. You'd look so much better with long hair, Ruth."

Meryl Dennison was a bitch, but she was impossibly pretty, with blue eyes, a tiny nose, long, slender legs, and blond hair—which was only shoulder-length. She didn't need her hair to be her one good feature.

Ruth should have ignored her. She'd told herself she *had* ignored her. But she still grew her hair in long.

She wondered what Meryl Dennison would say if she saw Ruth seated next to Danny Fortuna in his van. She wondered what Meryl Dennison would think if she knew that Danny supported and believed in her, that he fed her fragile ego on a regular basis to keep it from starving to death.

"Do you think I need to be more girlie?" she asked Danny now.

He laughed. "Nah. You need to be who you are." He steered across the railroad tracks and added, "Girlie girls wind up with football players and then they get knocked up."

Once again, Ruth puzzled over whether this was a compliment or a criticism. Was Danny saying boys only wanted to have sex with girlie girls? If so, was that a good thing? Ruth didn't want to have sex with anyone—yet—but it would be nice to think boys wanted to have sex with her.

"I could write a song about being on the rag," she said.

Danny laughed again. "If you do, I'm not singing backup."

They were still laughing as he reached her block. Her laughter withered when she spotted her mother standing on the front porch. She wore what she called a house dress, which really looked more like a cotton nightgown with snaps closing it down the front. Her hair was frizzy—and short, not her best feature—and she held a glass half-full with what was probably her second or third martini of the day.

Until now, her mother had never seen Ruth in Danny's van. She'd stopped asking how Ruth was getting to and from rehearsals and gigs—Ruth had told her two members of the band had licenses, which was true even if Danny wasn't one of them. He'd scheduled his road test for the day after his birthday in September, but he was still driving illegally. Ruth didn't care, and her parents didn't have to know.

But being confronted with the reality of Ruth sitting in a vehicle with a boy—a VW van, one of those hippie vehicles with the back seat flattened to increase the cargo space but also conducive to sex, or at the very least smoking pot—was not going to go over well with her. "Shit," Ruth muttered.

"Is that your mom?"

She nodded.

He pulled into the driveway. "You want me to get out and introduce myself?"

She looked at Danny. What would her mother think if she met him? That his hair was too long, that he was too good-looking, that he drove a van, that he was in that stupid band that had interfered with Ruth's mastery of the Chopin etudes and Gershwin preludes, and of course Debussy's "Clair de Lune," which Ruth tortured as much as it tortured her. "You don't have to," she said cautiously.

"I don't mind."

"It might be better if you didn't."

Too late. Her mother was storming down the front walk, her sandals clapping against the soles of her feet. Before Ruth could speak—before she could even open the passenger-side door of the van—her mother called through Danny's open window. "Get out. We have a situation."

"A situation?"

"Your grandfather died this afternoon."

"Grandpa died?" Rather than get out of the van, Ruth leaned back into the leatherette seat and sighed. She assumed her mother was referring to her paternal grandfather. If it had been her maternal grandfather, her mother would have said, "My father."

Ruth liked her father's mother, who cooked all those delicious Thanksgiving feasts and urged Ruth to eat as much as she wanted. But she'd never had much of a relationship with her father's father. He was a cranky old man who smelled of camphor and always had yellow crusts in the corners of his eyes. He was in his eighties, and he'd suffered several strokes over the past few years. She couldn't say she was shocked or devastated by the news that he'd died.

"Get out, Ruth," her mother said again. "We've got a lot to do. The funeral is tomorrow, and then *shiva* at Aunt Edith's."

"Tomorrow?" Danny murmured, frowning. "Isn't there, like a wake or something?"

"No wake. Jewish funerals happen within twenty-four hours of the death," Ruth explained. "And then *shiva* afterward. All the relatives sit around on stools, mourning and stuffing their faces with food. It's not like my parents are really religious or anything, but my Aunt Edith will insist."

"We have a gig tomorrow evening," Danny reminded her. "At Mack's Clam Shack." That was a regular job for them, setting up on a boardwalk area near the ocean and playing for the people who crammed the picnic tables to eat steamers, and who played beach volleyball in the sand beyond the boardwalk. Mack, the Clam Shack's gruff, bearded owner, said that when Trouble Ahead played, people hung around longer and bought more beer. Jimmy had talked him into letting them play for free back in June, and enough extra beer got sold to convince Mack to pay them to play every other week.

Ruth sighed. "I can't," she said. "You'll have to work out a play list where you don't need me. I've got to sit *shiva*."

"Yeah, well...sure," Danny said dubiously.

"Who *are* you?" her mother growled at Danny.

"Mom, this is Danny Fortuna. He's in the band."

"Of course he's in the band." She clearly wasn't impressed. "Get out, Ruth. We have to find something suitable for you to wear to the funeral. You can't go in those ragged bellbottom jeans you're always wearing."

As if her mother was such a fashion plate in her house dress. "I better go," she whispered to Danny. "Thanks for the lift."

"Let us know if you can make it to the Clam Shack tomorrow," he said. "If we don't hear from you, we'll figure you're doing that Sheba thing."

"*Shiva*," she corrected him, then smiled. She wished he'd told her to call *him*, not just the band in general. But that would have been asking for too much.

~

She didn't make the gig. Instead, she spent hours stuck inside her Aunt Edith's house, dressed in a short black skirt, a paisley blouse, pantyhose and her dress black shoes with the French heels. She'd wanted to go bare-legged, but her mother said that would be disrespectful. So instead, Ruth was very respectfully sweating as she sat *shiva*.

Aunt Edith's house in Cranston was crowded with relatives and well-wishers, and stuffy even with a couple of window fans whirling. The air was thick with the smell of roasting meat and onions, inexplicable since the only foods available for mourners were cold cuts, rye bread, dill pickles, and plates of bland vanilla cookies, all arrayed on Aunt Edith's dining room table. The table in Aunt Edith's kitchen held several bottles of cheap, sweet wine, along with bottles of soda and seltzer that had warmed to room temperature. Ruth filled a paper cup with wine for herself. It tasted like cough syrup, but what the hell. No one was paying any attention to her.

David remained in the living room with the older cousins, the aunts and uncles, and Ruth's newly widowed grandmother, who didn't seem terribly grief-stricken about the death of her husband, given how eagerly she'd devoured two sandwiches and a fistful of cookies. Ruth's younger cousins sequestered themselves inside Aunt Edith's bedroom, where they played Chinese checkers and Clue.

Ruth was the only sixteen-year-old among all the cousins, and she mostly spent the long, dragging hours by herself in the kitchen, sipping the cloying wine and worrying that Trouble Ahead would do just fine without her at Mack's Clam Shack that evening. They'd realize they didn't need her and her girlie songs, after all. Without her, they could split their earnings four ways instead of five, and keep it all instead of letting her bank it in the band's savings account and dole out ten or twenty dollars to each of them every week like a mother handing her children an allowance. They could make snide comments about whether Ruth was on the rag, and roll their eyes, and wonder why they'd ever thought she should be their keyboard player.

By the time Ruth's family arrived back home, it was ten p.m., much too late to join the guys at the clam shack—as if Ruth could convince her father or brother to drive her all that way. And it was too early to phone any of the guys to ask how the gig had gone. Not that she especially wanted to know. If they told her the gig went poorly, she would feel guilty. If they told her the gig went well, she would be devastated.

The truth was, she didn't want to know. She didn't want to hear that they didn't need her, didn't want her anymore, didn't think a girl belonged in their band.

She peeled off her sweat-sticky nylons, massaged her high-heel-sore feet, and slipped her nightgown over her head. Too restless and anguished to fall asleep, she settled on the floor of her bedroom, rested her back against her bed, and opened the notebook in which she wrote song lyrics. If her career in the band was doomed, she might as well write more girlie songs.

I want to design a tower, tall enough to scrape the sky, but they say I'm a girl and my voice is too high, she wrote. *I want to be a soldier, to fight for my country and die, but they say I'm a girl and my voice is too high. I want to be an astronaut and learn how to fly, but they say I'm a girl and my voice is too high. They tell me to be a homemaker, to cook and vacuum and dust the shelf, but I don't want to make a home unless I can build it myself. And I can't build a house, even if I try, because I'm a girl and my voice is too high.*

Maybe she would start her own band. An all-girl band, with all high voices. She would have to buy an electric keyboard, and despite the money she'd earned with Trouble Ahead, she didn't think she could afford one—not without raiding her college savings. And she would have to start from scratch, paying to enter a Battle of the Bands, writing a song as good as "Tom" so her band could win. *Damn it*, she shouldn't have let Trouble Ahead do that song. She should have saved it for when she herself would need it.

At eleven-thirty, the phone rang twice. A minute passed, and she heard a knock on her door.

"Yeah?"

Her father opened it. He stood in his pajamas, his hair mussed, his eyes half-closed, and his mouth set in a grim line. "Tell your friends, no calls after nine o'clock."

"We weren't home at nine," she said, shutting her notebook and hoisting herself to her feet. "Who is it?"

"Some boy. I nearly hung up on him. Tell him never to phone here this late again."

"I will." She brushed past her father and raced down the stairs to take the call on the kitchen extension.

"Ruth?" Danny's voice buzzed through the line.

"Hi," she said. Her heart pounded, and she told herself that was from her sprint down the stairs. But it wasn't. It was from the thought that Danny Fortuna had telephoned her.

"How was your Sheba thing?"

She didn't bother to correct him. "It was boring. There was bad wine. I'm so sorry I couldn't make it to Mack's Clam Shack tonight. We just got home a little while ago, and—"

"We stank," Danny said. "I mean, we weren't awful. But we weren't good. Mack said he doesn't want us playing without you. He said guys buy more beer than girls do, and the guys want to look at a chick singing when they're buying their beer."

I'm a chick, Ruth thought, ridiculously pleased. Even more pleased that Danny Fortuna himself had used that word in reference to her.

So much for the feisty manifesto she'd been penning in her bedroom. Build a skyscraper? Don a uniform and go to war? Hell, no. She wanted to be a *chick*.

When the fall term started at the high school, Ruth's wish came half-true. Danny greeted her in the corridor. He chatted with her at her locker. He slung his arm around her shoulders when they reached the door to the glee club room together, and ushered her inside, his gesture a public acknowledgment, visible to the entire student body—or at least those members of the student body who sang in the glee club—that he and Ruth Pinchas were friends. He continued to chauffeur her to band practices—legally, once he got his license. Ruth couldn't take her road test until late October, but even after she passed, she didn't have access to a car, so Danny continued to drive her.

That was the good part. The bad part was that right around Thanksgiving, he started dating Meryl Dennison.

Of course he did. She was the prettiest girl in the school, and he was the best-looking boy.

Ruth pretended to be happy for him. When Mike, Nick, and Jimmy teased him about his girlfriend, she defended him and told the others to grow up. When Nick asked if Danny was the king of the world, she cringed and kept her eyes focused on the dingy carpet covering Nick's basement floor. She didn't want to know if Danny was having sex with Meryl. If he was, she certainly hoped he wouldn't get her pregnant.

Danny was still her buddy. When he drove her to and from band practices, they talked about school or music or sometimes Ruth's mother, who, Danny insisted, was an alcoholic even if she didn't get fall-down drunk or puke in public. "If she drinks every day, she's an alcoholic," he said. "I read that in an article. One of my father's girlfriends was an alcoholic, and I found this article about it in the school library and gave it to my dad to read."

"You gave him a school library book?"

"Not the whole book," Danny clarified. "I just tore out the pages with the article and gave him that."

Ruth wasn't sure if he was joking, and decided she'd rather not know. "My mother drinks a lot, but it's not like she slurs her words or anything."

"Do you knock yourself out to keep from angering her?" Danny asked.

"Of course. She's awful when she's angry. It's easier just to do what she wants me to do and then steer clear of her."

"That's what the article said. If you knock yourself out to keep from angering the drinker, it's because the drinker is an alcoholic."

"I don't know." She didn't want to think of her mother as an alcoholic. She preferred to think of her as simply an annoying person.

Occasionally Danny would ask Ruth for advice about Meryl. "I guess I have to give her something for Christmas," he said during one late night drive home from a gig. They didn't have as many gigs during the school year, because they couldn't work weeknights. But schools and YMCA's still hosted dances, and a millionaire family hired them to play at their twin daughters' sweet-sixteen party on a Saturday evening. That had been a fun job, even though most of the twins' friends flirted shamelessly with Danny.

The night he raised the issue of Christmas presents, they were driving home from a dance at a junior high a couple of towns away. It was a low-paying gig, but the band didn't have anything else going on that night, and money was money. And Danny would need money if he was going to buy Meryl a Christmas present. "I have no idea what to get her," he said.

"I'm not really friendly with Meryl," Ruth said cautiously, not bothering to add that she thought Meryl was a bitch. "But I think she'd like something expensive."

"If I was dating you, what would you want for Christmas?"

If Danny were dating Ruth, she would have everything she could ever possibly want. "I wouldn't care about how much you spent. But Meryl is different from me." She pondered for a moment. "You could give her some jewelry."

"Would *you* want jewelry?"

"No, but I think Meryl would."

"Jewelry is too intense."

"I'm not saying you should give her a diamond ring," Ruth clarified. "Earrings would be okay."

He shook his head. "I'm not giving her jewelry."

"Flowers?"

"Flowers die."

"Chocolate? Every girl likes chocolate."

"Yeah?" He shot her a glance. "Do you like chocolate?"

"I love it. But I can't eat it very often. I'd get fat." She thought for a minute. "Maybe a record. She must like music. She's dating you, and you're a musician."

"Yeah. I guess I could give her an album. Too bad Trouble Ahead hasn't cut a record. I could give her that."

"Does she like our music?" Ruth asked. A couple of weeks ago, Meryl had accompanied Danny to a dance at the local community center where the band was playing. She'd sat in a folding metal chair off to one side while Trouble Ahead performed, and during each break Danny had hovered by her side. But she'd never complimented the band, or even talked to any of them besides Danny. When Jimmy and Mike gave Danny some grief about his groupie, Ruth didn't tell them to grow up. He'd deserved a little bit of grief for dating someone as stuck-up and nasty as Meryl.

Ruth believed she was handling the situation as best she could. She hid her feelings. If she couldn't have Danny any other way, she'd have him as a friend. She told herself this was better than nothing.

Sometimes, however, alone at night, she poured her emotions into her notebook, composing soulful lyrics about love and grief and jealousy. *I stand in the shadows*, she wrote. *She's the only one he sees. I wish he would love me, but love is a disease. It causes a fever, it makes you ache. He's sick in love with her, and I'm sick with heartbreak.*

Maybe she would write music to go with the lyrics she scrawled across the pages of her notebook. Maybe she wouldn't. Either way, these were not songs she would share with Trouble Ahead. They would complain that the songs were girlie—which, of course, they were. Even worse, they might figure out that she was sick with heartbreak for Danny. And she couldn't have that. It would destroy the band.

It was weird, this node of pain lodged inside her, this tightly sealed emotion she couldn't share with Danny. They could talk about music, about their parents, about school and driving and money and the band. But the most important thing in Ruth's life was the one thing she could never tell him.

In the spring, the bubbly cheerleader-types planning their class's junior prom asked if Trouble Ahead would play at the prom. "They're hiring a band from Boston," Jimmy reported during a break in Nick's basement, the air blue with smoke from Nick's cigarette and Mike's joint. "But Sally O'Donnell told me they'd like us to play, too, since we're their classmates."

Trouble Ahead had played at less formal dances at their high school. The prom would be a bigger event—but they wouldn't be the only band. "How much are they paying?" Ruth asked, ever the bookkeeper.

"We didn't negotiate a fee yet. She wanted to see if we were interested, and then she said she'd check the prom committee's budget."

"The only way I'd ever go to the junior prom is if I was playing," Nick said. Seated on the stool of his drum kit, his shoulder-length hair stringy with sweat and his barrel chest covered in a gray T-shirt with Che Guevera's image silkscreened on it, he didn't look like the sort of boy who would don a fancy suit and go to a prom.

Actually, none of them looked like the sort of person who'd go to a prom. Even Ruth, to her mother's everlasting fury, no longer wore make-up and no longer ironed her bellbottoms. She was as shaggy as the guys were, although unlike them, she wore dangly earrings and a few rings. She'd gotten adept at playing the keyboard with three rings on each hand. They were all silver and cheap, but she liked the way they made her fingers look special. Her fingers *were* special. They made music.

"Meryl expects me to take her to the prom," Danny said. His words were greeted by hoots and razzes from the guys. "No, seriously—I could go to the prom and still be in the band."

"But you're going to be all dressed up," Mike pointed out.

"A carnation in your *lapel*," Nick said, emphasizing "lapel" so it sounded like a French swear word.

"I think playing at the prom would be a gas," Jimmy said. "All our classmates hearing how good we are. I could get into that."

"What do you think, Ruthie?" Danny asked.

She shrugged. "Whatever you guys decide." She still hadn't mastered the art of assertiveness.

"I vote that we do it," Jimmy said. "If Danny wants to take Meryl, no big deal."

"I'm not bringing a date," Nick said.

"Ruthie, do you have a date for the prom?"

"No." You had to have a boyfriend to have a prom date.

"Why don't we all take Ruthie?" Mike suggested. "Danny, you can take Meryl. The rest of us can take Ruthie. She can be everyone's date."

Everyone except Danny's—but Ruth liked the idea. She would arrive at the prom escorted by three cool guys. They would play, and when the fancy band from Boston was playing, they would hang out. Or even dance, maybe.

"Do I have to wear a carnation in my *lapel*?" Nick asked, still sneering when he said that word.

"No," said Mike.

"You could carry a rose between your teeth," Jimmy suggested. "And dance the tango."

Nick contemplated the idea. "Yeah, that'd work."

So even though Ruth didn't have a boyfriend, and even though the only boy she'd want to have as a boyfriend went to the prom with Meryl Dennison, Ruth did attend her junior prom. She wore her fanciest dress, a fussy concoction of navy blue satin with an empire waist and white lace trimming the neckline and sleeves, and she was escorted by Jimmy, Mike, and Nick, all of them wearing dress pants, blazers—with *lapels*—and neckties. The guys gave her a wrist corsage which she had to take off to play the keyboard, and they asked if they could be reimbursed for the corsage with money from the band's savings account.

When Trouble Ahead played, Danny joined them on the stage, a shallow platform at one end of the high school gymnasium. When the band from Boston played, he returned to Meryl's side. She resembled an angel in a flowing white dress and silver high heels, with a silver tiara poking through her meticulously coiffed blond curls. She said hello to the band, her voice as cool and tart as lemon sherbet, and then ignored them. Once Danny returned with Meryl to their table, Nick called her a cunt and Ruth told him to shut up.

The Boston band was slick and smooth, but Trouble Ahead didn't embarrass itself, and their classmates seemed to enjoy their music more, if only because they knew the band members. The gymnasium was bedecked with crepe-paper streamers and balloons, the polished hardwood floor covered with canvas tarps so it wouldn't get scratched, the circular tables draped with paper tablecloths. A long buffet lined with aluminum bins filled with rubbery chicken, boiled vegetables, rolls as hard as hockey pucks, and squares of golden cake topped with white frosting, ran the length of the bleachers on one side. But it still looked like a high school gym, and Trouble Ahead seemed to fit into that setting better than the fancy Boston band.

Two weeks after the prom, Danny and Meryl broke up. He never told Ruth what happened, but he acted moody and mopey, so she figured he was grieving over the end of the relationship. "If you want to talk about it, let me know," she offered, but he stoically shrugged and said he was fine.

He poured his emotions into his singing, however. He sounded better than ever, and Ruth tried harder than ever to convince herself she wasn't in love with him. There was no point. Dreaming and hoping would be a waste of time. Why wish for something impossible? She would never be in Meryl Dennison's league—which meant she would never be in Danny Fortuna's league.

But his singing was gorgeous, his voice edged with sorrow and anguish even when the band played songs about getting wasted and getting laid. Ruth decided she had to write a song that would capture his heartache while it was still fresh. If a song about a broken heart was girlie, too bad. She was going to write one, and like "Tom," it was going to be a signature song for the band.

Every evening, she raced through her homework—pre-calc, chemistry, world history, Joseph Conrad's *Heart of Darkness* (which she absolutely loathed)—and cooked dinner because if she didn't, her mother sure wouldn't, and she and her parents would wind up eating something out of a can. She put forth the effort to be nice to her mother, staving off any maternal eruptions before they could occur. As soon as the dishes were washed and dried and her mother was safely settled in front of the TV with a fresh drink, Ruth retreated to her bedroom, closed the door, and jotted ideas for lyrics in her notebook, searching for just the right words, the right sentiment.

What I want, I can't have. What I need, it isn't there. She walked out of my life, and my world seems bare. I don't want this anger, I don't want this pain. I only want her, but my want is in vain.

Too prissy? Ruth wondered. Too schmaltzy? Too girlie? *In vain* had to go. *I don't want this anger, I don't want this sorrow. If the pain's bad today, it'll be worse tomorrow.* Much less girlie.

She wrote. She crossed lines out, wrote new lines, hummed melodies in her head. She wondered if Meryl had ever given Danny a gift. This song would be Ruth's gift to Danny. She hoped he'd appreciate it more than anything Meryl might have given him.

She played with the melody. Something in a minor key—but no, that was too obvious. The contrast between a sad song and a major key would work better for Danny. Ruth preferred blues songs in major keys. They played with your expectations, tossed you a curve.

It took her a few weeks, but she finally had the song where she wanted it. She wrote out the chords for guitar, wrote a bass line for Mike—who couldn't read music, but he could play by ear what she'd teach him on the keyboard—and added a few flourishes for herself. She could hear the whole thing in her head, even Danny's voice. He would wring tears out of this song—if he liked it.

She hoped with all her heart that he did.

At their next practice, she played it for the band. They listened respectfully, even nodded. "Yeah," Jimmy said. "It's good. But maybe you should sing it, Ruthie."

"You could change 'She walked out of my life' to 'he walked out of my life,'" Mike suggested.

"Or leave it 'she' and it could be a dyke song," Nick said helpfully. Jimmy threw a guitar pick at him, popping him in the nose.

"I wrote it with Danny's voice in my head," she told them, handing the sheet music with the melody line on it to Danny. "Of course, we could still change the 'she' to 'he' and make it a gay song." Jimmy threw another pick at her. As a guitarist, he always had a lot of picks stashed in his pocket.

Danny studied the page of music for a long minute, then shrugged. "All right. I'll try it," he said—and of course he sang it beautifully, his voice husky and plaintive, exactly the way she'd imagined it.

"We'll work on it," Jimmy said. "I think it's really pretty cool."

"It made me cry," Nick said in a wobbly, high-pitched voice. Then he grinned at Ruth. "It really is good, Ruthie."

All Danny said was, "Let's try it again."

A half-hour and four times through the song later, they ended their rehearsal. Ruth and Danny strolled down the cracked driveway to his van, Danny lugging his guitar and amp, Ruth hugging her notebook to her chest. He still hadn't said he liked the song. He hadn't said it was good. Nick had said it was good, and Nick never said anything was good.

But from Danny, silence—other than the way he sang the song. So beautifully. So poignantly.

"Hey, Ruthie?" Jimmy shouted to her, chasing her and Danny down the driveway. "You said you'd reimburse me for those long-distance calls I made to get us that restaurant gig."

"Oh. Right." She tossed her notebook onto the passenger seat and jogged back up the driveway to settle the phone bill with Jimmy.

When she returned to the van, Danny was seated behind the wheel. Her notebook was in his hands, open.

"Hey," she said, reaching to pull it out of his grasp.

He swung his hands away, beyond her reach, then glared at her until she subsided in the passenger seat. "I'm reading this."

"You're not supposed to. Those are my notes."

"They're song lyrics."

"Yes—and they're not done. I don't let anyone see them until I decide they're done. Most of them are terrible."

"No." He settled the notebook against the steering wheel and turned the page.

Ruth cringed. Which lyric was he reading? The one about how girls couldn't do anything exciting because they were girls, or...

Oh, shit. "*I wish he would love me, but love is a disease,*" he read aloud. "*He's sick in love with her, and I'm sick with heartbreak.*" Twisting in his seat, he gave her a hard look.

She stared at the cracked vinyl covering the dashboard, the hinged door of the glove compartment, her knees. Her hands were clenched so tightly in her lap her fingertips started to tingle. "That one's a piece of crap."

"No, it's not." He closed the book and placed it in her lap. "Who's the asshole?"

"Huh?"

"The asshole who broke your heart?"

"No one you know."

"Hey, come on. It's me you're talking to."

"I know who I'm talking to," she snapped. "Can you take me home? I'm tired."

He ignited the engine, peeled away from the curb and drove down the road. They bumped over the train tracks, and he pulled into the parking lot by the station. At this hour, it was empty, all the commuters home for the night. He shut off the car and turned to her again. "Who's the guy?" he asked. "I want to kill him."

"Don't be so dramatic," Ruth said. "It's just a song."

"I'm always dramatic," he argued. "You heard how I sang the song you wrote. Dramatic. Like I wanted to kill someone. Well, now I want to kill that guy." He jabbed his finger at the notebook.

"Well, then, obviously, I *can't* tell you who it is. I don't want you to wind up in jail." She managed a smile. Maybe she could joke her way out of this conversation.

"All right. I won't kill him. I promise." He lifted her book and flipped through the pages again. "All these songs—so many of them. All this heartbreak. I thought we were friends."

"We are."

"Then why'd you keep all this from me? All this pain? I mean, come on! How could you not let me know you were hurting?"

"Because you—" she cut herself off before she could blurt out the truth.

But Danny heard the truth in the silence enveloping the car. "*Me*?"

"It's stupid," she mumbled. Her cheeks grew hot, her eyes hotter as they filled with tears. She turned her head to stare out the passenger window and blinked hard. "Just forget it."

"*Me*? Why didn't you tell me?"

"Tell you what?"

"If I knew you felt that way—I mean, fuck Meryl. I would have taken you to the prom."

Okay. He wasn't going to embarrass her. His willingness to camouflage the sheer awkwardness of this discussion with a light comment eased her tension slightly. "I appreciate that," she said, manufacturing another phony smile. "Fortunately, I had three cool guys as my dates."

"It should have been me." He snapped the notebook shut, tossed it back onto her lap, and cupped his hand around the back of her head. Pulling her to him, he kissed her.

Really kissed her.

Kissed her fiercely, with tongue. With as much passion as he put into the song she'd written for him.

And oh, God, she fell more deeply in love with him than ever.

Chapter Eighteen

We still joke about it, how it's thanks to Professor Leidicker that we've wound up where we are. If I'd been walking across campus after a class I loved—music theory, for instance, or nineteenth-century American literature—when Danny had confronted me, I might not have said yes.

But I'd just emerged from Leidicker's microeconomics survey, which I'd foolishly signed up for because I'd enjoyed being the band's bookkeeper and I figured this would be something similar. Stupid move. The material was as dry as a desert, and every exam was like a forced march across the Sahara, barefoot. I hated that class.

So when Danny appeared outside Green Hall and blasted me with a smile, I was receptive. When he said, "Wanna take a ride?" I was even more receptive. One thing I didn't want to do was return to my dorm room to try to make sense of my notes from Leidicker's lecture.

"What are you doing here?" I asked him once we were inside his van. Our lives had moved in such different directions after graduation, or more accurately after the summer after graduation. Trouble Ahead had broken up. Jimmy had enrolled at UMass Boston, although he said he'd still play in the band if we wanted to keep it going. I was at Wellesley. Mike surprised us all by saying he was heading to Canada, even though he couldn't get drafted since his family had already lost his brother to combat in Vietnam. "I hate this country," Mike said in his quiet, solemn way. "I'm going up to Canada, see what happens." As a drummer, Nick was in demand. He said he'd find another band to play in.

Danny was at loose ends. "No idea," he'd said whenever I asked what he was going to do next year.

We'd kept our romance a secret all that time. But once I left for college and the band no longer existed, we didn't have to hide it from anyone.

Then again, my classmates at Wellesley didn't get Danny. They all thought he was gorgeous—which, of course, he was—but he wasn't in college. How could I be a student at one of the top women's colleges in the country (actually, Wellesley thought it was the top college; we were pretty full of ourselves) and date a guy who wasn't even in school, who was living with his father and doing odd jobs and clearly floundering? Sure, they'd all like to sleep with him—at least the straight girls would—but date him? Seriously?

They didn't understand. I loved Danny. That was all that mattered.

"Where are we going to take a ride to?" I asked him.

The sun spilled through the windshield, glazing his face with light. "I was thinking California."

It was crazy. It was ridiculous.

I said yes.

So here we are now, nearly fifty years later. He's still the best-looking man I've ever known. He still has the most soulful voice. I still love him.

It took us a while to find our footing. And even longer for my parents to forgive me. David, of course, was delighted: "A great idea, putting three thousand miles between you and Mom," he said. "I'm going to join you in California as soon as I graduate." And he did.

Danny and I have talked about retiring, but we're still enjoying our work too much. He's a record producer, a virtuoso on the audio console. Musicians demand his services and pay generously for them. Sometimes, he'll sing backup or add his guitar to the tracks he's recording and mixing. Sometimes he'll ask me to sing backup or play keyboard. But mostly I compose songs—songs his clients love and record. I don't really want to sing them myself. I'm happy to write them for other people and collect my royalties. Sometimes Danny hires me to doctor a song someone else has written, but mostly I write original pieces, and between him and my *agent, they get picked up and recorded, and I make good money. Thank you, copyright law and ASCAP.*

No one ever complains about my music being girlie.

Danny and I have a wonderful life. Self-employment means we march to our own drummers—or our own guitarist and keyboard player. We work when we want. We work with whom we want. Danny owns the sound studio and rents it to others when he isn't using it.

We live in one of the canyons northwest of Los Angeles, in a cozy house with so much glass, I sometimes feel as if I'm residing in a terrarium. Cooking dinner, or reading a book, or playing the piano, I can glance up and view the woods and scruffy shrubs that surrounded us.

Our children are grown—golden, long-limbed California creatures, so much mellower than Danny and I were when we were growing up in the Boston suburbs. We've taken them to the mountains so they know what snow is, and of course they visit their grandparents in New England. But they're Californians, cool and easy, comfortable in their skin.

Miraculously, our house hasn't been consumed by fire or crushed in a mud slide. The kids have moved on, but they come to visit all the time. This wonderful abode in the canyon, filled with musical instruments and beautiful views, is still home to them.

And Danny...

~

No. This fantasy didn't work. Ruth didn't, wouldn't, couldn't run away with Danny. Not even in her dreams.

The afternoon he'd appeared on the Wellesley College campus and asked her to drive to California with him, she'd been tempted. She'd feared—correctly, as it turned out—that if she said no to him that day, seated beside him in his van, which was parked illegally in one of the permits-only lots, he would leave without her, and she would never see him again.

But she'd been more her parents' daughter than her daughter's mother. She could never have done what Maddie had done.

Not only because she'd wanted to get a top-drawer education and earn a prestigious degree or because she couldn't bear to think of the fury she'd unleash in her family if she said yes to Danny, but because she didn't trust him.

Oh, she trusted him enough. She trusted that he cared deeply about her, maybe even loved her. They'd been a couple starting soon after the junior prom and lasting throughout their entire senior year—secretly, which added to the exquisite romance of it. She'd lost her virginity to Danny, and learned, in time, how to enjoy sex. Those first few times were painful and embarrassing, but he didn't give up on her, didn't shrug and say the problem was hers, as a couple of college boyfriends who failed to bring her pleasure did. She and Danny figured it out together in the back of his van, parked on secluded dirt roads outside town, and eventually Ruth started to enjoy it.

Not that she would have cared if sex continued to hurt. She was mad about Danny. Smitten. Infatuated. Intoxicated. Pain in her crotch was a small price to pay for Danny's love.

But she didn't trust him to love her forever. He was too handsome. Too sexy. Too charismatic. When Trouble Ahead played their gigs, girls would stick to him like black flies to flypaper, and Ruth could not imagine his attraction to females ever waning. Sooner or later, he would realize the wide variety of beautiful, sexy, charismatic women available to him, and he'd wonder why he was still with Ruth Pinchas, the A-track girl with the small boobs and the thick waist and the slightly bumpy nose—the girl plain and drab enough that she'd felt obliged to grow her hair long so she would have one attractive feature.

When Danny had been dating Meryl Dennison, Ruth had understood that she wasn't in their league when it came to beauty and charisma and all of that. She'd accepted it. She had her own strengths: good grades, self-discipline, a willingness to do what had to be done, an aptitude for minimizing chaos and conflict whenever possible. She could write songs, and a few of them were pretty good. She was smart enough to dream the kinds of dreams that had a chance of coming true.

Danny Fortuna hadn't been that kind of dream. So she'd told him no.

It was the right decision at the time. She had looked down both roads and chosen the one that made the most sense to her, the one smooth enough that she wouldn't risk tripping and breaking her leg, the one that wouldn't lead her into the underbrush, where she would get stranded and lost and would eventually die of starvation or hypothermia. She would have loved a life where she could fall asleep in Danny's arms every night and wake up beside him every morning. But that was never going to happen.

Still, Danny was worth a deep sigh or two. A moment of wistful wondering.

No more than that, however. He was probably bald by now, his elegant cheeks saggy with jowls, his eyes underlined with pouches of puffy flesh. He probably wore the belt of his jeans low to accommodate his beer gut.

You can find anyone on the internet, Rainie had said. Which was why Ruth was seated at the desk in Noah's old bedroom—now the guest room; Rainie had taken over Jill's bedroom, and Maddie still slept in her childhood bedroom—with her laptop open on Noah's desk.

She started to type "Daniel Fortuna" into the Google search box, then chickened out. Better to start small, she thought, typing "Nicholas Montoya" instead. Nick wasn't small, but he occupied very little real estate in her mind.

Not surprisingly, Google listed several dozen Nicholas Montoyas. Ruth perused the list, dismissing most of the Nick Montoyas without further investigation. Many were too young. A few were too old. She assumed any Nicholas Montoya who was a doctor, a professional athlete, or a financial services executive wasn't the right one.

"I should have gone to my high school reunions," she muttered as she scrolled slowly down the list, clicking a few links, rejecting the Nick Montoyas they led her to, and then moving on. She'd missed her forty-year reunion because she'd had the flu, and her thirty-year reunion because she'd been in California that weekend for David's daughter's bat mitzvah. If there had been a tenth or twentieth reunion, she had never received an invitation.

One Nicholas Montoya looked promising. He had a LinkedIn profile which she couldn't access without an account, but he was also on Facebook. The photo didn't look much like the Nick she remembered from high school, but then, she didn't look much like the Ruth she remembered from high school either.

This Nicholas Montoya was the right age, and the banner photo showed him seated behind a drum kit. Ruth wasn't officially his Facebook friend, so she couldn't see much. But she could type "Nick Montoya drummer" into the Google search box.

There he was—playing with a band called the Boston Starlites. According to the band's website, the Boston Starlites were available for weddings, conferences, anniversaries, and "all the special moments in your life."

A wedding band. Ruth grinned. Of course Nick would have kept drumming. Drummers were always in demand.

Imagining Nick playing at all the special moments in other people's lives filled Ruth with a happy warmth. She pictured him in a tuxedo with a ruffled shirt—a lot frillier than the suit he'd worn when he'd been one of her three dates to the junior prom. She pictured him playing covers of current pop tunes for the younger attendees at whatever special event his band had been hired for, and covers of songs from his own and Ruth's era for the older attendees. She imagined plump septuagenarians tossing down their linen napkins, ignoring their hunk of filet mignon, whipped potatoes, and four stringy asparagus spears, and crowding the dance floor so they could boogie to "Bad, Bad Leroy Brown" or "Crocodile Rock" while Nick pounded on his drums.

Finding him online—finding out that he was still a drummer, still making music—brought Ruth an unexpected joy. Nick had turned out well. She couldn't wait to see how the rest of the band was doing.

Still apprehensive about looking up Danny, she typed "Michael Radowski" into the Google search box. Google produced fewer Michael Radowskis than Nicholas Montoyas, but she still had a list to plow through. She added "Canada" to the search box in the hope of narrowing down the list a bit.

Her ploy worked. She found a Michael Radowski in Vancouver, British Columbia. From the photo on his Facebook page, he looked about the right age, and he had that same thoughtful, melancholy shadow darkening his eyes. He'd never gotten over the death of his brother, she realized. *All of them over in Vietnam, never coming home, just like Tom.* Apparently, Mike never came home either.

Her cell phone rang, and she turned from the laptop to answer it.

"Mom?" Noah's voice.

"Hi, Noah," she said cautiously. Noah rarely phoned her—he used to leave it to Laura to make all the family plans when his marriage was intact—and he ought to be at work right now. She hoped he wasn't calling with bad news. "What's up?"

"I was wondering, what do you know about Rainbow going skiing in Aspen with my family?"

In the distant recesses of her brain, she could almost hear the pulse of a butterfly's wings fluttering. "She mentioned something about that," Ruth admitted.

"So, okay. *I'm* supposed to go skiing over the winter break with my family. Not Maddie's daughter."

"Well, I guess, since you moved out—" *to that ghastly little apartment, where you're shacking up with a physically fit woman closer in age to Rainie than to yourself* "—Laura must have decided to make other plans."

"Kim and I are through. I heard everything you said, Mom, and okay, you were right. I belong with Laura, with my boys. We're a family. We can make it work. But we can't make it work if Laura's flying off to Aspen with Rainbow."

Ruth would have pointed out that Noah's marital crisis was not her business, except that it was. Laura had made it her business, and then Ruth herself had made it her business when she'd stormed the ghastly apartment with Maddie, Jill, and Rainie. "Did you talk to Laura about this?"

"Of course I did. I told her I'd made a mistake; I apologized; I wanted to come home and go skiing with the family. She said too late. She'd already invited Rainie."

"Do you think she should un-invite Rainie?"

"As a matter of fact, yes. *I'm* Laura's husband."

"Rainie certainly isn't her husband," Ruth agreed. "Well, Noah, maybe just apologizing isn't enough. Maybe what you did hurt Laura terribly, and she has to heal before she can forgive you."

"How can I make her heal? I want to ski with my boys. They're my sons."

True, Aaron and Ezra were his sons. Ruth wondered how attached to those two precious boys Noah had felt when he'd been screwing around with skinny Kim.

"Honestly, Noah, this is between you and Laura."

"And Rainbow."

"Rainie received an invitation. She accepted. That's also between you and Laura."

"She doesn't even know how to ski."

"She told me Laura said she could use the bunny slope and take a few lessons."

Noah let out a long hiss of breath. "Not to be mercenary, but Aspen would be wasted on her. You don't fly to Aspen to go on the bunny slope."

"Maybe you could buy another ticket and join them," Ruth said, even as the butterfly wings in her skull fluttered so dramatically, she could almost hear them clapping together, like hands applauding a marvelous accomplishment. Were marital disharmony and disorder marvelous accomplishments? "Rainie could babysit with the boys in the evenings, giving you and Laura a chance to get away by yourselves and work through your issues."

No hiss of annoyance this time. "That's a good idea," Noah said.

He shouldn't sound so surprised that his mother could come up with a good idea. But Ruth probably shouldn't have suggested it. By suggesting it, she'd yet again made Noah's disintegrating marriage her business even more than it already was. "You'll have to talk to Laura. She may not think it's such a good idea."

"I also need to see if I can buy a ticket now. I mean, Aspen over winter break... I'll have to pay a fortune."

Not to be mercenary, Ruth thought. "If you want to repair the damage you've done, Noah, you probably shouldn't be calculating the cost in dollars and cents."

He sighed. "You're right." Another pause. "I can see why Dad would never want to leave you. You're so smart."

Ah, that must be it, Ruth thought once Noah said goodbye and she tapped her phone back to sleep. Despite the fact that their marriage had stagnated and was comfortable rather than exciting, Barry stayed with her because she was so smart.

She swiveled the desk chair back to the laptop screen. So Mike had left the U.S. and never come back. And her husband stayed with her only because she was smart. If only she'd run away with Danny—

Who wouldn't have stayed with her, probably *because* she was so smart.

She clicked her way back to Google and typed James Grogan into the search box. The list of James Grogans Google served up to her was lengthy. One was an attorney. One was a stuntman in Hollywood. She couldn't imagine her Jimmy being either of those.

Then she came upon an obituary, dated a few years ago. "James Grogan, sixty-five, after a courageous battle with pancreatic cancer..."

Oh, God. This was her Jimmy. She read the obituary through a blur of tears. Graduate of UMass Boston, rose to become a partner in a PR firm, representing local musicians, writers, and artists. Known for his friendliness, his humor, his eagerness to pull out a guitar and entertain friends at parties. Survived by his wife, two daughters, three grandchildren.

He'd lived a full life in those sixty-five years, she thought. Ah, Jimmy.

She shouldn't have listened to Rainie. Being able to find anyone online was not necessarily a blessing.

Chapter Nineteen

"That boy is not allowed in my house," Barry fumed.

"First of all, he's a man, not a boy," Ruth said. She was perched on the edge of the mattress, keeping Barry company as he changed from his business attire to jeans and a plaid flannel shirt. He'd removed his suit and dress shirt but hadn't yet donned his jeans and the flannel shirt. Ruth watched him storm around the master bedroom in his boxer briefs, his belly jiggling slightly with each step and his dark socks emphasizing the pasty winter pallor of his legs. They'd been hairier when he was younger, but as with his scalp, the hair on his calves and thighs had thinned a bit over the years.

"Second of all," she continued. "It's not just *your* house. Maddie and Rainie live here too." *And so do I*, she considered adding, but she thought it best to remain a step removed from this latest explosion, which had been triggered by Maddie's announcement, when she'd arrived home from work, that she had invited Kyle to come to the house after dinner that evening so Rainie could meet him.

"I pay the mortgage," Barry said.

"You and I both paid the mortgage, past tense," Ruth shot back, trying to keep her voice calm and level, cold water to douse his blazing anger. "We made the last payment a long time ago. And Maddie does contribute to the cost of the utilities."

"She should move out." Barry was clearly not ready to have his fire extinguished. "Right now. She should move in with Warren. She wants to entertain Kyle Jarvis? Let her entertain him there."

"He's Rainie's father," Ruth reminded him.

"Some father. He never paid a dime in child support."

"He sent Maddie some money and she refused to accept it."

This news clearly took Barry by surprise. "What?"

"Kyle told me that once he found steady work and started earning money, he sent a child support check to Maddie. She returned it and blew him off."

"Well, then, she's as much of an idiot as he is."

"She wasn't being an idiot," Ruth defended Maddie. "She was trying to prevent Kyle from staking a claim on Rainie. She didn't want him to be a part of Rainie's life."

"And now she does?"

"People change," Ruth said. "And they change their minds. I think she figured that with or without her permission, Rainie was going to meet Kyle. It would be better for all concerned if that happens here, with Maddie chaperoning."

"Some chaperone." Sniffing in disgust, he reached for his jeans and yanked them on. "*I'll* chaperone," he declared as he fussed with the fly and then the belt buckle.

"It's your house," Ruth said, relieved that he seemed to be cooling off just a little. "If you want to chaperone, who's going to stop you?"

As it turned out, Barry was going to stop himself. After a dinner which Ruth wound up making because Maddie was too busy running a load of laundry and fussing with her hair and makeup to concoct anything out of her Asian containers, Barry announced that he was going to spend the evening in the den, watching sports—basketball or hockey, or maybe both, switching back and forth with compulsive clicking on the remote control—and if Maddie wanted to entertain that son of a bitch, she could do so in the kitchen or the living room.

"You're so mature, Dad, calling him names," Maddie said, shooting her father a withering look. She picked at the chicken and roasted vegetables Ruth had thrown together, but Barry ate as enthusiastically as if he himself was going to be playing basketball or hockey.

"I call him what he deserves to be called," Barry fumed.

"His daughter is sitting here at this table," Maddie countered.

"I love being talked about in the third person," Rainie said. Unlike Maddie, she hadn't gone to special lengths with her appearance. Her hair was still dark brown with pink and blue highlights. Her face, as usual, was scrubbed clean. She wore the skinny jeans and tunic sweater she'd worn to school, and her thick-soled black boots, which Ruth believed would look more appropriate on a lumberjack than on a nearly fifteen-year-old girl.

Maddie had gone all out, however: mascara and eyeliner, rosy lipstick that remained on her lips because she was barely eating, a lace-trimmed top and slim black trousers that showed off her long legs. And high-heeled shoes, which made her legs look even longer.

Ruth hoped Barry wouldn't comment on Maddie's appearance. Ruth herself wouldn't. She doubted Maddie had any desire to seduce Kyle. More likely, she wanted to make him jealous. She wanted to remind him that he'd once desired her, that she'd once been his, and that she would never be his again, even if he still desired her. She'd opted for an eat-your-heart-out look.

Despite the tension crackling like static electricity around the kitchen table, Rainie seemed unaffected. She polished off her dinner and asked about dessert. "Do we have any Oreos?" she asked.

Barry huffed. He thought they were *his* Oreos, just as he thought this was *his* house. "We sure do," Ruth said, smiling at her granddaughter and ignoring Barry's scowl.

Everyone fled the kitchen as soon as it was time to clean up. Just as well, Ruth thought. She'd rather be alone right now than caught in the crossfire among Barry, Maddie, and Rainie—who'd done nothing wrong except help herself to his cookies and contact her long-absent father. Barry brooded and seethed, and Maddie preened and snapped. Ruth wanted to be done with all of them. Rainie less so than the others, but whenever Rainie ate cookies, she left a trail of crumbs in her wake. For some reason, she couldn't seem to eat the cookies sitting down, or place them on a plate as she walked around with them. She held a stack of them in her palm and went about her business, crumbs leaking from her mouth and hand. Ruth had taught her how the hand-vacuum worked ("You press this button and run the nozzle over the mess, and then you empty the crumbs into the trash can"). But Rainie rarely demonstrated her mastery of that challenging skill.

Fine. Let there be crumbs all over the house. Let Barry simmer and sulk and watch overpaid athletes ice-skate or bounce a ball. Let Maddie practice her most coquettish looks in the mirror. Let Rainie dribble crumbs. As long as they steered clear of Ruth, she would be happy.

No, she wouldn't. She couldn't be happy. Jimmy Grogan had died and she hadn't even known about it. Jimmy, who had plucked her out of a crowded school corridor and invited her to be in his band, who had seen beyond her A-track status and let her hang out with a group of boys she would never have spoken a word to otherwise, who had told her to play the keyboard standing up so she wouldn't look like Liberace. Jimmy, who was gregarious and fearless and who convinced stodgy restaurant owners like Mack from Mack's Clam Shack to hire Trouble Ahead. Jimmy, whose smile was so easy, so natural.

He had died, and Ruth hadn't known because she'd chosen a different path. She'd lost touch with all of them. She'd done the safe, sensible thing and become a music teacher, and married a businessman, and raised a family, and lived in a house with central air conditioning.

And still she felt chaos lurking at the edges of her vision, nibbling at the periphery of her senses. Tiny, pretty wings fluttering, churning the air.

If it weren't seven thirty at night, and dark, and December-cold, she would take a walk. Instead, she finished loading the dishwasher and wiped down the table. In the distance, she heard the doorbell ring.

"I'll get it, Dad," Maddie shouted.

"I've got it," Barry shouted back.

Ruth braced herself.

She heard the familiar squeak of the door hinges, and then Barry's voice: "Kyle Jarvis."

"Hello, Mr. Singer," Kyle said, his voice so low Ruth almost couldn't hear it.

The clamor of footsteps on the stairs. "Is he here?" Rainie hollered.

Ruth didn't want to listen to this, any of it. She toweled her hands dry, then left the kitchen and ducked up the stairs, doing her best to avoid the front hall. Voices drifted up from the first floor, everyone talking at once, a jumble of sound. She could make out only a few scattered words, for which she was grateful. Honestly, this was one mess she didn't want to clean up.

Instead, she entered Noah's old bedroom and closed the door. Her laptop was still on his desk. She settled in the chair, tapped a key to wake it from sleep mode, and Googled "Daniel Fortuna."

Chapter Twenty

"If a farmer and the Marshmallow Man from *Ghostbusters* had a baby, this is what it would look like," Rainie said as she emerged from the dressing room and modeled the ski pants she'd tried on. Her expression was sour. But the dark blue ski pants, well insulated and waterproof, with adjustable suspenders looped over her narrow shoulders, looked adorable.

Ruth would never say so. In Rainie's mind, "adorable" applied to pink teddy bears, not apparel she would actually have to wear. "It's a good fit," Ruth said.

Rainie wrinkled her nose. "I don't see why I can't wear jeans when I ski."

"Jeans would get wet."

"I could wear leggings under the jeans."

"The leggings would get wet." Ruth shrugged. "Aunt Laura said you need ski pants and a parka for the trip. If you don't want to wear those things, you can tell Aunt Laura, 'Thanks for the invitation, but I'm going to stay home.'"

Rainie's nose returned to its usual unwrinkled state, but her lips curved in a pout of resignation. "All right. Can I get the ugly parka that matches these ugly pants?"

"Yes. You can have the ugliest outerwear on the slopes."

Rainie vanished into the dressing room and Ruth pulled out her credit card. Maddie ought to be paying for Rainie's ski togs, but she was at work right now, and somewhat detached from the entire Aspen trip. In fact, she'd seemed somewhat detached from the world ever since Kyle Jarvis's visit.

Ruth had been eager to interrogate Maddie about her reunion with Kyle, but she hadn't dared. She knew Maddie would fly into a fury and tell Ruth to mind her own business.

Picking Rainie up after school today and driving her directly to the sporting goods store on Route 9, she'd attempted to ask her a few discreet questions about Kyle's visit, but Rainie had been too busy ranting about a surprise quiz in her biology class to answer.

Maybe once Ruth spent a boatload of money on the farmer-Marshmallow-Man skiing outfit, Rainie would be more forthcoming.

The bill paid and the ski pants and parka crammed into a handled shopping bag with the store's outdoorsy-sports logo printed on it, Ruth and Rainie strolled out to the parking lot. "Happy Hanukkah," Ruth said dryly as Rainie climbed into the car and balanced the bulky bag in her lap.

"Is this my Hanukkah gift? Seriously? Because I didn't even want these things."

"You'll want them in Aspen, and you should behave graciously when I spend money on you. And yes, you'll get something else for Hanukkah."

Placated, Rainie fastened her seatbelt.

Ruth wondered whether Noah had been able to score a plane ticket to Aspen for himself. She wondered whether he'd discussed with Laura his desire to accompany her and the boys to Aspen. She wondered where Rainie would fit into all that.

But those questions were for another day—and for Laura and Noah, not Rainie. Instead, Ruth said, "You still haven't mentioned how you feel about meeting your dad the other day. Are you glad he came by?"

"Yeah. He seems like a nice guy."

Ruth steered out of the parking lot, remaining silent, giving Rainie room to expand on her answer.

"He got teary when he saw me. I thought that was...I don't know. Corny but kind of sweet."

Ruth nodded.

"Mom got teary too. Mostly, they looked at each other and got teary. Every now and then, they looked at me and got teary." She shrugged. "I don't know why my mom left him."

"They were young," Ruth said tactfully. "Probably too young to have a baby. And they didn't have much money."

"Mom said they didn't have any money at all. Kyle said she should have given him a chance. He would have found work. Is it okay if I call him Kyle? I don't think I'm ready to call him Dad."

"Of course."

"Mom told him about Warren. That was pretty boring. But what can you expect, if Warren is the topic of discussion?"

"Warren is a nice guy too."

"Nice and boring. He's an *accountant*," Rainie said, as if accountants were on a par with pimps or proctologists or biology teachers who sprang surprise quizzes on their students. "Kyle runs a bar. That's cool."

"Terrible hours," Ruth said. "Bars are open late at night."

"If you're a night owl, those aren't terrible hours," Rainie said sensibly. "He had to go back home—he lives in New Hampshire—but he said he wants to see me again. He said he wants to spend more time with me."

"How do you feel about that?"

"I think it's cool. Maybe he'll teach me how to mix cocktails."

"You're too young."

Rainie laughed, leaving Ruth to realize she'd been joking. "After he left, Mom told me he was her first love. As if I couldn't figure that out." She fidgeted with the bag on her lap for a moment, the paper rattling as her fingers pinched it. Her smile faded. "What makes first love different from second love?"

"Everything about first love is new," Ruth said. "Like new clothes the first time you wear them. First love is all clean and sparkly, no damage. It seems perfect."

"But it isn't?"

"No love is perfect. First love is exciting—and then you get older and realize that exciting isn't necessarily what you want."

"I want exciting," Rainie declared.

"You do now. When you get older, you might feel differently."

"Then I hope I never get older. I guess I don't have much choice, though. Either I get older or I die young, and I don't want to die young." Rainie contemplated the idea for a moment, then asked, "Was Grampa your first love?"

Ruth shook her head.

"I didn't think so. I love him, but he's not very exciting."

"No, he's not." *Not the way Danny Fortuna was.*

"There's this boy," Rainie said. "Nina told me she heard from Matt Selzner that he might like me."

"Matt Selzner might like you?" Ruth scrambled to recall if she'd ever heard his name before.

"No. Matt told Nina this *other* boy might like me."

"I see." Ruth suppressed a smile. "Do you like this other boy?"

"I don't know him. I mean, I know who he is, but we've never talked or anything." Rainie stilled her hands on the bag and leaned back in the passenger seat, her gaze on the road ahead. "I guess that's kind of exciting, right?"

"I suppose so." Ruth patted Rainie's shoulder. She was wearing only a hooded sweatshirt over her long-sleeved T-shirt and jeans. Given a choice, she'd probably wear those very garments on the slopes in Aspen. As it was, Ruth shivered just looking at her. According to the dashboard screen, the air temperature outside was twenty-eight degrees. "If you want to get to know this boy," she told Rainie, "you don't have to wait for him to make the first move. You can walk over to him and say hello."

"You don't think that would be too—what's the word? Forward?"

In Ruth's day, approaching a boy and making the first move would have been considered heresy. An aggressive girl was labeled a slut, or maybe a dyke. Fortunately, Rainie was growing up in a much more enlightened era. "Being friendly is never a mistake," she said.

"I don't know if I'd like him," Rainie conceded. "He's kind of cute, though."

"Cute is a definite plus."

Rainie lapsed into thought for a moment, then said, "I think I'm ready for my first love. But if the idea of first love is that it seems perfect, I have to make sure the guy is perfect, right?"

"No guy is perfect," Ruth pointed out.

"Okay, but he should be clean and sparkly. He should be exciting."

"You won't know if this boy is all those things if you don't say hello to him."

"He should say hello to me." Rainie studied her fingernails. They were polished with a glittering turquoise enamel. "Or maybe Matt Selzner made the whole thing up."

"Maybe Matt Selzner is the one who has a crush on you," Ruth suggested. "Maybe he concocted a story about this other boy as a way to test the waters, to see how you'd react to being the object of a boy's interest."

That possibility clearly hadn't occurred to Rainie. She mulled it over. "Matt's cute," she said.

When you were fourteen, *cute* was essential. *Cute* remained crucial well past fourteen too, Ruth acknowledged. She was still sighing about how cute Danny was when she'd been a freshman at Wellesley. Still mooning about his cuteness after she'd sent him away, aware that her decision not to flee impulsively to California with him would mean she would never see him again.

Barry was cute, too, in his own way. But she didn't want to think about him as cute. She was still angry with him for declaring that their house was *his* house. Old-hippie Barry was a terrific person. Grampa Barry was a teddy bear. Businessman Barry, no. When he barked orders, when he spoke as if he were the expert, the only person in the vicinity with the wisdom to evaluate the situation accurately, she didn't find him the least bit cute.

"Maybe I shouldn't go skiing with Aunt Laura," Rainie said. "What if Matt calls me over winter break and I'm halfway across the country?"

"You'll have your cell phone with you. He can call you there as easily as he can call you in Brentwood," Ruth assured her. "And if you're halfway across the country, you'll seem more interesting to him. More exotic."

"More exciting," Rainie said, her smile now warm and genuine, her eyes as sparkly as new love itself. "Yeah, that sounds good."

~

Maddie seemed distracted as she meandered around the kitchen, performing a dinner-preparation ballet graceful enough to appear on the Boston Opera House stage, even though dinner wasn't exactly being prepared. She glided to the refrigerator, pulled several plastic containers from a shelf, pirouetted, and deposited the containers on the center island with an unselfconscious flourish of her fingers. When she bent over to pull a pan from a lower cabinet, she extended her leg behind her, pointing her toe.

"We bought ski clothes," Rainie reported as she followed Ruth into the kitchen from the garage. "They're ugly but Aunt Laura says I have to wear them when we go to Aspen."

"They'll keep her warm and dry," Ruth said, wondering whether she should present Maddie with the charge card receipt.

Given Maddie's lack of focus, she probably wouldn't even look at it.

"I'm going to cut the tags off this stuff," Rainie announced, then departed from the kitchen with her bag. Her footsteps were light and bouncy on the stairs. She was probably contemplating whether Matt Selzner might like her, whether he might turn out to be her sparkly first love.

Ruth remained in the kitchen, unbuttoning her jacket and watching Maddie wander around the room in a daze. "Is your father home yet?" Ruth asked.

"I don't know."

"Are *you* home?" Ruth asked.

Maddie flashed a look of annoyance her way.

"You seem out of it," Ruth said.

"I'm trying to figure out what I'm going to do when Rainie is in Colorado. Dr. Bromberg is closing the office for a week between Christmas and New Year's."

"I assume you'll spend New Year's with Warren," Ruth said, her voice twisting into a question when she realized, from Maddie's expression, that this might not be a safe assumption.

"I've been talking to Kyle," Maddie said. "He's back at his bar in New Hampshire—" she wrinkled her nose at the word *bar* in exactly the way Rainie had wrinkled her nose at the way she looked in the ski pants "—but we need to work some things out. I don't know if I'll have time to see Warren."

Ruth experienced a twinge of apprehension. "What things do you need to work out?"

"Well, visitation rights. He still wants to contribute child support—"

"Which would be very nice," Ruth interjected, thinking of the charge slip in her wallet.

"But it would give him a say in Rainbow's life. He and I have to work through that."

Would it take a week? The full week between the Christmas and New Year's holidays? Couldn't they figure this out with a couple of phone calls? Ruth sincerely hoped they wouldn't have to hire lawyers.

"Does Warren know that Rainie's father has surfaced?" Ruth asked, choosing her words carefully.

"Rainbow is *my* daughter, not Warren's," Maddie snapped.

Well, that was a change. Hadn't Maddie been campaigning to get Rainie to move in with her and Warren, to feel as if Warren's house was her new, true home?

"I'm sure you'll be able to hammer out a reasonable arrangement with Kyle," Ruth said, if only to turn down the heat under Maddie's boiling mood. "He's a lot more mature now than he was when Rainie was born. You are, too," she hastily added when Maddie shot her another irritated look.

"What did I do with the edamame?"

The non-sequitur startled Ruth, but she didn't comment on it. Maddie's thoughts clearly weren't on the plastic tubs she'd pulled out of the refrigerator, none of which contained edamame. "What are you planning to cook?" she asked instead, keeping her tone light and cheerful.

"How the hell do I know?" Maddie retorted. Her cell phone, sitting on the counter by the sink, played a lilting jingle and she glanced at the screen. "Shit," she muttered. "It's Warren." She scooped up the phone, swiped to connect the call, and pressed it to her ear. "Hi," she said in an unhappy voice as she wandered into the dining room.

Ruth gazed at the food containers on the island. Would any of them spoil if they were left out of the refrigerator too long? Did she care?

No. She wanted to be done caring about Maddie's meal preparations, Kyle's childcare proposals, Rainie's incipient love life, and Barry's grouchiness. She wanted to be done with all of them.

She wanted a turret room with a door that locked. And she wanted all those damned butterflies halfway around the world to find contentment by landing on pretty Asian flowers and sitting perfectly still, not daring to flutter their wings.

Chapter Twenty-One

While the rest of Brentwood plunged into the frenzy of the Christmas holiday, with residents stringing lights from the eaves of their houses and the branches of their trees, wrapping their mailbox posts with garlands of fake greenery, and adorning their front yards with wrought-iron reindeer and inflated Santas, Ruth felt her life devolve into disorder. Rainie was alternately freaking out about her ski trip—"I'm gonna look like a dork on the ski slope, and I don't even know how to ski"—and her nascent love life, spending hours texting with her friends about whether Matt Selzner was cuter than the other boy who, according to Matt, liked her. Ruth had to drive her to school several times when she missed the bus because she was dithering over whether to wear eyeliner. "Do I look like a raccoon, Grammy?" she'd ask, squinting at her reflection in the mirror above the bathroom sink. "Do I look too Goth?"

"You look like a girl who's going to miss the bus," Ruth would mutter. This was more often than not an accurate critique.

Maddie was behaving weirdly too. She wasn't her usual mercurial self. Too often, she abandoned a project without completing it, whether that project was fixing dinner or running a load of laundry or pulling her car all the way into the garage when she arrived home after work. She sighed heavily. She spent long stretches on the phone in her bedroom, her voice too muffled by the closed door for Ruth to figure out whom she was talking to.

Barry fumed. "I don't know what's gotten into her, but it sure as hell better get out of her soon," he'd rage as he paraded around the bedroom in his boxer briefs, transitioning from his office persona to his home persona, although lately the office persona held sway no matter what he was wearing. "She's acting like an idiot."

"She's worried about allowing Kyle into Rainie's life," Ruth explained.

Barry scowled. "She should have been worried about allowing Kyle into her panties sixteen years ago," he said. "It's a little late in the day to worry about his being a part of Rainie's life now. Do you know what she did this morning? She turned on the coffee maker but forgot to put water into it. If I hadn't come into the kitchen and noticed that the brew light was on and nothing was dripping into the pot, she probably would have set the house on fire."

Ruth didn't think the coffee maker could overheat enough to ignite the engineered stone counter on which it sat, let alone the entire house, but she agreed that Maddie could have destroyed the coffee maker.

"When I yelled at her, she gave me this blank stare, like I was speaking Swahili. Where were you this morning when all this was going on?"

"Trying to wake Rainie up," Ruth told him.

"And that girl..." He wagged his finger in the general direction of the bedroom door, as if Rainie were standing on the other side. "Her head is in the clouds. Her jeans are too tight. She's wearing makeup."

"I'm trying to guide her away from the makeup," Ruth said. "I keep telling her less is more."

"Less. Ha. I think she's added some orange to her hair too."

"No, that's just the pink. It looks sort of orange in some light."

"I never thought I'd say it," Barry muttered, "but I can't wait for that fucking wedding. I want them out of my house."

It's not your house, Ruth wanted to shout, but she pressed her lips together and took a long, deep breath. What good would riling Barry further do? She wanted peace and calm, not high-decibel fury.

Noah phoned her while she was walking with Coral the following morning and said, "I'm going to Aspen." She told him she was happy to hear that and asked how Laura felt about it. He told her he had to meet with a client and would call her back. He didn't call her back.

Coral spent the rest of their walk moaning because she'd gained three pounds. "I'm so ashamed," she confessed. "I went to Hilda's for dinner with Lee last week and I put dressing on my salad."

"At least you were eating a salad," Ruth said.

"Not just vinaigrette, either. Roquefort dressing. All that cream, and chunks of cheese. God, it was so good. And a steak, which Lee gave me grief about. And I put butter on my baked potato. I guess I'm lucky I only gained three pounds. You and I need to go to Hilda's for lunch so you can make sure I don't put any dressing on my salad."

More crazed days. More of Rainie oversleeping, overthinking her eyeliner, overanalyzing her social status. More of Maddie wandering around the house in a daze, making Ruth wonder how she was functioning at work. Was she scraping tartar off her patients' teeth or puncturing their gums with her dental implements? Would Dr. Bromberg fire her for endangering his customers?

And more of Barry raving, growling, declaring he wanted his daughter and granddaughter out of *his* house, which in turn infuriated Ruth, although she suppressed her anger. No point in venting. The atmosphere of the house—*her* house—was already choked with resentment and indignation, as if it were a toxic smog. She could barely breathe.

She phoned Jill. "Everyone's driving me crazy," she said.

"I hope you don't expect me to make you sane," Jill responded. "That would take years of therapy. And I'm not supposed to treat my next of kin. Professional ethics and all."

"The next of kin I'm most worried about is Maddie. She's acting like a ditz."

"She's always been a ditz," Jill said.

"No, she hasn't. She's been argumentative and egotistical and impulsive, but not ditzy. Lately, though, she's zoning out, forgetting things, neglecting things. I'm afraid she's going to lose her job if she keeps this up."

"Do you think she's on drugs?" Jill asked.

It occurred to Ruth that Maddie might have access to painkillers at the dentist's office. But she doubted that was Maddie's problem. "It's more that she seems distracted and unfocused. Almost as if she doesn't know where she is, or who she is."

"Like she's in a fugue state?" Jill said.

Ruth wasn't sure what a fugue state was, but it sounded lovely. Musical. Once she mastered the Bach inventions, maybe she ought to tackle some of his fugues and get herself into a fugue state.

"Just kidding," Jill said. "I'm sure she's not experiencing a dissociative fugue. It's probably just drugs."

So Ruth decided she was done. Done with all of them. Done with the volatility of her loved ones—assuming she still loved them, which was open to question at the moment. Done with the moods, the madness, the plunges in barometric pressure that warned of a destructive storm blowing her way.

~

Fortunately, the house emptied out over the winter break. The day after Rainie's final day of the fall semester, Laura and her sons pulled into the driveway to pick up Rainie and her carry-on suitcase and backpack, into which she'd managed to pack enough clothing for a week, recharging cords for a half-dozen devices, and her puffy ski apparel. They'd driven off to the airport, Ruth standing on the front porch and waving at the car as it receded down Jefferson Road.

Not long after Rainie's departure, Maddie packed a travel bag as well and announced that she would be spending the week with Warren. "We have stuff to deal with," she'd said cryptically. Ruth was relieved that Maddie didn't enlighten her on what that stuff might be. Her guess was that Maddie didn't want Rainie to know she was sleeping with her fiancé before the wedding, which was ridiculous because Rainie surely could guess that this was what adults on the cusp of marriage usually did. Rainie wasn't a fool.

But Ruth felt much less wistful as she waved Maddie off than she'd felt waving Rainie off.

Barry opted to work during the holiday week. If Rainie had been home that week, he might have taken a few vacation days so he could enjoy some Grampa time with her. He used to take the entire week off when Ruth was teaching. That week had been a vacation week for her, and as school children, Noah, Jill, and Maddie were home for the week as well. The family would play in the snow, or go to the movies together, or enjoy their Hanukkah gifts. Barry would reset his emotional thermostat to old-hippie and be the playful dad, popping jumbo bags of popcorn in the microwave, challenging the children to marathon games of Monopoly, teaching the dog to catch snowballs between his teeth and then laughing when the snowballs vanished in a puff of white.

But since everyone was gone this year, he told Ruth he saw no point in wasting vacation days by staying home that week. Hanging out with Ruth, apparently, would have been a waste.

She was pleased with his decision. One week alone in the house, without anyone to take care of, anyone to rouse out of bed, anyone to monitor to make sure the coffee maker wasn't turned on when there was no water in the reservoir, seemed like bliss. For one blessed week, she could be rid of all the drama.

She had grown used to having an empty house during the daytime, when Rainie was in school and Maddie and Barry were at work. Four months into her retirement, she relished the peace that descended upon the house—which became *her* house, not Barry's, when she was the only person inside it. The first few weeks of September, she had felt addled and rootless, not sure of how she was supposed to spend time she used to spend teaching second- and third-graders how to sing rounds, teaching fourth-graders the physics of overtones and harmonics, and teaching fifth-graders the mathematical structure of Bach's fugues. "They're kind of like those rounds I used to have you singing in second and third grade," she would tell her older students, at least half of whom seemed intensely interested. The other half were simply happy not to be in their home classrooms, learning about fractions and the mass migrations spawned by the Great Depression.

But Ruth was comfortable in her retirement now. She could enjoy her long exercise walks every morning when the weather allowed, and read books in the den without hearing the babble of sportscaster voices spilling from the television set, and she could play the piano as loudly as she wanted.

Barry's mood was practically jovial when he arrived home from work the first night after Rainie and Maddie had both decamped. Maybe he was thinking about Maddie's romantic week with Warren. Maybe he'd had an especially productive day at work. Maybe, like Ruth, he appreciated the tranquility of the house when only he and Ruth were in it. In any case, when they were upstairs in their bedroom, Ruth seated as usual on the bed while he stripped off his suit, dress shirt, and tie, he didn't reach for his jeans and flannel shirt. Instead, he plopped himself down onto the bed next to her, clad only in his briefs, and nuzzled her neck. "Alone at last," he murmured.

Alone, yes. Also tired, and distracted by thoughts of Rainie with Laura and the boys so far away, and Noah hoping to join them, and Maddie and Warren and Kyle and how chaotic it all seemed. "I've got dinner in the oven," she told him. "Chicken, baked potatoes, steamed green beans." A regular dinner, nothing out of containers with Asian writing on them.

"Go turn off the oven," he whispered. "We'll eat later."

They could eat later. They didn't have to schedule dinner around when Rainie would be home from her afterschool activities, how much time she would need to do her homework, whether Maddie had a plan with Warren or an appointment with the wedding planner to discuss menus and seating arrangements and strapless dresses for the bridesmaids.

Maybe some gentle sex—or some wild sex—would cheer Ruth up. It had been a while.

She went downstairs to turn off the oven. When she returned to the bedroom, Barry was already naked, lying on his back, his head cushioned by the pillows. He was still a good-looking man, despite his paunch. Yet the paunch annoyed Ruth—not in and of itself, but because it reminded her that she abstained from salad dressing and took her walks and went on a diet if she gained more than a few pounds, while he indulged in potato chips and Oreos and whatever else his appetite demanded.

Not a romantic thought.

She got undressed and ducked into the bathroom to find the lubricating cream that made this activity possible. Once she was greased up, she joined Barry on the bed, climbed on top of him to spare his aging knees, and brought him pleasure. Afterwards, he closed his arms around her, kissed her hair, made soft, soothing noises, told her he loved her.

This should have made her feel better. It just made her feel... tired.

The next day, Ruth walked her usual Wednesday route, paying homage to the Victorian that she and Barry didn't buy and waving to the house across the street, where she imagined Maddie's friend Anne—the un-Kyle—had lived. She reminded herself that Kyle had grown up, that he'd been very polite the morning he'd visited her, that Rainie seemed to like him. That if Maddie hadn't met Kyle, Rainie wouldn't exist.

That was the trouble with wishing things had been different. Taking the other road would mean missing out on everything, both good and bad, on the road you *had* taken.

Back home after a brisk five-mile power walk in the frigid late-December morning, she showered, washed her hair, and dressed in soft jeans and a thick wool sweater. The house was still and silent. No one to take care of. No one to make demands on her. She was happier alone than she'd been in Barry's arms last night.

She entered the living room and strode directly to the piano. Pushing the piano bench out of her way, she played "Tom" standing up, belting out the vocals, her voice resounding through the living room. She played a song Jimmy had written about getting stoned on Saturday night, and teared up a little when she acknowledged that he was dead. She worked her way through all the original songs in Trouble Ahead's repertory, ending with "King of the World."

The songs she'd written back then weren't bad. Why had she stopped writing songs?

She hadn't stopped completely. In the first year of her contract with the Brentwood School District, she'd written a school song for each of the three primary schools where she worked. They were simple, bouncy songs in major keys, reflecting joy and exuberance, not angst and adolescent misery. *We go to the Oak Street School, where the teachers are great and the students are cool!* And *English, math, and science, too! Longford School's the place for me and you!*

Damn, they were really bad. Even as she played the simple chords on the piano, she had to laugh.

If she had to write a song now, what would she write? Not about boys taking sexual advantage of girls. Not about loved ones lost in the Vietnam War. Definitely not about how cool a primary school's students were.

She abandoned the piano for the basement, moved directly to the shelf where she stored the box containing her memorabilia from her high school years, and lowered the box to the floor. Her yearbook was no longer in it—it was still somewhere in the clutter of Rainie's bedroom—but the notebook in which Ruth used to write her songs ought to be inside the box. She rummaged through its contents—the diploma, the mortarboard tassel, gold-embossed certificates she received for being inducted into the Honor Society and for her invaluable contributions to the school's Glee Club—until she found the weathered old notebook, held shut by a desiccated rubber band that cracked and dissolved into crumbs when she touched it.

She gathered the brittle bits of rubber band off the floor, hoisted the carton back onto the shelf, and carried her notebook upstairs.

She could still write a song. At least she could try.

She detoured to the kitchen to grab a pencil, then carried the notebook to the living room and settled on the piano bench. What mattered to her now? What tapped into her deepest feelings? What *were* her deepest feelings? Weariness? Resentment? Longing?

Bewilderment at how she'd wound up here, instead of in a turret room, instead of on a concert stage, instead of with her first true love?

New love is scary. Old love is wary, she wrote. *It's the faded sofa in the den, lived in, worn out. It's less passion than doubt, a sigh, not a shout. It's not cheap wine but expensive gin, it's "this is what is" rather than "could have been," New love is chaotic. Old love is hypnotic. It puts you in a trance. But you know all the steps, so you keep doing the dance.*

As if she were fifteen again, she played with the words, crossed a few out, added a few, scribbled question marks in the margins. She felt her mouth twist in disgust, then spring into a smile. She played chord progressions on the piano—less ordinary, more daring progressions than in the songs she'd written for the band. This was *her* song, and she was older and, if not wiser, at least more knowledgeable. More experienced. More cynical.

If it was a girlie song, so be it. In the life she was living, the life she'd chosen, the road she'd taken, there were no boys to criticize her for writing a girlie song. There was no band. No Trouble Ahead.

Only Ruth.

Chapter Twenty-Two

The second time they had sex that week, Barry paid attention enough to question Ruth afterward. "You didn't come?"

"It's all right." Five minutes ago, rocking up and down on him, she'd made him happy. She didn't want to make him happier by engaging in an awkward conversation with him. Couldn't he just let her cuddle and doze? She'd done all the work, after all. She was tired.

"You always used to come."

"No I didn't."

"Most of the time," he insisted.

She sighed. Fine. Barry wanted to have the awkward conversation, so they'd have the awkward conversation. "Probably half the time. It's all right, Barry. I'm older. My body doesn't do what it used to do."

"Maybe you need to take some hormones."

Anger flared inside her, but she shoved it back into its little box in her soul. She'd gotten through menopause without taking hormones. She certainly wasn't going to start taking them now.

Couldn't a woman just get older? Couldn't she let her body be what it was? Wasn't taking synthetic estrogen to make her ovaries younger the same thing as getting plastic surgery to make her face younger? Why couldn't she look her age, both inside and out?

She reminded herself that Barry was simply trying to be helpful. This was his idea of concern. Either that, or he felt guilty because he had come—he always did—and she hadn't.

In any case, she was now too agitated to cuddle and doze. She rolled out of his arms, off the bed, and strode into the bathroom to wash up. Tomorrow Rainie would be home. So, presumably would Maddie. Ruth could focus on accommodating Maddie and Rainie as well as Barry. She would be back in wife-mom-grandmother mode, stagnant and comfortable. She wouldn't have to be sex-goddess anymore.

"What did I say?" Barry called after her. He sounded annoyed, too—irritated that she wasn't overwhelmed by gratitude thanks to his sensitivity and solicitousness.

She could spin around and tell him exactly what he'd said: that there was something wrong with her, some malfunction, because she was here, living this life in this body. But then they would have a fight, and she didn't want to fight. She just wanted the conversation to end. She wanted peace and calm.

"It's fine," she told him. "I'm fine. Just tired."

~

When she heard a car slow to a halt by the curb in front of the house the next evening, she prepared herself for the surge of noisy energy she was sure Rainie would sweep into the house. While she'd been in Aspen, Rainie had sent Ruth daily texts so brief, reading them was like deciphering a foreign language. "Snow pants rock!" "Off the baby hill today!" "Out to dinner, steaks on Uncle Noah." "It IS Matt!" "Aaron wants me to explain Emily Dickinson." As best Ruth could figure, Rainie had a good time.

But instead of letting herself in—had she forgotten to bring her house key with her?—she rang the doorbell. Ruth abandoned the bunch of romaine she had been tearing into a salad bowl and hurried to the front door to let Rainie in. Swinging it open, she found herself face to face with Jill and the twins. "I'm sorry I had to bring the kids," Jill said, stepping inside and moving out of the way so Emma and Nate could race into the house, shrieking about some cartoon they wanted to see on TV.

"Grampa's watching the news," Ruth warned them as they vanished into the den. Turning back to Jill, Ruth said, "I didn't know you were coming. What's going on?"

"Maddie told me to come. She didn't tell you I was coming?"

"Maddie isn't here. She said she'd be here in time for dinner, but she's been staying with Warren this week while Rainie was in Aspen with Laura and the boys. And Noah," she added, although she couldn't tell, from Rainie's cryptic texts, whether Noah had been welcomed into the condo with his family or had been relegated to the overpriced-hotel equivalent of a doghouse.

"Well," Jill said, unwrapping a watered-silk scarf from around her neck, "Maddie said she needed me here, it was very important. *Essential*, that was her word."

"Everything's always so emphatic with Maddie," Ruth reminded Jill. She couldn't help wondering why, if it was essential that Jill be here, Maddie hadn't bothered to mention anything to Ruth.

"Ben's playing in his weekly basketball game," Jill continued, "and I couldn't find a babysitter on such short notice."

As if on cue, the twins screamed something unintelligible. "Indoor voices," Barry reminded them.

"We're starving!" Nate's shrill outdoor voice pierced the air, and then the twins bounded out of the den and back into the entry hall. "Grammy, we're *starving!*" Emma announced.

"I didn't have time to fix them dinner," Jill said apologetically. She pulled off her coat and stuffed the scarf into a sleeve. "Kids, please take off your jackets."

Emma and Nate did as they were told, shoving their jackets into Jill's hands. "We're starving, Mom," Nate said.

"We're starving, Grammy," Emma added.

"So I hear." Ruth glanced helplessly at Jill.

"Just throw something together," Jill suggested. "They'll eat it. They don't have sophisticated palates."

"What's that, Mom?" Nate asked. "A *fisticated pallick?*"

"Sophisticated palate," Jill enunciated, clearly amused by her son. "It means you care what things taste like."

"I don't care," Nate said. "I'm so hungry, I could eat dog food."

"You could not. You're such a liar," Emma yelled. "I'm so hungry I could eat a stick."

"I'm so hungry," Nate yelled even louder, aiming to top Emma in both hyperbole and volume, "I could eat two gorillas!"

"All right," Ruth said, patting the air with her hands to quiet them down. "I guess I can throw together some spaghetti."

"I'm so hungry I could eat spaghetti!" Nate bellowed, and then he and Emma tore down the hall and back into the den.

They nearly knocked Maddie over as she entered the hall from the kitchen. She must have parked in the garage—an improvement over those weird days when she'd forget to pull her car into the garage and left it sitting in the driveway, leaving barely enough space for Barry to steer his Audi past her Toyota and into his own garage bay. "Oh, good," she said to Jill. "You're here." Her vibrant scrub top, visible when she unzipped her parka, brightened the entry. To Ruth, she asked, "Have Rainie and Noah arrived yet?"

"Not yet."

Maddie fished her cell phone out of her oversized hybrid tote bag/purse and tapped the screen. "I've been monitoring their flight. They landed—" she squinted at the screen "—a half hour ago. They should be here any minute. I'm going to change into some real clothes. And then I have to run a load of laundry. I've been gone all week," she added for Jill's sake.

"I don't know what's going on," Ruth told Jill, pivoting and heading for the kitchen to start the spaghetti. She could brown up some chopped beef for meat sauce, and sauté diced garlic in olive oil for anyone who didn't want meat. She could expand the salad, although the twins probably wouldn't eat any of that.

Jill joined her in the kitchen. As usual, she was dressed too nicely to perform any messy tasks, but Ruth welcomed her company as much as she could welcome a sudden influx of family after a week when she had to take care of only one person and the butterflies in Asia were apparently tucked peacefully inside their cocoons.

"Maddie does not seem to be in a dissociative fugue state," Jill declared. "A bit manic, perhaps."

Ruth shrugged as she filled her biggest pot with water. "This is the first I've seen her all week."

"The prospect of doing laundry never makes me manic," Jill said dryly.

Ruth shrugged again. "Dr. Bromberg is a stickler for clean scrubs. Which, I suppose, is a good thing. I wouldn't want a dental hygienist in a dirty uniform messing with my teeth."

A rattling noise in the front hall alerted her to the arrival, finally, of Rainie and Noah's family. Ruth set the pot on one of the larger burners, clamped the lid on it, and turned on the heat. Then she peered down the hall. Noah and Laura stood together, their sons swarming around them, as Rainie called out, "We're home!"

The next fifteen minutes were bedlam, everyone speaking at once. The twins and Ezra chased each other around the dining room table. Rainie declared that ski pants were the greatest invention since the computer because they kept her so warm and dry while she was skiing, and she wanted to take ski lessons now so she could qualify for Black Diamond trails. Barry nagged her to go upstairs and unpack her bag. Aaron quietly asked his Aunt Jill if liking poetry meant he was gay. Laura, when Ruth discreetly asked her how she and Noah were doing, answered, "Let's just say we're doing."

Noah overheard the question and elaborated: "We're doing great."

Laura shot him a lethal look, then turned back to Ruth, who had broken several pre-shaped hamburger patties into a skillet to brown. "He broke up with Kim and gave me flowers, which he bought at the Aspen airport. Obviously, all is forgiven." Sarcasm bathed her voice in a bitter, sticky sauce.

"We're working on things," Noah explained. "I'm committed to our marriage."

"He needs to atone some more," Laura said, then reached into the salad bowl and plucked out a black olive, which she popped into her mouth.

"I'm sure you guys want to go home," Ruth said. "It's been a long trip and you've got unpacking to do too."

"Maddie sent me a text and said she needed us here," Noah said.

"I'd rather be home unpacking," Laura muttered. "In case you were wondering, Madelyn is not my favorite sister-in-law."

"I'll let Jill know," Ruth joked. "She'll be thrilled."

Eventually, Ruth produced enough food to satisfy eleven people, including two six-year-olds who were hungry enough to eat gorillas and sticks. At the head of the dining room table, Barry beamed at the food as if it were another gourmet Thanksgiving feast instead of what Ruth had managed to scrape together—two heaping bowls of linguini, two sauces, salad, and three previously frozen submarine rolls, which she'd cut into small circles and topped with garlic, oil, and grated Romano cheese. She would have scolded Maddie for inviting people to dinner without alerting her, but then, this was still Maddie's house, and would likely be her house for another few months. Unless her week with Warren had been so sweet and romantic that she decided to move in with him in advance of the wedding.

"So," Maddie said once everyone was settled and Jill had fixed plates of spaghetti for her twins and Ezra. Maddie's eyes were bright, her cheeks rosy. She definitely didn't seem fugue-ish, or even detached and disoriented, the way she'd been behaving a week ago. "I'm so glad everyone is here."

"We do have a lot of unpacking to do," Laura reminded her as she spooned thick red meat sauce onto her pasta.

"And we have news for you too," Noah said. "Laura and I can be figurines on your cake."

"That's great," Maddie said rather unenthusiastically. A distant buzzer sounded. "Oops—that's the washing machine. Gotta put my clothing in the drier. I'll be right back."

"Why are you doing your laundry here?" Barry called after her as she bolted from the table. The laundry room was just beyond the kitchen, and he leaned back in his chair so he could holler to her. "Why didn't you do your laundry at Warren's house? He doesn't have a washing machine?"

"Does it bother you that I want clean clothes?" Maddie hollered back.

"It bothers me that you bring your laundry here." Barry straightened his chair and scowled down the table to Ruth. "Like a college kid, she comes home with a bag of dirty laundry."

"You want me to pay you for the detergent I'm using?" Maddie shouted. "Send me a bill. Plus fifty cents for the electricity."

"She has no idea what electricity costs," Barry grumbled.

"She contributes toward the electricity bill," Ruth said in Maddie's defense.

"She should buy her own damned detergent," Barry groused.

Maddie returned to the table, shooting her father a lethal look before she surveyed the rest of the table, her eyes once again bright, her cheeks once again glowing. She took her seat and smiled at Noah and Laura. "I'm glad you're working things out. But forget about being figurines on the cake." She paused theatrically, then said, "I'm not marrying Warren."

"Yay!" Rainie hooted reflexively, then glanced around the table and subsided. From where Ruth sat, no one else seemed at all thrilled with Maddie's announcement.

"What do you mean, you're not marrying Warren?" Ruth asked.

"The wedding is off," Maddie said. "Kyle and I are getting back together."

"That son of a bitch?" Barry roared. "You're getting back together with him?"

"He's my soul mate, Dad." She circled the table with her gaze. "Kyle is my soul mate," she repeated, apparently so enamored of the idea she had to say it twice. "He always was and he still is. I never should have left him."

"You left him because you were dead broke," Barry reminded her. "You left him because you didn't have a pot to piss in."

Aaron tried unsuccessfully to suppress a snicker. "Who pisses in a pot?" Ezra asked, peering up at Noah. "Why don't they use a toilet?"

"It's an expression," Noah said.

"I can't believe this," Barry growled, tossing his napkin onto the table. "What the hell is wrong with you, Maddie?"

"Nothing's wrong with me. I've finally come to my senses."

"Yay," Rainie whispered, barely loud enough for Ruth to hear her.

"When did this happen?" Ruth asked, keeping her voice calm, trying to lower the chaos level. "When did you decide this?"

"I've spent the week with Kyle."

"You told us you were staying with Warren."

"I lied," Maddie said simply, then glared at Barry. "If I'd told the truth, you would have reacted just like you're reacting now."

"You're damned right I would have reacted," Barry said. "I put down a huge deposit for that fancy venue you booked for your wedding. First you screw me out of the deposit I paid Oberlin College to hold your place there, and now you're screwing me out of the deposit on that fancy-schmancy mansion overlooking the ocean."

Ruth considered reminding him that they'd both put down the deposit. Theirs was a joint bank account. True, Barry had always earned more than she did, but then, she performed a great deal of unpaid labor. The money was theirs, not his. Just like the house.

"Okay," Maddie said, her voice rising as her anger matched his. "You won't waste your big, fat investment in my wedding. Kyle and I will get married instead." She smiled at Laura and Noah. "You can still be on the wedding cake."

"I suspect Warren's friends aren't going to want to be groomsmen with me and Ben."

"We'll find other groomsmen," Maddie assured him.

"And we can still have a bridesmaid party?" Rainie asked. "At a spa or something?"

"Of course."

"Have you discussed this with Kyle?" Ruth asked. "Does he have any idea of the elaborate plans you made for your wedding to Warren?"

"We'll work it out. He'll do anything for me."

"Will he give you a pot so you can go to the bathroom?" Ezra wanted to know.

Everyone laughed except Ruth and Barry. Barry twirled his fork through his linguini, scowling so deeply she wasn't sure he'd be able to open his mouth to eat the pasta coiled around the tines.

He was furious. He'd never been Warren's biggest fan, but he despised Kyle.

And Ruth... She had no appetite, not even for the salad she'd prepared. Not even if she doused it in dressing. She stared at her plate, feeling as if the air around her was pulsing and pounding, the barometric pressure plummeting again, a tornado sweeping through her house.

All of this craziness. All of this turmoil. If only she could be somewhere else, living some other life, wandering down some other road.

If only she had a turret room to shut herself up inside.

Chapter Twenty-Three

If Only I'd Taken the Road Not Taken...

"What do you mean, you're driving to Vermont?" Barry sounded outraged, as if she'd told him she'd booked a seat on a rocket ship to Mars.

"I'm going to visit an old friend from high school."

"What old friend? You never have anything to do with your high school friends. You don't even go to the class reunions."

Ruth had considered lying to him, telling him she and Coral were driving to visit a friend of Coral's, or someone they'd worked with before they'd retired, or...anything. She could have come up with a wide variety of lies that wouldn't have set off alarms in Barry's brain.

Then again, everything seemed to set off his alarms lately. She might have told him she was driving to the supermarket and he'd go ballistic. *What do you need at the supermarket? We have a house full of food. Tomorrow's Thursday. You always shop on Mondays.*

He barely spoke a word to Maddie these days, and instead said to Ruth everything he should be saying to Maddie. "She's throwing away a nice, stable relationship with a nice, stable accountant for that good-for-nothing SOB," he ranted nearly every evening, once they were shut up inside their bedroom so he could shed his business suit. "What the hell does she see in him? Why can't she make the right choice for once in her life?"

"She thinks she *is* making the right choice," Ruth would say.

"Then she's an idiot."

All right, maybe he shouldn't be saying these things to Maddie. But Ruth was tired of listening to him. She couldn't change

Maddie's mind. She didn't want to. Maddie was an adult. She could choose for herself what shape she wanted her life to be, what road she wanted to take. Ruth didn't need to insert herself into Maddie's decisions. If they were bad decisions, Maddie would cope with them. Or she wouldn't—but that was up to her.

Ruth decided, for the sake of her own fragile sanity, to change the subject whenever Barry launched into one of his tirades. After a few days of Barry's daily diatribes about Maddie's love life, Ruth announced that she would be driving to Vermont tomorrow. "I shouldn't have to justify myself to you," she said. "I'm allowed to reconnect with an old friend, and Vermont isn't that far away." She did her best to filter her resentment from her voice, but he could probably sense it even if he couldn't hear it.

"What old friend?" he asked. "Who is this friend?"

If she weren't so profoundly annoyed, she might have laughed at the sight of her husband, his face flushed and his hair mussed, parading around the bedroom in his underwear. He'd tossed his suit onto the bed, and Ruth was damned if she'd arrange it on its hanger for him. Let it sit there and get wrinkles.

"You don't know my friends from high school," she reminded him. "I just found out recently that one of them died of cancer, and I want to see another friend before we're all dead. I'll be gone for most of the day. You'll survive. Maddie can make dinner if I get home late."

"I wouldn't trust Maddie to find her own nose. I sure as hell don't trust her to make my dinner."

"Then you'll make your own dinner. Maybe Rainie will help. She likes to fuss in the kitchen."

"She's always home late from school these days. What the hell is she doing after school? How many times does the ski club meet every week?"

Ruth suspected Rainie was hanging out with Matt Selzner after school, but she didn't dare mention that possibility to Barry. That would set off enough alarms inside him to summon the Brentwood fire department, and perhaps a few fire trucks from neighboring towns.

"You know where the refrigerator is," Ruth told Barry. "You know where the microwave is. You won't starve to death."

Barry fumed, and Ruth wondered whether he considered her insistence that he make his own dinner while she was in Vermont proof that their marriage was stagnating. It sure as hell wasn't proof that they were comfortable with each other.

She didn't care. For one single day, she was done. Done with him, done with her children, done with her grandchildren. Done, done, done.

~

Rainie had said you could find anyone online, and it turned out to be true.

Ruth hadn't found Danny Fortuna on Facebook, LinkedIn, or any of the other social networks. She'd found plenty of Daniel Fortunas, Danny Fortunas, and Dan Fortunas, but none of them were *her* Danny Fortuna. Most were too young, a few were too old, a couple were the wrong race. A Daniel Fortuna in Manila was a ceramist. A Dan Fortuna in Kirkland, Washington, was the CEO of a high-tech company. A Danny Fortuna in Alabama posted a selfie on Twitter in which a Confederate flag hung on the wall behind him. Definitely not her Danny.

She found the right Danny Fortuna in an article in the Rumson Gazette, a weekly newspaper serving the town of Rumson, Vermont. Its online edition had run a story a few months ago, now archived, about the town's deliberations over whether to install parking meters on Main Street. At the zoning board hearing, Daniel Fortuna, the proprietor of Watson's Hardware on Main Street, had spoken out against the parking meters. "We count on people parking their cars, wandering up and down the street, and browsing," he was quoted as saying. "If they have to pay to park, they'll only come to Main Street if they're running a specific errand."

She Googled "Watson's Hardware, Rumson, Vermont." The store had a website, with a picture of the store's front façade, its cluttered showcase windows, its green-and-white striped awning, and a large white sign reading "Watson's Hardware" above its open front door. Under the awning, next to the door, one hand in the pocket of his trousers and the other gesturing toward the open door, stood her Danny Fortuna.

He'd changed, of course. She'd changed. After fifty years, you don't *not* change. But he was still lanky, his hair neatly trimmed but still wavy, his eyes—now framed in wire-rimmed eyeglasses—still riveting. Mostly, she recognized him by his chiseled cheeks and his lips. She had watched him sing so many songs when they were teenagers. She'd kissed him so many times. She knew that mouth.

The photo had presumably been taken in the summertime, given the bright sun and the absence of snow or ice on the sidewalk. But the store's website must have been updated recently, because it advertised specials on windshield scrapers, snow shovels, and halite crystals for melting ice on driveways and walkways. According to the website, the store had the widest selection of screws and bolts this side of Burlington. It specialized in certain brands of power tools. You could order snow blowers or lawn tractors and it would arrange for delivery. Best of all, you could download a twenty-percent-off coupon, good for purchases over one hundred dollars.

Danny Fortuna was running a hardware store on Main Street in Rumson, Vermont. And Ruth was going to visit him. She was going to see what her life might have been like if she'd zagged instead of zigged, if she'd run off with Danny that day he'd shown up at Wellesley, if she'd become a rock star. If she'd chosen the road not taken.

That was all she wanted—to see what might have been. If only she hadn't chosen safety and stability, if only she'd learned to embrace chaos. If only she'd taken a chance. If only she'd risked everything.

~

After enjoying a spectacular career doing whatever, I'm now retired. Still happy with Danny, who continues to enjoy running the hardware store and doing battle with the town's zoning board. Our children are perfect. Our home is perfect. Life is perfect.

No.

Life is a mess, because no matter what you choose, no matter which road you take, life is always a mess. There's always a butterfly somewhere, doing what butterflies do.

After I left college and ran off with Danny, he abandoned me for a gorgeous woman who had an exquisite nose, a nipped-in waist, long, slim legs, and platinum blond hair. I broke my leg skiing. I never amounted to anything musically, neither a rock star nor a classical pianist, and now I earn a meager living playing schmaltzy pop songs in the cocktail lounge of a motel on Route 9, where the patrons are too stewed to pay any attention to me. I often find myself wondering why I didn't opt for a stagnant but comfortable life with Barry Singer, that smart, funny guy I met only because after Danny dumped me, I returned to college, got my degree, and enrolled in graduate school in an effort to salvage my life and justify my existence and get my mother off my back. Barry was studying economics in the same grad school, and so we met. If only I'd married him, I could be living in a house with central air, and we would bicker sometimes because he can be presumptuous, but we would be comfortable, if somewhat stagnant, and my kids would be mostly okay although they would generously contribute to the graying of my hair. Thank God for hair-coloring products.

If only I'd thrown my lot in with Barry.

~

Located about halfway between the Massachusetts state line and Burlington, Rumson was the sort of town Vermont might use to illustrate travel brochures. Obeying when the dulcet-voiced woman who resided inside her GPS as well as Jill's instructed her to exit the interstate, Ruth drove past rolling hills blanketed with snow so white she wouldn't have been surprised to hear that it was scrubbed daily with bleach. In the distance she saw sturdy wooden barns, no doubt filled with dairy cows who would produce rich, delicious milk, which would be transformed into dense, flavorful cheddar cheese and decadent ice cream. White clapboard houses adorned with black shutters and red front doors and flanked by evergreens stood along the numbered route into town.

Rumson's downtown—if that wasn't too grand a name for the three-block-long commercial district—was lined with brick and brownstone shops: a general store, a craft store, a gift shop, a clothing store, a pharmacy with a big red "Rx" sign protruding from its flat roof, and a café that looked homey and probably catered to tourists seeking a genuine Vermont experience, with a menu that included ten flavors of herbal tea and ice cream made from the milk of all the cows occupying the barns Ruth had passed on her way into town. Christmas decorations had not yet been removed. Wreaths hung on some of the doors, and star-shaped lights arched overhead from one side of the street to the other at regular intervals. Right now, with the lights turned off, they were mere skeletons of wrought iron, wiring, and bulbs, but she imagined that when they were lit up at night, they looked festive.

Her breath caught in her throat when she spotted Watson's Hardware in the second block. She recognized it from the store's website home page. *You can find anyone online*, she thought, although it had taken her a two-hour drive to find this store—where Danny might or might not be. Did he work on-site? As the store's proprietor, did he just own it or did he actually run it?

Did she really want to see him?

She found a parking space half a block from the store's entry. Danny had apparently prevailed in his dispute with the town's zoning board last summer; no parking meters lined the sidewalk.

After turning off her car, she remained seated, breathing deeply, trying to figure out what she hoped to accomplish with this trip. It had all seemed so clear to her when she'd left Brentwood that morning, and before then when she'd conceived of the trip, planned for it, tuned out the constant, chronic sniping between Maddie and Barry—as of last night, he was threatening to pull the plug on her wedding extravaganza and demand reimbursement for his lost deposit, although Ruth had later reassured Maddie that he wouldn't really do that—and Rainie's histrionic moods, seesawing between giddiness and despair over whether she'd passed her biology midterm, whether she would make the girls' varsity soccer team, whether she could go skiing with the school ski club so everyone could see how cute she looked in her puffy ski pants, and whether Matt Selzner *really* liked her or was just saying he did.

Even if Danny didn't run a hardware store in Vermont, Ruth would have wanted to escape for a day—or a week, or the rest of her life.

But now she was in Rumson. What was she supposed to do?

See if Danny was working at the hardware store. See if he remembered her. See if he even recognized her, now that she was fifty years older. Her eyelids were a little baggy, her cheeks a little saggy. She no longer wore her hair long and parted down the middle. It was the same boring brown it had been in high school, thanks to those hair-coloring products, but she wore it in a chin-length bob. To avoid the worst tragedy that could befall a woman, she'd always been disciplined about her weight, forgoing dressing when she ate a salad, and she still had the thick-middled, small-bosomed build she'd had in high school. Her breasts were a lot softer and her tush spongier, but Danny would not have the opportunity to see those body parts.

Assuming he did recognize her, would he want to talk to her? She had turned him down that afternoon at Wellesley. For all she knew, she was the only girl in the universe who had ever said no to him. He might loathe her. All these years later, he might still be nursing a grudge.

Assuming he did want to talk to her, what would they talk about? The good old days? The bad old days? The fact that Mike had left the country and Jimmy had left the planet—and Nick was playing in a wedding band?

Would they talk about what was, and what might have been?

Should she put on some lipstick first?

Or should she pull away from the curb, drive around the block, and head back to the interstate?

She had taken this road. She had made this choice. She had embraced uncertainty and risk.

She would walk into Watson's Hardware and ask for Danny.

Chapter Twenty-Four

Drawing in a deep breath and squaring her shoulders, as if full lungs and straight posture could give her courage, she climbed out of her car and locked it. Rumson seemed like the kind of town where the locals left their doors unlocked, but she wasn't a local. Better safe than sorry.

The air was a crystalline, biting cold. She tightened the scarf around her neck—not an elegant silk fashion statement like what Jill would wear, but a utilitarian muffler Coral had knitted for her out of the yarn she'd had left over from an elaborate abstract collage she'd created as her first retirement art project. Drawing in another deep breath and ignoring the way the icy air chafed her lungs, Ruth strolled down the block to the hardware store and stepped inside.

Like the town itself, Watson's Hardware was emphatically charming—or as emphatically charming as a hardware store could be. It featured a scuffed wood floor, long, narrow light fixtures hanging from the ceiling, and rows of shelves stacked with everything a person might need to survive in a rustic Vermont town: carpentry tools, plumbing pipes, coils of wire, light switches, sheets of Plexiglas, seed spreaders, shower heads, suede-palmed work gloves, bottles of 3-in-1 oil, tubes of super glue, slabs of bluestone, toilet plungers, stacks of roof shingles, cans of interior and exterior paint, and sorted bins containing all those screws and bolts the website bragged about. The air smelled faintly of sawdust. A couple of men in stained jeans and fleece-lined denim jackets deliberated over a selection of blowtorches; she doubted they were discussing which one would be best for browning the crust of their crème brûlée. An elderly woman wearing a vintage pea jacket and a ribbed gray watch cap stood at the checkout counter.

The clerk had his back to her as he operated a key-duplicating machine, which issued a metallic drone as he manipulated the key.

The task done, he turned around.

Danny!

No, he couldn't be Danny, unless Danny had discovered the Fountain of Youth and chug-a-lugged its entire contents. This man looked to be no older than mid-thirties. But he had the same soft, tawny waves of hair as Danny did, the same chiseled cheeks, the same deep-set eyes and slightly pouty lips.

Danny's son.

If only I'd married Danny, I could have had a son who looked like Danny.

Or not, given that her genes might have something to say about the appearance of her offspring. Besides, her children were just as good-looking as that young man was, even if none of them could pass as a Fortuna. Jill looked the most like Ruth, with the same sharp intensity in her features, the same dark eyes and slightly bumpy nose. Noah was hunky for a guy settling into middle age—hunky enough to catch the attention of a skinny, inappropriately younger paramour. And Maddie was ravishingly beautiful, which was lucky for her. No one would put up with her crap if she weren't such a joy to look at.

Ruth waited until the woman had paid for her duplicate key and strode through the door and out of sight. After eyeing the two men assessing the blowtorches, Ruth approached the counter. She opened her mouth to speak, felt her voice catch, and cleared her throat. And smiled. "Hi," she said a bit too brightly. "Is Danny Fortuna here?"

"You're looking at him," the young man said.

"I'm looking for an older Danny Fortuna."

The young man grinned. "My dad? He's busy in back. Is there something I can help you with?"

"No. I mean, you have a lovely store, but I don't need any hardware." She silently admonished herself to stay cool and act normal, and began again. "I'm an old friend of your father's. I just happened to be in town, and I thought I'd stop by and say hello."

Did that sound as absurd to him as it did to her? At least it conveyed that she was more or less sane.

"Well. Hmm." The young Danny checked his watch. "He told me not to interrupt him, but for an old friend..." Lifting his cell phone from a shelf behind the counter, he tapped its screen and then raised it to his ear. "Hey, Dad? There's a lady here who says she's an old friend of yours, visiting in town. She wants to say hello." He listened for a few seconds and shot Ruth a conspiratorial grin. "Yeah, she's gorgeous," he said. He listened again, then chuckled and tapped his screen. "He'll be out in a minute."

"Thank you for lying on my behalf," Ruth said, concluding that Danny had done a fine job raising his son.

The blowtorch men approached the counter, carrying their selection, and Ruth stepped out of their way. Two women entered the store, chattering as they gravitated toward a display of sink faucets. An empty-handed man emerged from the house paint area, waved at the young Danny, and exited onto Main Street. Ruth focused on the red bandanna dangling from the back pocket of his overalls, visible beneath the edge of his fleece-lined jacket. It was easier than focusing on the back of the store, where the older Danny was alleged to be busy.

She heard footsteps behind her, growing louder as they neared her. One more deep breath—would all these deep breaths cause her to hyperventilate? Would she faint?—and she forced herself to pivot to face the man who approached, working his way along the narrow aisle between two floor-to-ceiling walls of shelves. As he drew nearer, Ruth saw he was the senior Danny. She wasn't sure she would have recognized him if she hadn't seen his picture on the store's website. He was still a good-looking man, but not the Danny Fortuna he'd been in high school—as, of course, he wouldn't be. His hair was more silver than brown, long for a man in his late sixties but nowhere near as long as it had been when he'd been the heartthrob of Trouble Ahead. The eyeglasses suited his face, but except for the website photo, she'd never seen him wearing eyeglasses before.

Her heart, she realized, had been thumping like a pile-driver inside her ribcage until he was about ten feet away from her, at which point it settled back into its usual healthy rhythm. He was a man, that was all. A hardware store owner in a shirt and navy blue crew-neck sweater, khakis and the sort of thick-soled boots hardware store owners in northern New England would wear. He was just...Danny.

He saw her waiting a few steps from the counter and slowed his pace slightly. A frown crossed his face for a moment; he seemed to be trying to place her. She gave him a hesitant smile. "Danny?"

"Holy shit," he murmured, breaking into a smile much more robust than hers. "Ruthie?"

She nodded, feeling her tension ebb a little more.

A few long strides brought him to her side. "I can't believe this! Ruthie Pinchas? What are you doing here?"

"Well, I saw you owned this store, and I was in the vicinity..." Her feeble excuse again.

"Wow." He spun around to his son. "Hey, D.J.! This is Ruthie Pinchas."

"It's Ruth Singer now," she said, returning Danny's son's smile.

"We were in a band together in high school," Danny the Elder said.

And so much more, Ruth thought, but she was relieved that Danny didn't bother to share with his son that he'd deflowered Ruth in the back of his rusty, dilapidated van when they were high school seniors.

His son smirked. "What, the school marching band?"

"Give me a break. I've told you about my rock band. Ruthie, did you meet my obnoxious son?"

"He seemed very nice to me," Ruth said, giving young Danny another smile. "You called him D.J.?"

"Dan Junior. Why I thought he deserved to be named after me, I'll never know." It was clear he and his son were teasing each other. Their grins matched. Their eyes glinted with shared humor. "Listen, D.J., I'm gonna take my lunch break now. Ruthie and I have some catching up to do."

"What about the inventory lists?"

"They can wait." Danny turned back to Ruth. "Let me grab my coat."

Ten minutes later, they were seated facing each other at a table inside the cute, touristy café down the block. The waitress, a thin young woman with a silver eyebrow ring and blond hair that fell in a braid to her waist, knew Danny. "Hey, Dan," she said, then smiled at Ruth.

"This is a high school friend of mine," he told her. "Just visiting in town. Have you got any specials today?"

She wheeled over a blackboard and left them to peruse the dishes listed on it. Ruth ordered a salad with an assortment of greens and veggies and some grilled chicken, and—since she'd already taken one huge risk in coming to Rumson—a maple vinaigrette dressing. Danny ordered maple-glazed salmon on a baguette. In Vermont, apparently, many recipes included maple syrup.

They both ordered hot tea to drink—and Ruth's guess had been correct; the café had a dozen different herbal teas to choose from. Just seeing the steam rising from her heavy ceramic mug helped her thaw out from the chilly January air outside.

"So," Danny said, his smile growing gentle. "You look terrific."

"*You* look terrific," she said. "I look like an old lady."

"A mature woman," he assured her. "How've you been?"

"Fine," she said automatically, then decided her answer was close enough to the truth. He didn't have to know her husband and youngest daughter were reenacting their own version of World War III, her son had very nearly destroyed his marriage, her other daughter was a shrink who didn't know how to discipline her children, and her oldest grandchild had pink and blue hair and was currently in the throes of her first romance. He didn't have to know that since retiring, Ruth had had enough time on her hands to imagine a multitude of other lives for herself, lives she'd failed to live. He didn't have to know that her marriage was stagnant and her husband had a potbelly and she no longer came when they had sex.

"So, you just happened to be passing through town?" His laugh conveyed that he didn't believe her.

She conceded with a smile. "I was in a nostalgic mood, looking up old friends, people I'd lost touch with. You can find anyone online," she quoted Rainie.

"If you look hard enough, yeah."

Did that mean Danny thought she'd looked too hard? Had he wanted her not to find him?

Was she overanalyzing his every utterance?

"I just found out recently that Jimmy died, and...I thought it would be nice to get in touch with other friends before they died too. Or before *I* died."

"Yeah, Jimmy." Danny lowered his eyes and shook his head. "That was a shock. He went so fast."

"You knew about it?"

"I travel down to Boston sometimes. He and I used to go out for a beer or two, or smoke a number in his basement."

She nodded.

"One time..." Tiny crow's feet edged his eyes as he smiled in reminiscence. "We saw Nick playing drums with this band he's in—Boston Starlites. They were playing at a wedding at this hotel in Natick, and we could see them from an open doorway in the lobby. They were playing shit like 'The Macarena.' What a hoot!"

"At least he's still playing," Ruth pointed out.

"A drummer can always find work," Danny said. "How about you? Are you still in a band?"

"Ha." She snorted. "I just recently retired after teaching music in the Brentwood school system for thirty-two years. All that experience playing the piano standing up paid off. When you're banging out chords and conducting a children's chorus at the same time, you've got to stand so the kids can see you above the piano."

"Wow! You kept doing music. That's cool. Probably cooler than playing 'The Macarena' at a suburban wedding." He pondered her words for a minute. "Brentwood, Mass.?"

She nodded.

"That's not too far from where we grew up."

"I never made it to California."

"Neither did I." He gestured vaguely toward the tinted glass pane that formed the front wall of the café, overlooking Main Street and its meter-free sidewalks. "A music teacher. That's really cool, Ruthie. And you conducted the chorus?"

"I taught primary school kids," Ruth told him. "Besides leading the chorus and organizing the school concerts, I taught them basic music theory, introduced them to Bach and Beethoven—and the Beatles. I encouraged them to learn how to play instruments. I enjoyed it."

"I bet you were great at it. You were so smart. It figures you'd be a teacher."

"I wasn't so smart," she demurred.

"Wellesley College? They don't accept stupid girls there."

So he remembered Wellesley. Did he remember charging onto the campus, parking illegally in the permits-only lot, daring her to run away with him?

Of course he did. He'd already confessed that he, like her, never made it to California. He remembered.

The waitress arrived with their food, and they sat in silence as she handed them coarse linen napkins wrapped around silverware and held together with macramé napkin rings. Ruth gazed at her salad, which looked delicious, glistening with salad dressing. Worth gaining a pound or two, she thought.

"How did you wind up here?" she asked. "Rumson is a beautiful town, but I never would have predicted you'd be running a hardware store."

"Kind of like, the wind stopped blowing and this was where it dropped me?" he asked more than said.

She wondered whether the wind that had blown him here had been a tornado, whether a butterfly had steered him to this place.

"I went up to Burlington. College town, lots of kids, clubs." He took a bite of his sandwich, chewed, and swallowed. "I thought maybe I could join a band there, or start one. But the world wasn't looking for a kid who'd barely made it out of high school and knew a bunch of basic chords on the guitar. I was never a real musician like Jimmy or Mike—or you."

"You played the guitar well."

"I played chords. Jimmy played lead." He shrugged. "So I was up in Burlington. I took odd jobs, got tired, got broke, hitched around when the van died, saw a 'help wanted' sign in the window of Watson's Hardware and asked them to hire me. Bob Watson—the owner of the place—was a good guy. He had a nice daughter. I wound up marrying her, and I guess I wound up marrying the store too."

"And now your son is working there. That's wonderful." It sounded sweet to Ruth, homey and cozy. Something that could be depicted in a Norman Rockwell painting, just like the town itself. If only she'd stayed with Danny, she could have lived such a life, the wife of a shopkeeper in a small, charming town where the snow in December was whiter than white.

"One son. My other boy..." Danny shook his head. "God knows where he is. He wants to see the world. Dropped out of college, flew off to Kathmandu, wherever. He sends us emails now and then. He's in New Delhi. Or Nairobi. Or Amsterdam. Grass is legal there, he tells us."

"Grass is legal in Massachusetts."

"I guess it's legal pretty much everywhere these days." Danny shook his head. "It's amazing none of us got busted back in high school, when it wasn't legal."

Ruth thought briefly of Kyle's misadventures with illegal drugs. If she had run off with Danny, the way Maddie had run off with Kyle, would he have gotten busted? Would they both have? Would he have realized that she wasn't so terribly smart, if they'd wound up behind bars?

"Do you ever wonder," she asked, "what would have happened if I had said yes that day you came to campus and asked me to go to California with you?"

He worked on his sandwich, buying time to consider his answer. "I probably would have been shocked," he said. "You were so much more together than me. You would never have done anything that stupid."

"I didn't think it was stupid."

"But you said no."

"Because..." Why not be honest? "Because I thought eventually you'd leave me. I'd go to California with you, and you'd see all those beautiful California girls, and you wouldn't want to be with me anymore."

His eyes widened behind his stylish eyeglasses. "Oh, come on, Ruthie. Do you really think I would have done that?"

"You were Danny Fortuna. You had gorgeous girls throwing themselves at you all the time. Half the kids in high school had crushes on you. The other half were straight boys."

He laughed and shook his head. "They didn't all have crushes on me."

"They did. When we played gigs, all those little groupie girls would gather around you, and giggle and sigh and ask you for your autograph."

"They were just...silly," he said.

"Why me, Danny? When you could have had any girl you wanted, why did you want to run away with me?"

In the silence of the pause before he answered her question, she heard silverware clinking against dishware at neighboring tables, murmured conversation, the jingle of someone's cell phone ringing. Danny's expression grew solemn, intense as he sorted his thoughts. "You were so..." He groped for the right word. "*Grounded.* So stable. So smart. You knew about bank accounts and budgets and stuff like that. And you were...calm." He lowered his sandwich and leaned toward her. "My life was a mess. Things were out of control. I thought you could save me."

She'd grant that Danny had seemed a bit lacking in direction that fall after high school, but he'd been so handsome. She never would have believed he needed saving. He could have glided through life on his looks alone, his smile, his soulful voice, his magnetism. "You mean because you weren't in college?"

"I was sleeping with my father's girlfriend," he said.

Well. That was a conversation stopper.

"She was about halfway between my dad's age and mine, and she came onto me, and I was an asshole. So I said yes. And then...I just knew that was so fucked up—pardon my language."

"I know the word," Ruth assured him. "If I didn't, my granddaughter would have made sure I learned it."

He smiled fleetingly, then grew somber again. "I knew I had to get away from all that. Away from her and my father too. It was just... Crazy. And sick. And I thought, who can make it right? Who knows how to clean up a mess? Who fixes things? Who's the stablest, most grounded person I know? You."

"Oh, Danny." He'd supposedly been her boyfriend at the time, and she wondered if she ought to be upset that he was having sex with another woman—let alone his father's girlfriend. But that was all so long ago. How could she be upset? She hadn't known about it at the time, and now it no longer mattered. Besides, even then, she'd known he would be tempted by other girls, other women, and he would give in to that temptation. That was why she had said no to him, even though she'd been crazy-in-love with him. She had known he could never be hers.

"So, I just ran away on my own. I ran north instead of west. Same thing." He leaned back, the level of intimacy between them dropping now that he'd told her why he'd wanted her to run away with him. Not because he was crazy-in-love with her but because he'd gotten himself into a messy problem and he'd thought she could clean up his mess for him.

He'd believed she could tame the chaos of his life. That was what she did, after all. That was who she was.

"It all worked out pretty well, though," he said. "I found my place in life, a place where I belonged. I like Rumson. I like selling hardware. I married a good woman. We've got two good sons—well, one and a half. The jury's still out on my younger boy."

"My youngest has been a challenge, too," she told him. They shared a smile.

She felt something lift off her—a weight, a shadow, a tint like the café's tinted-glass window that made Main Street appear just a little darker than it actually was. No longer would she imagine how different her life might have been if she'd run away with Danny. Oh, sure, it would have been different—but he belonged here, in Rumson, with his good wife and his one-and-a-half good sons.

And Ruth... If she had run away with him, she wouldn't have wound up living with him in a beautiful house in a canyon north of L.A., operating a recording studio, producing records, writing songs, gazing out at the flora and fauna of Southern California through the glass walls of their home. Because he didn't belong there, and neither did she. The wonder of Rumson, Vermont's Main Street was who Danny was. The wonder of the colonial on Jefferson Road was who Ruth was.

"After I told you I wouldn't go to California with you," she confessed, "I went back to my dorm room and sobbed for hours. I actually missed dinner because I was crying so hard."

He seemed surprised. "Why? That was probably the smartest decision you ever made."

"I was so in love with you, Danny. And I knew that if I said no, I would never see you again."

"But you thought if you said yes, I'd leave you."

"I cried," she acknowledged as the truth came to her, "because I was forced to accept that sometimes things will never work out the way you want them to."

"I loved you too." From his tone, she could tell he'd said that to make her feel better, to reassure her that he might have also cried for hours over losing her. But she knew he hadn't really loved her, not the way she'd loved him. He had been gorgeous, and male. Any woman—even the daughter of a hardware store owner—could have saved him and set him on his feet. Ruth or someone else; it hadn't mattered.

Yet thinking back, she realized that after she had stopped crying, she'd wound up on her feet too. The tornado had stopped blowing and dropped her where she'd landed, just like Danny.

They lingered over lunch. They talked about their grandchildren—D.J. and his wife had two little girls, and as far as Danny knew, his other son hadn't fathered any children yet. Ruth told him about her five grandchildren. They pulled out their cell phones and oohed and ahhed over photos.

They caught up on the past half-century. They talked about Mike in Vancouver. They commiserated over Jimmy's death;

Danny had traveled down to Boston for the funeral and sat beside Nick in the church. "I wish someone had let me know," Ruth said. "I would have wanted to be there."

"Yeah, well, we'd all lost touch with you," Danny said, looking sheepish. "And we figured you'd gotten married and changed your name. Nick tried looking you up, but he couldn't find a Ruth Pinchas."

Of course not. Rainie was right; Ruth should have kept her maiden name.

Danny insisted on paying the bill. "You taught me money management," he reminded her as he produced his credit card. "You were so good about keeping us all on a budget."

"I was a shrew," Ruth argued. "I was a nerd. I was Miss Goody-Two-Shoes."

"You were a girl. All girls were kind of like that. At least that's what we guys thought." Chuckling, he shook his head. "We took a lot longer to grow up."

She thanked him for the lunch and they stepped outside the café. The afternoon sun was winter-white but brilliant, causing Ruth to squint after the atmospheric dimness of the café. "Do you have to run off?" Danny asked. "I could show you around town a little. Rumson is really pretty."

She didn't have to run off. She didn't want to. "Don't you have to deal with your inventory?"

"It can wait," Danny assured her. "Come on. I'll give you the grand tour. I've got to drop something off at my house, anyway."

He led her down a narrow alley to a parking area behind the row of shops. The asphalt was eroded in spots, and potholes filled with snow had melted and refrozen, creating slick patches of ice. Ruth wished she had worn shoes like his, with treaded soles, instead of her stylish ankle-high leather boots. Twice he reached out and took her arm, steering her around a stretch of ice.

He led her to a van—a nicer, newer van than the VW van with the balky passenger door that he'd driven in high school, although pretty much any van on the road today would be nicer than that one. This one was shiny and white, with "Watson's

Hardware" painted on the side, along with a telephone number, a website URL, and "Nuts and Bolts and Everything Else" in vivid green letters. He pressed his key button to unlock the doors and helped her into the passenger seat. Then he climbed in behind the wheel.

"I take it you have a driver's license these days?" she asked.

He sent her a grin. "I was a good driver even when I wasn't legal."

"You were." She had been his passenger so many times. She remembered how he always braked to a near full stop at the railroad crossing in town, checking to make certain a train wasn't approaching, even though the gate was up and the lights were off and the warning bell wasn't clanging.

"Rumson's a funny town," he said, coasting out of the lot. "Fifth-generation locals. Rich city folks who buy second homes here so they can go skiing. Old hippies. Here's town center." He drove past the stores on Main Street until he reached a town green—although it wasn't green at the moment, given the snow covering the open square. It was bordered by a spired white clapboard church, a squat white clapboard building with brass letters reading "United States Post Office" above the door, and a sprawling white clapboard building with a sign that said "Rumson Town Hall." Someone had shoveled paths through the snow on the green, most of which converged on a white clapboard gazebo at the center of the green. If not for the towering pines and spruce and bushy yews adorning the expanse, all that white, illuminated by the cold sun overhead, would have blinded Ruth.

"It looks like a Christmas card," Ruth said.

"My wife is active in that church," Danny said as he cruised along the road that formed the green's perimeter. "Congregational. I'm still not sure what that's all about. It isn't Catholic, I'll tell you that."

Danny had been about as Catholic in high school as Ruth had been Jewish. As far as she knew, he never went to church, but she supposed the memory of Catholicism was in his genes, just as the memory of Judaism was in hers.

"I go with her for Christmas and Easter. Other than that, she's on her own when it comes to God." He steered away from the green, onto a two-lane road cutting through a copse of trees. Modest houses stood among the trees, some closer to the road and some set at the end of lengthy driveways bordered by ridges of snow left by plows. If only Maddie had grown up in one of those houses, Ruth thought, the walk across the street to visit Kyle would have tired her out. After a while, she might have decided he wasn't worth the hike down such a long driveway.

Or else she would have been a hardy Vermonter, used to miles-long treks to get anywhere—especially to reach her soul mate, the hopefully reformed drug dealer/bartender.

Danny turned down one of the shorter driveways, which ended in a compact saltbox colonial—also white clapboard. That was clearly the architectural trend in this part of Vermont. "I've just got to drop this shelving off. Angie—my wife—said she needed more storage space in the cellar. I was going to bring it home this evening, but if I drop it off now, she can probably get the shelves assembled by dinnertime."

"No problem," Ruth said.

Danny climbed out of the van. As he circled to the rear of the vehicle, the front door of the house opened and a woman emerged. Clad in loose-fitting jeans and a baggy cable-knit sweater, she was stout in a healthy, hearty sort of way. She had a round face with deep creases framing her mouth and ending at her jawline, and her hair, a shade somewhere between ash blond and mop-head gray, hung in a crooked ponytail down her back. "Hey, honey," she called, descending the porch steps to greet Danny. "What are you doing here?" She glanced toward the van and her eyebrows rose.

Ruth smiled faintly.

"I had a surprise visitor," he said, leaning through the van's rear doors. Ruth twisted in her seat to watch him as he heaved a broad, flat box nearly as tall as he was out of the back of the van. "An old friend from high school was passing through town and stopped to say hello. So I'm playing hooky this afternoon."

Danny's wife leaned through the open driver's side door and grinned at Ruth. "Hi, there, old friend of Dan's."

Danny balanced the box against the side of the van and joined his wife at the door. "Ruthie, this is my wife Angie. Angie, Ruth—not Pinchas anymore?"

"Singer," Ruth said. "Hi, Angie. Nice to meet you."

"Ruth Singer," Danny corrected himself. "Perfect name. Ruthie was in my band."

"That high school band?" Angie rolled her eyes and let out a bark of a laugh. "Oh, dear God. That band of his!"

"He talks about it a lot?"

"Enough to drive us all crazy," Angie said.

"Those were the best days of my life," Danny said in his defense.

Angie narrowed her pale gray eyes on him. "I thought the day you met me was the best day of your life."

"That was definitely in the top ten," he said with a grin. "Let me carry this inside. I'll put it together this evening if you don't want to tackle it yourself."

"Nonsense." Angie turned back to Ruth. "I know more about how to use a screwdriver and a hammer than Dan does. My dad made sure of that. Why don't you come on in, have a cup of coffee."

Curiosity tempted Ruth to say yes. This woman was so unlike the sort of woman she would have expected Danny Fortuna to end up with. Not gorgeous. Not glamorous. Not giggly and fawning and swooning with adoration. Not insecure and moody and yearning, the way Ruth had been in high school.

On the other hand, did Ruth really want to know who this woman was, how she'd won Danny's heart, why the wind had dropped him to earth in this spot? Did Ruth want to poke around inside his house? Did she want to search for the solution to the puzzle of what he'd become?

He answered his wife for her. "I'm going to show Ruth around the area a little, and then maybe we'll come back for coffee."

"Well, I'll be here. I'm not going anywhere." Angie eyed the box, which Danny hoisted off the ground and lugged up the walk to the front door. "I'm just going to be putting together these shelves this afternoon. If you want to stop by later, I've always got a pot brewing." Her smile seemed genuine. "Nice meeting you, Ruth."

"You too."

Ruth sat by herself in the van for a few minutes as Danny and his wife vanished into the house. Closing her eyes, she allowed herself a small laugh. Had she refused to run away with Danny because she'd been fearful he would dump her for a woman more beautiful and sexy, a woman as charismatic as he was? Angie seemed like a lovely woman, but—*and*—she was none of those things.

Either Ruth hadn't known Danny very well at all, or he'd changed. Or both.

He returned to the van, climbed in, and turned on the engine. Ruth welcomed the blast of hot air from the vents. "Your house is very pretty," she said.

"Standard-issue Rumson," he blew off the compliment as he backed down the driveway. "This time of year, the prettiest thing about it is the wood-burning stove in the living room. We have a furnace, but the stove keeps things toasty."

The houses thinned out, the road narrowing as it wound through a forest of evergreens. Ruth wondered whether Danny had intentionally dropped off the shelving because he wanted Ruth to meet his wife, to see her, to know that he wasn't the shallow sex object she'd assumed him to be.

She had never assumed he was shallow, of course. But when a boy overflowing with testosterone had so many females flinging themselves at him—even, as it turned out, his father's girlfriend—how could she not think he'd been a sex object? How could he have resisted all those eager women?

Maybe he could have resisted them, even as a randy teenager. Maybe Ruth had misjudged him. Or maybe she had just been so insecure and so determined not to get hurt that she had exiled him from her life before he had a chance to hurt her.

Maybe she'd simply played it safe, because she had been too afraid to take a chance on him, too afraid to wander down a risky, possibly dangerous path.

The road climbed and the trees thinned out. "Here we are," he said, pulling off the pavement and onto the gravel shoulder. "My favorite spot in the world."

She could understand why. Through the van's windshield, she viewed below them a breathtaking vista of gentle hills, snowy slopes, spear-shaped fir trees, and a small pond like a rounded tile of silver glass embedded in the snow. "Wow," she said.

"Pretty amazing, huh." Danny smiled proudly, as if all that glorious scenery belonged to him.

She nodded her agreement.

"I drive up here whenever I need some quiet time. It's just—like the whole world is spread out below me. Or at least anything in the whole world that's worthwhile. Angie doesn't think there's anything special about this view, and my boys always thought I was being a goof when I drove them up here. So I come by myself and just drink it in."

"It's magnificent," Ruth said.

They sat together in silence for a long moment. "Did you really think our time in the band were the best days of your life?" she asked.

He laughed. "Nah." He reconsidered his answer. "The best days and the worst days. Isn't there some famous book like that?"

"'It was the best of times, it was the worst of times.' Charles Dickens."

"I must have cut that class." He shot her a look that was half contrition, half mischief. "I loved being with the band, but those days weren't so great. You had a mother who drank too much and drove you crazy. I didn't have a mother at all. I had no idea where I was going or what I was doing."

"Did you ever think *this*—" she gestured toward the panorama beyond the windshield "—was where you were going?"

"Are you kidding? A sleepy little town in central Vermont?" He shook his head. "But you know, sometimes, if you're lucky, you wind up where you're supposed to be."

After admiring the view for a few more contemplative minutes, Danny eased the van back onto the road. He asked her if she wanted to stop at his house for coffee with Angie, but she declined. "You probably have to do your inventory," she reminded him. "I've taken up too much of your time."

"Don't be silly. This was great. Much more fun than reviewing our stock and ordering more shovels and rock salt."

Back in town, he asked where she had parked, and when she pointed out her car, still sitting happily beside the meter-free curb, he double-parked next to it and let her out. "Door-to-door service," he said.

"Thank you. And thank you for lunch, and for sharing your view with me."

"We should stay in touch," Danny said, leaning across the console and giving her cheek a light, friendly kiss.

"Yes, of course."

There was no *of course* about it. By the time she reached the entrance ramp onto I-91, she was certain she would never see or talk to Danny again.

The realization pierced her, a pain in her chest so sharp she momentarily believed she was having a heart attack. However, her heart was beating steadily, and her arm and jaw felt fine, and she had no indigestion, not even a hint of heartburn from the maple vinaigrette that had drenched her salad. But her eyes watered, her vision blurred, and she had to pull off the road to collect herself.

Sometimes we just wind up where we're supposed to be. Not in Montana. Not in California. Not on a ski slope, not in a sprawling apartment on Central Park West with a concert-grand Steinway. Not a mother of two.

A mother of three. That was where Ruth was supposed to be.

And maybe *here*—where she was supposed to be—meant not being anywhere else. Not wandering, not wondering. Not regretting the road you didn't take but accepting the road you did take. More than accepting it—enjoying it. Embracing it. Appreciating the view.

The shadows lengthened and the sky faded from pink to lavender to dark blue as the sun slid behind the gentle mountains to her west. The digital clock on her dashboard read six and then six-thirty and then six-forty-five. Barry wouldn't starve. He could rustle up something for dinner. He could open a can of soup or fix himself a sandwich, or perhaps even eat strange green things from one of Maddie's Asian-market containers. Or he could retire to the den with a bag of potato chips and a bag of Oreos, and leave a residue of crumbs behind when he went to bed.

She herself wasn't hungry. Her brain kept churning despite the fact that it was exhausted. Shapeless, elusive thoughts flitted in and out, a mental pandemonium. Yet all around her, as the night closed in and the highway lanes stretched smooth and straight ahead of her, the lane lines distinct and bright as they reflected her car's headlights, the world seemed tranquil. As tranquil as the view from that bluff where Danny had driven them.

What had she expected? A road as bumpy and serpentine as this highway was smooth and well-marked? Just because two roads diverged didn't mean the left fork was markedly different from the right, or that they didn't both wind up in the same place.

It was after eight o'clock when she finally crossed the town line into Brentwood. To reach Jefferson Road, she would have to turn right at the Baker Lane intersection, but she turned left, instead. Just a quick detour, not a major one.

She followed the route of her Wednesday walk. The streets were quiet and dark; in January, children didn't fill the roads with their bikes and scooters. Parents didn't sit on their porches, enjoying a cold drink while they watched their kids shoot hoops in the driveway. The scent of meat roasting on grills didn't fill the air. The sky was a deep, deep blue, smudged with random gray clouds. The half-moon was edged in haze.

She reached the Victorian and braked to a halt. A light was on inside; although the shades were drawn, the front windows glowed amber. That was where the living room was located, she recalled from when Patti, their realtor, had given them a tour of the house. Was someone in the living room now, living?

She craned her neck to see the second floor. The turret was dark...and then someone turned a light on there. Those windows also had shades drawn across them, but they glowed brighter, as if the lamp illuminating the room was the maximum wattage. Someone had entered the turret and wanted to fill that lovely round room with light on this dark, mildly overcast winter evening.

If only Ruth was the one who had turned on that light.

But she wasn't.

She was in her car, and it was time to drive home, to Barry and his simmering anger at his youngest daughter. To Rainie, hyperventilating about Matt or else—Ruth hoped—reviewing her biology class notes. Maybe to Maddie if she wasn't up in Portsmouth with her soul mate, recalibrating her wedding. Now that she had the Noah and Laura figurines worked out, she was going to have to do something about the Warren figurine.

To the staid, symmetrical colonial that contained her family, contained her life, contained who she was right now. The house that had a piano—not a concert grand, but a decent instrument that she could play sitting down or standing up, with the score of "Clair de Lune" or her notebook of lyrics propped on the music stand. The house with its refrigerator filled with tubs of mysterious foods marked with unreadable labels, the house with its depleted supply of laundry detergent on the shelf above the washing machine, the house with an attached garage and a backyard where a dog once romped, and central air.

On a chilly January night, the air conditioning was irrelevant. But come summer, she would be grateful for it.

Acknowledgments

My "if only" house is a white colonial with brick trim. Whenever I pass it on my power walks, I imagine what my loved ones' lives would be like today if we had made our home within its walls. But we didn't buy it when we had the chance. Like Ruth Singer's husband, my husband vetoed that house because it lacked central air conditioning.

If Only isn't autobiographical, but I did borrow a few experiences from my life for Ruth's story. When I was a teenager, I—like so many other teenagers—was in a rock band. More than one, actually, but none of them were anywhere near as accomplished as Trouble Ahead. Still, I would like to thank my very first bandmates: Emma Joy Jampole, Louie Agiesta, and Ernie Germano. Being in a band with them was a glorious rite of passage for me.

Even as a teenager, I didn't spend much time fantasizing about rock stardom. I knew from an early age that I wanted to be a novelist. I have many people to thank for helping to make that dream come true, first and foremost my editor, Lou Aronica, who freed me to write this book and loved it as much as I did. Thanks, also, to my copy editor, Stacy Mathewson, whose keen eye and light touch brought *If Only* a little closer to perfection.

I am grateful to the teachers who guided me along the way: Eugene Murphy and Michael Stoller in high school, Len Berkman, V.S. Pritchett, and Gladden Schrock in college, George Bass and John Hawkes in graduate school, and Candy Volin, my marvelous third-grade teacher, who urged me to spread my wings and fly.

Each of them taught me something vital, and each of them encouraged me to keep going.

Thanks, as well, to my community of writer friends—the Romexers, the Savvies, the Discussers, the Saturday Pizza Group—and my Smith Sisters, who surround me with support and affection. And immeasurable gratitude to my family—my husband (who makes the pizza for the Saturday Pizza Group), my two wonderful sons, and my lovely daughter-in-law. They keep my feet grounded in fact even when my mind is lost in fiction, and they remind me that, as a somewhat more successful rock band once sang, all you need is love.